Daniel Church

THE HOLLOWS

ANGRY
ROBOT

ANGRY ROBOT
An imprint of Watkins Media Ltd

Unit 11, Shepperton House
89 Shepperton Road
London N1 3DF
UK

angryrobotbooks.com
twitter.com/angryrobotbooks
A pale, thin hand

An Angry Robot paperback original, 2022

Cover by Kieryn Tyler
Edited by Simon Spanton and Andrew Hook
Set in Meridien

ISBN 978 1 91520 238 3
Ebook ISBN 978 1 91520 239 0

Printed and bound in the United Kingdom by TJ Books Ltd.

9 8 7 6 5 4 3 2

MIX
Paper from
responsible sources
FSC
www.fsc.org   FSC® C013056

Dedicated to Debbie Pearson and Gus Lambert, without whom this book would not exist.

PART I
Came the dread Archer

19th December
Sunrise: 0817 hrs
Sunset: 1549 hrs
7 hours, 32 minutes and 38 seconds of daylight

1.

White sky stretched from Wakeman's Edge, across the wedge-shaped valley of Thursdale, to Slapelow Hill. Drystone walls and bare black trees marked the blanket of snow; nothing broke the silence. The only signs of life were a police Land Rover parked halfway up the hill road, and a policewoman in a grey fur hat, peering over the crash barrier.

Ellie crouched and squinted down the slope. The man lay on one side, doubled up around the base of a tree in the beech coppice below. He wore a donkey jacket, jeans and Wellington boots, dusted by the snow that clogged his tangled hair and covered his upturned face.

The air was clear and sharp, the afternoon cold and still.

The two hikers who'd called it in were huddled together in the back of the Land Rover. Only idiots went blundering around the Peaks in this weather; at least stumbling over the corpse had stopped them from getting lost in the snow while Ellie and Tom Graham spent the night out looking for them. Or adding two more bodies to this year's total, because some idiot always thought he or she knew better – especially, for some reason, when it came to this part of the Peak District. It was usually hikers who came to grief, although a couple of years ago some amateur archaeologist looking for the ruins of Kirk Flockton had drowned in the marshes on Fendmoor Heath. Every year, it seemed, there was always at least one.

But a body was a body: somebody's husband, somebody's son. Someone, somewhere, would be missing the poor sod.

3

Hopefully. There was always the possibility that nobody was, a prospect so depressing Ellie never cared to contemplate it for long. Either way the body would be retrieved, but not just yet. Ellie had no intention of risking a Christmas in hospital by trying to shift the body single-handed. Tom was en route, with Milly Emmanuel; Milly would help her move the body and cast an eye over the scene besides.

Ellie tramped back over to her vehicle. She was a small, sturdy woman in her forties, her dark hair salted grey, and there were days where she felt every one of her years and every degree of cold. This was one of them.

In the Land Rover, the boy was crying, the girl hugging him. Ellie softened a little: they were kids, after all. Seventeen, maybe eighteen at the outside: Richard would be that old now, if he'd lived. Better she was called out for them because of this than because they were injured or dying.

Ellie opened the Land Rover's tailgate, making the kids start at the sudden sound. Knowing she'd be out for a while, she'd filled two flasks before setting off and stowed them in the back; she took them out and shut the tailgate, then opened the driver's door. "Hot chocolate?"

"Please," the girl said.

Ellie handed her a cup. "Careful," she added. "Hot." Which should have been obvious, but she'd learned long ago never to take the general public's intelligence for granted.

The girl cradled the cup and sipped. The boy, wiping his eyes, eyed it with some envy, so Ellie sighed, took the cup from the other flask and poured out a measure for him. "Let's go over it again," she said.

"We weren't going far," said the girl. "I just wanted to show Rick the Height."

Rick: an unwelcome jolt passed through Ellie at the name. Just coincidence, but still unpleasant, after the similarity in the boy's age. The moment passed, and Ellie was glad to see it gone; she leant against the doorframe and breathed out.

"Are you okay?" said the girl.

"Fine," grunted Ellie. The wind was blowing hard along the hill road and making a low, dull moan. She climbed into the front seat and shut the door. "So," she said, "the Height."

"Yeah. You know –" The girl gestured up the road.

"Yeah, I know where it is." Ellie tried not to sound snappish. "Where were you coming from?"

"Wakeman Farm," said the girl, now gesturing down the road.

"Grant and Sally Beck?" said Ellie, then remembered they had a girl away at university. "You're the daughter?"

"Kathleen Beck. Kate." The girl took the boy's arm. "Rick came up to stay. I wanted him to see it."

Ellie nodded. Maybe the girl, at least, wasn't as thick as she'd thought. Wakeman Farm was close by on Spear Bank, which ran from the bottom of the hill road across Thursdale to the Edge. Even that wasn't without risk in these conditions, but it wasn't as dangerous as a longer hike. "You tell your folks where you were going?"

Kate shrugged.

"You need to," Ellie said. "Main roads are gonna be cut off for the next couple of days, and there's more snow coming. You get caught out in it and get in trouble, right now there's exactly two coppers in the area." Or one, if she included Tom Graham.

The girl's story was simple enough. They'd stopped for a short rest, as the hill road was pretty steep; before setting off again, the boy had gone to the road's edge to study the view, and seen something lying in the snow.

"Took me a few seconds to realise what it was," said the boy, wiping his eyes again and giving Ellie a shy smile. "Sorry about that. Gave me a bit of a shock – never seen anyone dead before."

Town lad – a bit soft, maybe, but polite. Well-mannered. The kind you'd bring home to meet your parents.

"Happens sometimes round here," said Ellie at last. "You get used to it. What happened then?"

"Managed to get a signal," Kate said. "So we called it in."

"Lucky again," said Ellie. "Reception's a nightmare round here, specially when it's like this."

She had no idea what else to say, so she looked out through the windscreen. To her relief, an olive-green BMW X5 came round the hill road's bend and drove down towards them. Barsall Village had two full-time officers and one official vehicle, so at times like this Tom Graham's own 4X4 – a seven-seater SUV, no less, a proper Chelsea tractor – was pressed into service; a blue police light had been hurriedly mounted on the roof, but, as usual, he'd forgotten to switch it on.

The BMW halted beside Ellie's, and Tom got out. "All right, Ell. What have we got?"

Ellie trudged over and pointed. "Body, Sarge."

"Oh, yes." He scratched the back of his neck. "You did say."

He looked lost – as usual – so Ellie, once again, stepped in. "The young lady and gentleman over there found him. I thought if you took them back to the station and got their statements, Dr Emmanuel and I can retrieve the body."

"Oh. Yeah. Makes sense." Tom gave the kids an amiable if vacant smile, then frowned at Ellie, or more accurately the fur hat. "For God's sake, will you stop wearing that bloody thing on duty?"

"It keeps my head warm and the regulation cap doesn't. I like having ears."

"I wouldn't mind so much if you'd take *that* off it." He had a point, given that the hat was Soviet-era Red Army surplus, complete with a hammer-and-sickle-emblazoned red star badge Ellie had never trusted herself to remove without tearing a gaping hole. "Ernie Stasiolek's gonna think you're the bloody Stasi one of these days and take a pot at you."

"Ernie Stasiolek's Polish, Tom. The Stasi were East German."

"All right, clever clogs." Tom took a step towards the kids

and called out. "This way, you two. Nice cup of tea when we get in, eh?"

He probably hadn't even noticed the cups they were already holding, but you could never have enough hot drinks on a day like this. The kids followed him back to the X5 as Milly Emmanuel climbed out of it, hidden under multiple layers of clothing culminating in a neon pink puffa jacket and matching ski-hat that rendered her almost globular. She waved to Ellie and waddled over as Tom managed a clumsy three-point turn before driving back up the hill road towards Barsall.

"Afternoon, Constable," she called.

"All right, Doc. Got enough layers on?"

"It's all right for you. My Dad was from Jamaica, remember? I'm not half fucking penguin like you are. So where's the patient?"

Ellie pointed. Milly peered over the crash barrier. "Think we might be a bit late to help."

"What would I do without you?"

"Many a true word."

"Oh, sod off."

"So what's the plan? Please tell me you can call someone in."

Ellie shook her head. "Phone and radio reception's up and down like a whore's drawers and the main roads are snowed up anyway."

Milly groaned. "Don't suppose we could just shovel a bit more snow over him and leave him till the spring?"

"I wish."

"Great. So, heavy lifting duty, then?"

"That and your medical expertise, Doc."

"I'm not a pathologist –"

"You're the closest I've got."

"Fair enough." Milly's breath billowed in the air. "But you'd better have some decent wine in for later."

"Do my best. Got some hot chocolate in the meantime, if you want it."

They got in the Land Rover and Ellie drove down to the bottom of the hill road. She cleared space in the back, spread a blanket out there, folded another over her arm and picked up a small black pack. She opened it and checked the contents – latex gloves, evidence baggies, a pair of small flashlights – then slung it over her shoulder and turned away. Ellie wasn't expecting to find any evidence of foul play – chances were a drunk had slipped and fallen on the path, and the cold had done the rest – but it was best to be prepared.

Milly had already climbed over the crash barrier and was waiting. Ellie climbed after her. Intermittent snow drifted down. Ahead of them a narrow footpath ran along the hillside, past the edge of the Harpers' land, towards the silent trees.

2.

Pinched between the hillside on the right and drystone walls and wire fences on the left, the path, rocky and uneven at the best of times, was slippery with ice and impacted snow.

The body lay at a point where the hillside bulged and became a gentler slope, which a brave soul might be able to climb up to the hill road. The slope extended down beyond the path, over about thirty yards of woodland, before flattening out at the edge of the drystone wall encircling the Harpers' fields.

Ellie saw a wide deep furrow, not quite hidden by last night's snow, scoured through the drifts on the path and down the slope to the trees. "Watch your step here," she told Milly, and picked her way down the incline, following the slide mark.

While the body was clearly visible from the road, once among the trees Ellie could barely make out the fields or the farmhouse beyond. Chances were the Harpers hadn't ventured outside all day, but even if they had, they could have stood at the very edge of their property without seeing the dead man. Ironic, really, as Ellie was fairly certain who this was.

"Wonder if they've even noticed he's missing?" she said aloud.

Milly frowned, then followed her gaze. "Think it's one of them?"

"Pretty sure it's Tony Harper."

"Shit. He was all right."

"Comparatively. When sober."

Milly chose not to get onto the topic of the Harpers, or Ellie's long and not entirely pleasant history with them. She crouched by the body and tugged experimentally at the booted feet; the legs were stiff as wood. "He's well into rigor mortis."

"So, time of death?"

"Guesswork at this stage, Ell. You know that."

"I'm not gonna hold you to it."

"Rigor sets in two to six hours after death – it's usually complete within twelve, and this fella's stiff as. So – tentatively –" she glanced at her watch "– I'd say he died around two a.m. today at the latest. Although that's not factoring the cold in. Could have been here longer, but there's no sign of animal predation."

"Plus," Ellie looked at the furrow in the snow, "if it'd been before last night there'd be no trace of this. Or him, probably – he'd have been buried and those kids would never have seen him."

"Probably should have been," said Milly. "But any snow covering him would have been knocked off when he fell."

"Come again?"

"Gimme a flashlight." Ellie handed one over and Milly shone it over the corpse. "Look at his posture. One leg's out straight. The other's pulled up at the knee. See? And his back's straight too."

"And?" Then Ellie saw. "He was sitting up?"

"Yeah. He died somewhere else, rigor set in, and then he fell."

"Or someone brought him out here and dumped him." Ellie groaned. "Why couldn't the snow have fucking buried him? Then I wouldn't have to deal with this bollocks until it was warm."

"If it wasn't him, it'd be someone else," said Milly. "You know what it's like. Every sodding year, like clockwork." She sighed. "People never seem to learn."

"I know. I know."

Neither spoke for a few seconds. Snow drifted down and settled on the body.

"Why dump him here, though?" Milly said. "Not exactly the perfect spot."

Ellie shone the other flashlight along the slide mark. Then she frowned and followed it back to the footpath before moving the beam up the slope above. "Milly? Think I might've found the answer."

Milly floundered back up to her side, catching her arm for balance. "What you got?"

Ellie played the flashlight beam over the dead vegetation on the slope above the path. Snow had clogged it since last night, but they could both see that a section of it was badly crushed.

"He fell from above?"

"I reckon. Maybe somebody slung him from the road?"

"Maybe." Milly sounded doubtful. "What's that, though? See? There?"

She pointed. Ellie moved the beam further up the slope. The snow hadn't covered it as extensively as the lower section, so she couldn't see any slide marks, but there was a ledge about ten feet below the road barrier. It was twelve feet across, and looked as though someone had chiselled a neat oblong out of the rock.

"Remember his posture?" Milly said. "Back straight, one leg out, one drawn up..."

"Like he was sitting down," said Ellie. "How wide's that ledge look? Couple of feet?"

"If that."

"So you pull a leg up to brace yourself, make sure you don't topple off. But what was he doing there to start with?"

Milly didn't have an answer. The cold was creeping in, along with the awareness of what lay ahead, and Ellie didn't like either. She'd have to visit the Harpers, which wasn't her idea of fun at the best of times. And it mightn't be just the standard death knock either. "All right. Let's get some pictures of the scene then get back."

Milly nodded down at the body. "What about him?"

"I'll have a word with Plant-Pot at the Co-op. See if he's got any room in the meat freezer."

Milly grimaced. "That's turned me veggie for the duration. Hey! Where you going?"

Ellie pointed up. "I'm gonna head back up the road, get some shots of that ledge from above. If he was up there –"

"Fair enough." Milly eyed the body and grimaced again. "Just don't be too long, okay?"

"Quick as I can."

Ellie made better time heading back to the car; negotiating footpaths like this was another thing she had more experience with than her friend. She parked by the spot overlooking the woods, leant over the barrier till she had the ledge in view, then took a series of wide-angle shots on her phone, with and without the flash, before zooming in for close-ups.

Tom Graham would have bothered with none of this. He'd already have decided he was dealing with an accident and nothing more. But Ellie believed in doing her job. She didn't have much else. Besides, she still had some instincts left, and they were prompting her to look more closely.

She zoomed in on sections of the ledge, again photographing both with and without the flash, moving from one end to the other. Harper would have been sitting against the end to her right – it'd been his right leg drawn up for balance, so the drop would have been on that side of him.

She zoomed in closer, and if she hadn't she'd have missed it. One area of rock .that had remained clear of snow was smudged with what looked like soot and patched with lichen, against which smears of dried blood showed. To capture those Ellie had to straddle the crash barrier and lean out to an almost life-threatening degree, but she managed.

When she did, she saw that the soot wasn't a smudge at all, but a symbol of some kind: a straight vertical line, with three shorter horizontal ones pointing off from it to the left. Made using charcoal, maybe. She didn't recognise it, whatever it was. She tightened the focus on the symbol and took more pictures.

"You quite finished up there, David fucking Bailey?" Milly shouted up from the path.

Ellie climbed back over the barrier. "I'm done. You?"

"Been stood here watching you like piffy on a rock bun for the last five minutes."

Ellie drove back down and trotted up the footpath to Milly. "Anything?" she asked as they ventured back down through the trees.

"Yes and no."

"What?"

"There's some cuts and scratches – one on the forehead that bled a bit."

"A fight?"

"Or just a fall. Easy enough in this weather, especially if you've had a few."

"Which, knowing Tony, he had."

"Bit of a piss-head?"

"Only at weekends, but last night was Friday night. So if I know him, he'll have been up past closing time at..." Ellie stopped and frowned, peering through the trees.

"What's up?"

"Tell you in a sec. You were saying – why's it yes and no?"

"The injuries are inconclusive. But look at this."

Milly shone her flashlight. She'd brushed the snow from the dead man's face. He'd been swarthy – although less so now, with death's pallor – and handsome in a sharp, bony, not-quite-conventional way. Blue-black stubble, long black hair, a gold ring gleaming in one earlobe. Tony Harper, and no other.

Milly had cleared the snow from his right arm, too, which had been half-buried. His hand was clenched around an open clasp-knife with a handle made from an old shotgun shell.

"Let's get him on the blanket and get out of here," Ellie said at last.

It took them nearly twenty minutes to carry the body back to the Land Rover, manhandling it over the crash barrier before loading it onto the blanket in the back. Ellie covered Tony with the second blanket and slammed the tailgate shut.

By the time Milly got into the passenger seat, her teeth were chattering. Ellie turned on the heater and passed her a Thermos. "Get some of that down you."

"Thanks."

Ellie waited till Milly had filled her cup and restoppered the flask before beginning the drive back to the village.

"What's up?" Milly said.

"Nothing."

"Come on, Ell. I can always tell."

"Rhyming now?"

"I'm a poet and I didn't know it. Come on. What?"

"For a start, Tony Harper's the only half-decent – *was* the only half-decent – bloke out of that family. Until he's had a few, and then he gets rowdy. But I've never known him pull a knife. I mean, he'd have killed someone by now otherwise, and there'd be one less Harper to worry about."

"Well, there *is* now."

"Huh." They passed the slope above the coppice. "No, but when it comes to fighting he's always used his fists. Well, and the odd boot."

"Not last night he didn't."

"You know he made them himself?"

"Huh?"

"The knives. Used to flog 'em round the village for beer money. I've got a couple at home." Ellie snorted. "Course, you can guess who had to deal with him when he drank the money and got in a fight. Talk about making work for myself. Plus, there's two pubs in Barsall and Tony's barred from 'em both – only place he can go drinking is the *Bell* up on the North Road. He'll get rat-arsed there, then walk home. But the track to the farmhouse is on the other side of the valley, and..."

"And he ends up over here, freezing to death halfway up the hillside," Milly said. "Someone chased him?"

"Yeah. And he didn't fight them. He tried to run and hide..." Ellie thought of the slope. "If he'd got the rest of the way up to the hill road, he could have made it to Barsall. So there must've been more than one attacker. He was surrounded, and got the knife out to keep them back."

"Keep who back?"

"Well that's the big question, isn't it?"

Ellie had, despite herself, rather liked Tony. There'd been a good lad in there under it all, despite a family background practically designed to beat it out of him. And rowdy or not, he'd been brave. He'd got into a brawl with his brothers when Paul Harper had tried to assault a local girl, come out of it with a broken arm and still been struggling with them when Ellie had arrived on the scene. And yet he'd been driven back from his own front door and died cornered on the ledge.

They reached the bend in the road, near the hill's summit. "Oh my Lord," said Milly, and pointed.

The Height was a flat shelf that stuck out beyond the bend, dotted with snow-caked litter bins and picnic tables, with a safety railing round the edge. The view from there, over Thursdale, Wakeman's Edge and Fendmoor Heath – marred only by the pylons that marched from the Edge over Fendmoor, in a line that grew crooked where it skirted the Heath's marshes – fetched in a small horde of tourists every summer, but what commanded Ellie's attention now was the wall of black cloud advancing towards the peaks across the valley.

"More snow tonight," said Milly.

Ellie didn't answer. Around the bend from the Height, the hill road became Halliwell Way: the road to the village. Closer to home. She pressed down on the accelerator. She had work to do, and it would soon be dark again.

3.

Andy Brailsford had shaken Barsall's dust from his feet twenty years earlier, vowing never to come back. Whether he'd really shouted "Later, losers!" from his car window while departing was open to debate, but no doubt the attitude had been there: at twenty-one you thought you knew it all and could conquer the world by sheer force of will.

Five years ago he'd moved back, complete with pot belly, male-pattern baldness and a family. He'd done a number of things in the interim, but among them had been managing two failed garden centres, as a result of which someone – possibly someone who remembered his alleged parting words – had christened him "Plant-Pot", a dubbing so popular that even his wife was now rumoured to use it.

Plant-Pot had become a store manager for the Co-Op; how willingly or otherwise he'd accepted the posting to the same store he'd once stacked shelves in for an out-of-school Saturday job was another debatable topic, but there was no disputing his lack of enthusiasm at using the Co-Op's freezer for body storage. He cleared a space for Tony Harper's body nonetheless; Milly was a GP, not a pathologist, so there'd be no post mortem until the roads were clear.

The unpleasant task of searching the body yielded a wallet containing a driver's licence and National Insurance card in Tony Harper's name; Ellie sealed them into separate evidence bags and slipped them into her jacket pocket.

"Still on for tonight?" Milly said.

"'Spect so. Couple of stops to make first."

"Harpers?"

"Yeah."

Milly poked her arm. "Just be careful, okay?"

"Don't worry about that." Ellie grimaced. "Pity sometimes we can't go armed."

"Don't forget to get some decent wine in."

Ellie drove on to the station, to find Tom Graham setting off with the girl and Rick. "All right there, Ellie. Just running them home."

"I'm heading up to the *Bell*, then I'll go break the news to the Harpers."

"Fair enough." If Graham wondered why she was going to the *Bell*, he didn't ask. To him, coppering was a simple job that Ellie overcomplicated by worrying too much. He'd have missed half the things she and Milly had noticed at the scene, and even if he hadn't, he'd still have decided Tony Harper had got lost in the snow and frozen while drunk. "Don't be too long. Latest weather report says it'll be another bad one tonight – worst yet. Even the hill road might get cut off. Don't want to get caught in that."

"Any word on when?"

"Six-ish at the latest."

"Kay. Thanks, Tom."

In the back of Tom's X5, Rick and Kate huddled together. The girl gave Ellie a wan smile and raised her hand in a wave. Ellie nodded back, and watched them drive away.

Light, intermittent snow continued to fall. It was just after three o'clock; one and a half to two hours before dark, and – in theory – three before the snowstorm hit, but Ellie knew better by now than to gamble her life on the accuracy of weather reports. She wanted to be home no later than five, and even that felt as though she was cutting it close. "Better crack on then," she muttered, and drove to Longhowe Road.

Derbyshire's little local police stations had closed years earlier in favour of larger central stations, like the one in Matlock Ellie and Tom were nominally based at. They were usually assigned the Barsall area anyway since they lived there; knowing the territory could be crucial when searching for those lost hikers.

The old station should have been sold off, but there'd been trouble finding a buyer and then the council decided to turn it into a museum or heritage centre. But nothing came of that either, so although the blue lamp and any other identifying signs had been removed, Longhowe Road Station was still the Derbyshire Constabulary's. It mainly served to store emergency equipment and, when weather cut the village off, as now, as a base of operations. A relic of a different time, stuck in a kind of limbo; Ellie could relate to that.

Julie Robinson was behind the old sergeant's desk with a cup of coffee. She ran the Post Office with her husband Phil, but mucked in at times like this as an impromptu dispatcher and point of contact. "Oh. Hi, Ellie."

"You heard about Tony Harper?"

"Mm." Julie sighed. "Poor lad."

"He was in the *Bell* last night, so I'm gonna go get a statement off the Famuyiwas. After that I'm doing the death knock at Barrowman Farm."

"God." Julie grimaced. "Rather you than me."

"Yeah."

Serious crime was rare around Barsall; the standard gear of pepper spray, extendable baton and handcuffs usually left Ellie feeling over-equipped, but since those rare serious crimes were usually the Harpers' work, not today. She picked up a two extra pairs of cuffs, just in case. Until earlier this year, they'd had a couple of tasers in storage, but Matlock had taken them back. More was the pity, right now.

On her way back through the village, she stopped at the Co-Op again to pick up two bottles of Merlot. A promise was a promise, and she'd need a drink later anyway. She grabbed a cold pasty too, and ate it as she drove.

***

Ellie overtook Tom, who was proceeding at his usual snail's pace, and followed the hill road past Wakeman Farm and along Spear Bank, to the North Road that ran along the foot of Wakeman's Edge.

The hills and passes the North Road led through were vulnerable to the winter storms, often cutting Barsall off from the outside world. One of the reasons for the strong sense of community in the village – which was one reason Ellie liked it – was that you had little choice but to look to one another to survive. According to the local vicar, Madeleine Lowe, even that hadn't always been enough, as one particularly prolonged and harsh winter – the "Bad Winter", as she always called it, the capital letters always clearly audible – had left the village almost depopulated back in the Middle Ages, with only a handful of survivors left by the spring.

Still, this section of the North Road, at least, was still clear. Even in better weather than this, though, it could seem long and unfriendly, and the prospect of breaking your journey for a pint or pub lunch was always appealing, especially if you were stopping to refill your tank anyway. The *Bell* dated back to the seventeenth century, but the landlords had moved with the times, hence the petrol station next door.

The Famuyiwas had bought the roadside inn from the previous owners five years ago and kept it going, but the reliance on passing trade meant they couldn't afford to be choosy about their clientele, especially not in winter. Which was why it had been Tony Harper's usual watering-hole.

Ellie couldn't see anyone inside the petrol station, but the pub's windows were lit and a brand-new Volvo, clearly a city car, was parked outside. The place was a welcome sight given the weather, and did a decent pub lunch, too; under other circumstances, she'd have abandoned the remains of the pasty and gone in to order the bangers and mash. But there was the weather warning to consider, and the Harpers still to see. She couldn't spare the time. Ellie locked up the Landrover and entered the pub.

The snug was empty, apart from an elderly couple sipping coffee over the remains of a meal in one corner – presumably the Volvo's owners – and Charlotte, Joda's daughter, polishing glasses at the counter. Ellie stopped at the old couple's table to confirm their destination; they were heading for a village three miles to the south, the road to which was so far still clear. Having made sure they knew about the weather warning, she crossed the snug.

The worn red carpeting really needed replacing, but it had been hoovered and shampooed; the oak-panelled walls and the brasses hung on them were polished and bright. From beside a heavy old pendulum clock mounted above the fire, a stuffed pike glared at Ellie from its glass case as if it were her fault it had ended up here. *Don't look at me, pal: you should've had a closer look at what you were putting in your mouth. As the bishop said to the actress.*

Ellie leant on the counter. "Hi, Charlotte."

"All right."

"You on the bar last night?"

"No. Thank God. Dave took me out for dinner." Dave Chapple, at twenty-three, was six years older than Charlotte. He worked for his dad, who owned half the rental properties in Barsall, so he wouldn't have been a bad catch if he'd shown any signs or even any understanding of the concept of sexual fidelity. Ellie had no idea what Charlotte knew or suspected about that, but the poor girl still seemed to think Dave was her ticket back to the bright lights of Manchester. Ellie had thought of saying something more than once, but what seventeen-year-old listens to her elders? You think you know everything at that age. Ellie had.

"Would it've been your Dad, then?"

"Wouldn't have been Mum, would it?"

"Oi." Ellie had always liked Charlotte and would put up with a certain amount of cheek, but there were limits. "No need for that."

Charlotte sighed theatrically. "Soz. I mean," she added with exaggerated formality, "hang on, Constable Cheetham, I'll go and get him for you now."

She came out from behind the bar. Beyond it were an extra half-dozen dining tables for the rare busy times that came with the summer trade, a pool table and the stairs to the upper floor. She lifted, then replaced, the chain with its sign marked PRIVATE – STAFF ONLY and ran up. Ellie wished she could allow herself a drink. Or that she still smoked. Or that you could still smoke in pubs.

A cold draught, and a voice called "Bye." Ellie turned to see the old couple slipping out through the door. It clicked shut, cutting off the moaning wind, and outside the window, a few seconds later, the blue Volvo pulled out onto the North Road. *Safe journey, folks.* The snow was falling steadily now, and thicker than before. She turned back to the bar as someone clumped across the landing overhead and started down the stairs.

Joda Famuyiwa stepped over the chain at the foot of the staircase and clomped over to the bar. He wasn't a giant, but it was close: he stood six feet five in his socks and nearly three feet wide at the shoulders, and although just past fifty, he was still mostly muscle. He had the same model of home gym as Ellie – in fact, she'd bought hers on his recommendation, given that he clearly knew whereof he spoke. The only signs of softness on him were the small paunch straining his lumberjack shirt and his plump round face.

"Hello, Ellie." He looked tired, but then he often did. Between the pub, his wife and his daughter, there were a lot of demands on his time. There were crow's-feet at the corner of his eyes Ellie was sure hadn't been there the last time she'd seen him, and a little more grey hair at his temples and in his neatly clipped moustache.

"Joda." They shook hands, as always; he was curiously formal like that. "How's Barbara?"

"Much the same. Maybe a little worse."

"I'm so sorry."

He shrugged. "It is what it is. How can I help?"

"Charlotte said you were minding the bar last night?"

"She had to go out with her *young man*." Joda placed a pause before, and an emphasis on, the words to indicate that he could think of several better terms to describe Dave Chapple, none repeatable in polite company. "It was quiet, and Barbara was having one of her better nights."

"Was Tony Harper in?"

Joda sighed. "What's he done now?" Like Ellie, he'd always had some time for the black sheep of Clan Harper. Tony had reciprocated his respect, at least to the extent of only getting into fights in the car park, rather than inside the actual pub.

Ellie evaded the question. "Any bother from him?"

"Actually, no," said Joda. "And I thought there would be a couple of times. We had three or four boys in from the village. Don't know why they were here – maybe they're barred as well – but they were mostly playing pool in the back, and Tony just sat there –" Joda nodded at the snug "– drinking in a corner. One of the boys even spilled his drink – accidentally, I mean, they weren't looking for a fight – and he let it go."

"How many had he had by then?"

"Six or seven."

By that stage of things, Tony was usually on the fine border between being everybody's friend and decking anyone who looked at him the wrong way. "Something bothering him, maybe?"

Joda shrugged. "He didn't really talk except to ask for another drink, but that's how he looked."

"What time did he go?" Joda often stayed open till the early hours of the morning at this time of year, to get the most out of the reduced trade.

"Midnight exactly." Joda pointed to the pendulum clock. "You know what that thing's like – strikes the hour like Big bloody Ben. He was sort of slouched over the table and I was wondering what to do about him – I was starting to think he'd fallen asleep."

"Tony, fall asleep in a pub? That'd be new." Pity, really. He mightn't have been barred from as many. "How much had he put away by the time he left?"

"His usual – ten, eleven pints. But he seemed to wake up when he realised the time. Finished his drink, said 'goodbye' very politely, and out he went."

"What about the other drinkers?"

"Hardly noticed he'd gone. They were all here until nearly two o'clock."

By which time Tony Harper would already have been dead. "Got names for any of them?"

Joda remembered two, which Ellie jotted dutifully down. "Thanks, mate. Give my love to Barbara."

"Will do. What happened? Is he in trouble?"

She shook her head. "Couple hikers found him out by the hill road this afternoon. Looks like he froze to death."

"Oh, God. That poor young man."

"Yeah."

Joda didn't bother to spare a thought for his mother, but then, like Ellie, he'd met Liz Harper. If he wondered why Tony had been out by the hill road, he didn't ask. He had problems of his own.

Outside, Ellie jogged to the Land Rover. The snow was thicker still, and the sky above even darker. She didn't know if that was because of the approach of night or that of the storm, but either way, time was limited, and as little as she wanted to, she had to get to Barrowman Farm.

Ellie was briefly tempted to drive back to Barsall and leave the death knock for tomorrow. But that wasn't fair: the Harpers had the right to be told; if they had any idea what Tony had fallen foul of Ellie wanted to know; and there was no telling if the roads would be passable by tomorrow. So instead she took a dirt track that led off the hill road onto Thursdale, opened the gate with its crudely lettered signs (*PRIVATE PROPERTY* and *PISS OFF – THIS MEANS YOU*) and shut it behind her having coaxed the Land Rover through.

The track was rocky and potholed and she was glad of the Land Rover's suspension as it bounced and rocked along. She turned the headlights on, full beam, as she pushed on through the gloom and whirling snow. She should turn back now: by the time she was done here, driving back to Barsall would be near-suicidal.

"Fuck it," she muttered.

Finally she was level with another gate. Ellie pulled back the bolt and dragged it open, against the weight of the half-breezeblock chained to it to keep it shut.

She drove past tangles of mud and weeds that might have been intended as kitchen-gardens, heaps of rusting machinery the Harpers couldn't be arsed disposing of, old leaking sacks of cement and a teetering shell of a barn, then finally into the potholed asphalt yard in front of the brick and stone huddle of Barrowman Farm.

They'd given the house a coat of white plaster over a decade ago; large chunks of it had flaked off, while the rest was discoloured with dirt or mould. The roof was missing a quarter of its slates and bowed in the middle, and two windows had plastic sheeting taped over holes in them. The whole thing was dirtylooking, sagging and somehow menacing, like a huge grey toad waiting with cold, patient greed for its prey.

Christ, she *had* been working too hard. Ellie should be back home with her feet up, sipping a mug of black coffee with rum. Or whisky. Still had a few inches of Lagavulin left in the bottle Milly and Noel got her for her birthday. Normally she'd have said Irishing her coffee with that was a terrible waste of good single malt, but just now it sounded exactly the kind of decadent treat she should be enjoying by her fireside with her doors locked tight.

Well, you're here now.

She could still turn around and go.

But then a curtain twitched. They'd seen her.

Even if you did *leg it now, you'd still have to come back sooner or later. Someone's got to tell 'em.*

Ellie double-checked her utility belt. She didn't usually envy the American police's penchant for heavy armaments, but there'd be firearms in the house and there was no predicting things with the Harpers. She took off the fur hat and put it on the passenger seat; the ear flaps might limit her peripheral vision, and she'd rather not risk that.

The grim grey bulk of Barrowman Farm squatted there, as if crouched to spring. Ellie got out and locked the car. From the dark sky, the snow spiralled slowly down.

4.

The heavy wooden door was still solid, but rotten beneath its years-old crust of red paint: at the bottom it was crumbling away. Ellie banged the verdigrised brass knocker, and a dog started barking, a ferocious, almost rabid sound, which grew suddenly choked, no doubt because the chain around the animal's neck was being pulled tight, ready to be released if Dom Harper received an order from Liz.

A baby began squalling – screaming, really – and a woman's voice, coarse and jagged-sounding, yelled "Shut that fucking brat up or I fucking swear I'll fucking –" There was more shouting – men's voices this time, and a young girl – then scuffling and a cry.

A second woman shouted. "Jess! Leave her alone!"

A third: "But Mam, it was her who –"

"Shut up, you dumb fucking slag," spat the first woman. "Do as you're fucking told – shit!"

A crash – something had been thrown, Ellie guessed, and hit the wall. "And you can pipe down too, Keira Lucas." The second woman sounded older than the other two. A growling, phlegmy voice. "That's enough from all of you! Jess – shut the fuck up and go get the door."

Footsteps in the hallway. The baby's screaming came nearer. A voice mumbled, trying to shush the child. Ellie breathed out slowly. She had to be calm and relaxed. *Don't go looking for a fight. You're here to break bad news to a family. That's who they are. A family. People. Whatever else they might be.*

26

A key turned in the lock. The door part-opened, then stopped, secured by a brass chain. A dark eye and a pale, heart-shaped face showed in the gap, framed by lank brown elf-locks. The eye blinked at Ellie. The baby squalled.

"Sh," said a soft breathy voice – the third woman Ellie had heard. She was talking to the baby. "Sh now. Shut *up*." The voice cracked, close to tears. The baby quieted a little, probably out of breathlessness. The dark eye focused on Ellie again. "What do you want?"

Ellie forced a smile. "Hiya, Jess. Your Mum in, love? Need a word."

The baby squalled again; the half-seen face tightened in frustration. Jess rocked the baby, clumsily and too fast. "What about?"

Ellie was afraid – for the baby, in those arms, not herself. "It's about your Tony. Can I come in, please?"

Jess blinked, bit her lip and nodded. Out of all her family, she was closest to Tony. This would be hard for her. Tony aside, Jess was the only Harper Ellie had any time for, being the closest thing to an innocent possible for anyone who'd grown up at Barrowman Farm. She took off the chain and reopened the door, kicking aside a draught excluder made from the leg of a pair of tights stuffed with newspaper and cotton waste, then stumbled down the dim hallway.

It took all Ellie's composure not to recoil from the stench as she followed Jess. The house was warm – a thick damp heat – and stank of sweat, rotten food, mildew, unflushed toilets, wet dogs and their acrid piss. Which reminded her of the barking she'd heard.

Jess rocked the child, but it kept screaming. It wore an old, dirty romper suit and gave off a horrible smell; its little face was red and scrunched-up. Jess whimpered, almost crying with frustration. The child looked too big for her; she was tiny, barely five feet tall, small-boned and very thin, with a hunched shoulder due to scoliosis. Practically a child herself, in every sense. Ellie edged forward, holding out her arms. "You're rocking him too fast, love. Want me to show you?"

Jess shrank back, clutching the baby to her. The outside world would steal her child if she gave it any excuse: her mother had told her. "I won't hurt him," Ellie promised, "and I'm not gonna take him away. Just want to show you how to rock him."

Jess was, in her own way, as unpredictable as Tony. She could be kind-hearted and gentle, but she was also a Harper, with all that went with that – most notably, distrust and hostility to anyone outside the clan. She'd been brutalised in other ways, too. A six-month-old baby, and she wasn't seventeen yet. Father unknown – according to the birth certificate, anyway – but the social worker who'd dealt with Jess had voiced suspicions about her brother Paul. Paul Harper had raped three women, assaulted four more, and those were the ones Ellie knew about.

With the Harpers, though, there was always a gap between what you knew and what you could prove, not least because anyone who pissed them off brought the whole clan down on them. Paul had only done time for one of his many assaults, and Jess herself had always denied he was the child's father, not that anyone expected her to do otherwise.

After the last assault, when little Tara Caddick had refused to testify against him, Ellie made it clear to Liz Harper that Paul's safety couldn't be guaranteed if any more local girls came to grief. That would have brought the big guns out with a vengeance, but by that point she hadn't given a shit. In her redder dreams she sometimes thought of coming out here with a shotgun and a can of petrol and cleaning house once and for all, but the thought of Tony and Jess had stopped her.

Paul was more careful now, went to the nearest town to gratify his appetites – with prostitutes, Ellie hoped – but her warning him off fitted all too neatly with the timeline of Jess's pregnancy. She half-hoped Paul gave her trouble today; the thought of applying her baton to his head was all too appealing.

Ellie hoped her bloody thoughts didn't show in her face. If they did, Jess didn't notice them, but put the baby in her arms.

"Hush now." Ellie rocked the child slowly. Her eyes stung; her throat clenched. *No. You're here to do a job. This is a sideshow to the main event. Nothing else. And for Christ's sake, stay alert.* Jess was harmless enough, but the rest of the brood weren't.

But when she focused on the baby, things became easier. Like riding a bike, it seemed; some old habits were too well-ingrained, even at nearly two decades' removed, to easily forget. She rocked the child, cooing, and he became quiet. Even smiled. Now he was calmer and his face less red, Ellie could see he was a beautiful baby, with fair hair and blue eyes. He reached out towards her, and Ellie saw there were only two digits on his right hand. Poor little sod.

The baby gurgled happily, and Ellie handed him back to Jess. The girl smiled, blushing. "Thanks."

"You just need to –"

"Fucksake, you stupid little slag. Fuck're you doing, letting her in?"

Keira Lucas' voice was high and harsh and grating at the best of times, and rarely – never, in Ellie's experience – free from spite and anger. The baby started wailing again, and Jess's face closed on itself like a fist.

"You!" said Keira. "The fuck do you want?"

Rage had lived with Ellie ever since Richard's death, like a cruel, ill-tempered animal. She bound and bridled it so it couldn't attack anyone, was so used to doing so she'd forget its existence for days. But it was a cunning beast, and would break free given half the chance. Everything about Liz Harper's de facto daughter-in-law made it struggle to escape, and more than once Ellie had been tempted to let it.

"Oi, I asked you a fucking question," Keira shouted. "The fuck are you doing in our house?"

She was a sinewy woman in her early twenties whose

small, hard eyes and wide, thick mouth made her look like a
predatory fish, gormless and malevolent at once. Not for the
first time, Ellie treasured a mental image of her gloved fist
smashing into Keira's ugly mouth and scattering her carious
yellow teeth in all directions. But it could never be more than
an image. Acting it out would cost Ellie her job, and while she
mightn't have much of a career, her job was all she'd got.

"I need to speak to Liz," she said out loud.

"Liz, is it? When'd you become her best mate?" Keira
wobbled over; she wore carpet slippers but walked as if in
eight-inch heels. She'd been at the gin again. Ellie managed
not to flinch from its juniper stink and her sour breath. "Eh?
Asked you a fucking question, Cuntstubble." She always called
Ellie that; it was her idea of wit. "Eh? Bit of fucking respect, eh,
under Mrs Harper's roof."

"Okay, Keira." Ellie did her best to address a spot on the
ceiling. "I need to speak to Mrs Harper. Actually, I need to talk
to the whole family if I can."

"Oh, *actually*? Will you, *actually*?"

"Keira," said the second voice Ellie had heard through the
door, and Keira fell silent, her mouth clamped tight. "Show
her in. Get Frank and the boys."

"Right." Keira tramped up the stairs. "Frank! Dom!" She
didn't shout Paul's name; probably wanted to make sure the
other two were summoned and downstairs and her halfway to
the ground floor after them before hailing the Rapey Cunt of
Thursdale, as she was known to call him.

"Come on," Jess Harper whispered, motioning down the
hall and – a little less clumsily than before – rocking the child
in her arms.

Ellie made her way down the stinking hall, over threadbare,
dirty carpet and walls spotted with black mould and a few
cheap 1970s-era art prints, bought, like the faded, decaying
wallpaper, when someone at Barrowman Farm had cared
about such things. Every breath made her want to cover her

mouth and nose; everything and everyone in sight made her itch. A shower or hot bath would be in order when she got home.

Jess pushed open the kitchen door and stepped to one side. Liz Harper sat at the head of a long wooden kitchen table, with half a dozen shotguns laid out on old newspaper – side-by-sides, over-and-unders, single-barrels and a lone pump-action weapon.

The Harpers owned ten shotguns and at least two rifles – legally, anyway. No doubt there were others, but it wasn't the time to ask how many of the weapons on the table appeared on either of the family's shotgun certificates; Liz was cleaning a twelve bore with an oily rag, a box of cartridges at her elbow.

Behind her, below the big kitchen window (dirty, cracked and mended with gaffer tape), was an Aga range and a Belfast sink. An ancient yellow-painted fridge in a corner. A dog chained to the Aga cooker – brawny and lean, with ugly white scars under a cropped sandy coat, pacing on more old newspaper stained with piss and littered with turds. It lunged at Ellie, barking again, but the chain pulled taut.

"Dog!" Liz shouted, and it cringed, whining. "Dog," she said again, more quietly: it fell silent and lay down on its filthy paper bed. Most of the poor animal's scars would be from the dog-fights Dom Harper organised, the rest from the family. But brutalised as it was, it would attack whoever the Harpers pointed it at. It was what they did: whatever beast or human strayed into their orbit they caught and coarsened, abused any kindness out of them, then made them part of the clan, so they fought in its defence, only unleashing their pain and anger on the targets Liz Harper selected.

"Well?" said Liz. A cigarette hung between her lips. There was a scuffed plastic ashtray on the table, the kind they had in pubs back when you could still smoke in them. Ash speckled her old cardigan and the blue Slazenger jersey underneath. "Can I do for you today?"

Upstairs, Keira was shouting, and heavy footsteps were stamping around. "It's about your Tony," Ellie said.

Liz sighed. She was a thickset woman, shapeless in her sweaters and cardigans. A pallid, doughy, jowly face. Stringy, greasy-looking hair, the colour of dishwater, eyes the dull hard grey of wet stone. Like her house, she always put Ellie in mind of a squatting toad. But half her bulk was down to her layers of clothing; the rest was muscle. "What's he done now?" she said, folding her arms and wearing her usual expression when she learned one of her kids had been in another fight, caught in another theft, accused of another rape: indifference, angry victimhood and smugness. It made her face almost as punchable as Keira's.

"He hasn't done anything," said Ellie. She shouldn't have come here: the Harpers pushed her buttons at the best of times. But she had to break the news. And Liz Harper was still a mother. "We found a body this afternoon." Liz opened her mouth – *My son never killed anyone, typical police, always blaming us every time anything happens* – and Ellie carried on before she could speak. "It was Tony, Liz. He's dead. Looks like he got caught outside and froze –"

Jess howled in unbelieving grief, and the sounds from upstairs stopped. Liz stared at Ellie unblinkingly, the slack face blank. Then she shouted – not grief, not even rage but outright horror. The movement above started again, and footsteps came charging down the stairs.

"It's that fucking pig," Keira shouted. "That fucking pig's done something –"

The dog was barking, hauling on its chain, rearing up on its back legs, forepaws slashing at the air. Ellie turned sideways, stepping backwards towards the wall – keep the door on one side, Liz and the dog on the other. She'd still be penned in and trapped, but her back would be safe. She put one hand on the pepper spray, the other on her baton; if necessary, she'd fight her way out.

Outside it was dark; the air whirled with snow. God knew if she could even make it back to Barsall in that, but right now she only hoped she'd get the chance. And then the kitchen door flew open, and the Harper boys burst in.

5.

First in was Frank, biggest and eldest of the boys – man of the house and head of the family, as he liked to fancy himself, but in reality his mother's obedient lapdog, though no-one ever said so to his face. He was just over six feet tall in his trainers, with his mother's jowly face and hard grey eyes in a square, shaven head. A stained vest with a Union Jack design showed off arms and shoulders thick with steroid-boosted lifter's muscles and dotted with blue-ink prison tattoos.

"You." He jabbed a thick forefinger at Ellie. "What you doing to our mum?"

Keira bobbed at his elbow, teeth bared in a grin, and Dom Harper darted across the kitchen, surprisingly fast for his bulk. The next eldest after Frank, he had the same shaved head but was far shorter, with Liz's toad-like build, none of the muscle, and a wide, flat-nosed face. Foetal Alcohol Syndrome: Liz had suffered a terrible thirst for the gin while carrying him. His blue hooded top and grey leggings were stained and filthy; Ellie caught their stink as he passed. He crouched by the dog, muttering, fumbling at the chain around its neck.

Paul Harper pushed the kitchen door shut and leant back against it, eyeing Ellie and smirking. He was the least impressive of the men to look at; gangly-thin with prematurely receding hair, a greasy ponytail and smudged glasses fixed with tape, but as his victims could testify – or had, before recanting their statements – his strength belied his looks. Ellie was keeping clear of him most of all.

"Oi," Frank shouted. "Talking to you! Fuck do you want?"

"Stop it!" Jess screamed, over the baby's squalling. "Stop it, just stop it –"

Keira rounded on her. "Shut the fuck up, you stupid cunt, and shut that fucking mutant of yours up –"

"Quiet!" Liz thumped the table, and the kitchen fell silent, except for the baby's whimpers and sobs. Jess did her best to rock it as Ellie had shown her, and it quietened a little. Dom cradled the dog, still muttering; it licked his face. Paul took one of Tony's shotgun-shell knives out, using it to clean his nails.

Keira had retreated behind her partner, hiding from Liz's potential wrath. For his own part, Frank stared at Liz. "Mum?" he said. "Mum? What?"

To Ellie's unease, Liz picked up the shotgun and began cleaning it again. Her face was ashen, and there was a tremor in her hands. "It's your brother," she said at last.

Frank looked around the kitchen, then at Ellie. "Tony?"

The Harpers were all staring at her now. The baby whimpered, batting at the air with its cleft hand; Jess whispered to it, and Dom muttered to the dog. Paul Harper stopped picking his nails, and held the knife flat against his thigh.

Frank flexed his meaty hands, knuckle tattoos writhing. "What you done with our Tony?"

Ellie looked to Liz, but she said nothing – just continued to clean the shotgun, her face empty and slack. *Thanks a bunch, you old sow.* "We found a body earlier this afternoon," Ellie said. "The coppice outside your boundary wall, by the hill road?"

Frank gave a reluctant nod. "Yeah. There. It was your Tony."

"No," said Frank.

Ellie thought of showing the picture of the body from her phone, but felt that would have been too brutal. Instead she took out the driving licence and NI card in their evidence bags. Frank took one in each hand and held them close to his face, staring.

"Frank?" said Keira.

"They're Tony's," he said. He made to put them in his pocket, but Ellie held her hand up. "Need 'em back for now, Frank. They're evidence."

"They're our family's."

"You want whoever did this caught?"

She knew at once it'd been the wrong thing to say; once again they were all staring, and Liz snapped the shotgun's barrels shut with a clack.

"Who did it?" demanded Frank.

"Shut up, Frank." Liz banged the shotgun down and leant forward. "You told us he got stuck outside and froze."

"I –"

"She's a liar, Mum," Paul had a thin nasal voice, like a perpetual whine. "All coppers are liars, you know that."

"He froze," said Ellie, "but –"

"Shut the fuck up, Cuntstubble," Keira said. "Fucking liar."

"Needs teaching a lesson, this one," Paul smirked at Ellie. Loose wet lips. *Really?* Ellie thought, and put a hand on her baton.

"Paul," said Liz, eyes closed, voice hardening. "Keira." She opened her eyes again, staring at Ellie. "Talk."

"Looks like he froze to death outside," Ellie said. "But there's some circumstances –"

"*What* circumstances?"

"He had his knife out, for a start." Ellie nodded at Paul's. "One of those."

"Tony never pulled a knife on anybody," said Keira, "you lying c –"

"*Keira*," said Liz. She was quiet. Restrained; determined to keep control. "Change the fucking record."

"I know he didn't," said Ellie. "He was in the *Bell* till midnight, then set off home. But he ended up on the other side of Thursdale, and given how we found him, he was cornered."

"Bollocks." Dom spoke for the first time, thick and lisping. "Our Tony'd never back down. He'd a fought." He blinked, wet-eyed, stroking the dog's head. "Our Tony was brave."

"He was, love, he was. But –" Liz broke off.

"But what?" said Ellie.

"But nothing." Liz's hands had settled on the shotgun again. *Empty. It's empty. Isn't it?* She took them off the gun and rested them on the table. "Go on."

Proceed, by permission of the Queen. Ellie ploughed on, knowing she'd get nothing from them, wanting only to be back in her car heading home. She took out her phone, opened its picture gallery and swiped through the crime-scene pictures.

"Now what you fucking doing?" said Keira. "Liz, she's checking her fucking texts in the middle of –"

"Does this symbol mean anything to you?" Ellie asked, holding out the phone to Liz. She'd settled on the best and clearest image she'd been able to find of the charcoaled sign on the ledge. "We found it at the scene. Trying to determine if there's any connection."

Liz stared at it, and Ellie could literally see her face turn white. "Liz?" she said again. "Have you ever –"

"Nothing," said Liz. She was still pale – paler than usual – but the slackness had gone out of her face, which was pinched now and hard. "Never seen it before in me life."

A lie, but meaning what? Ellie showed the picture to the others. "Any of you recognise this?"

A chorus of mumbled negatives answered her. Keira shook her head and shrugged, which was politeness by her standards. Their reactions seemed genuine enough – although they'd have probably said nothing even if they had recognised it. Ellie put the phone away, and carried on. "He must've been set on as he came home. Probably on your land."

"What you tryna fucking say now?" demanded Keira.

"Chances were, they were mob-handed," Ellie went on, looking straight at Liz. "You're right, Tony'd never back down from a fight otherwise. Unless he didn't want to fight them for some other reason."

"*Now* what are you tryna –"

"Do you know anyone who'd want to harm Tony, or your family in general?"

"No," said Liz.

Wouldn't tell you even if she did. Christ's sake, what a waste of time. The next question was one any copper would have to ask, but would be the equivalent of lobbing a grenade across the kitchen. There'd be no straight answers anyway; much more sensible to offer her condolences, ask Liz to make a formal ID and get out. It was what Tom Graham would have done. Anything for a quiet life.

But it would have been the coward's way out, and Ellie wouldn't take it. "Where were you all last night between midnight and two a.m.?"

Even the baby stopped crying, and Dom Harper rose from his crouch beside the dog.

"You. Fucking. What?" said Keira.

"Keira," rumbled Frank.

"She's saying we killed him – Liz, the bitch is saying we did our Tony in –"

"I have to ask this question for –" But Keira chuntered on.

"She's saying one of youse did your own brother in. You gonna let her stand there and say that, Frank? Under your own roof?"

Liz said nothing, not meeting Ellie's eyes. Had Ellie actually hit a nerve there? People surprised you all the time if you were a copper, and rarely in a good way. Nature of the job, after all; you spent most of your time dealing with the consequences of greed, stupidity or just plain viciousness, and she could believe pretty much anything of the Harpers at the best of times.

But not this. The Harpers' one positive feature, pretty much, was their sense of family unity, even if it was warped and didn't draw the line at actual sibling incest. They'd fight among themselves, sometimes viciously; Ellie might have just about believed Tony falling and cracking his skull in a family brawl gone wrong, but not this. Whoever did it had surrounded him and watched as he'd died. You couldn't get more cold-blooded than that. And that wasn't the Harper way, least of all with one of their own.

So what didn't Liz want to say? What was she hiding?

"She needs a lesson," Paul said again. He moved towards Ellie; Keira came out from behind Frank and went for her too.

Ellie drew the pepper spray and baton together, pushing the baton's catch so it shot out to its full length. Keira clawed for her face and Ellie sprayed her in the eyes from a foot's distance. Keira shrieked and fell; Ellie spun towards Paul, but he had his left arm up to shield his eyes and the knife ready in his right.

Was this real? Was this happening? *I'm a fucking police officer, you –*

She swung low with the baton, catching Paul across the knee. He fell sideways, screaming; Ellie jumped over him and ran for the door.

A hand grabbed her baton arm and swung her round. Frank's thick face was red and bloated with rage, his free hand drawn back in a fist. Ellie pepper-sprayed him too; he bellowed in pain, staggering, but clung onto her arm, dragging her back into the kitchen. Keira was screaming and cursing, trying to get up and clawing at her own eyes now; Paul rolled around clutching his knee and had vomited on the stone floor. Liz remained motionless: saying nothing, doing nothing. Dom huddled against the Belfast sink, letting out thick-voiced wails and fumbling with the dog's chain, and Jess was sobbing, trying to push herself back through the kitchen wall while her baby howled.

Ellie stamped on Frank's foot twice, thumping at his wrist with her free hand till his grip slackened. She pulled free and hit him across the stomach with the baton, then again when he doubled over. *Self-defence, Your Honour, he'd attacked me and I couldn't give him a chance to do it again. Any enjoyment I got out of it is purely coincidental.*

"Get her, Sabre! Get the bitch!" Dom shouted, and Ellie saw he'd got the chain off the dog. It ran towards her, snarling. Jess screamed, hunching protectively around the baby. And Liz

Harper sat at her table, stubbing out her cigarette, doing nothing.

Ellie pulled the kitchen door shut behind her and the dog slammed into it with a force that shook the house. *Let it all fall fucking down, the whole rotten ruin of it.* She ran down the hall to the front door. Please let it be unlocked. She'd smash her way out through the windows if necessary. It opened a few inches, then jerked to a halt. The security chain. *Fuck.* From the kitchen came muffled bellows and screams and the baying of the dog. Then they grew suddenly louder as the kitchen door opened.

She slammed the front door and fumbled at the chain – *come on, come fucking on* – till it came free. She flung the door open and ran out – should have slammed it behind her – pelting over to the Land Rover. Snow was falling heavily now, and the ground was slippery; she slipped and nearly fell.

Keys – the keys –

She fumbled for them as the dog ran across the yard. *Oh shit. Oh fuck.* She didn't want to hurt it. She liked dogs; they were preferable to people on the whole. But it was barking maniacally, lips rolled back from its teeth and covered in foam.

She swung up the baton and screamed, "Come on then!" It halted, but kept barking.

Keys, keys, fucking keys –

She found them, pushed the button and the Land Rover bleeped. Lights flashed and locks clunked, but the dog rushed her as she turned away. She lashed out with the baton and it leapt back – no doubt the poor beast had plenty of practice dodging blows.

Dom staggered out of the doorway, bellowing. Ellie scrambled into the Land Rover, slammed the door and started the engine, throwing the gear into reverse and accelerating backwards. The dog chased after her, then stopped.

The gate was coming up, but she refused to stop to open it: Ellie wanted a solid metal shell between her and the Harpers until she was clear of Thursdale. She floored the accelerator; the Land Rover hit the gate doing fifty and tore it off its hinges before fishtailing across the dirt-track and tearing halfway through a hedge.

For one appalling moment she was sure it would roll over or stall, but it kept its balance and the engine continued running. Ellie threw the gear into forward and the car lurched free of the hedge back onto all four wheels, rocking slightly. She accelerated up the track: it was nearly dark now and all she could see in the Land Rover's headlights were swirling mandalas of snow.

She didn't look at the rearview; couldn't spare the time or concentration, and the Harpers were unlikely to give chase. Keira, Frank and Paul would be no threat to anyone for now, Jess couldn't drive and Dom wouldn't have the gumption unless Liz told him.

As for Liz, Christ alone knew what she was thinking. She wasn't thick; she knew Ellie would have had to ask the family to account for their movements. She'd just sat there and *let* things kick off. Why? Didn't she want Tony's killers finding?

Might already know. Either way, she'll want to deal with them herself.

Probably true, but still not the answer. They could have all confirmed their whereabouts without giving Ellie anything concrete. Even by Harper standards, what had just happened was extreme, especially if Paul had had his way. They were the ones with the injuries and they'd all no doubt blame Ellie, but once the roads were clear again there'd be court appearances, fines – maybe even jail time, though not as much as they deserved.

So why?

Ellie reached the other gate. She hesitated, then got out and opened it the normal way, looking back through the snow for approaching headlights. None came.

Liz got what she wanted: you off her property before you could ask too many questions.

She drove through, closed the gate, then set off homeward at the fastest crawl she dared, through a tunnel of whirling snow.

6.

She'd been tempted to stop at Wakeman Farm till the storm passed, but she'd have been stranded for the night and badly wanted the comfort of her own four walls. She felt too raw right now, too many buried things threatening to surface. The anger and violence and loss. No. She needed safety. Shelter. Sanctuary. Home.

Properly speaking, she should have gone straight to the station to fill out a report on the incident at Barrowman Farm. But she was shaking from the adrenaline rush and from negotiating the hill road in the snow. Fuck it, basically.

Ellie's house was one of the first you passed entering Barsall Village, a few doors from the crossroads and the conical war memorial. Ellie let herself out of the Land Rover, locked it and stumbled to her front door, stepped through and slammed it shut behind her.

The house was warm and quiet. A sweatshirt and leggings were draped over the living room radiator, ready for her return. She shucked off her stab vest, utility belt and the rest of the uniform, tossed it on an armchair and pulled on the soft, warm clothes.

Ellie's hands were shaking and she was desperately hungry; in the kitchen she put the kettle on, ate four slices of bread and made a mug of heavily sugared instant coffee. Normally she was a tea drinker, but this was her comfort drink. The crockpot and rice cooker were steaming away, ready for Milly and Noel; Ellie filled a bowl with chilli and rice and took it upstairs.

Enough. Easy. Rein it in.

She breathed in, then out. Slow. Steady. Control. Ellie ran the hot bath she'd promised herself, poured in a capful of Radox, undressed, then sank into the hot water to work the day's chill out of her bones and cleanse her of the contact she'd had with the Harpers.

Could have been killed back there. Beaten anyway. Maybe raped.

No maybe about it, when Paul Harper was involved.

Breathe in. Breathe out. She didn't want to think of that right now. Or the adrenaline rush. The thrill of sudden danger and excitement. Or the fight.

The violence, too. The release of it.

You enjoyed it. Admit it.

Of course she had. Before this, Ellie had worked one of the toughest beats in inner-city Manchester; you had to be hard, the people you were dealing with, but she'd always found that easy; the difficult part was reining it in. After Richard died and Stan left, it only got worse. Sooner or later, she'd known, she'd go too far. So she'd transferred out to the sticks. It'd meant goodbye to CID and promotion, but losing your child and your marriage in quick succession made you re-evaluate your priorities.

Breathe in. Breathe out.

She lay back in the water and chuckled weakly. Over and above the release of the action, there'd been satisfaction in giving the Harpers some well-deserved pain, especially Paul. They got away with ninety percent of the shit they pulled; a few baton blows at least dealt out a small measure of justice.

Jesus, Ellie.

She didn't particularly like herself at times like this, seeing how her inner clockwork functioned so clearly. Then again, she wasn't sure how well she liked herself full stop. She climbed out of the bath, dried herself off and dressed again.

She towelled her hair, typed up incident reports on Tony Harper's death and her visit to Barrowman Farm, then emailed them to Tom Graham. The hourglass icon hovered and spun, but just when she thought it was about to time out, the message showed as having been despatched. She sighed in relief, then flopped back onto the bed to relax before –

The doorbell rang.

Ellie went downstairs, then stopped. Her address was no secret; the Harpers could easily know where she lived. She went into the living room and picked up the baton.

The doorbell rang again, and someone started pounding on the door. "Ellie!" Milly shouted. "Let us in, for fuck's sake."

Ellie peeped through the spyhole, just in case: the image of Paul Harper holding a knife to Milly's throat was as insistent as it was unwelcome. But she only saw Milly and Noel; the street behind them was empty apart from the snow.

"Ellie!"

She opened the door. "Sorry –"

"Bloody hell." Milly bustled past her down the hallway. "Trying to fucking kill us?"

"Hi, Milly," Ellie called after her. "You okay, Noel?"

"Not bad, Ell. You?"

"Yeah. Yeah."

"Where's that bloody wine you promised me, Cheetham?" Milly called.

"Shit. Left it in the car."

Milly snatched the keys from her as Noel wandered into the room and tossed them to him. "Jones! Wine. In the Land Rover. Go fetch."

"Whereabouts?"

"Passenger footwell," Ellie said. "In a Co-Op bag."

"Roger and wilco, Red Leader."

Noel went out. A cold draught blew into the living-room and outside the Land Rover's locks beeped and clunked. Milly took Ellie's hands. "What happened?"

"Nothing."

"Ell."

She shrugged. "It's the Harpers, you know?"

"It's not *just* that. Come on, what?"

The car door slammed. The locks beeped and clunked again, and the front door banged as Noel came back through.

"Fucksake. You born in a barn, Jones?"

He held up a bottle of wine, and a dripping Co-Op bag. "Other one was broken."

"Well get it in the bin then. Don't drip it on the carpet." Milly grinned as Noel trotted into the kitchen. "Got him well-trained."

Ellie managed a smile.

"Your Land Rover's been in the wars a bit," said Noel as he came back in.

Milly raised her eyebrows. "Well? Come on, Ell, talk to me."

"Chilli's in the cooker."

"Fuck the chilli."

"You're supposed to eat it."

"Jones. Chilli." Noel went into the kitchen. Milly raised her eyebrows. She wasn't letting it go. Ellie sighed.

"All right. Fine. Things kicked off a bit."

"A bit?"

"Want some wine?"

Milly finally dropped the topic until the chilli, the rice and the bottle of wine were gone and they'd switched to Scotch. By that point in the evening Milly was stretched out on the sofa, her head in Noel's lap. He gazed down at her with an expression either of befuddled joy at having found so perfect a soulmate or bewildered terror at how the hell he'd ended up in this particular trap. Ellie was leaning back in an armchair with a pleasant buzz on and had almost convinced herself the subject was forgotten when Milly piped up: "So come on, Ell. What happened at the farm?"

"Nothing much."

"*Ell.*"

Ellie finally gave her a bowdlerised version of events, downplaying the violence – although, booze or no booze, it visibly didn't fool Milly for a second. "And Liz H just let it all kick off?"

"Yeah."

"So you gonna have to go back there?"

"Not if I can help it."

"Won't someone have to ID Tony?"

"Tom can deal with that. And questioning them can wait till we've got some outside help in. I'm not going back there without the heavy mob."

For nearly a minute, the only sound in the room was the CD she'd put on earlier. "Anyone want topping up?" Ellie said at last.

The bottle went round the room. "Think she let it kick off on purpose?" Milly said.

Ellie didn't fence around this time. "Yeah."

"What for?"

"Well," said Ellie, "that's the big question, isn't it?"

"Could it not be some sort of family feud, got out of hand?" said Noel.

"I wondered that," Ellie said. "If he got his head bashed in, I could see it – he gets into a scrap with Paul or Frank – someone lands a lucky punch, or he falls and cracks his head…"

"And they're still family, so Liz wouldn't want them getting done for it." Milly pursed her lips. "His injuries didn't *look* severe, but he could've had a bleed on the brain. Can't always tell without digging a bit deeper. But you'd need a proper pathologist for that. And it still doesn't explain how he ended up where he did. Right?"

"I know. A brawl's one thing, but –"

"But someone chased him down," said Noel. "Cornered him. Then stood around and watched him die."

"Yeah."

"That's cold-blooded," said Noel softly. "I mean, that's *really* fucking cold-blooded." He reached for the whisky, and no-one spoke. Noel hardly ever swore; when he did, it hung in the air.

"Exactly," Ellie said. "And that mark."

"What mark?"

Ellie took out her phone and showed her. "That was on the ledge where we reckoned Tony Harper'd been. Would have been just over his head. Liz said she didn't recognise it, but –"

"Think she was lying?"

"Liz Harper, lie to the police?" said Noel. "Surely not."

"Shut up, Jones."

"She looked as if she was about to shit bricks," Ellie said. "Not to put too fine a point on it."

"Who does something like that? A gang? There anyone else around here like the Harpers?"

"Christ on crutches. Don't go there."

"Ellie."

"Sorry." Milly swore like a sailor, but drew the line at blasphemy. "One lot's bad enough. Besides, who'd try starting a gang war in all this? Practically been blizzards blowing all week, roads getting blocked as fast as they can clear them. And come on, you ever seen a gang killing like that?"

"No," Milly admitted, "and I've seen a few, worse luck." Like Ellie, she was originally from Manchester. She'd been raised in Hulme, in a vibrant Afro-Caribbean community, among friends and family she still dearly loved, but there'd been a bad gang problem when she'd been growing up there. "He'd have been shot or stabbed or beaten. They wouldn't just stand around and let him freeze."

"No," agreed Ellie.

"So," said Noel, "who does?"

No-one had an answer, Ellie least of all. She reached for the Scotch and poured them all another. Outside, the wind blew waves of snow down the High Street. Ellie was glad it wasn't visible through the curtains, except for the way it made the streetlights' dim glow flicker; she kept thinking she could see shapes moving in it.

7.

Liz Harper sat and smoked in the front room at Barrowman Farm. In the kitchen, the dogs were barking. almost drowned out by the sound of hammering from there and upstairs.

Paul had boarded up the front room window from the inside, moaning and complaining all the while about his knee, while Frank and Keira bathed their eyes and Jess got under everyone's feet. That'd only left Dom – thickest and most useless of her brood next to Jess – for the last job, so she'd sent him out with shovel and pick. She should've stayed off the gin when she was carrying him. Still, better risking Dom than Frank or Paul.

If there *was* a risk; if Nan's stories turned out to be anything more. The cold hard logical part of Liz said they weren't and couldn't be. Tony had got into a fight down at the *Bell* which had followed him outside (but would Cheetham have come, asking the questions she had, if she'd already known who it was?) Or some other gang with either a grudge or an eye on the Harper's business, had come after him (but in this weather, in these storms, with snow blocking the roads every night?)

There was more cold hard logic in Liz than people guessed – one reason the family had far less prison time between them than most would say they deserved – but that hadn't been all that'd kept them free and healthy over the years. There was another part of her, an older, darker voice. It'd warned her away from the undercover copper from Nottingham, and the dog-fight the police had raided.

She'd learned to heed it for the best and simplest reason; whenever it spoke, it was *right*.

Soon as Cheetham'd told her how Tony'd died, that old dark voice had told Liz Harper that all Nan's tales were true. She couldn't, mustn't think of Tony now. She'd the rest of her family to worry about. Easy to start howling and sobbing, or take to her bed and not come down for a week, but there wasn't time for that, for her or anyone else.

She'd told the old voice it was talking shite, and cold hard logic had agreed. Tony had got drunk. Maybe slipped and knocked his head, dizzied himself and wandered, off-course and dazed, till the cold got to him and down he went. Stupid, tragic, a senseless fucking death for her little boy, but it made sense at least. Explained it without having to believe in Nan's fairy tales.

But then Cheetham had shown her the mark, and –

Something banged on the front door. Liz tied a bandolier around her waist, trying and failing not to think of Tony again, and picked up her shotgun.

Always starts with one, Nan had told her. *Some poor sod, out after dark in the dead of winter – it's always then, when* They *wake up.* They *go out hunting. Never touch whoever it is – just chase them down and watch them freeze. Some folk read tea-leaves – or remember that old ghost story, about drawing the sorts? Well,* They *do the same thing by watching how you die of the cold.*

Liz remembered *the sorts*: you opened a Bible at random, put your finger down the same way, then read the line you'd found to discover what you had to do, or what was going to happen.

Bible. Yes – the Bible, that was what Liz needed now.

But there was someone at the door, and that needed seeing to first. She slotted two cartridges into the twelve-bore and snapped the barrels shut.

If the death goes well – for Them, *I mean,* They *leave their sign*, Nan had told her. They *gather and meet, to talk about what* They've *seen. About the portents, to see whether it's time yet. And if*

They *decide it is – there'll be two nights, just two more nights – and then on the third, the Dance.*

Liz remembered that, and the old rhyme Nan had taught her: *Board your window, keep on your light, when the Tatterskin walks at night.*

But they were stories. Fairytales. They weren't real.

So cold hard logic said. But the old dark voice had disagreed.

And Liz had paid attention to it. Keira was nailing up the other downstairs windows, Frank attending to the upstairs ones and Paul keeping watch from the attic skylight with a pair of night-vision binoculars as he could see straighter than either of them just now. Jess was supposedly nailing up the window in the pantry, but most likely just keeping out of everyone's way. *Worthless.* Liz'd miscarried twice; sons, both times. Couldn't one of them have lived, and Jess been born dead and half-formed? Waste of space. Maybe her kid would be worth something.

Someone banged on the door again.

Just in case. It was all just in case. Let them think she was going mad if they wanted. Let them get through tonight, and in the morning she'd see. The boards would come down from the window easily enough, and they'd never speak of it again – they could carry on as normal, and this would be a blip. Let them, let any of them, try making out Liz was losing the plot, and she'd make them sorry. She would. But for now, for tonight – just in case, the windows would be boarded and all the lights on.

Tony. Her little boy, her handsome boy, her favourite. He'd driven her half-mad with his ways – never seemed to get that it was family first and last and always and the rest of the world could go fuck itself, that you never stood against your own. Like he'd done with Paul over that silly girl, although Paul was enough of a trial in his own right – fuck anything that moved and half the things that didn't – but of course she'd loved Tony best, how could she not have? She'd give both Jess and Dom for Tony back again.

Enough of that, you silly old crow. Liz edged into the hallway, raised the shotgun towards the door, relaxing only when Dom bellowed: "Mum? Mum? S'me."

She broke the shotgun and let him in. "Why didn't you say, you spastic?"

Dom grinned and dragged in a dirt-covered barrel bag. Liz slammed and locked the door after him. "Kitchen table. Jess, get your brother a brew. *Jess!*"

The pantry door opened with a click and Jess padded into the hall, still holding the baby. "Coffee," said Dom.

In the kitchen, Liz unzipped the barrel bag. The Harpers owned their share of legal guns – half a dozen 12-bores, an old .303 army rifle and a .22 self-loading rifle that looked like something the SAS would use (and was therefore coveted by all the boys despite being a glorified popgun as far as Liz was concerned) but there were a few others for special occasions that the law didn't know about (although that bitch Ellie Cheetham no doubt suspected), which were kept buried out back unless required.

Along with a folding poacher's gun – just a .410, but it had its uses – and a deer rifle were another half-dozen shotguns with highly illegal modifications. Five were standard double-barrelled guns with the stock cut down to the pistol grip and the barrels sawn short. The sixth was an Ithaca pump-action. The barrel and stock were cut down too, and it had a five-shot magazine. Just the job for close quarters. You had to be ready for whatever came.

There was a little .22 target pistol, as well; they'd used it for rats before the handgun ban. Liz shoved that through her belt, put down her twelve-bore and picked up the Ithaca: that was hers. She loaded the magazine, chambered a cartridge and loaded a sixth, then applied the safety catch.

Frank plodded down the stairs. "All done."

"Good. Any sign?"

"Paul thought he saw something near Wakeman Farm. Can't be sure though in all this."

"No," she said. Not much point having a lookout in this weather, but at least she'd tried. "Anything happens tonight, I reckon it'll be the outskirts. Wakeman, maybe the *Bell*, and then..."

He doubted her, though he was doing his best to hide it, but that'd pass. Long as he did as he was told tonight – tomorrow, he'd see for himself. "But not here?"

"No, 'cos we'll be ready."

He still looked doubtful.

"Maybe I'm just being a mardy old bag, our Frank, and maybe I'm not. We'll see tomorrow, won't we? But for tonight, we're doing this. Better safe. Got a problem with that? Say so now."

He didn't, of course; she'd known he wouldn't. Frank was rock-hard in every other way, but he'd never go against his Mum. Liz smiled. "Now, pair of you – one shotgun, one sawn-off each, and load 'em. And *Dom* – keep 'em broken till you're ready to use them."

Frank chose the other pump-action gun. Dom picked an over and under; each took a sawn-off and scooped up a bandolier. Dom pottered through to the front room, his coffee in one fist. Frank followed.

Liz remembered something. "Jess!"

"Mum?"

Dumb cow eyes, scared rabbit eyes. "Go to me room and fetch the Bible."

"Bible."

"The *Family* Bible, Jess."

"The big 'un?"

Give me strength. "Yes, Jess. The big 'un."

Jess dithered, holding the baby. "Give that here," said Liz. "Now go, fetch."

"Yes'm."

Liz sat down at the kitchen table. Baby Steven fussed and mewled, but she tucked him under one arm and rocked him, using her free hand to get herself a fag and light it, occasionally moving her head back so as not to let that disgusting deformed hand touch her face.

Jess came back, huffing and puffing under the weight of the book. "Ooh, Mum, don't smoke around J – round Steven." She'd wanted to call the kid Joel, and still might when no-one was listening, but Liz'd put her foot down. Not giving the kid a stupid name like that. He was Steven, after Liz's granddad. She'd have to watch the girl and listen out, come down on her if she caught her calling the kid by the wrong name. Fucking thing was probably retarded as well as deformed, like Jess herself and Dom; giving it two names'd just make things worse.

"Stop your whining." Liz handed Baby Steven back. Jess retreated, cuddling the child. Liz scowled and slammed the target pistol down on the table. "And get that loaded."

"But Mum –"

"But nothing. You're doing your bit. Take a shotgun too."

Jess grabbed a box of .22 ammunition, sat at the far end of the table and clumsily began loading the pistol.

Liz hung one of the sawn-offs around her neck on a rope sling and ground out her cigarette on the kitchen floor. "Get us a brew," she told Jess.

The girl ran to the kettle; bullets rolled across the table. The wind roared outside. *They* were out in it somewhere, looking for a way in.

Six adults, if Jess and Dom counted. They'd cope. Work in pairs – one upstairs, one down. Watch and listen.

She'd grown up on Nan's stories and loved hearing them – who didn't like a good scare on a dark night? But if she'd ever believed, she'd stopped long before she started bleeding of a month. This wasn't a life for the soft and dreamy – like useless bloody Jess. Christ, imagine if Liz'd been like that. She nearly *had* been, but her Mam'd toughened her up, mean old lush though she'd been. Least Nan'd been there; she'd been kind, and she'd had her stories to tell. But that was all they'd been;

never real. Oh, Nan had claimed to have seen *Them* when she was young, but who'd really believed her?

But now there was Tony and how he'd died.

Her baby. Her child. No. No weakness. No –

Liz slammed a fist on the table. Jess give a little cry.

"Stop fussing," said Liz, more harshly than she'd meant. The girl was only scared. *So what? Scared doesn't stop anything happening. You've got to pull it together and be ready to act.*

Tony had died like a cornered rat. No, not even that: a cornered rat died fighting. Tony hadn't been a coward, he'd known how to fight. Her beautiful boy; she'd been proud of him. His wilfulness had only made her love him more, even knowing it had to be broken and broken by her.

It never would be, now.

He must have been so scared, dying alone in the cold and the dark.

Liz's eyes were suddenly full of tears and there was a scream stuck in her throat, but she dragged her sleeve angrily across her face and choked the scream down. There'd be a time to grieve, a time to cry. So much still to do. She'd have to talk to the police again, in order to see him and claim him back for burial. Have to identify him – that was her job and no-one else's – but that would have to wait.

The lights flickered. Was it *Them*, or just the storm? Liz told herself it was only the second, and she'd keep doing so till she knew better. She lit another cigarette, laid the shotgun across her knees, then put on a pair of reading glasses and began to go through the family Bible.

They just had to get through to the morning; by then she'd have combed every page of this and, between that and whatever the daylight showed, she'd know what their survival would take. Because survive they would. The Harpers knew how to take care of themselves. Against the world. Against the night.

8.

Joda Famuyiwa watched his wife sleep, wondering if tonight she'd finally die.

He'd watched the sickness take almost everything from her over the past six years. She'd survived far longer than the doctors had thought, but it was nearly over now. Her chestnut hair was almost white, her oval face gaunt, and her once-smooth skin, now lined, had gone from creamy white to dull waxy grey.

She was horribly thin now too; the hand Joda held was a claw of knuckle and bone. He squeezed gently, and her breath caught. The pain was almost constant, despite the drugs; she tried to hide it, but he could always tell.

Barbara had grown up not far from here, and it had never let go of her; she loved the landscape and had always hoped to return. After her diagnosis – once they'd known it was not if but when the cancer won – Joda had wanted to give her that at least. Perhaps he had, but what had he taken away from Charlotte in doing so?

Joda released Barbara's hand and stroked her forehead, biting his lips: his eyes were stinging, his throat constricted. He might cry, and mustn't; she depended on him.

As did his daughter. But he must forget Charlotte, at least for the moment. A heart could only bear so much at a time. God never supposedly gave anyone more than they could withstand, but lately Joda had come to suspect his Creator had overestimated him. As he did every night, he uttered a silent prayer that his wife sleep peacefully.

He'd closed the pub early, unable to face another late shift. Besides, no-one had set foot in the *Bell* since Ellie had come to tell him about Tony Harper. That poor boy. Troubled, yes, but not wicked. Frozen in the snow. Lost and drunk, most likely, on Joda's beer.

Joda's hand became a fist, but he relaxed his fingers and continued stroking Barbara's face instead. He had guilt enough without holding himself responsible for every drunk who staggered in and out. It was a struggle to stay afloat, especially in the winter months, and they had nowhere to go if they lost the pub. He had a family to provide for. But he could never shake the fear that he'd somehow failed his only child.

Charlotte ate, had clothes on her back and a bed to sleep in. That mattered. But summed up that way, it sounded cold as well; Man didn't live by bread alone, and children looked to their parents for affection and care as well. And the more of Barbara her illness had taken, the less Joda had had to give to his daughter.

Barbara was still now, almost at rest. When her face relaxed in sleep, some of the lines on it faded. Joda ran his thumb across a sparse, wiry eyebrow.

He provided, as a father should. For the rest, if anything, he was too forbearing. Joda's father would never have allowed one of his daughters to see – as if seeing was all that happened – a boy like David Chapple. Joda had seen a hundred boys like that – might even have become one, in his wilder days. At least his fathers – earthly and heavenly – had prevented that. But what was he to do?

Joda's father would have ordered Charlotte to have no more to do with the boy, and yes, might have beaten her if she'd disobeyed. But that wasn't how things were done – not here, not now. Besides, if Joda ordered Charlotte not to see David, she'd only become more determined to. As for raising his hand to her – Barbara would be furious if he did that. It might kill her, for which Charlotte would likely hold herself as guilty as him. More to the point, it wouldn't keep her from the Chapple boy – it would guarantee she ran away to him, if anything.

It was like trying to grip jelly in your hand; the more tightly you squeezed, the more surely it slid between your fingers. All he could do was cup it gently and hope that was enough.

Barbara was snoring. Joda tried not to think or feel it, but it was only the truth: if God were merciful, He'd let Barbara pass tonight as she slept, with no more pain.

He thought that almost every night now, and every night hated himself for it: he was asking God to murder his wife, because he couldn't face the burden of caring for her. In sickness and in health, their marriage vows had said. Barbara would care for him without question were their roles reversed.

But he was afraid she'd ask him to do it. He knew the thought had occurred to her, but doubted she still had the strength or clarity of mind for it. Suicide was a dreadful sin. But she was suffering without hope of recovery or survival, and just wanted it to end.

He'd often prayed for guidance on the matter, but received no answer. He could always ask Pastor Williams, but Joda had little confidence in him. A priest should offer not only kindness but authority, too, and he couldn't picture Pastor Williams displaying any sign of *that*.

Barbara mumbled, then lay quiet. Joda suddenly couldn't look at her without seeing her as she'd been, and the contrast was too painful to bear. He got up and went onto the landing.

Charlotte had just finished primary school when they'd moved here; it had seemed a good time to relocate. But she'd left her friends behind and was, he suspected, a city girl by nature; for all their beauty, the Peaks would always be a poor substitute for that.

Joda eyed the door to his daughter's room. The light was out, or he'd have been tempted to knock. Go in and try, at least, to talk to her. He'd almost done so in the past, but his courage had always failed him. She was like a foreigner to him now, and he had to mend that; she'd soon be all he had. And who would she have but him? David Chapple?

Joda shook his head, but the knowledge wouldn't go away. The boy was worthless, empty, a taker and nothing more; when would she see that, and what would be left of her by then? And what would become of her, if she'd cut herself off from her family?

Barbara would have said he worried too much. He wished she still could. She might have helped him see things clearly, and what to do. But so little remained of her now.

He turned away from Charlotte's door and plodded downstairs. He didn't know what to do with himself, but he couldn't be upstairs any longer. He needed – guilt slid through him at the knowledge – to be away from his dying wife. Just for a little while.

The snug was dark and silent. The fire had long gone out; despite the central heating, there was a chill. When he went behind the counter, the faint smell of spilt beer was oddly comforting.

Joda rarely drank. What was that saying? *One's not enough, and three's too many*. Yes. Far too easy for it to become a habit. Barbara having a bad night? Drink. Don't want to think about her dying? Drink. Worried about Charlotte? Drink. Sorry for yourself? And so on.

But tonight he'd make an exception. He held a glass under the appropriate optic and decanted first one measure of Scotch, then a second. Then he came out from behind the counter and crossed the snug.

He didn't turn on the main lights. There was a table lamp in an alcove by the fireplace, so he switched that on and sank into a soft leather armchair, swirling the whisky in the glass. He took a sniff of the fumes and winced; he'd never understand why Ellie Cheetham went on about this stuff. But then he felt that way about most spirits; when he drank them, it was for their effect, nothing more. The whisky burnt his mouth and throat;

a trail of fire etched its way to his stomach like a falling star. Lucifer, falling from Heaven. That wasn't a comforting train of thought, and Joda needed some peace and reassurance – especially tonight, when God seemed so silent.

Above him, the stuffed pike gawped, waiting for a passer-by to meet its black eyes in order to transmit its mute resentment to the world: *There I was, minding my own business, trying to sort out dinner, and next thing I know some joker's stabbing me in the mouth and drowning me in the air.*

Joda chuckled to himself. The whisky was taking effect. Beside the pike, the pendulum clock ticked slowly and steadily. He closed his eyes, settled back in the chair. The ticking was a soothing sound: it spoke of something constant and ancient, that had been here before him and would remain long after. He took another sip of whisky.

Another night, he might have gone outside. Just a short stroll. The quiet, the fresh air, the stars. You saw so many of them on a clear night: there was so little light pollution out here. But on a night like this you'd see nothing.

Wind buffeted the pub, rattling the windows, eclipsing the sound of the clock. *Old? Eternal? I've been here forever. Before you, or the clock, or this building. I've been here since 'here' was only stone and earth, and I'll be here when it is again.*

No more whisky, Joda decided, at least not just now. He leant forward again, and opened his eyes.

If he'd turned on the main lights, the windows would have been black mirrors, and he'd have only seen himself. But as it was, he could see through them. Not that there was much to see but the whirling, billowing snow. A clump of it had somehow massed in the middle of a window, clinging to the glass.

Then he realised that it wasn't stuck to the window, but outside it. Not snow, then. Whatever it was, it was hunched and immobile, and a thin fabric flapped loosely around it. Some kind of windblown debris, but he had no idea what.

The window misted. It faded almost at once, but as he watched, it happened again, fanning out on either side of the object. Spread and faded. Spread and faded. Almost rhythmic, like the clock's ticking or his heartbeat –

Or like breath.

Joda blinked, and stared; the warm condensation rhythmically spread and dispersed, again and again, across the glass.

He stood up and took a step towards the window. What was he doing? He moved closer, reminding himself that this was a living thing, maybe even a person. It might need help, like Tony Harper had last night. What kind of a man wouldn't help, if he could?

The patch of condensation continued to pulse in and out as he neared the window. He could see his visitor, or its outline, more clearly, but was none the wiser for doing so. It was very thin, and hunched; Joda thought of a hairless, emaciated dog. Or perhaps an ape. He couldn't decide; his impression of its form wavered between the canine and simian, even humanoid. It must be the thinness of its front legs that made them look so long; its skeletal shoulders stuck up like blades on either side of its head.

The flurrying snow also confused matters, but not as much as the fabric that swaddled the creature. It was a pale, thin material that surely couldn't offer any protection worth speaking of to the hairless, fleshless form beneath, and appeared ragged and tattered. Joda's confusion gave way to unease: who'd dress themselves in that, in any weather? Someone desperate, who'd had no choice in what to wear – someone who'd been held against their will and managed to escape? Or someone whose reason was so distorted that such clothing might seem a rational choice? In other words, either a maniac or a refugee from one.

Assuming this creature *was* a person, clothed or not; Joda still couldn't decide if its shape was human or bestial. He moved to one side, trying to view it in profile, but the shape of its head only added to the confusion. It definitely wasn't a dog, because it had a very human-like high forehead and large round skull, but instead of a mouth and nose it seemed to have a snout or muzzle. Joda couldn't decide whether it looked more like a man, ape, dog or even an impossibly huge insect with a stubby proboscis.

The creature's head turned – swivelled – in a single smooth, precise motion, then stopped; less like an animal now than a machine. It made a small movement up, then to one side, then down again – like a remote-controlled weapon, adjusting its aim – until it pointed directly at him.

The wind blew; the fabric flapped and billowed. Otherwise the creature had resumed its earlier motionlessness.

Joda retreated slowly, and the head swivelled to follow him. Mist bloomed and faded on the window. Then two new creatures appeared; gigantic white spiders with repulsively long thin legs that made a faint pattering sound as they crawled up the glass. As they rose to hang on either side of the creature's face, its shoulders also rose, moving away from its body.

They weren't shoulders at all, Joda realised, but the creature's elbows; they'd been sticking up straight in the air because its hands had been resting on the ground, which meant its limbs were even longer than they'd appeared.

Joda detested violence in all its forms – another reason he'd never raised a hand to his daughter. He had witnessed it more than once, as a child and as a man, both in Nigeria and in Britain: there was no glamour to it, only pain. So even though it would have been relatively easy, out here, to purchase a shotgun or smallbore rifle, he'd rejected the idea out of hand. Not even a baseball bat in case of burglars or rowdy customers. For the first time ever, he regretted that decision.

Again the thing's head altered its position with small, shifting movements, until it pointed directly at him. Then it was still again, apart from its flapping shroud – yes, a shroud – but the wind was no longer the only sound. There were thin, pattering noises, like soot falling in a chimney. But the fireplace was to Joda's left, and the sounds came from his right.

He didn't want to look away from the thing, fearing both what it might do if his attention left it, and what he might be about to see. But he had to know what he faced if he was to cope with it. He had Barbara and Charlotte to consider.

And so he turned and looked.

There were four front windows on the ground floor of the *Bell*, and each was now occupied by a creature like the first. The same crouched, emaciated forms and snouted heads, the same thin, long-fingered hands splayed on the glass. Joda retreated across the bar, and their heads swivelled, tilting towards him. A gust of wind brushed the shroud partially away from one of them, revealing more of its face – if you could call it that – than Joda wanted to see, but also revealing that it had no eyes.

Blind; the things were blind. They must hunt by sound and scent. Perhaps it was safer to remain still. But every instinct he possessed told him to get away from them and find a weapon to keep them from his family.

The lamp in the alcove went out; the wind seemed to grow louder as well, and Joda realised that the faint hum from the refrigerator behind the bar had stopped. The power had gone.

Something slammed into the pub's front door. The noise was shattering, and Joda leapt. The door shifted in its frame; another blow followed, and then another.

The long pale fingers clawed at the windows. How long before they realised the glass was so much weaker than the wooden door? A weapon; Joda must find a weapon. If only he'd put even a sawn-off pool cue under the counter –

A pool cue. He ran across the snug, around the bar. The pool balls went into the table's pockets at the end of the night, but the cues were left on the table. He snatched one up. It would make a serviceable club; in a pinch, he could stab with the narrow end. Better than nothing.

The front door was struck again; another, answering crash sounded from the rear of the building.

They were behind the pub, too: of course they were. The *Bell* was surrounded. They'd be at every entrance, trying to get in. He saw those long thin fingers crawling up the outside walls like the spiders they resembled, drawing the rest of the creatures after them, to the bedroom windows – his and Barbara's window, Charlotte's –

Behind Joda glass shattered, and the wind blew into the snug. The first creature had driven a hand through the window; it groped over the wall and then across the floor, on the end of an impossibly long, thin arm.

Joda stepped forward, raising the cue to strike, but another window burst inwards as a second intruder drove both arms and its head through.

More blows struck the front door, getting louder and faster. Before it had sounded as though one intruder was flinging itself bodily against the door; now it sounded like several. By the time the third window shattered it sounded like a machine-gun, and Joda heard the wood begin to crack.

The first two intruders already had their arms and upper bodies inside the snug; their arachnoid hands crawled across the walls and sank into them, dragging the rest of their pale, bony bodies through. The third intruder thrashed and writhed, caught on the broken glass. Pointed shards snapped off as it struggled, but if they cut it, it didn't bleed, and nor did any pain it felt deter it. As a fourth window broke, a final blow cracked the oak door vertically down its centre, top to bottom. The intruders' long limbs spread out across the snug and they advanced, those jerky robotic movements accelerating so that their crawl became a spiderlike scuttle. Their heads swivelled in short arcs. They were searching.

He couldn't fight this – not here, at least. But he had to believe there was some defence against them. Barbara deserved to die quietly in her bed. And there was Charlotte. His child. The future.

He fell back towards the stairs. More glass shattered at the rear of the building, and more wood splintered. The back door was giving way.

The intruders were breaking through on every side. Why? What had he done? What had been their offence? But how many millions had asked that since time began, without any answer?

Joda stumbled over the chain at the bottom of the stairs. He fell, sprawling, dropping the cue. Things slithered and scuttled over the worn carpeting of the snug.

The cue – he needed the cue. Had to be able to defend his family. However hopeless the fight, he had to try. Joda clawed across the stair carpeting, reached down and found the cue. As he grasped it, something long and thin brushed his hand.

Joda hadn't made a sound of his own since seeing the first creature outside his window; shock and disbelief had made him speechless. But his silence ended now, and he was shocked how high and shrill his cry of revulsion was. He lashed out with the cue and kicked down at whatever was below him for good measure, not looking back for fear of what he'd see crawling behind him like an immense pallid spider.

Cue in hand, he went up the stairs on all fours – like a spider, like a dog. Like a bug, fleeing a boot that wanted to crush it. No. He had to be a man – stand straight and face the Devil. That was his job.

Joda reached the top of the stairs, clutched a newel post and stood. Barbara. Charlotte. He had to protect them.

Glass was breaking upstairs too.

Something was coming up the stairs behind him.

His wife's room, or his daughter's? He couldn't be in both at once.

Charlotte. It had to be. He'd bring her into the main room, to Barbara, and make his stand there if he could, but if not, if it had to be one or the other, it wasn't a choice. Barbara would expect no less of him, he knew that as he ran across the landing, but still felt a distant flare of sclf-disgust at the ease with which he'd written off his wife of more than twenty years.

It remained distant, though. Guilt and expiation were for the future, if there was one.

He already knew, in his marrow, that there wasn't.

Joda reached Charlotte's door and threw it open –

On an empty room.

He stared in disbelief at the unoccupied bed and shut, unbroken window, outside which snow swirled as two more white-spider hands crawled up the glass and another eyeless, shrouded head rose between them. His child was gone. His baby; they'd taken her.

The head rose into full view; the windowpane shook as its fingers clawed and scratched. There was movement on the landing behind him, but he couldn't bring himself to turn.

And then he realised.

Barbara had always told Joda that he had a beautiful laugh, loud and rich and booming. *Full of life and light,* she'd told him once. He hadn't laughed in a long time, but he did now.

Charlotte's bedroom window wasn't broken. The creature had only just appeared outside it. There was a fire escape on her side of the building; she'd used it to slip out, to meet thc Chapple boy. Not the first time she'd done so, but the first time Joda had been glad of it.

And the last.

He stopped laughing when he heard the window give way in the main bedroom next door. And when his wife began to scream.

Sounds behind him, from the landing: stealthy, scuttling movement, but louder, and still he couldn't turn.

Barbara screaming, more loudly than she'd seemed capable of in months. Things crashed and broke in the main bedroom.

And still he could not turn.

His wife would die alone, and for nothing, because his

daughter had run away. He had failed her, and his family, in the profoundest sense imaginable.

He couldn't turn. He couldn't turn.

He must.

The window in Charlotte's room began to crack, and that spurred Joda to action at last. The intruders were in front, below, behind, beside him. There was no escape, and so he'd face them. He'd be a man. Make his dead father proud.

He would fight his way to his wife's side, and die trying to protect her.

He could do no more.

Joda Famuyiwa, always a quiet and contained man, now bellowed and whirled, lashing out with the cue, and struck towards the bedroom door only yards away.

He never got there.

There were screams, and other sounds.

Then only the wind.

PART II
As the desolate weep

20th December
Sunrise: 0817 hrs
Sunset: 1550 hrs
7 hours, 32 minutes and 24 seconds of daylight

9.

The last of the storm passed over Thursdale just before dawn. That was officially Jess' watch – weak link or not, the girl was a Harper and she'd do her duty with the rest – but Liz was awake too, sitting in the kitchen while Jess dithered around upstairs. Someone with a brain needed to be there.

Even in the darkness, there was white: the snow had fallen thick and heavy, blanketing the grounds. Liz could see that through the chinks in the boards across the windows. You had to leave a gap to spy through, however tiny – better to see and know, however frightening the truth, than drive yourself half-mad imagining. Everything not touched by the snow was black.

Liz squinted through the gap in the boards until the black turned grey, then put the kettle on, brewed the biggest pot of tea she could find and let it stew. She filled a mug, added plentiful sugar and the smallest splash of milk, then drained half of it in a scalding gulp. When she looked again, the grey had turned silver.

Dawn, or near enough as made no difference. By the time Keira and the boys were ready the sun would be well up. There'd be a few hours of safety. Time enough. Liz nodded to herself, then stamped out into the hall. "Jess!"

The girl appeared on the landing, pistol in her hands. "Mum?"

"Point that fucking thing at the floor, I've told you. Get your brothers and Keira up. There's work to be done."

***

The freezing air was utterly clear; the tractors' growls echoed off the peaks as they lumbered, one after the other, from the farm towards Spear Bank.

Heavy snowdrifts choked the road, but both vehicles were fitted with ploughs. The first, driven by Frank with Keira beside him, a shotgun broken across her knees, turned left along Spear Bank, rumbling towards Wakeman Farm and the hill road to Barsall. The second, driven by Dom Harper – simple or not, he had a sure touch with heavy machinery – turned right, towards the *Bell*.

Liz Harper, meanwhile, trudged through the snow with a walking-stick for balance and a piglet under her arm, puffing out clouds of breath. Thursdale was wide in the west and narrow in the east, and Liz was going eastward, through her fields to the thick woods at the tip of the wedge. Oak, beech and ash, bare black and naked in the snow. Barrow Woods.

Her stomach was tight and clenched; she didn't scare easily, but she was this morning. It was one thing remembering the stories Nan had told her; believing them was another.

Well, she wasn't there yet, just hedging her bets. But if she ended up believing, what then? If she'd kept up all the rituals the family used to follow – according to Nan, anyway – would Tony be alive? Liz couldn't afford to think that. Better to believe he wouldn't. Nan had always been clear that the rituals were a help, but never a guarantee.

She shouldn't think of Tony at all just now. She kept seeing him, not as she'd seen him last, sloping out the door with a fag in his mouth, but as the little boy he'd been. He'd always been the handsomest of her kids. Different father from the rest, a notch or two above them in looks and charm. She'd felt something for Tony's dad. Might even have been love. Maybe that'd made the difference in him.

Now Tony was dead, and she hadn't even seen the body. Might never get the chance, if Nan's stories were true.

But she mustn't panic. Nan had told her: *Mostly They sleep, but sometimes They wake. Always in winter, because that'll be Their time.*

How could she have told Ellie Cheetham Nan's stories? Dumb cow would've laughed in Liz's face.

Liz had never seen the inside of a church if she could help it, but of all the people who went in every Sunday, hearing the vicar prattle on, how many of them *really* believed? Oh, if you asked them, they'd tell you they did – believed in God and Jesus, maybe even the Devil too – but miracles? Even the ones in the Bible they'd probably claim were really parables or symbols, or some other bollocks. Whatever it took to avoid facing it. Show them a *real* miracle – an angel, or a demon – and they'd run screaming.

And who could blame them? There was the world you lived in, and the one you hoped for.

Or, if you weren't so lucky, the one you feared.

Last night Liz had read the family Bible. A *real* Bible, one with things in it that'd make the vicars and pastors back in Barsall soil their jeans and cassocks. Things Jesus never talked about; those things weren't in ordinary Bibles, which was why those Bibles wouldn't do them any good.

We've our own faith, Nan had told her. *Always have had. Had to learn it for ourselves. It's all in here*, she'd say, and pat the family Bible.

Liz wanted to believe Tony had been drunk – that he'd slipped and cracked his head, wandered off all dizzy and dreaming, waving his knife at something that wasn't there. But she couldn't. He'd been chased and cornered, left to freeze: so said Ellie Cheetham, and bitch or not, she knew her job.

And that was how it began. Liz had wanted to believe she'd remembered Nan's lessons wrong, that there was something else she'd missed, but she'd checked the Bible and it was right. The first one died without a wound: *They* let the winter do the killing. A test, like a soothsayer reading chicken guts.

And afterward, *They* left *Their* mark. *Their* sign of jubilation, because it was *Their* time.

Knowing the story was one thing, but it didn't prepare you to see it coming true, least of all with your own child.

Liz stopped and leant on the stick. The weight of all the grief and fear made her buckle at the knees, ready to fall down and give up. But she couldn't, any more than she could let herself believe she was just being an old fool. Not yet. No-one in Barsall knew about the mark. No one outside Barrowman Farm. If she was wrong, well and good; her only worry'd be making sure no-one in the family thought she was losing her grip and tried to push her aside. But if she *wasn't* wrong or mad, she had to be ready to get her children through this. They'd look to her.

Liz trudged on.

The piglet kicked and wriggled. Liz squeezed hard to quell it; it kicked harder, squealing, then gave up. Liz peered down to check it was still breathing. If she'd killed it she'd have to go back for another: the Bible said it had to be live. They'd penned the sheep and pigs up last night, the lights on full around the pens, wire mesh around the bulbs to protect them. That'd kept the animals all safe, but *They'd* be hungry – always were, so the Bible said – which made the offering all the more important.

The piglet blinked at her and grunted. Liz nodded to herself and stamped on through the snow.

Long night last night. Least Frank and Dom did as they were told. Jess didn't count – too scared to do a thing but go along with the rest and keep out of the way. Paul she'd have to watch – him most of all of them. She'd seen him smirking, when he'd thought she couldn't see. *Old bat's finally going doolally.* Danger there in more ways than one: if he didn't challenge her outright, he might not bother following the precautions that would keep them safe.

Keira wasn't blood, more was the pity. She had teeth, that girl, a fucking spine, and enough respect to trust Liz's word, for now at least. She didn't *believe*, but then none of them did: why should they, when even Liz wasn't sure?

Yet.

If Liz hadn't read this wrong – if this didn't all begin and end with Tony – perhaps she should've brought Keira with her, to see the truth for herself. Someone'd have to keep the Bible in the future – watch for the signs, know what to do. Liz couldn't trust Paul with that, and Frank had no more gumption than Dom or Jess.

Her boots thumped on through the snow. The earth sounded hollow, like a drum. Imagination, that was all. Would she never reach the woods?

At last she stepped across the treeline. She puffed for breath. Her cheeks burned from the frost. The piglet kicked feebly. The path through the woods lay ahead; the old holloway, beaten out through time. She followed it easily, even in the snow.

Further on, the path forked. The right-hand track carried on ahead, to the end of Thursdale and then up to the higher ground of Fendmoor Heath, where they said the old town of Kirk Flockton had stood till the earth one day swallowed it up. Liz smirked to herself: oh, she could tell folk a tale or two about *that*, though not one they'd want to hear. The other, almost overgrown path led towards the North Road and Wakeman's Edge, through the densest part of the woods.

Liz took the left-hand fork, using the walking-stick to snap off protruding twigs. Even in winter, the trees tried to grow across the path, as if it was a wound the world wanted closed.

Soon she reached a clearing. A few yards into it was a steep grassy embankment, a little higher than Liz's head, that Nature – never one for straight lines or corners – had clearly had no part in shaping.

There was a gap in the embankment, cut or broken long ago, and Liz went through it, to the Hollows.

Behind the embankment on either side, sinkholes dotted the ground. Two had filled with water, now frozen over so they shone like eyes. Their exact depth remained unknown, not least because no-one trying to plumb them had ever been known to survive the attempt. Beyond the sinkholes was a second embankment, crusted with snow, set into which was a slab of pinkish rock unlike any stone Liz had seen in these parts. Below the slab was another hole, about two feet across.

The pig kicked and squealed in earnest, thrashing its bound trotters. Liz shook it, irritated, and thought of Jess' brat – that'd please *Them* more than any pig. She shook her head. Idiot though its mother was, however it'd been conceived and born, it was still blood; still a Harper. But if certain stories were true, *They* might want more than piglets now; the family might have to give up one or two to save the rest. Maybe she should have let Jess name the kid after all, 'stead of making her name it after Grandpa Steve.

The piglet stopped squealing. The woods were silent, too, as if the world had died.

Liz advanced to the far embankment and the edge of the hole, then raised her stick and banged it on the slab. Clumps of snow fell loose, exposing the stone in full: the stone, and what was on it.

Liz's stomach cramped; she wanted badly to run back to the farmhouse and bar the door behind her, but that would do no good. The stone had been marked with charcoal, scored by a chunk of charred and blackened wood. There was a triangular symbol, like a jagged, back-to-front capital D, and below it, three short, vertical lines. Or rather two lines and one smudge, where the third had been rubbed away.

The piglet squealed again, squirting hot piss down Liz's trouser-leg. She cursed and shook it, stabbing the walking-stick into the ground. It squealed louder, then fell silent. Liz stopped and looked down at the sinkhole, trying to convince herself she'd heard no sounds from the shaft.

Do it, quick, and go.

She gripped the piglet's front legs in one hand, the back legs in the other, then raised it in the air and said the words as it squealed and thrashed and shat itself, liquid turds running down her gloved hand. It didn't matter. She'd dealt with worse. She said the words again, then a third time, then tossed it down.

It squealed again, sounding almost human. There was a thud of impact from the bottom of the shaft, and a clatter of loose things. Then nothing. Nothing. The fall must have killed it. Waste of good meat. But those marks had come from somewhere.

Anyway, it was done. Best go now. But she could hear movement in the shaft. The piglet; the unlucky beast had survived the fall and was thrashing in pain and fright. But the noises were too loud and numerous for something so small. It began squealing again, sounding more human than ever before as its shrieks became louder and higher and more anguished, to a crescendo that was like the sound of a drill in Liz's ear; then it was cut off, and there was only the sound of things being torn and snapped.

Liz fumbled blindly for her stick and pulled it out of the ground. She stumbled backwards, gathering speed as she went, not daring to turn around until she backed into something.

She cried out in fear, then realised it was only the first embankment and stumbled sideways through the gap. One last look back, at the slab above the hole and the three black charcoal lines, and then she broke into a shambling run, faster than she'd gone in years, gulping at the searing air till she tasted blood. She had to slow down, before she gave herself a cardiac. But it was a long time before she could do so, what with the sounds coming out of the hole, that carried so clearly on the winter air.

10.

The inside of the Land Rover was pleasantly warm, but it was the sight of Wakeman Farm, rather than the cold, that made Ellie want to stay inside. Or, better still, turn around and drive back home to her bed. She'd had a late shift scheduled today, hence the all-night drinking session with Milly and Noel: she'd intended a lie-in, followed by a fry-up to counteract the consequences.

But the road to Matlock was still cut off, and until it was clear, she and Tom were all the village had. That was the job, and she'd signed up for it, so Ellie pulled on her hat, opened the door and got out, shivering at the cold.

Wakeman Farm was a farm in name only, had been for years. It was clean and whitewashed, with a paved drive, rockery and floral garden: Sally Beck liked her home to look pretty. In summer the rose trellises on the front of the building turned the plain white frontage, grey stone and black earth into a riot of colour. Whenever Ellie drove past in summer she'd slow down to admire it.

It was always hard to imagine the land being warm again at this time of year, but more than ever today. Only one trellis remained attached to the house; the other lay scattered over the front drive. The wooden frame hadn't just been pulled down but torn apart, along with bundles of rose creepers that had been twisted and snapped.

The storm last night had been fierce, but the trellises had withstood worse winds than that. Grant Beck was a builder and joiner by trade, and knew his job; he'd put them up himself. Besides, smashing up the trellises was one thing, but the roses would have taken serious work. Strength. The wind wouldn't have done that; nothing short of a tornado would, and climate change or no, there'd been none of those last night.

It took serious application – anger, or outright hate – to put that kind of work in, especially on something as innocuous as a rose trellis. Likewise, the wind might have smashed one or two windows if the storm turned to hail, but not every single one. Let alone the door.

The Becks had replaced their old oak front door with a brand-new uPVC one – tradition was all very well, Grant had told Ellie, but you wanted to keep the cold out in winter and the gas bills weren't coming down any time soon. It had five lever mortice locks that made it next to immovable, but move it had: the frame was empty, and the door, torn off its hinges, lay inside the dim hallway.

Ellie popped two paracetamol from a blister pack and swallowed them dry.

"See what I mean?" Bert Annable climbed down from his tractor cab. He was a big, grey-bearded man of sixty-odd in waxed jacket, wellies and cords, a woollen cap over his bald patch. He ran a smallholding on the far side of Barsall – his family had lived there for centuries, and had allegedly been among the few survivors of the 'Bad Winter' that had almost wiped the village out – and used his tractor to clear the smaller local roads after heavy snow, which was why he'd been driving along Spear Bank at eight a.m. He'd seen the state of the place, and come banging on Ellie's door.

Ellie nodded. "Grant?" she shouted. "Sally?" What had the daughter's name been, again? "Kate?"

No answer. There was no wind; the morning was silent, without even a birdcall. If anything had moved or made a noise inside the house, it would have been audible.

"See the state of the door?"

"Yes, Bert, I can." If Bert Annable had a fault, it was a tendency to state the obvious.

"And that thing over it?"

"Yes, Bert." The charcoal symbol was stark against the whitewash: a long black vertical line with a shorter diagonal one pointing down and to the left from the top. Different to the one by Tony Harper's body, but made the same way and equally incomprehensible.

"Not an animal, then," said Bert.

"Well, obviously," said Ellie, then remembered – every winter, almost like clockwork, Bert would lose sheep from his flock and mutter darkly about animals roaming the moors – escaped dogs, big cats or whatever. Only a matter of time, he'd always scowl, when in that mood, before they attacked a person. "How are your sheep?" she said. "Missing many of them?"

"Strangest bloody thing is, I'm not. Lost two or three, no more than that – and a couple of those I found later. One had tumbled down a gorge and the other one'd drowned in a stream. Usually a sight worse than that by this time of year. That's why I thought it might've been the dogs or cats or whatever the hell they are here to begin with – buggers deciding to go after bigger game. But animals can't draw."

"Yeah." Ellie sighed and turned away, looking out across Thursdale towards Fendmoor Heath and trying not to think of how many bodies the landscape had yielded up over the years. Or how many it might still conceal: it seemed vast and desolate on mornings like this, capable of hiding anything. A pack of wild dogs would almost be a relief, if that was the worst they had to deal with: certainly more comprehensible and less of a threat than whatever had happened here.

"I mean…" said Bert; Ellie turned to see him gesture to the doorway. "The hell did that?"

A good question. "Big red doorkey, maybe."

"Big red what?"

"You've seen them on the telly, Bert. Those battering-rams we use for door-breaching."

"Oh. Right." Bert stuck his hands into his jacket pockets. "Don't suppose there's many of those knocking around here."

Once again, the bleeding obvious. But another good point. "Got one in the Land Rover, as it goes," she said. "We had a spare at the old station, but the powers that be took it back."

"Glad you've still got one. Bloody need it one of these days for that lot." Bert motioned with his head in the direction of Thursdale and Barrowman Farm.

Ellie eyed the front of the house again. The Harpers were the only locals who sprang to mind as potential culprits, but this would've been extreme even for them. And what motive would they have had? She was certain she hadn't mentioned who'd discovered the body during yesterday's visit; even if she had, why would the Harpers go after the Becks?

For information, maybe. Find out who'd done it, then settle things their own way. Ellie looked again at the house, at the mark above the door. What kind of face would Liz Harper show if she saw that?

"Should we go in?" said Bert.

"Best had," said Ellie, grateful for the 'we'. She still had her baton; the spray, too, but she wasn't sure how much was left in it. The house's silence, plus its gaping door and windows, made her wish she'd brought her twelve-bore with her.

Now she was being stupid. The Becks could still be inside, injured or hiding from whoever attacked them. They mightn't have heard her calling out. Ellie went towards the house, halting a couple of yards from the entrance; the darkness in the hallway looked thick as smoke. She shone her torch into it. "Sally? Grant? Kate?"

There was broken china on the floor – the remains of one of the commemorative plates Sally had mounted on beams and shelves in the hallway. Something shone among the debris; Ellie stepped over the threshold and saw it was a copper warming pan, the handle snapped in half. On the wall, a painting Ellie had always liked, of a city street on a rainy autumn evening, had been defaced with soot or charcoal. Ellie shone the torch on it; it was the symbol from above the doorway.

A floorboard creaked behind her.

"Bert?"

"Aye."

Ellie breathed out. "I'm checking the ground floor. Keep an eye on the stairs for me, okay?"

Bert frowned, then swallowed. "Think they're still here?"

Ellie knew he didn't mean the Becks. "Better safe than sorry."

Despite the whitewashed walls, the hall remained uncomfortably dim. Ellie flicked the light switch on the wall, but the Art Deco lamp on the ceiling didn't come on. She went forward. There were markings on the beams, under their black paint: rings of overlapping circles. Witch marks, Sally Beck had told her. She'd been proud of them. A little piece of history. People carved them onto walls, doors and beams to keep out evil.

How did that work out for you, Sally?

She found no sign of the Becks, alive or dead. In the front room, the TV was missing; in the dining room, the stereo. In the kitchen, the floor was wet, but it was only water: the fridge-freezer had been tipped over and dragged into the middle of the kitchen floor, the lead ripped out of the back. On top of it was the missing TV, its screen smashed in, and the stereo, its casing prised open, the electronics pulled out and broken apart. On top of those were three laptops, each of which had had its screen bent back and snapped off, the motherboards broken in half. The kitchen clock lay in pieces on the same heap, along with the carriage clocks from the living room and dining room mantelpieces.

Vicious, but systematic, too: cold hate rather than wild rage. Always more frightening, and more dangerous, but Ellie couldn't imagine anyone feeling that way towards the Becks, not even the Harpers. Maybe the daughter had made worse enemies who'd followed her out here, her or her drip of a boyfriend.

There was another black mark on the wall where the kitchen clock had been. Despite her vow not to return to Barrowman Farm without full backup, Ellie would have dearly loved to drag Liz Harper in here and shove her face up against it, demand to know what it meant, what had happened –

For a second she was back in the kitchen at Barrowman; she could smell the sewage and dog piss, the mildew and the gin on Keira's breath, see the knife in Paul's hand and feel Frank's bruising grip on her arm. The dog barking as Dom let it off the leash at her. Her chest tightened. She saw herself with an assault rifle, forcing the whole pack of them back down the kitchen and then firing into them. *Jesus, Ellie. You're meant to be a professional. Fucking well act like one.*

Breathe. In and out.

"Right," she said. "Upstairs."

"What about –"

Ellie followed Bert's gaze to the pantry door under the stairs. "Good point. Forgot."

Thoroughness. Doing the whole job. That was who she was meant to be. *Focus.*

The door hung ajar, battered and splintered, and the bolt on the inside – why on the inside, in a pantry? – had been torn out of the wall. Ellie pulled the broken door open. There were shelves stacked with jars and tins – jams, pickles, canned meat and fruit – and on the wall directly opposite, another black mark.

Ellie stepped over the threshold to inspect the rest of the narrow space. When she did, the floor gave slightly underfoot, with a very faint creak, and another sound came from underneath it. In a built-up area, with traffic and passers-by outside, she mightn't have heard it, but in the silent house on that silent morning, it was just audible: a high-pitched noise somewhere between a whimper and a sob.

Ellie pressed down with her foot again, and once more felt the floor shift. It was covered by a thin, coarse piece of loose carpet. She crouched, pinching a corner of the material between her gloved fingers, and threw it back.

A square trapdoor had been cut into the floorboards, with a metal ring set into it. A cellar?

"Bert?"

The big man shuffled forwards. "What can I do you for?"

"Just hold this for me." Ellie handed him the torch and took out her baton, putting her thumb on the release catch, then hooked a finger through the metal ring.

As the trapdoor lifted, another muffled cry came from underneath – pain or fear, Ellie couldn't tell which. She kept her hand on the baton all the same.

Bert shone the torch down as Ellie pulled the trapdoor away. There was no cellar; under the trapdoor was an earth-floored crawlspace about three feet high. Kate Beck was crawling painfully away from the torchlight, her right hand held up to shield herself from it. Her left arm was immobile, twisted at an angle that made Ellie feel sick.

"Please," the girl said, her voice a croak. "Please."

"It's all right, love," said Ellie. "You're safe now."

"Please. Please. Please."

Her eyes were unfocused, with none of the alertness they'd had yesterday. Shock or a head injury, maybe both. She was shivering. Ellie took the torch from Bert. "There's a foil blanket in the back of the Land Rover," she said.

"I'll grab it."

Ellie sheathed her baton and swung her legs into the gap. "Please," the girl said. "Please."

"It's all right, love," Ellie said again. "You're safe."

"Please."

Ellie lowered herself into the crawlspace. It smelt of damp earth. A sudden fear of attack gripped her and she swept the torch around, but there was only the earth floor and the stone pilings propping up the house. The girl shrank back. "Please."

"Kate," said Ellie. "It's me. Constable Cheetham. You remember me, right? From yesterday?"

If the girl did, it didn't show. "Please. Please."

"Ellie?" Bert called from above; he sounded slightly nervous to have entered the pantry and found it empty.

"Down here."

"Phew." He handed her the blanket. "Had me worried for a second."

Ellie wrapped the girl in the blanket as best she could. "Can you stay with her? I need to check upstairs."

She went up, baton drawn and ready, wishing again she'd brought the twelve-bore from her gun cabinet at home. The second storey told the same tale as the first. Broken windows, a black mark on a wall in every room, but no bodies. She found a coin-sized spot of blood on a pillow in the main bedroom, but that was the only direct evidence of any harm having come to the Becks themselves.

Ellie went back downstairs. Bert had climbed down into the crawlspace beside the girl; his head and shoulders poked out of the trapdoor. "She said anything?" Ellie said.

"Please," said the girl's muffled voice.

Bert shrugged. "Just that."

"All right." Ellie took out her handset. "Mike Whisky, from Sierra Four Five, urgent call, over."

The set crackled. "Sierra Four Five, this is Mike Whisky, go ahead, over."

"Need you out at Wakeman Farm now, over."

"What?"

"We've a break-in, and two –" she remembered the boy "– no, *three* missing persons. One injured, possible head trauma. So get hold of Milly, and see if you can call in an air ambulance. Over."

"Received. Break-in at Wakeman, three mispers, one injured. Collect Dr Emmanuel, contact air ambulance."

Tom sounded out of breath, not to mention surprised he'd remembered it all. "Um, over."

Ellie turned to Bert. "Can you hold the fort till Tom turns up?"

"Can do. What's up?"

"I want to make sure Joda and Barbara are okay." Ellie spoke into the handset again. "Mike Whisky from Sierra Four Five, proceeding to the *Bell* public house to check on occupants. Out."

"Please," she heard the girl saying. "Please."

It was seemingly the only word Kate Beck still knew, and God knew if she was aware of anything happening around her. But this time it sounded as if it had been meant specifically for Ellie. But please what? *Please don't leave me? Please come back so I can tell you what happened?*

Or – Ellie didn't know where this interpretation came from and tried to dismiss it entirely as she got into the Land Rover – *please don't go to the* Bell?

For some reason that was what lingered with Ellie as she drove along Spear Bank, and it wouldn't go away.

11.

Liz heard them shouting long before she reached the house; even stone walls couldn't muffle everything. Trouble of some kind.

She should've taken a shotgun or a rifle with her. Although the trail across the fields led to Barrowman Farm's back yard, Liz circled round to the front; the only vehicles in sight were the tractors. Safely home, and no police. That was a good start to the day. But then what was the commotion about?

The row was coming from the kitchen, so Liz returned to the back and let herself in to face the latest drama.

Jess huddled in one corner rocking the baby, Dom in another shaking his head; always a bad sign. Frank and Keira were shouting at Paul, who sat at the table with that silly .22 rifle he liked to pose with in front of him, his tongue pushed into his cheek. He was drumming his fingers on the table-top, uncomfortably close to the gun.

"The fuck were you thinking, you stupid prick?" Keira shouted, and waved at Dom. "You're as thick as that fucking spastic."

They hadn't heard Liz come in, which let her make a dramatic entrance; when she crashed the stick down on the stone-flagged floor its metal ferrule made a crack like a rifle shot. Jess shrieked, Keira yelped "Fuck!" and Frank grabbed for his shotgun on the kitchen counter.

Liz pointed at Keira. "Don't you fucking dare call my son that. You don't say that about any child of mine." Keira had said far worse and Liz hadn't cared, but it was a good way to lay down the law and shut everyone up. "Now what the hell's going on?"

"He's gone and –"

"*Keira*. Not now. What about Wakeman and the *Bell*?"

"Yeah, what about the *Bell*?" Keira muttered, smirking at Paul. Liz gave her a look; she fell silent, moving back behind Frank.

"Place was empty at Wakeman," Frank said. "Windows'd been put in, door was gone."

"Any marks?"

"Above the door," said Keira, trying to get back on Liz's good side. "Like you said."

Liz nodded. "Paul?"

He looked sullenly up. "Same at the *Bell*. No-one there."

"Well," said Keira.

"*Keira*," said Liz. "Paul, any marks?"

"Yeah."

"Show us."

"Didn't get any pictures."

"I told you to get pictures."

"Yeah, well, stuff happened."

For fuck sake, what now? "What stuff?"

Frank glared at his brother. "They're in the front room."

Paul banged the table, turning red. "They showed up while I was checking inside. What was I supposed to fucking do?"

Liz swept through the kitchen into the hall. Muffled noises came from the front room. What had that perverted idiot done now?

The first thing she noticed, entering the front room, was that the old coffee table was shunted up against the far wall. Daft, really: first thing she should have clocked were the two people lying gagged and hog-tied on their stomachs. One man, one woman. Once she was over the initial shock, Liz recognised them: that stuck-up little cow Charlotte Famu-whatsit and

David bloody Chapple. The girl didn't matter – if the rest of her family had been taken she'd be assumed to have gone the same way – but Ron Chapple's son was a different matter. It was a Saturday, so he'd be meant to open up the office. Ron Chapple'd most likely assume Dave was in bed with some little tart, so it'd take a while before he worried. But sooner or later he would.

The Famu-whatsit girl sobbed and screamed through her gag, staring up at Liz. Red eyes, full of tears. But she wasn't family, so she didn't matter. Nothing would, soon.

Liz strode back into the kitchen. "What happened?"

"Told you," Paul said. "They drove up while I was checking upstairs at the *Bell* and Little Miss High-And-Mighty started kicking off. Couldn't just leave 'em, could I? Have the pigs down on us again."

Like it or not, that was hard to argue with. "What about their car?"

"Eh?"

"They drove up, you said. Where's their car now?"

"Uh," said Paul, and looked down at the table. Liz closed her eyes.

"Oh," she said, "you stupid cunt."

12.

The windows were broken and the door smashed down. A silver car sat in the *Bell*'s forecourt, doors open, and two sets of footprints led through the snow to the doorway. A third set, and maybe a fourth, approached the doorway from the other side.

There were tyre-marks too. Big, heavy ones: a tractor, Ellie guessed, but not Bert Annable's: he'd driven back to Barsall as soon as he'd seen the state of Wakeman Farm. Someone else had cleared the rest of the hill road, and the North Road as far as the pub.

The Harpers; had to be. Anyone coming from outside would have cleared more of the North Road, and no-one else nearby owned a tractor big enough for the job. Although they weren't normally so public-spirited, unless they were being paid.

The car was a silver Audi with a personalised plate. DAV3C1: Dave Chapple, of course, either picking up Charlotte or bringing her back. Utter insanity, slipping out in this weather, but Dave was used to getting away with everything, and Charlotte was in love with him, or thought she was. Ellie had done things every bit as stupid at that age.

She grunted, and looked again at the scene. There was a mark on the wall above the doorway; she wasn't surprised to see it was the same as the one at the Becks'. The Harpers' work? Some kind of response to the one by Tony's body? But if there was a feud, how had the Becks and Famuyiwas been pulled in?

The tyre tracks were fresh; they'd been made that morning, after the snow had stopped. And, since the bar's floor was covered in snow, presumably after whatever had happened there. So the Harpers might not have caused the damage; even so, they couldn't have missed it.

There were footprints on the bar floor. Ellie took out her phone and photographed the scene; she really needed SOCO here, the full circus, but there'd be no chance of that till the roads were clear.

Whoever was responsible for what had happened here and at Wakeman Farm last night could have lingered to capture Dave and Charlotte too, along with whichever Harpers had shown up at the pub. But then the tractor would still be here. Ellie sighed; no point second-guessing herself to death. She took a deep breath, and went inside.

The snug was empty. Thin drifts of snow glittered on the carpet. Some of it might be glass. The pendulum clock lay in pieces, and the stuffed pike, free at last from its glass case, had been torn in half, stuffing strewn across the floor. Its glass eye stared ceilingward, jaws gaping in a last protest. The charcoal symbol was on the wall above the fireplace.

Ellie's feet crunched in snow and splintered glass. The row of optics glinted behind the bar. She went through the snug and past the pool table. Cold wind blew in her face. The door by the toilets, the one marked PRIVATE, had been smashed down. At the end of the passage beyond it, another doorway gaped open into the back yard. There was snow on the floor.

Be thorough, she told herself. Be methodical. She checked the toilets, then went down the passage and checked the kitchen. All were empty. No sign of anyone, or – except for the doors and windows – of a fight.

More glass crunched as she climbed the stairs; when she reached the landing, a door clicked shut at the end and Ellie went very still. There was snow on the landing carpet. Ellie breathed out. Only the wind.

But she should make certain. As she went towards the closed door, Ellie saw blood on the carpet outside it. Two or three spots, nothing more. But all the same, it made her wish – yet again – she'd brought her shotgun.

Ellie shoved the door wide and stepped back, just in case. But the room was empty. More glass and snow, this time sprayed across the single bed by the window, over the bright yellow duvet. A laptop on the floor, snapped in two like plywood. Books. Posters on the wall: pop stars, film stars.

Charlotte's room. There was another of the marks, on the wall above the bedhead. But no blood.

There were five rooms upstairs. Ellie hadn't been up here in years but remembered the layout clearly enough: four bedrooms, one bathroom. When Ellie checked them she found all the windows broken, front and back. One bedroom had been an office: filing cabinets, a desktop computer. The computer had been overturned, the monitor smashed. Another bedroom was bare and empty. More glass and snow on the floor. She left Joda and Barbara's bedroom until last, nerving herself for whatever she might find.

Empty windows, gaping open to the sky. Clean cold air had blown in, that didn't smell of anything. Under it were whiffs of soap, air-freshener, perfume and shampoo. The room was dim. Ellie flicked the light switch, but nothing happened. Torn sheets on the floor; blood spots on the mattress. And that mark yet again, scratched on the wall.

Ellie was still for nearly a minute, thinking of Joda as she'd last seen him, the weary sorrow in his eyes, and of Barbara as she had been. She clenched her fists, then opened them. Then she pulled out her phone and took pictures of each room, before going back downstairs.

Outside, it had started snowing again, and the tyre-tracks and footprints there were already fading.

Ellie studied the ones in the snow inside the bar. There were her own, and another set, made by large, heavy boots. The kind a farmer wore.

Harpers. They'd been here, and at Wakeman Farm. Dave and Charlotte had arrived while they were at the *Bell*; Dave and Charlotte were no longer here. Their current location wasn't hard to guess. Which meant Charlotte Famuyiwa was almost certainly with Paul Harper.

Ellie's fists were clenched. *Hello fury, my old friend.* It had been close to slipping its leash last night, and now here it was again.

Deep breaths, Ellie. Control yourself. Think it through. Go in half-cocked, you'll make it worse.

Ideally, she'd have Tom call for back-up from outside, up to and including an armed response team. But in an ideal world the roads would be clear, and they weren't. Of course, an ideal world wouldn't contain Paul Harper to begin with. Either way, she'd have to work with what she had.

So: back to Barsall, liaise with Tom, and plan the next move. Whatever happened, chances were she was going back to Thursdale again. She climbed back into the Land Rover, and reached for her AirWave.

13.

"Jess," said Liz, "make us all a brew."

The girl dashed away from the wall towards the kitchen range. Keira, more from habit than anything else, feinted a swipe at her as she went.

"Quit it," snapped Liz. "No time for that now."

She sighed, unfastened her coat and hung it over the back of the chair, then sat and began to roll herself a cigarette. She normally preferred tailor-mades, but always kept a tin of baccy and papers in case she ran out. She hadn't, but it gave her fingers something to do, and that relaxed her.

Paul mumbled sulkily. "Pardon?" Liz glared.

For a moment, she thought he'd pretend to have said nothing, but instead he scowled. "What was I supposed to do?"

He always sounded like he was whingeing, and doubly so just now, but he had a point – he'd done as he was told and checked the *Bell* out. Nobody else's fault the Famu-whatsit girl hadn't been able to keep her legs together last night. They'd have gone screaming to the police, and Liz didn't want to see Ellie Cheetham's face again any time soon.

She licked the cigarette paper, sealed it, then tore a piece of cardboard from the Rizla packet for a roach. If she *didn't* see Cheetham's face in the next two days, she never might again, not if those markings in the Hollows told the truth. But even if they hadn't been seen clearing the roads, it wouldn't take Cheetham long to guess who had.

Yesterday, the day before, Liz would still have been raging

about that. But not today. The rules had changed. They'd worse than the pigs to worry about.

She poked the roach into one end of the cigarette, sparked up and took a long deep drag, held it then breathed out. First fag of the day, always the best; after that it was all diminishing returns. "So. Looks like we'll have callers soon."

"Fuck," muttered Keira.

"We'll handle it," said Liz.

Keira stared. "How? The pigs are gonna be round – what you gonna do, shoot 'em?"

Liz shrugged.

"Have you gone fucking –"

Liz stared Keira down, daring her to finish. Keira looked away; Liz had known she would. "Sorry."

"You don't believe it yet," Liz said. "That's all right, Keira. Don't blame you for that. It's a lot to take in. Wasn't easy for me, either. Paul, fetch the scanner."

Paul rooted in a kitchen drawer, took out a radio scanner and plugged it in. He switched it on, but all they heard was a mush of static. "It's fucked."

"No, it's not." They'd last used it a few days earlier – before Tony's death had changed everything – to listen for chatter while Dom was setting up a dog-fight, to make sure the pigs hadn't been waiting to jump in. They hadn't been; retard or not, Dom was always careful setting things up. "*They're* doing it."

Keira made to speak, then subsided.

"You saw what they did at Wakeman," said Liz, "and you've heard what they did at the *Bell*. Wasn't fairy stories did that, Keira Lucas. Not me going mad. Or d'you think I sneaked out last night and did it?"

"No," Keira said at last.

"Well, then."

"Can't get the pigs on scanner anyway, now," said Paul. "They're all encrypted and shit."

"Doesn't matter," said Liz. "No bugger's talking to anyone, that's the point. Now," she turned back to Keira, "something's out there. You admit that? Not robbers, 'cos they took nothing. Not some gang, cos they'd've come after us, fucked with something we gave a shit about. Yeah?"

"All right, but Liz – even still, shooting at the pigs?"

"Tell you what," said Liz. "Pigs come round, say you were a hostage too. Tried to stop us, but we tied you up. We'll all say the same."

And Keira would be out if she did, and nowhere else to go. Liz saw her looking to Frank and was proud to see the stone face he showed; when you came down to it, Frank always put blood first.

Keira shook her head. "No. Whatever needs doing, I'll do it."

"Good girl," said Liz, and meant it. She'd have broken Keira if she'd had to, but the girl was loyal. She might not be a Harper by blood, but she was in every other way. This had tested her, but she'd stick. Long enough to see all Liz said was true.

The scanner crackled and squealed. Liz gestured, and Paul switched it off. "They won't be calling any of their pig mates in," she said. "So it'll just be Cheetham and Tom Graham, and he's about as much use as a concrete parachute. Maybe a few locals, if they're feeling hard enough. Nothing we can't handle till it's dark. And after that –" Liz pictured Ellie Cheetham's face when she saw what she was really up against, right before she died, and smiled "– they'll have a sight more than us to worry about."

She looked at the others, daring them to challenge her. No-one did.

"What about those two, then?" Keira motioned to the kitchen door.

"Come tomorrow we won't have to worry about the pigs or anyone else. All we'll have to worry about after tonight's *Them*. We'll take the boy to the Hollows in the morning. Give 'em the girl the next day. *They'll* want more than piglets now. We wanna keep *Them* happy."

"No!" Everyone jumped: the cry had come from the last place anyone had been expecting to hear a peep from. "You can't do that," said Jess. "You can't."

"Shut up, you thick cunt," Keira said.

"It's murder." Jess' face was red, her eyes glistening.

Keira gave a jagged, cawing laugh. "Ooh, no. Listen to the little cry-baby. Mustn't do anything against the *law*. That'd be dead naughty and we'd get in trouble."

"By tomorrow it won't be murder," said Liz, as if Keira hadn't spoken. "It'll be sacrifice. Survival."

A big leap, she knew, but one they'd all have to make, as a family, else they'd never survive.

"But the police –"

"Fuck the pigs," said Keira. "Right? Right?"

Dom laughed. "Fuck the pigs."

"Two days," said Liz. "That's all that's left. Tonight, then tomorrow night it's the Dance and –" she ground out her cigarette "– police won't matter anymore."

"Mum, you *can't*. They haven't done anyth–"

"Just shut up," Liz snapped, all patience gone. "Enough bloody snivelling. The boy goes down tomorrow, the girl the day after. End of story. Fuck everyone else, Jess. This is about the family."

And normally that'd have had Jess slinking away like a whipped dog, but she wasn't just scared or sad any longer – for the first time Liz could remember, she was angry. The red face, the tears, weren't grief or fright but rage. "You wanna give Charlotte and him to the *fuckers* who killed our Tony?"

"Shut the fuck up!" Liz was angry too now, and raised a clenched fist. Good thing the shotgun hadn't been in reach. "This isn't about wanting, you stupid little cow. I told you, it's survival. Tony'd no business going out at night. It was his own stupid fault." Her voice cracked. No; no tears. She mustn't cry. "If it hadn't been him, *They'd* have found someone else."

And if *They* hadn't? Would *They* have taken it as a sign that the time wasn't yet? If Tony had stayed in night before last, would they have been spared all this?

No point thinking on that – the past was past and done. What mattered now was dealing with what came next. Liz knew from the family Bible what that was, and what to do.

She made her voice a shout. "What's gonna happen's gonna happen. Our job's getting through it, and we won't do that by whining. We'll do it by doing what's gotta be done. Giving *Them* what we've got to give *Them*. We do that, we'll live." And more than just live, too. She knew what the old parchments – as old as any Bible if not older – promised those who kept the faith. Adore Tony though she had, this was about the whole family now.

Jess had hunched back, bright red in the face, head down, humiliated. "All right?" said Liz. "Then shut up."

"Ha-*ha*," sang Keira – a last little jab at her sister-in-law, and the straw that broke the spine of Jess's restraint; the girl spun and, with surprising skill given how ineffectual Liz had always thought her, punched Keira in the face.

It sent Keira flying, as much due to the element of surprise as to its actual force, and she'd have gone sprawling if Paul hadn't caught her. She kicked free of him, shouting, "Keep your fucking hands to yourself, pervert," (in fairness, Liz was sure she'd seen Paul's fingers groping towards Keira's breasts), in a muffled voice. Her mouth and chin were slick with blood. "Fucking bitch!" she shouted, and lunged for Jess.

Frank stepped between them and Paul grabbed Keira from behind; she yelled and thrashed, kicking. Liz grabbed the big shotgun and jacked the slide, hard. "Enough!" The harsh *shucklack* of the action froze everyone in place; there'd been a cartridge in the chamber and Liz heard it tinkle on the stone flags.

"We're a family," she said. "We stay together. Not fight each other, at a time like this. Keira, get yourself fucking cleaned up."

Keira elbowed Paul aside and stumbled from the kitchen. "Thought she'd knocked me fucking teeth out, the bitch..." she mumbled. "If she had I'd fucking..."

Liz almost smiled at Jess: *Might make a Harper of you yet.* "Paul, do one thing, eh? Get some plastic sheeting down under them in the front room. They'll be pissing all over the carpet 'fore we know it, and probably worse. Rest of you, get on watch and be ready. We'll have guests soon."

14.

"Matlock from Sierra Four Five, urgent call, over. Matlock from Sierra Four Five, urgent call, over."

The radio's only answer was a hissing, mushy scream of static. Ellie checked her smartphone again, but there was still no network.

Beyond the windscreen, veils of snow blew across the Height. The Land Rover's wipers beat, wiping away the flakes that accumulated between each arc. The lights of Barrowman Farm, down in Thursdale, gleamed through the snow. So close; so distant.

She wouldn't think of that. Or Charlotte Famuyiwa. Nor Dave Chapple, although that bit was easier. Serve him right if something bad happened to the smug little sod; God knew it would be about time.

No way for a copper to think. You protected all the public, not just the ones you like. Even so, if it came down to either getting Charlotte out of there intact, or Dave...

Well, it won't. Your job's to make sure it doesn't.

"Matlock from Sierra Four Five, urgent call, over. Matlock from Sierra Four Five, urgent call, over."

But still no answer, only static. And if Dave and Charlotte were at Barrowman Farm –

Still an 'if', Ellie. You can't be sure.

Maybe not sure, but close enough. There'd been fresh tracks in the snow: Dave and Charlotte had shown up in the morning, after the storm, and so had the Harpers. Unless whatever had happened to Joda and Barbara had happened to all of them, too.

But then where's their tractor?

She was second-guessing herself again. Whatever the truth, it meant a trip to Barrowman Farm.

If Charlotte was there, with Paul Harper –

Keep it together, Ellie. Clear head. Looks like you might be the only chance she's got.

"Matlock from Sierra Four Five, urgent call, over." But it came out in a dead, flat mumble, no reply was expected or even hoped for now. And there was none. Only static.

So what'll you do, Ellie?

An idea was forming. It'd give Tom an embolism, but the one advantage of having a superior that useless was knowing how to get round him easily. Especially if she demanded he come up with a better idea. If it came down to it, she'd assume full responsibility. Might mean the end of her career – criminal charges, even – but better that than risk Charlotte's safety.

Ellie's breath billowed white in the air; she replaced the handset, started the engine and reversed back onto the hill road.

Tom Graham stared glumly at his desktop, willing it to give him better news, but it refused to.

Usually they only lost the internet connection during a power cut; the office lights were still on, so that wasn't the problem, but the computer still refused to connect to the web.

A tower or a line must be down. They'd no mobile phone signal either; even the landlines were out.

Cut? Jammed? His imagination threatened to take flight in half a dozen directions – terrorists, earthquakes, floods, a nuclear bomb on London (he was fairly certain they wouldn't see the flash out here in Derbyshire, but didn't honestly know) or just the Harpers escalating their skulduggery to hitherto-unexplored levels – but as Tom himself would have been the first to admit, had his imagination been a bird, it would most likely have been an ostrich. He loved a good book – couldn't beat an old-fashioned adventure, like Alistair Maclean used to write – but he read them in childlike wonder, knowing a mind existed that could just *make things up* like that.

Too much imagination, he'd told Ellie more than once, was the kiss of death to a copper. You were meant to stick to the facts and establish what'd happened; too much imagination was a recipe for spinning random facts into grand conspiracies, like Alistair Maclean did. Fantastic if you were writing a book, which Tom was first to admit he couldn't and more power to anyone that could, but the last thing a copper needed because nine times out of ten the obvious answer was the right one: the husband did it, or the wife. Or, in Tony Harper's case, he'd wandered off-course while pissed, had a fall and frozen to death. Very sad – to the extent any bloody Harper dying could be – but hardly a threat to the community as a whole, whatever Ellie reckoned. That was too much imagination in action, right there.

But Wakeman Farm hadn't been imagination, Ellie Cheetham's or anyone else's. The smashed-in windows, the state of the place, not to mention the state of Kate Beck. He'd only met the girl once or twice before yesterday, but she'd seemed to have her head screwed on – a bit up herself, maybe, thinking she was better than everyone else, but that was what University did for kids these days, and the real world knocked it out of them soon enough. Except it looked as though something else had already done that, and knocked a shedload of other things out of her too. She was still rocking back and forth, last he'd heard, burbling "please" over and over again. Milly Emmanuel had burbled in her turn about shock and dissociative fugue states and Lord knew what else besides, but in plain English whatever'd happened at Wakeman Farm had sent the girl doolally-tap, at least for now.

And then there was the scene at the *Bell*. He'd love to tell Ellie that was too much imagination as well, but that was easier said than done with Ron Chapple stamping around demanding to know where his lad was.

Another reason too much imagination was the last thing a copper needed was that in the absence of proper answers you drove yourself potty trying to work out what was going on. And again, you'd end up filling in the gaps in your knowledge with any number of barking mad ideas – monsters, ghosts, Lord knew what else.

Not that Ellie had mentioned any of those, but Tom didn't like to think what conclusions she might jump to, or explanations she might dream up. Not that the evidence they pointed to was anything reassuring in itself. It looked as though the Harpers had collectively flipped out – or Liz Harper at least, mad with grief over her son. Ellie's encounter with them yesterday had been OTT even by their standards.

So they'd – what? Declared war on the world, or at least Barsall? Gone after the Becks and Famuyiwas because Liz thought they'd had something to do with Tony's death, or were witnesses? It was the only explanation Tom could think of that fitted the evidence; even so, it was hard to square. But otherwise, what was the answer? Even if some other mob were trying to muscle in on the Harpers, why go after the *Bell* or Wakeman Farm? They'd have to be nutters, not criminals. And that was getting into the kind of speculations Ellie Cheetham went in for – that or actual novels, although even Alistair Maclean gave his villains a better motive than "being bloody lunatics".

Then again, in real life people sometimes had no better reason.

So round and round it went, driving him up the pole. There was a reason Tom had never wanted promotion – he'd only applied for a sergeant's post under protest because Thelma had kept on at him about the salary and pension. He should, he knew, have been the constable and Ellie the sergeant: he'd be happier in a nice simple job where you could understand and predict things, and pass them on to someone better paid if you couldn't.

He'd always done his best to do so, sergeant or not, with any problem he couldn't solve himself, but this time he bloody couldn't, could he? No radio, no phone, no flipping internet even. Once again he wished Ellie was the one with the rank: then *she'd* be the one wondering what the hell to do. Maybe she'd have more luck calling out from the Height, raising Matlock – or someone, anyone else – and she'd come back with instructions on how to proceed. He was close to outright panic, because he was buggered if he knew what was going on or what to do about it –

He jumped at a sudden roar of wind, then realised the station's door had opened, letting in an icy bloody draught that came into his office even under the closed door. "Ellie?" he shouted.

The door banged shut. The office went quiet, apart from the sound of footsteps. Tom's hand crept towards his desk drawer, inside which was one of the old wooden truncheons that'd been standard issue till the mid-'90s. "Ellie?"

The footsteps approached his office door and the handle turned; Tom grabbed the truncheon, but its butt caught on the drawer's interior and yanked it out of the desk in a shower of staples, paperclips, post-it notes and drawing-pins. The truncheon clattered to the floor with the rest of the drawer's contents, and the door swung open. Tom yipped in alarm and scrabbled for the weapon, then yelped in pain as he accidentally seized a handful of pins.

"Sarge?" said Ellie Cheetham.

"Christ, woman." Tom rubbed his smarting hand against his trousers and yelped again: two of the pins were still embedded in his skin. "Didn't you hear me shouting you? You scared the daylights out of me."

"Sorry, sarge. Wind was a bit noisy."

Ellie slumped into the chair across the desk – they never really stood on ceremony – and Tom could already tell from her face what the news would be, but asked anyway as he struggled to reinsert the drawer. "Any joy?"

She shook her head. "Just static. You?"

"No radio, no phones, no bastard internet, even." Tom slammed the drawer back home so hard that Ellie jumped. "Sorry," he muttered.

"Forget it. So we're on our own."

"Not necessarily." In his desperation to avoid a decision, an idea had come to Tom. "Could always try and reach Matlock by road."

"Are you on crack?" Ellie coughed. "Sarge."

The "Sarge" almost made Tom crack up laughing, which was a good job; normally he'd have let the first comment go, but the state he was in he'd likely have taken her head off. As it was, the two things cancelled one another out, and he just sighed. "Think about it, Ellie. Get to Matlock, tell 'em what's happened, they'll get an Armed Response straight down here. Simple."

"On these roads? In this weather? Sarge, have you seen it out? Just getting to the Height was a nightmare. Normally I'd even hold off going as far as Barrowman Farm in these conditions, never mind anywhere else. Might as well try and drive to Berlin."

"Well, what do you expect me to do, Constable?" It was the first time Tom could ever remember pulling rank on Ellie, and it felt like admitting defeat. And it didn't impress her; she just folded her arms as if to say *All right then, Sarge, what* do *we do then?* The very spot he hadn't wanted putting in. "You're telling me that we've civilians in danger at Barrowman Farm, and we need to go get 'em. How we supposed to do that? There's two of us with batons and pepper spray, and according to you the Harpers've gone loopy, and they've got guns. So how, exactly,

do you expect me to sort this short of getting extra bodies in?"
And finding someone else to make the decisions? he didn't add.

Ellie looked down, and Tom thought he'd shut her up – not
that he considered that a victory as it still meant he'd have
to come up with an answer. But he *had* an answer – get to
Matlock, get help, bring them in. If things at Barrowman *were*
that dangerous –

"If one of us tries to get to Matlock," she said at last, "we
won't make it. And that leaves one officer here on their own.
We'll be worse off than before."

"What, then?" Tom demanded. "Do it ourselves?"

"Well, yeah, Sarge." Ellie was angry now, her patience gone.
"It's our fucking job."

Tom flinched, then rallied. "Don't you talk to me like that."

"There are civilians in danger at Barrowman Farm," said Ellie.
"That's my professional judgement. It's also my professional
judgement that the roads to Matlock are impassable, and we
can't contact Division. So we'll have to deal with it ourselves,
because that's what we're paid for."

Tom wanted to shout at her to shut up – but that wouldn't
do any good, would it? He couldn't think straight. He raised his
hands to ward her off. "Just – just –"

"Sarge, we can't just –"

"All right!" He shouted it. Christ. Might as well have run up
the white flag. He held up his hands again. "Just – just – give
me a minute here, all right?" He couldn't look at her. He felt
wretched. Useless. *Call yourself a copper, Graham? Bloody pathetic.*
He took deep breaths. He wished he could stretch this moment
out, so he didn't have to think or decide. But he couldn't.
So. "All right," he said. "So, Constable Cheetham, in your
professional judgement, how should we proceed?"

Ellie hadn't smoked in years, but craved a cigarette right now,
felt that tickling itch at the back of her throat only a lungful of

tobacco smoke (or certain other kinds) could assuage. No time for that now, though. Had to focus on the matter in hand.

"We'll have to go to Barrowman Farm ourselves," she said. "Search the house for Charlotte or Dave, or any clue where they've gone."

"And if they won't let us in?" said Tom. "Or if – look, you've already said things got out of hand there yesterday. Now you reckon they've graduated to kidnapping, maybe worse. I mean, what's happened to the Becks and the Famuyiwas?"

That was the big question. It was purely instinctual on her part, but Ellie was as certain that the Harpers *weren't* responsible for the scenes at the *Bell* and Wakeman Farm as she was that they *were* for Charlotte and Dave's disappearances. The last was easily explained – the Harpers had been at the *Bell*, Dave Chapple had driven up and caught them, and things had gone from there. But the rest, like Tony Harper's death, had no explanation she could think of that made sense.

The Harpers knew something, though. The way Liz had reacted to the charcoal sign – and ensured Ellie couldn't question the family in any depth – suggested something to hide, and since when were the Harpers so public-spirited as to clear the roads? No: they'd been looking for something, and maybe they'd found it. Another reason to visit Barrowman Farm again.

But she was going off instinct, and Tom was right: she couldn't ignore the evidence. Maybe it *had* all been the Harpers. Maybe they'd gone to the *Bell* on a return trip to get Charlotte, having missed her the night before.

"I don't know," she said.

"No. And they've got guns. Probably including a few we don't know about."

"We've got guns too."

"What?"

"I've a shotgun and rifle at home, fully licensed –"

"So what, we just go down there, the two of us, and –"

Tom waved his arms helplessly. "Neither of us are Authorised Firearms Officers."

"I used to be." Back in Manchester, a hundred years ago.

"Used to. Besides, it'd be us two against –"

"We ask for volunteers," said Ellie.

"Volunteers? Now who's on bloody crack? You get volunteers to help search for missing hikers, not for a sodding armed response."

"I know it's not ideal –" Understatement of the bloody week "– but I can name a dozen people round here with firearms licences, just off the top of my head. A dozen more who could use a shotgun if they needed to –"

"Jesus Christ, Ellie –"

"Tom, they probably wouldn't even *need* to use them." As soon as she'd said it, Ellie wished she'd dropped the *probably*. "Just hang round in the background looking hard. All right, none of the Harpers are the full shilling, but they're not going to want to reenact the flipping Alamo."

"You just said yourself, you weren't sure what they'd done. Come on, Ellie. You want to show up with a bunch of civvies waving guns around? If someone starts shooting –"

Anything for a quiet life, and this as far from one as Tom could imagine. That was what worried him, Ellie knew. And she wasn't. Maybe it would be to the good, if this cost her her job. Milly was always saying there was more to her than that. It was the last part of her old life, the life that'd ended when Richard died. Her marriage had certainly died that day; it had taken Stan the ironic time span of nine months to leave, but that had been a formality.

Hadn't her police career died then, really, too? Transferring out here had been a convenient way of relocating without any interruptions to her pay packet. But she was good for more than police work, surely? Maybe it would be an opportunity. Do the right thing and get a new start all at once. Worth a go.

Most importantly, it was the best chance to get Charlotte Famuyiwa out in one piece.

Yeah, yeah. Tell yourself you're doing it for her.

Tom's face was grey; his eyes were darting. He wouldn't look at her. He wanted someone else to come and take the cup but no one would, not unless the radio miraculously started working again. And she knew it wouldn't. Poor bastard looked close to a heart attack.

And then it came to her.

"You feeling okay, Tom?"

"Fine. I'm bloody fine."

"You sure?" He scowled at her. "I mean, you're really not looking well, Sarge. Like you're coming down with something."

He frowned, looking at her.

"Look, Tom – if you're not well, get home and rest up. I'll handle things here. My responsibility, okay?"

He looked down. "I've not been feeling that great, that's true. Might be the flu."

"No joke at your age, that, Sarge."

"Less of the 'your age', you cheeky mare." He was already putting his coat on. Still not looking at her. "If you're sure."

"I'm sure, Sarge."

"I'll – I'll head home, then."

"Do that."

Ellie couldn't look at him as he shuffled to the door. He looked suddenly very old.

The door clicked shut. Tom had wanted a way out, and she'd given it to him; she still wasn't sure she'd wanted to be in charge, but like it or not, she now was.

In charge, and responsible.

Ellie straightened up and breathed out. Then sat behind his desk, grabbed pen and paper, and wrote a list of names.

For a small community, Barsall wasn't short of churches. There was the old Anglican church, St Alkmund's, down on Church Street – where else? – and there was a Wesleyan Methodist Chapel out by Blackfield Park, on Spring Bank.

The newest stood close to Ellie's house: the Assemblies of God church, which resembled an inner-city community centre more than anything else. Still, it had four walls, a roof and the facilities to produce tea and coffee in quantity, and that was enough. Whatever Ellie might think of Matt Williams privately, he'd been glad to help.

Ellie stood at the plywood lectern. Around twenty people sat in the rows of cheap plastic chairs before her. She knew them all by sight. Bert Annable was in the front row, along with Noel. Not Milly, though; she detested anything to do with guns and was busy looking after Kate Beck. Ellie would need to look in on her shortly.

Also present was a man in a Barbour jacket over designer outdoor wear. His hair was salt-and-pepper grey at the sides and reddish-brown and woolly-looking on top as the result of a hair transplant that no one other than himself found impressive, but he still had something of his son's Mediterranean good looks. Ellie hadn't particularly wanted Ron Chapple there, but hadn't had much choice.

"All right." She knocked on the lectern; the church grew quiet. "We need some volunteers."

There were sighs, more of weariness than reluctance. Barsall didn't lack community spirit; it was a necessity in a place so easily cut off from the outside world. People mucked in and pulled together on one another's behalf; one of the things Ellie liked about the village. The sighs were because they were expecting to hear some stupid bloody townies had got in trouble and needed saving. Ellie had a surprise for them on that score at least.

Briefly, she outlined what they'd found at Wakeman Farm and the *Bell*. "We're still not a hundred per cent clear what happened, but we do have reason to believe at least two people are being held against their will at Barrowman Farm."

That provoked a few mutters; Ron Chapple bit his lips, clenching and unclenching his fists on his knees. "Harpers," said Ernie Stasiolek. "Big bloody surprise."

"We know who they've got?" asked Bert.

"Charlotte Famuyiwa and David Chapple."

There were a few more mutters at that, and a few glances in Ron's direction. He closed his eyes, fists still clenched, plainly hating to be the object of whatever mixed emotions were being directed at him. Except among the more easily impressed local girls, Dave Chapple wasn't a popular lad, even if his blend of smug good looks, piss-taking 'charm' and (above all) Ron's money always got him out of trouble. Most would be thinking it served him right to be in some real bother for once; some would be considering the benefits of Ron's gratitude to anyone involved in getting his son and heir out of said bother, and mixed in there would be some genuine pity, which Ron would probably hate the worst of all.

Chances were, Charlotte was a distant fourth in their thoughts, and Ellie hated that. Even now, Dave's rich dad was getting him special treatment. "We don't know what's happened to Joda and Barbara Famuyiwa," she said, "or Grant and Sally Beck. Charlotte's probably scared to death and we haven't even a family to get her back to. And I don't have to tell you that any girl shut up with Paul Harper's in big trouble."

That silenced the murmuring and pulled everyone's attention away from Ron, no doubt to his relief. Ellie saw a few faces set hard; at least three people there had loved ones who'd suffered at Paul Harper's hands, including little Tara Caddick's mother Laura. Ellie had hesitated to include Laura Caddick, but she wasn't really in a position to pick and choose.

"What is it you need, Ellie?" asked Bert.

"We can't contact Matlock and the roads are impassable. We don't know when that'll change, and I'm not prepared to risk Charlotte or David's safety by waiting. So we're looking for volunteers to accompany us to Barrowman Farm to determine whether they're there and, if so, get the Harpers to release them."

"Armed," said Bert. It wasn't a question.

"Any luck, we won't need them," said Ellie. "Liz Harper's not thick. If we can get her to let them go, and no more said –"

"No more said?" cried Ron Chapple. "They've kidnapped my lad!"

"Right now we're short-handed, Ron," said Ellie. "Priority's getting him and Charlotte out of there in one piece."

"This is how the Harpers get away with everything, every bloody time," muttered Ernie Stasiolek.

"They won't get away with *this*," vowed Chapple.

"Oh yeah," said Chris Brailsford, aka Son of Plant-Pot. "Now Money-Bags Chapple's got the hump, we might finally get shot of them. Us bloody peasants just had to lump it, didn't we?"

His father, embarrassed, elbowed him in the ribs, but there was a widespread mutter of agreement.

"No-one's lumping anything," said Ellie. "As soon as the snow clears I'll get onto Matlock and call in the heavy mob. They're all involved, the lot of them, and this is our chance to throw the book at the sods."

Although she wished she was more confident about that: Liz might let Paul take all the blame, say it'd all been his doing and they'd have called the police themselves if the phones had been working. It was an old Harper tactic – one of the clan took the fall for the rest, leaving them free to intimidate the witnesses and so on. Still, a raid might turn up other incriminating stuff.

Enough.

"That'll wait till the weather clears," said Ellie. "Priorities, people. Charlotte and David. Now, I need this clearly understood – the weapons are for show unless otherwise instructed. No-one fires them or even points them at any of the Harpers without my express authority. Is that clear? I don't want the shootout at the OK Corral here."

"Thought you said they should just hand them over," said Laura Caddick.

"I'm hoping they'll see sense," said Ellie, "but this is the Harpers we're talking about. We all clear?"

"It's clear," said Noel. "So when do we go?"

"Straight away. No time to waste. Who's on board?"

Virtually every hand went up.

"Right then," said Ellie. She was afraid, but it was the kind of fear that went with giddy excitement, like riding a roller-coaster or bungee-jumping. At least, she supposed so, never having done either. She *was* jumping into the unknown, though. A gamble. A risk. She felt alive for once, instead of existing. That could become addictive, which mightn't be a good thing, but that was another day's problem. For now, she'd work to do. "Let's go."

15.

Liz saw the approaching headlights as she peered between the boards of the front room window, through the snow and the winter-stripped hedges. Here any second. "Frank!"

On the front room floor, Charlotte Famu-whatsit jerked at the shout, then gagged as the movement pulled the noose tight around her throat, while Dave Chapple let out a whimper. The pair of them were shivering, although that was as likely to be from cold as it was from fear; they were stripped down to their underwear after all.

Liz was glad she'd had Paul lay some sheeting down; the girl had managed to hold her water so far, but a glistening stain had already spread out around the Chapple boy. Not so high and mighty now, Little Mr King Of All The World. Probably soil those boxer shorts of his in a bit as well. Which would be a problem, given that the smell of his piss was already bad enough. Thank God he'd be the first one down the chute at the Hollows tomorrow.

"'Sup, Mum?" Frank shouted from the landing.

"I want you at the top of the stairs, 'case they try anything. Tell Keira to keep an eye on them, but just watch for now. I'll say if it's to be anything else." She'd stationed Keira in the attic, to watch for trouble; it'd been Keira who'd shouted a warning down about the approaching vehicles minutes earlier. Keira also had the rifle, since she was by far the best shot in the family, town-bred or not. All that worried Liz was how eager Keira might be to use it, especially on Ellie Cheetham. "Paul!

Dom! Kitchen. Watch the back." Safest to have Dom with one of his brothers, and it meant that would leave someone free to watch the hall lest anyone get past Liz. "Jess!"

The girl appeared, whey-faced and trembling, in the doorway, the baby on her hip and the pistol in her free hand. "Mum?"

Liz peered between the boards again. The cars rolled into the drive and parked up, spread out. Car doors opened and slammed. She jerked a thumb towards the prisoners. "Watch them," she said, and picked up the Ithaca.

The wind had dropped, and the snow was tumbling down. Ellie turned off the wipers and got out of the Land Rover, reaching inside to take out her shotgun.

Even with the wind gone, Barrowman Farm remained a shadow, a silhouette, looking more like a squatting, predatory toad than ever. Thinking of Liz Harper, Ellie wondered if some houses, like pets, could grow like their owners.

"Ernie?" she said, quiet as she could. "Round the back when I say."

Ernie Stasiolek nodded, motioning to Chris Brailsford and Phil Robinson. Ellie hadn't liked the idea of a second armed group not under her or another officer's direct control – not that she'd have had much confidence in Tom – but Ernie had a good head on his shoulders and apart from maybe Noel was the one person she'd felt she could trust with such a job.

She looked around, but both Bert Annable and Noel had already moved to flank her. Bert carried his twelve-bore over one arm, Noel his rifle. The wind picked up again, and snow billowed around them. Ellie held the shotgun behind her, against her leg. The others were turned briefly into shadows; faceless men and women with guns, come knocking at someone's door. "Ready?"

Bert Annable snapped his shotgun closed; Noel pulled back

his rifle bolt. "The rest of you, hang back and no shooting, unless I say otherwise."

"What if they shoot at us?" someone asked.

"First thing you do is take cover," Ellie said. "After that, you wait for my instructions."

No one thankfully asked the obvious question – *what if they shoot you?* – and Ellie took a deep breath. "Let's go," she said, and with a nod to Ernie Stasiolek, stepped towards the house, Noel and Bert beside her.

16.

Through the gap in the front-room window, Liz saw Ellie and two others advancing on the house. *Here we go*, she thought, and went out into the hall.

"All right," she shouted. "No-one do anything, not less I say."

Remembering how Cheetham had been holding her gun, Liz did the same with hers, resting it behind her thigh, just out of sight. If it came down to it, she wouldn't hesitate, while Ellie Cheetham more than likely would: she was still a copper, after all, with rules and procedures to obey. She certainly wouldn't be as ready as Liz, because she didn't understand what was happening around here; not what was *really* happening.

Liz checked the security chain was on, and waited.

There was a knock at the door.

Ellie heard the key turn in the lock, and the front door opened a few inches, the brass security chain pulled taut. Liz Harper's bulk filled the gap: half that doughy, sullen face; a coil of greasy hair; one stone-coloured eye.

The wind blew snow between them.

"Well?" said Liz.

"Morning, Liz."

"What do you want?" The face blank, the eye as stony as its colour.

All right, then. "Anyone from here been out today?"

"What if we have?"

"Clearing the roads with your snowploughs, that sort of thing?"

Liz smirked. "Yeah, that's right, Constable. Even though you're always saying we're scum and never do anything for anyone else. See? Bit of community spirit on show there. Not that it'll make any difference next time some –"

"So you went past Wakeman Farm? And the *Bell*?"

The smirk froze. "Might've. Well, not me *personally*."

"Who did, then?"

"What's this about?" No pause before the question; Liz had known it was coming. Playing games. Deflecting.

"So whoever went out clearing the roads didn't happen to notice the state of either of those places, then?"

"Dunno what you're talking about."

"Been a bit hard to miss, I'd've thought."

"Maybe they did see something. What if they did?"

"And they didn't report it?"

"What for? You lot'd just blame them for it, like you blame us for anything goes wrong round here. Give a dog a bad name and –"

"They didn't happen to see Charlotte Famuyiwa or David Chapple on their travels, did they?"

"Not that I heard."

"Just that the pair of them set off from Barsall this morning. Dave was taking her back to the *Bell*. And we found his car parked outside the pub with the doors open. Right next to some fresh tractor marks. So you can see how it might look."

"Like I said," said Liz, "give a dog a bad name. Can't blame the boys not wanting to get involved when you lot blame them if you stub your toe."

"Charlotte and Dave are both missing."

"Sorry to hear it."

Ellie shifted gears, into formal mode: "Are Charlotte Famuyiwa or David Chapple on the premises here?"

"Here we go."

"Simple question, Liz –"

"Here we go. Coming here accusing us of all sorts –"

"Simple question, Liz. Yes or no?"

"This is harassment. Pure and simple. I'll be making a complaint about –"

"Yes or fucking no, Liz?" Shit. Her control had slipped, and she saw Liz's eyes gleam at being given an advantage.

"Don't you talk to me like that. My own house. Who d'you think you are, eh? Who the hell d'you think you are?"

"Are Charlotte and Dave –"

"Not being insulted on me own doorstep. Do one!" And Liz slammed the door.

Or tried, at least. Ellie was wearing a good heavy boot, and she shoved it into the gap between door and jamb.

"Shift your foot," said Liz. Was that a gleam of sweat on her forehead?

"If they're not there, you won't mind us coming in and taking a look, will you? Prove to everyone you're on the level."

"You got a warrant?"

"I've got two missing persons." *More than two. Try six.* "Thought you'd want to help."

"You got a warrant?"

"Sooner we eliminate you from our enquiries, sooner we can –"

"Warrant."

"– find out where they really are –"

"War. Rant."

"– before something happens to them."

"Warrant," said Liz again, shifting position as she said it, and that was when Ellie saw the gleam of the shotgun she was holding against her leg.

"Fine," she said, turning as if to go. "I'll be back with one –"

She hadn't taken her foot out of the door, but she glimpsed Liz in her peripheral vision and saw some of the tension go out of her, the glint of the shotgun sink about half an inch as she relaxed, and that was when Ellie swung back round, gripped her own gun in both hands and shoved the barrel between door and jamb into Liz's stomach. "Don't fucking move," she said.

Liz blinked; the stonelike eyes widened in disbelief, then narrowed again in fury. Her mouth writhed and tightened.

"Keep still," said Ellie slowly. "I'll blow you in fucking half, Liz. I mean it." The shotgun's safety catch was still on, but Liz didn't need to know that.

"Mum?" shouted a voice – Frank, Ellie thought. "Mum, what's she doing?"

"Quiet, Frank," said Liz. Her voice was hoarse and her grey face might have gone a shade or two paler.

Ellie took her left hand from the shotgun, pushing the barrel harder into Liz's belly with her right, and reached down to her utility belt and the extra item she'd hung from it. She unhooked the bolt-cutters, brought them up and snipped the security chain. It dropped and clinked lightly; Liz breathed out through her teeth.

Ellie returned the cutters to her belt and resumed her two-handed grip on the shotgun. "Now," she said, "move back very, very slowly. Try to get away and I'll shoot. And tell your boys to take things easy. Don't want this going off, do we?"

"You'll fucking pay for this."

"Yeah, yeah."

"No. You will fucking *pay*."

"Step back. Slowly."

Liz pressed her lips together till they turned white, but obeyed. Ellie pushed the door wider with the toe of her boot. "Noel," she said. "Bert."

She stepped over the threshold, pushing Liz back with the shotgun. Frank Harper was on the stairs, pointing another shotgun down at her. Behind Liz, in the hallway, Paul was standing with what looked like a baby assault rifle at his shoulder. Ellie recognised it; it was one of the ones on their licence – just a .22, but even a .22 could kill, especially at that range.

"Tell your lads to put their guns down," she said.

"Fuck off."

Bert, then Noel, entered the hallway after her. "Do it, Liz," said Ellie.

The white mouth writhed. "Guns down, boys."

"Mum," said Frank.

"Down," said Liz. Glowering, Frank lowered the weapon to his side.

"Means you too, Paul," said Ellie. The rifle didn't waver. Was he going to chance a shot? He might manage it – have a better chance of hitting Ellie without damaging Liz than Frank would. Although even if he hit her in the head, the gun might fire. At least it might if she took the safety catch off, which Ellie now remembered to do. The click sounded very loud in the stillness. Liz looked down, then up. She licked her lips and half-smiled. Then it faded. "Do as she says, Paul."

"Fuck," muttered Paul, but lowered the gun.

"And I'll take that," said Ellie, taking the shotgun from Liz's grip. A sawn-off Ithaca pump-action – illegal, right there – and with a five or six-round magazine, which was illegal too. Another time, anything that could potentially get Liz Harper sent down for four years would be cause for celebration, but there were more pressing concerns just now. "Noel?" she held the weapon out. "Unload it."

He slung his rifle, pointed the shotgun at the floor and worked the slide to eject the cartridges. Noel threw the shotgun out into the yard, then unslung his rifle again.

Liz clenched and unclenched her fists, glaring back at Ellie. Ellie looked straight back at her, not blinking. "Where are they?"

She waited for more Harper bullshit from Liz, but there was only a mute stare. The stone eyes moved slightly, studying Ellie's face. Ellie wasn't certain what Liz was looking for, or whether or not she found it, but finally the other woman breathed out. "Front room," she said, nodding towards the door.

"Who's with them?"

"Jess."

"Jess?" shouted Ellie.

"Yeah?" The girl sounded scared. Better than belligerent, Ellie supposed, but scared people could fire guns too, whether they meant to or not.

"I'm sending someone in to get Dave and Charlotte," said Ellie. "Don't do anything stupid. If you've got a gun, put it down." A bead of sweat trickled over her temple. "I know you don't want to hurt anyone. Neither do we."

Liz sneered at that, but Ellie let it go. "Okay?" she said.

"Okay."

"Noel," said Ellie, and he went in through the door. "Christ," she heard him say.

"Noel?"

He stepped back through, slinging his rifle and took the bolt-cutters. "Need to borrow these."

"Okay, just make it quick."

Noel disappeared back into the front room. Frank and Paul glared at Ellie. Movement behind Paul, in the kitchen: Dom Harper, gawping at the scene. "Take it easy, Dom," she said. "Put the gun down."

Jess was in the front room, which just left Keira, the one who worried Ellie most right now. Bert moved his shotgun from Frank to Paul, ready for trouble. But he only had two shots. And where the fuck was Keira?

Ellie was about to ask Liz that, but before she could she heard what sounded like the bolt-cutters snipping through rope, a sort of twang, and a gasp. Then again. Moments later, she heard a woman coughing and groaning, then a man.

Noel came through the door, supporting Charlotte Famuyiwa against him. She was shaking – both with cold and fright, Ellie guessed, as she was clad only in her underwear. "Got a problem," said Noel. "Pair of them can barely walk." He glared at Liz. "Bastards had them hog-tied."

"Such lovely people," said Ellie. Glancing at Charlotte's bare feet and remembering the state of the Harpers' yard, she reckoned it was probably a good thing she couldn't walk across that lot. "Can you carry her?"

"Yeah."

"Want me to get the lad?" said Bert.

Ellie mulled it. "Can you manage Dave as well, Noel?"

"Not at the same time."

She smiled. "I was thinking more a second run."

"I can do that."

"Okay. Bert, if you can just keep an eye on the natives here, in case they get restless?"

The older man smiled. "My pleasure."

Noel checked the rifle's safety was on, then gave Charlotte his best smile. "Right, sweetheart. Fireman's lift, okay?"

Charlotte nodded, and actually managed a faint smile in response. Noel could be a charmer when he wished to be. He picked Charlotte up, slung her over his shoulder, toed the door wide and went out across the farmyard.

"I don't know what you were thinking," Ellie told Liz, "but you've gone and done it this time."

Liz just smiled, and shotgun or not, Bert Annable's presence beside her or no, Ellie wanted nothing more in that moment than to turn and get out. Liz wasn't stupid. There was something else here. Madness, maybe. Or – that conviction again – Liz Harper knew something Ellie didn't.

Noel came back, went into the front room and helped Dave Chapple to the door. Dave was wrapped in a blanket, and when Noel hoicked him up on his shoulder Ellie caught a glimpse of the poor sod's underwear and understood why; there were some stains Noel would rather not have to clean out of his coat this evening.

Noel slipped out through the door, and then it was just Ellie, Bert and the Harpers again. "We done?" said Bert Annable.

"Yup," said Ellie. "You go first."

"Ellie –"

"Bert, I'll be fine. Just go on."

"All right."

Bert went out into the yard. Now Ellie was alone with her gun pushed into Liz's stomach, with Liz still grinning at her. Up on the stairs, Frank was stealing glances at his shotgun. Over Liz's shoulder, she saw Paul sidle sideways, too. "Stay where you are, Paul," she said. "What about Joda and Barbara, Liz? What about Grant and Sally? Where are they?"

"Won't find them here," said Liz. "Don't you be trying to pin that on us, Ellie. That wasn't any of our doing."

"Whose, then?"

Liz didn't answer, just kept on grinning. "It's just you now, Ellie," she said. "Starting to get a bit worried?"

She'd pushed Liz too far back into the hall; now when Ellie backed towards the door, she'd be far enough from her that Frank or Paul might chance a shot. Especially if Liz dived for the ground or the front room. She could grab Liz's sweater, pull the other woman after her – but that would mean moving closer to Liz, and she didn't want to do that either. She didn't like that grin. She didn't like anything about Liz Harper or Barrowman Farm at the best of times, but that grin was in a class of its own.

So Ellie backed away, keeping her finger on the trigger and hoping that neither Frank nor Paul were stupid enough to risk the shotgun going off if they fired at her. But she could already see Frank reaching down for his gun. And Liz was moving too, advancing on her, still with that bloody smile in place.

"Won't be seeing you again, Constable Cheetham," she said, in a sing-song voice. "Think we're bad? You've no idea what's coming for you."

Ellie kept eye contact and carried on moving back at a slow

pace, pushing the heel of her back foot along the hall carpet in search of the door's sill. Last thing she needed was to trip over that and go sprawling, especially with Liz moving towards her. "What's that then, Liz? Enlighten me. What about those signs? What do they mean? At the *Bell*, at Wakeman's –" Liz's face tightened, but the smile stayed fixed on her mouth and she didn't answer. "What about your Tony?" Ellie tried. "What about the sign by him? What's that all about?"

"You'll see," said Liz. Ellie's heel caught the sill and despite everything she almost stumbled. Liz chuckled. Ellie stepped carefully back over the threshold. "Wouldn't want to spoil the surprise, Ellie. But you'll see. You'll all see. They'll come for you tonight. All of you."

Ellie took another step back, and Liz, still grinning, slammed the front door in her face. Clever. Maybe the crazy grin had all been an act so that she could do that – shut the house up tight again, so Ellie would have to either fight her way back in or leave them alone. Not that there'd been any need: Ellie had what she'd came for, and she'd happily wait until she could whistle up some aid from Matlock before coming near Barrowman Farm again.

"Clear!" she shouted. "All clear!"

It had started snowing again. A moment later she heard muffled voices and footsteps; Ernie Stasiolek and the others, making their way back round from the rear of the house. Her heart was pounding and she was panting for breath, but she was grinning. Adrenaline.

Even if a part of her was disappointed; even if a part of her was sorry she hadn't had a chance to hurt one of the Harpers. Or worse.

She wouldn't think of that now. The important thing was that they had what they'd come for, and no-one was hurt. She could live with that.

The snow was coming down thick and fast. Ellie turned away, and took a step towards the Land Rover.

She was never sure what she trod in, but whatever it was made her stumble. As she did, something flicked the top of her head, hard. She stumbled harder, tripped; as she fell, she saw her fur cap fly ahead of her through the falling snow, a ragged chunk torn out of the crown.

And then she heard the shot.

A second shot sounded when Ellie was five or six feet from the Land Rover and she let out an involuntary cry – *that's it, number's up Ellie* – before she realised the shot had missed, else she wouldn't have heard it. She realised too that it hadn't been the high crack of a rifle, and had come from ahead of her, and then she heard the high, drilling scream sounding from above and behind her.

Noel caught her arm and bundled her into the car. Bert Annable was scrambling into the back of the Land Rover as well, shoving in beside Charlotte and Dave – Dave Chapple let out a high-pitched cry of fright and might well have soiled himself again – and Ellie registered that the barrels of Bert's shotgun were smoking.

From the farmhouse came furious shouting.

"Best bloody go," said Bert, breaking the shotgun open.

He was right. They had the kids, someone had shot at her, Bert had shot back and Christ alone knew what was about to kick off. Ellie grabbed the radio mic from the dashboard, flicked on the speakers and shouted into it. "Everybody out! Everybody out! Into the cars and home!"

Ernie Stasiolek came pelting across the yard with Chris Brailsford and Phil Robinson at his heels. Bert reloaded his shotgun and leant out of the window, aiming at the house. He fired first one barrel, then the other, over Ernie and the others' heads. Not as loud as the first time he'd fired. That must have been both barrels at once.

Engines revved; wheels tore at the muddy ground. Ellie turned the key in the ignition. Something hit the windscreen, splintering the glass. A little white spider-web, up in one corner. "Everyone get down!" she shoutcd, throwing the Land Rover into reverse and flooring the accelerator – second time in twenty-four hours she'd done that in the front yard of Barrowman Farm.

She saw a muzzle flash twice more – the front room window, a gap in the boards – and felt something else hit the Land Rover's bodywork. A small bullet, like the first – a big one would have punched straight through the windscreen and made a far bigger hole. That farty little .22 rifle. Paul Harper.

The Land Rover shot back towards the demolished gate; Ellie floored the brake to avoid clipping another of the cars from the village, and the engine stalled. "Fuck. Fuck."

"Get us out of here! Get us out of here!" Dave Chapple was screaming, as she turned the ignition key again, and then again. The engine coughed and churned. *Turn over you bastard, turn over.* She could hear the twig-like snapping of the .22 from the house. On the first floor, a board was wrenched from one of the windows and a shotgun barrel was thrust out through the gap.

The engine caught as the last of the other vehicles from Barsall reversed out onto the farm road and slewed round. Ellie reversed too as the final vehicle shot off along the road towards Spear Bank; the shotgun boomed and she ducked reflexively. Something smacked hard into the Land Rover's side panel; the vehicle shuddered but kept moving. They swerved onto the farm road; through the snow she could see the taillights of the other cars, accelerating away.

17.

Ellie had to cut speed quickly after accelerating clear of the farmyard; the cars soon slowed to a crawl as the snow replaced the Harpers as the main danger.

They'd left the main gate (*PISS OFF – THIS MEANS YOU*) ajar but there was still a queue of vehicles there, negotiating the turn onto Spear Bank. Ellie doubted they'd be followed, but found herself checking the rearview. Bert Annable reloaded his shotgun once more, peering out through the rear windscreen. "No sign of 'em," he said.

Think we're bad? You've no idea what's coming for you. That was what Liz had said. Sounded like she expected someone else to deal with Ellie for them. Or something. No, that was daft. *You'll see. You'll all see. They'll come for you tonight. All of you.*

So Liz Harper had finally flipped. That was all it was. What else could it be?

Even if she had, though, what had flipped her? It all kept coming back to that charcoal sign. If she even had a clue what it meant –

The car ahead of them moved. Ellie eased the Land Rover after it, gratefully turning onto Spear Bank and following the procession through the falling snow.

Ascending the hill road was a slow, painful crawl, but at last it was finished and they were on Halliwell Way, nearing the outskirts of Barsall. As they entered the village and reached the roundabout, she saw Tom Graham's X5 parked outside the Assemblies of God building, along with several other vehicles. A couple of people stood outside; they waved when they saw the returning cars. One ran back in, and more people began emerging onto the pavement. She recognised Julie Robinson among them.

Most of the cars pulled in there – the 'posse' (Ellie had to smile at the word) reuniting with their loved ones to confirm they'd returned from their expedition in one piece.

Ellie halted the Land Rover and turned to Bert. "You want to get off here? I'm going on to Milly's."

"I'll hop off, if you don't mind," Bert said.

"Sure." Ellie pulled in. "Thanks for today."

"No problem."

"And thanks for… thanks for before."

He chuckled. "Always glad to help."

"Noel?"

"I'll stick with you."

"You sure? Bet Milly'll be pissed off."

"Might as well catch it now instead of later."

Ellie looked at Charlotte and Dave in the rearview mirror. "We're going to head on to Dr Emmanuel's now, have her look you over."

"I *did* hear," said Charlotte, with a hint of her old spikiness. Ellie hid a smile, glad to see some of the girl's spirit back.

"Charlotte – look, I need to ask here, in case… well, in case there are further charges. Did they… were you assaulted?"

"You mean sexually?" Her voice was flat. "No." It cracked slightly. "He bloody wanted to, though."

Ellie didn't need to ask who 'he' had been. "All right, love," she said, putting the Land Rover back in gear. To the right, Bert Annable was trudging up the High Street towards the church. Laura Caddick, walking alongside him, turned back and waved to Ellie. Ellie waved back. She'd forgotten Laura was there; she hadn't had to worry on that score after all.

"I wasn't either," said Dave, as they crossed the stone bridge over Groveley Beck. "You know, I'm sure you were gonna ask."

"Okay. Sorry."

"It can happen to men too, you know. I've seen *Deliverance*."

Noel suppressed what seemed to be a coughing fit and Ellie bit the inside of her cheek to keep her face straight. Dave had a point, but it was also entirely typical that he'd try to make it all about him.

"Oh," said Noel. "Think this is yours."

He held up her fur cap and put it in the well between the seats. Ellie saw the blackened gouge in the crown where the bullet had snagged it. She forced her gaze back to the road. She wasn't going to think about that now.

"Ellie?" said Charlotte from the backseat. Ellie couldn't remember the last time the girl had called her by her first name. It'd been *Constable* or *Constable Cheetham* or, if she was in a good mood and not in a strop of some kind, *Sheriff*.

"Yes, love?"

"What about my Mum and Dad?"

Ellie sighed. "I don't know, love. Didn't find any sign of them at the pub. Dunno where they are. But we'll find 'em."

Charlotte turned away, her face crumpling. Dave made no move to comfort her. The little prick. Ellie knew that wasn't a charitable thought, and that he'd been through a rough time today as well. But even so: the little prick.

She turned off Halliwell Way and pulled up in front of the surgery on Hollybeck Row. "Be right back," she said, then got out and went to the door. It was locked. She rapped on it. After a few moments, there were footsteps; the key turned in the lock and Milly opened the door. She glared angrily up at Ellie, then past her at the car.

"He's fine," said Ellie. "We both are. Everyone's back okay."

Milly's gaze shifted to the cracked windscreen. Then she breathed out. "Well, thank God for that. Did you find them?"

"Charlotte and Dave, yeah. No sign of anyone else."

Milly's eyes glistened, and she shook her head. She knew Joda pretty well from church, and Barbara from her surgery. "Okay," she said at last. "Get 'em in here."

Noel brought Dave Chapple in; Ellie gathered Charlotte in her arms, swiped the car door shut with her backside and carried her into the surgery. Milly shut the door behind them. "Consulting Room One," she said. "Now."

There were two consulting rooms; although Milly was the only permanent GP here, a locum doctor came in part-time. "Both of 'em?" said Ellie.

Milly rolled her eyes. "Yeah, both." She lowered her voice. "Got Kathleen Beck in the other one."

"Shit. Course." Wakeman Farm felt like a memory of something Ellie had done years ago.

"This way," Milly said. "Okay, Charlotte, you're on the couch. Dave, just park yourself on that chair for now, love. Right, you two – waiting room. Deal with you in a bit."

Which didn't sound promising, but what the hell. Ellie and Noel went back into the waiting-room and sat down, listening to Milly's soft voice from the consulting room. Noel let out a long slow breath, and studied his hands.

"You okay?" said Ellie.

He nodded. "Think so." He forced a smile. "Bit more excitement than I'm used to." His Welsh accent was stronger than usual; it tended to come to the fore in emotional moments.

Ellie's hands were cold. She tried rubbing them together, and realised they were shaking. Fucking hell. For the second time in twenty-four hours, she wished she still smoked. She could have badly used one right now.

What she remembered more than anything, in this moment, was the gentle flick against her scalp, and then the sight of her cap flying past her. A rifle bullet, meant for her head. A couple of inches lower –

Ellie had seen gunshot wounds before – in Manchester, and one or two up this way, but they'd been accidental injuries. Guns going off by accident, stray bullets. But this had been deliberate. And it hadn't been Paul Harper's .22, or one of the shotguns. Ellie had heard the crack of the shot; she was guessing a deer rifle, a .303 or .308. Two inches lower and she wouldn't have even heard it.

"Fuck," she said out loud. Her throat and stomach felt clenched; she was struggling to breathe and could only manage short, shallow gasps. Her heart – Christ, she could feel it pounding, at what felt like twice the normal speed.

"Ell?" A hand on her shoulder. Milly's small, heart-shaped face. Frowning. Worried. "Ell, what is it?"

"I think. Just." She couldn't even get the words out.

"Is she okay?" Noel asked.

"Yeah. Well, no, but – think I know what this is." Milly knelt, taking Ellie's hands. "Ellie, love, listen to me. You're having a panic attack."

"Delayed reaction?" said Noel.

"Probably. What happened out there?"

"Someone shot at her as she headed back to the car. Blew her cap off."

"Fucking what? Bastards. All right." Milly squeezed Ellie's hands. "Okay, sweetheart. You're safe now, okay? You're gonna be all right."

You'll see. You'll all see. They'll come for you tonight. All of you. Ellie shook her head.

"Ellie, it's okay. Now listen to me. You're hyperventilating. That's not gonna help. So I want you to take a deep breath in, slowly – slowly as you can. Count up to seven as you do it. Then let it out over a count of eleven."

Ellie tried, but she'd filled her lungs to capacity by the count of three and the air whooshed out of her almost as fast, leaving her wheezing and gasping. But Milly kept making her try again and again, and gradually her breathing stabilised. Ellie couldn't make out what Milly was saying half the time, but her voice was soothing and gentle. *Great bedside manner, doc.* One reason Milly was so well-loved in Barsall

As her breathing steadied, Ellie felt a little calmer and slowly the fright ebbed out of her.

"There you go," said Milly, and gave her a hug. "Jones? Get the bloody kettle on. Coffee with lots of sugar for this one. Decaf." She poked Ellie in the ribs. "Last thing you need is caffeine right now."

Ellie managed a smile. "Are they okay?"

"Charlotte and the Giant Twat?" Milly was no more a fan of Dave Chapple than most of Barsall's adult population. "No permanent damage – nothing physical, anyway. They were scared shitless – literally, in his case."

"So much for doctor-patient confidentiality."

"Nothing confidential about that smell. Make sure you get the backseat of the Land Rover cleaned before you go getting jiggy on it with your latest bit on the side."

"Piss off." There'd been no bit on the side, or anywhere else, in some time. Milly had teased Ellie more than once about getting her job descriptions mixed up: she was supposed to be a copper, not a nun.

"How you feeling now?"

"Better." Ellie started to get up. "I'd better crack on."

"Sit yourself down." Milly pushed her back into the chair. "You're getting that brew down you before you do anything else."

"Milly, I've got a lot to do."

"Yeah, and you'll get it done. But you need to take care of yourself. All right?" Milly sighed. "Fucksake. I thought I'd got away from this shit when I moved out here."

"You and me both, kid."

"Here we go." Noel returned with three steaming mugs on a tray.

"Helped yourself, I see," Milly said.

"Made you one as well."

"Bloody arse-kisser."

Noel kissed the top of Milly's head.

***

Ellie finished the coffee as fast as she could, then drove back to the Assemblies of God church. Tom's X5 was still outside, she saw with something approaching relief for the first time.

The church was packed, with most of the occupants rising to their feet as she entered. A couple of people clapped and someone even cheered, although they cut it short with an embarrassed silence when no-one joined in.

First person to come up and greet her was Ron Chapple – joy of bloody joys – shouldering his way up the aisle. "Constable Cheetham? Where's my son? What happened to him?"

"Dave's at the surgery now," she said.

"Surgery? What?"

"I did try to tell him," said Bert Annable, "but –"

"Just shut up, you." Ron rounded on Ellie again. "Well?"

"He'll be fine," said Ellie. "Just shock. No physical damage. He's had a bad scare, that's all."

"Scared the shit out of him, in fact," Chris Brailsford muttered, triggering an outburst of laughter. Ron wheeled round, furious; Ellie caught his arm and he pulled away, his arm coming up. The absurdity of the spectacle triggered more laughter, although nervier and cut short; were they about to witness one of their leading citizens decking the local constable, or at least attempting to? Ellie actually felt something approaching sympathy for Ron Chapple, for the first time ever. His son had been in danger, and he was angry and scared. "Ron," she said. "Dave's gonna be fine. He's at the surgery now. Milly's just finished looking him and Charlotte over. You can go see him now if you want."

Some of the anger went out of Chapple, and he lowered his eyes, then nodded. "Thank you," he said at last. "For – getting him back." And then he hurried out of the church, head down.

"Must have bloody hurt to say," Bert Annable said. "You all right, Ellie? Close shave back there."

She nodded. "I'm fine. I'm fine." *They'll come for you tonight. All of you.* She saw Julie's face in the group. "Any joy raising

Matlock?" she asked. "Sooner we can get some back-up here..."

"No luck, I'm afraid." Tom Graham – still in uniform, Ellie realised – stepped forward. "Julie's been on it, non-stop. I was thinking, now we've got the Land Rover back – I could try taking it out to the Height, see if I get any luck there."

Ellie nodded. It had been known to work – she'd tried it herself earlier, after all. "Worth a go." She handed him the keys. "Thanks, Tom."

Tom looked as though he wanted to say something else, but either didn't or couldn't. "No problem," he said, then passed her the keys to his vehicle. "Case you need it," he muttered. "Let you know if I get anywhere."

Bert Annable turned to Ellie. "Right then. What now?"

What indeed? *You'll see. You'll all see.* "Well," she said, "I've got a report to write, so I'm going back to mine to write it. Anyone needs me, just knock on."

A few people clapped her on the back as she passed them, and she did her best to smile. Heroine of the hour. She tried, unsuccessfully, not to think about what Liz had said, or what might be coming next.

18.

"You daft cow." Liz swabbed Keira's face with cotton wool soaked in hot water and Dettol. "The fuck did you think you were trying to do?"

Keira hissed and tried not to whimper at the pain. "Bitch walked in and held a gun on you. Your own house. Couldn't just – ow."

"Forget her," said Liz, but nonetheless felt a wave of affection for the girl. More of a daughter than Jess, who'd just cringed and whimpered when the pig and her mates had heifered into the front room. Keira gave a fuck about the family. Stood up for it. And as for having faith in Liz – well, she'd have been looking at a murder charge if she hadn't missed.

"Bitch slipped; would you fucking believe it?" Keira said. "I'd have had her otherwise."

"She'll wish you had," said Liz. "Come tonight, she'll bloody wish it. When *They* come out..."

"Just wish I could see it."

"Listen out," said Liz. "You might hear the screams."

In her room, Jess Harper huddled at the end of her bed while Baby Joel squalled in his cot.

It was the smallest bedroom. There seemed even less space now; she'd dragged the chest of drawers across and propped it against the doorway. Her back muscles throbbed from the effort.

Outside the door, Paul was singing: *"Hush little baby, don't say a word,*

Uncle Paul wants to shag a bird..."

She'd left the pistol downstairs, after the police had gone. It hadn't been a big gun and she wasn't a good shot, but neither would have been necessary, if she'd been close enough. But it wouldn't have mattered anyway. She couldn't have pulled the trigger, could she, useless as she was? Not least because if she shot Paul, she'd face far worse consequences than any he would for whatever he did to her.

Jess'd seen the fury in his face after the police had gone, and she knew why. She'd seen how he'd looked at Charlotte Famuyiwa, knew what he'd wanted to do.

She wasn't stupid. She knew what Paul liked doing, even if he hadn't done it to her. He'd like to, she knew that, but so far she'd been lucky. The one time she'd been stupid enough to trust him was over Andy, and that was where Baby Joel had come from.

The police had taken Charlotte away, so Paul couldn't do it to her. But Jess knew him; he'd want to do it tonight. Keira'd scratch his eyes out if he tried anything with her, and if there was anything left of him afterward Frank would stomp him into the floor. Never mind that Mum would have his hide for it. But Jess was different. No good to anyone – she'd heard Mum say that out loud. Frank had been nice to her when they were younger. Even looked out for her with Paul. But not now. He didn't give a shit. Dom – she wasn't even sure how much Dom understood. She wouldn't have thought he understood anything, but then everyone thought that about her.

Like the Family Bible. Jess'd taken a look in there, when Mum'd had her fetch and carry it back and forth. She'd seen the pictures of *Them*. She knew what it was about. Some of it anyway.

She knew what was coming.

"And if that golden ring turns brass," sang Paul,

"Uncle Paul'll get a black girl with a nice tight ass,
And if that black girl goes on the run,
Uncle Paul'll make do with your Mum..."

Jess shrank back.

Outside the door, Paul laughed. "Don't worry, Jess," he said. "I'm not coming in." He waited a moment. "Not unless you invite me."

Did that mean he'd given up? She waited to hear his footsteps creak away along the landing. But there was no sound.

"You're getting better at hiding that book of yours," he said. "Had a job finding it."

She was still.

"I *did* find it, though."

No. No, not that, not again. She scrambled across the room to where the chest of drawers had been. Pain pricked her under one fingernail from a splinter as she pried up the board she'd loosened. The plastic bag she'd wrapped the book in was still there, but it was empty. Her book was gone, and all her boys with it. Boys with warm smiles and smooth skin, kind dark eyes or bright blue ones. Boys who'd have taken her to bed because she'd wanted them to and only then. Boys who'd be nice to her. The kind of boys she had to clip out of magazines, because they could only exist in dreams for a girl like her.

Boys like Andy.

Andy'd been a mate of Paul's dealer, Degs. Turned up at the house with him sometimes, when it was summer, go and smoke some draw with him and Paul out in Thursdale. He'd looked nice. Come from a nice home. Clean, smooth skin and long hair. Like the boys in her scrapbook.

Jess would sneak out after them and watch. Andy hadn't been much older than her, and sometimes he smiled when he saw her, and didn't just tell her to fuck off like Paul did. Didn't mind having her around. And she'd used to tell herself that he'd want to go out with her, and she could live with him and get away from Barrowman Farm and Mum and Keira and Paul.

Only, it hadn't been like that.

She'd thought it would. There'd been one time she'd followed them and she'd heard raised voices. Degs was shouting at Paul, on at him about money. Paul had been shrinking back, head down between hunched shoulders, lower lip hanging out, the way he did when someone was having a go and he didn't dare have a go back. And then Andy had seen Jess watching and grinned at her and waved, and then looked at her for a bit, then spoke to the others, and they'd looked at her too. Jess had hunkered there, crouched painfully behind a tree, afraid to move.

Finally some agreement had been reached, and Paul had come over. Said they were going on to Andy's house in Matlock, because his Mum and Dad were away on holiday. A party. She could come if she wanted. And of course, she had.

The house had been lovely. Clean, and warm, with soft carpets and furniture. Jess remembered some music playing and drinking cider out of tins, which'd tasted horrible, but had made her feel pleasantly lightheaded. And then Andy had put a hand on her knee and she'd been scared and excited all at once, and he'd led her out of the room while Paul'd pretended not to notice.

She remembered him kissing her, then nothing else. Nothing that stuck. Not till she woke up that morning, sore and alone and cold and scared, and Andy wouldn't look at her afterwards, like there was something horribly wrong with her, or like she'd done something wrong. Degs neither. Paul'd told her to stop whingeing and making a fuss. She was the one who'd wanted to come to the party.

He hadn't said a word to her on the drive back to Barrowman Farm. Later when she was lying in bed, crying and desolate and wondering what she'd done wrong, she heard people shouting downstairs.

She'd never seen Andy again, nor Degs. Keira had called her a dirty little slag, even before she found out she was pregnant.

Mum'd told her it was her own fault, she'd been asking for it, but she'd know better in future, which was as close to kindness as Mum'd ever come, now she thought of it.

Jess hadn't even wanted the baby; she knew there were ways you could get rid of one, but when she'd said so to Mum, Mum'd hit her so hard across the face Jess'd thought she'd lose teeth. That was wicked, Mum said, fucking disgusting, to want to kill a helpless little baby. She should be ashamed of herself. Mum'd shouted at Paul when she'd found out Jess was pregnant, but she'd never said *that*. And so Jess had had Baby Joel.

Yes, Baby Joel. Not Baby fucking Steven. Joel was what *she'd* wanted to call her baby, but Mum'd said that was a shit name, a queer's name, so this was Baby Steven, after her granddad. Jess didn't even get to name her own kid. But she'd call him Joel if she wanted, when it was just the two of them. She fucking *would*.

"See you've put some new pictures in," said Paul. "Love the paper you use. Lovely sound when you rip it."

She heard the soft purr as paper began to tear.

"Love doing that. Go up lovely in the fire though too, it would. Can't decide which I'd like best. Which do you, think, Jessie? Or is there something better I could be doing? Mm?"

She bit her wrist, crying without sound.

"Nothing to say? Oh well. Off downstairs then. Poke the fire."

The floorboards creaked outside.

"Well, Jessie?"

She remembered how it'd hurt having Joel. She was glad of him now – most of the time – because at least he was hers and didn't treat her like shit, but she wouldn't have had him, given the choice, and wasn't having another if she could help it.

And least of all with *him*.

Jess stood up. Her legs shook. She clenched her fists tight.

"Do what you fucking like, Paul," she heard her voice say,

hating it for its cracked and weepy sound. "You're still not coming in."

A silence.

"All right." he said. "If that's what you want. All right."

Jess sat back down, and for long minutes afterwards she listened to the sounds of tearing paper, and Paul grunting with effort as he worked to tear the precious scrapbook into smaller and smaller pieces.

"There, you cunt," he said at last. "And now I'm gonna fucking burn it."

The floorboards creaked again; she heard him clomp away down the landing, then on down the stairs.

Joel was still squalling in his cradle. A moment later Keira shouted up the staircase "Will you fucking shut that fucking brat up!"

Jess went to the crib and gathered up Joel, then sat and rocked on the bed. At last he quieted; in silence, she cried.

Outside was wind and snow.

19.

Before Tom left, Ellie retrieved her shotgun from the Land
Rover and crossed the street to her front door.

She shut the door behind her and propped the weapon
beside the writing bureau in the corner of the room, fetched her
laptop downstairs and resisted the temptation to pour a large
Scotch; no doubt the sun was over the yardarm somewhere,
but God knew what else the day might hold.

Instead she made another hot, sweet coffee for herself,
powered up the laptop and began filling out another incident
report. A couple of times she got the shakes again, but
remembered her breathing and worked on it till the tremors
passed.

She'd better brace herself and toughen up. *You'll all see.
They'll come for you tonight. All of you.* Much as she wanted to
dismiss that as Liz Harper having finally lost whatever plot
she'd ever had, Ellie knew she couldn't; knew, with bone-deep
certainty, there was more to come.

She slogged her way through the report and saved it; there
was, of course, still no online access. Perfect.

She stood up, stretching, and her foot caught something.
She remembered the shotgun just as she saw it toppling, and
lunged to catch it in the nick of time. Jesus Christ. The safety
wasn't even on. If it had fallen, it could have fired. Probably
blown her own foot off, with her luck. She pumped the slide,
ejecting the cartridges, picked them up and put them on her
desk.

Madness. Criminally irresponsible. She should have put the safety on. She should have unloaded the shotgun. She should have locked both it and the ammunition back in its cabinet. She should be doing that now, but instead, after a moment's hesitation, she laid the gun across the top of the bureau, prodding it gently to make sure it wouldn't fall off. She wanted it close to hand. Beyond that, she had no idea, right now, what to do.

Been a long time since she'd had to deal with anything serious. Well, not that long – the Harpers had always prevented Barsall being too sleepily bucolic a beat – but in the past they'd gone quietly whenever they'd needed taking in. Not like today.

The rules of engagement have changed. The phrase began to circle round her head, along with Liz's words. *They'll come for you tonight. All of you.* Police didn't worry the Harpers, but something else did. Enough to make Tony Harper freeze to death in the snow in sight of his own front door.

Ellie yawned. She felt exhausted, and would have liked nothing more than to crawl into bed and pull the covers over her head. But that wasn't an option, especially not now. Instead she went into the kitchen and made another coffee with ridiculous amounts of sugar. Some days you just needed to treat yourself and sod the consequences.

As she pottered back through into the front room, there was a knock on the door. Bollocks. No peace for the wicked, a police(wo)man's lot was not a happy one, and any other quotes and clichés that suited the occasion. She went and answered the door. "Mill."

"Ell." A moment of silence. Snow settled on Milly's shoulders and in her hair. "Can I come in or do I freeze my tits off out here?"

"Sorry. Come in. Please." Ellie shut the door behind her friend. "Brew?"

"Please." Milly followed Ellie into the kitchen. "You okay?"

"More or less. Still a bit wobbly. Just feel knackered."

"Yeah, you will. I would say take it easy, but that's not sounding like an option, is it?"

"Too fucking right. How are the patients?"

Milly sat down at the kitchen table, rubbing her eyes. "They're okay. Jones is keeping an eye on them. Lord Chapple of Dogdickington turned up to collect the Golden Child, so it's just the girls left."

"How's Charlotte?"

"How do you think? She managed to get her head down, for now."

"You doping up everybody? If so, slip me a pill, will you?"

"Fuck off. Not given her anything. She just conked out of her own accord. It's been a rough day. Still no idea what happened to Joda and Barbara?"

"Not a clue. I mean, not really been a minute to investigate properly since this morning. God, the poor kid."

"Poor both of them, when you think about it."

"True." Kathleen Beck was in the same boat as Charlotte, even if Ellie hadn't known her since she was knee-high. "Whatever it is, the Harpers are a sight more worried about it than the cops."

"Know more than they're telling?"

"Don't they always?"

"True story." Milly cleared her throat. "Anyway, the Beck girl's awake. I asked if she was up to talking to you, and she said yes. Thought you'd wanna –"

"Too right." Ellie got up and went through to the front room. She paused on the way and picked up the shotgun from the bureau.

"What the fuck kind of interview techniques are you into now?"

"Sorry, Mill." She knew how much Milly loathed guns of any kind. "I'm keeping this to hand until we know what we're dealing with."

Milly breathed out angrily, but looked down and nodded.

"Fine. Come on, then."

They drove to Hollybeck Row in Tom's X5, and Milly unlocked the door. Noel was on one of the chairs in the waiting room, arms folded, legs outstretched and crossed at the ankles, chin on chest, eyes closed. Milly kicked the sole of his shoe. "Wake up, Jones, you dozy sod."

"Mm. Sorry." He yawned. "Must've crashed out a bit."

"They'd better be all right," said Milly, striding to the nearest consulting room. "Or else –"

"Dr Emmanuel?" called a voice. "What's happening?"

"That you, Kathleen? Don't worry, all good. One sec." Milly opened the second consulting room's door and peered inside.

"Charlotte?" said Ellie.

"Still dead to the world." Milly motioned to the first consulting room. "Come on. Jones, try to stay awake this time."

"Okay. Sorry."

Ellie followed Milly, bringing the shotgun in with her, but she propped it in a corner of the consulting room as they entered, the safety catch on, to keep it out of sight.

The couch had a screen around it. "Kathleen, love?" called Milly.

"I'm decent." Kate Beck pulled the screen back and forced a wan smile at them. "Hi."

"Hello again," said Ellie. "How are you feeling?"

"Well as can be expected, I suppose." The girl sat down in the nearest chair. Her left arm was in a sling, the forearm strapped up between splints. She was very pale, with a slightly dreamy look in her eyes; Milly had no doubt dosed her with the strongest painkillers available that wouldn't actually knock her out.

She didn't say anything else, and after a few seconds Ellie cleared her throat. "Kathleen –"

"Kate. Might as well." That smile again. "Kathleen's a bit of a mouthful. That's what my –" For a moment the dreamy composure of her face trembled, like a smooth pond disturbed by a ripple; then it calmed again. "What my friends call me."

"Okay. Kate. Do you feel up to talking to me now?"

"Well, I am doing, aren't I?" It wasn't said sarcastically; the girl smiled again. Ellie smiled back.

"Fair enough. But I meant about what happened at your house last night."

"Um." Kate nodded. "Yes. I know. Um. Yes. All right. I'll try."

"If it gets too much," Milly said, "I'm right here, love, and you just tell me. We can stop any time you need to, and pick it back up again whenever you're ready."

She was right, of course, and yet Ellie was annoyed with Milly for saying so. Night wasn't far off. *They'll come for you tonight.* They had to know what had happened before it got dark, in case it happened again. In case? No, there was no "in case" about it. *How do you know that? You don't know what happened.* Which brought things full circle.

"Thanks," said Kate.

Ellie took out her phone. "I'd like to record this. Is that okay?"

Kate nodded. Ellie set her phone to record and set it down beside her. "Interview with witness Kathleen Beck," she said, "carried out by PC Eleanor Cheetham on 19th December. Also present, Dr Millicent Emmanuel." Milly grimaced; she'd never liked her full name. Ellie looked to Kate. "Whenever you're ready."

Kate licked her lips. "Um. Could I have a glass of water?"

"Course, love." Milly filled a paper cup at a tap and brought it over.

"Thank you." Kate took a gulp and cradled the cup in both hands, looking downwards, for a few seconds. The silence stretched uncomfortably out; just as Ellie was about to gently prod her, the girl looked up and started talking.

"Mum and Dad had gone to bed," she said. "Rick and I stayed up." The smile again. "A little time to ourselves, you

know? We put a movie on and snuggled up on the sofa. We."
She stopped. Her eyes misted. When she sipped the water
again, her hand shook. "Sorry," she said. "Well. We were on
the sofa. And then. We heard something. Sort of scratching
sound. From the window."

"Course, love." Milly filled a fresh cup and took the empty
one from Kate.

The girl looked at Ellie. "I'm not mad. I'm not."

"No-one's saying you are."

"Huh." A different smile this time, almost a smirk. Bitter.
"Might change your tune in a minute. I know what it sounds
like. Been trying to say it to myself, before. So that you'd
believe me. But I can't. Just sounds mental however I." She
stopped, shuddered, drank more water.

"We're not gonna think you're mad, love," said Milly. "Just
tell us what you saw. What happened."

"You won't..."

"What?"

"Have me locked up?"

"What for?"

"For being mad."

"No. That doesn't happen anymore, love. Only if you're a
danger to yourself or others. And you don't look like one to
me. You just look like someone who's been through something
horrible and might feel better if she talked about it."

Ellie was afraid Milly had gone too far with that last nudge,
but Kate nodded and took another sip. "We tried to ignore it
at first. Sounded like twigs. On the windows. But there aren't
any trees that close to the house. And it got louder. So Rick
went to look. I was on the sofa. He pulled back the curtains
and..." She shook her head. "I didn't see it. Not then. He just
shouted and jumped back. When he did the curtain fell back
down. So I didn't see. Not then. Rick'd gone white. Well, you
saw him yesterday. Always was a bit of a softy."

Her voice choked as she said it; she'd begun to cry. She wiped her eyes on her sleeve. "But he looked really frightened. He said we should get Dad. And then something started banging on the door."

Something, not *someone*.

"Rick shouted up," said Kate. She began speaking rapidly. "I could hear Dad upstairs, moving about. He came down in his dressing gown. Rick was talking to him, babbling. Dad went towards the door but Rick grabbed him and said *Don't, don't*. The scratching sound was still going on. At the windows I mean. It was louder. Faster. You could still hear it. In between the banging on the door. Dad said something about people playing silly buggers." A smile. Different again this time. Like a little girl. "Dad went to the window and pulled the curtains open. He was starting to shout something but then he stopped. He'd seen them. I. I. I saw them too then."

Milly handed her a tissue. "Thank you," Kate whispered. She gulped the last of the water.

"Another?"

"Please."

Kate looked down at her other hand, which rested on her knee. Her thin white fingers scrabbled and clutched at her leg, balled into a fist and opened again. Milly brought her a second cup. "Thank you," she whispered again, and drank off half the water in a gulp.

"Kathleen?" Ellie prompted.

"Kate. I told you, call me Kate." A pause. "Please."

"Okay. Kate. What did you see? What did they look like?"

Kate shook her head. "Horrible," she said. "Horrible. Horrible. They were horrible. The most horrible things I've ever seen."

Ellie pressed on. "Anyone you recognised? Or *would* if you saw them again?"

"They weren't people. I told you. Weren't you listening? They were – I don't know what they were. Not people. *Things*. I don't know what." Kate shook her head. "And now you don't believe me. Think I'm mad. I'm telling you –"

"No-one thinks you're mad, love," Milly said.

"Yes you do. You do."

"Love, we're here to listen," said Milly. "You were there. We weren't."

"Please," said Ellie, after a moment – too many people talking at once and the girl would feel crowded. "It's what Dr Emmanuel said. You were there and we weren't. No-one's judging. No-one thinks you're mental." She winced and berated herself for using that term, but it was too late to retract it. "Please, just tell us what you saw."

Kate gulped the last of the water, then crumpled the cup in her hand. Milly brought her another one and put a box of tissues on a chair beside her. "Case you need 'em," she said. Kate's lips moved, but no sound came out.

The clock on the wall ticked; Ellie forced herself not to look at it, or at her phone. Don't push the witness; don't make her feel pressured. Just as she was wondering if she should suggest pausing the interview, Kate started speaking.

"Horrible," she said again, then shook her head. "Sorry. Keep saying. They – they were –" A pause, then a deep breath. When she spoke again, she was calmer, fighting to keep her voice level and to describe what she'd seen precisely. "Very – pale. Like maggots, or grubs. You know what I mean? Something you'd find under a stone. Thin, very thin. You could see the bones sticking up. They looked a bit like people, but they were on all fours, and their arms and legs –"

She broke off and took several deep, slow breaths. "They were very long," Kate said. "The arms and legs, they were very long. I mean, ridiculously. They would have looked silly, if they hadn't – been there, outside our house, and – trying to get in –"

She broke off again. "Do you need to take a break?" said Ellie.

Kate shook her head. "No," she said at last. "So, let me see. Very pale. Very thin. Mad long arms and legs. They went on all fours. Their fingers – they were scratching at the window with them. Their fingers were horrible. Must have been nearly a foot. And their faces."

She shook her head again. "Oh. And they wore – they were all wrapped in some kind of cloth. Just like a big sheet of it. Like a cloak or a – a cloak, or something. I know how it sounds. I know how it sounds."

Ellie said nothing; Milly, either. Kate blew her nose and wiped her eyes, then stared at the crumpled ball of tissue paper, turning it this way and that.

"They didn't have any eyes," she added. Very calm, very matter of fact. "No eyes at all. It was just –" she passed her hand across her own eyes. "Smooth," she said. "You know, like – like a forehead? No sign that there'd even been eye sockets. Just smooth. And snouts – and – and teeth. Like rats' teeth. Big sharp yellow teeth. And then –" A breath. Deep. "Then the lights went out."

Kate put the ball of tissue paper down on the chair, rubbing her palm against her thigh. "One of them put its hand through the window," she said. "No blood, not that I could see. Didn't seem to get cut or anything. Dad shouted at us to move – out of the living room, into the hall. Then I saw the front door – it was all – cracked, and starting to give way. Then – I heard more glass breaking upstairs. Mum. Was screaming. Dad shouted at us to get out – through the back. We ran into the kitchen – Rick, Rick and I did, I mean – but I could see one of them outside – through the windows. And then the front door went. It was just smashed in. It hit Dad. He was shouting. I mean in pain. And then one of those things came through. Like this huge horrible fucking spider. Its head just swivelled about – like it was listening. Or trying to smell. Maybe both. Dad was still scr – shouting." She'd meant to say *screaming*, but hadn't been able to use the word, Ellie realised; didn't want to think of her Dad as screaming. Screaming was a thing children did. Hysterical people. People who were terrified beyond all control. "Its head – turned." She mimicked the action with her own head: swivelling, as she'd said, then snapping to a halt. Mechanical. Robotic. "And then it went for him. And Dad was – Dad was." She stopped and shook her head. "He was screaming," she said finally, using the word at last.

The wall-clock ticked; again Ellie resisted the temptation to look. Moments passed, and still Kate didn't speak. Ellie cleared her throat. "What happened then?"

"There wasn't really anywhere else to go to," she said. Then, suddenly, she broke into song: "*Nowhere to run to, baby, nowhere to hide.*" She stopped and put a hand to her mouth. Her eyes welled up again. She took a deep shuddering breath behind the hand, dabbed her eyes, then continued as if nothing had happened. "Only the pantry. There was a bolt on the door. Thought that might… I dragged Rick in and shut the door. I thought they might…" She covered her mouth again, then took her hand away. "They might. Mum and Dad. And then leave us alone."

Ellie thought of telling the girl that there'd been nothing she could have done, that her parents were already done for by that point and the only thing she could have hoped for was that the impossible intruders she'd described would be satisfied with the prey they already had and leave them alone; that Grant and Sally would have wanted her to survive. But no amount of logic would take away the guilt. "What happened then?" she asked.

"You know what happened." The girl looked down, then went on. "They started battering the door. You could hear the wood start to crack. Wasn't exactly a heavy door. Just some cheap old thing Dad got from Ikea. Or was it B&Q?" She smiled, but it wavered. Then she began to cry again.

"Do you need to take a break, love?" said Milly softly.

Kate shook her head. "Get it over with," she said. She looked up at Ellie. "And you need to know about it, don't you?" She sounded very calm when she said that, and suddenly older.

A flash of the woman she'd be in a few decades. Then it was gone, and she was a shaking, traumatised girl again. "Rick was crying," she said. "He was really scared. They could smell us, that's what he kept saying. They could smell us. Or maybe they heard us instead – we weren't exactly being quiet, as you can imagine." A bright, brittle smile. "Bit freaked out. But then I remembered the crawlspace. The hatch in the floor. You saw it."

"I did, yes."

"So I pulled it back and I told Rick to get in. But he kept saying they knew we were in here. They could smell us. I grabbed him and..."

"What happened, Kate?"

"He grabbed me back, and he – we – fought. I didn't understand why. What he was doing. I thought he was hysterical. Funny. Supposed to be the girl, isn't it? And then he slapped me! He slapped me. I was – well, I was shocked." That strange brittle calm had returned to her voice; she sounded like a well-bred society lady discussing some minor local scandal over tea and cucumber sandwiches. "I was just stunned. And then he shoved me through the hatch." She motioned to her splinted arm. "That's when this happened. Then he – he pulled the hatch back into place. And then the door went and –" She shook her head. "He saved me," she said. "*He* saved *me*." Then her face crumpled.

Kate composed herself enough to tell the rest of what she knew, which wasn't much. She'd heard Richard – *Rick* – screaming, before, like those of her parents, his cries had died away. After that she'd lain in the dark and the cold for what had seemed like an endless time, in agony from her broken arm, hearing the intruders move about above, listening to her family's home being wrecked. And then the house, at last, had fallen silent, except for the wind.

She'd drifted in and out of consciousness, convinced the intruders were still lying in wait – they knew she was there and were waiting for her to venture out of the crawlspace. By morning she'd been half-delirious with pain and terror, and had thought Ellie and Bert were the creatures returning; when they'd pulled the crawlspace hatch back, all she could do was beg for a mercy she had no hope of receiving.

"I think that's everything," Kate said, at last. "Do you mind if I have a lie-down now? I feel quite tired." The brittle composure had returned.

"Get your head down, love," said Milly. "You've done great."

Kate gave a gracious smile, then went back to the couch, lay down and curled up on it with her back to them. Almost at once, she began to snore.

"Sure she's got a deviated septum or something," Milly shut the consulting room door. "Sounds like a pig giving birth. Wanna brew?"

"Love one."

They sipped their drinks in the waiting room. "So?" said Milly, finally.

"So what?"

"What do you think?"

"About what?"

"What the girl said."

"What am I supposed to think? Monsters with no eyes and arms and legs like..." Ellie gestured helplessly. "Love to see their faces in Matlock when I sent this one in."

"Could've been some kind of outfit. Masks, robes, that sort of thing. I mean, the poor kid's in shock, hurt, just lost her whole family."

"Still doesn't tell us who."

"Some sort of cult, maybe? Devil-worshippers or whatever?"

"Seriously?"

One of the few things Milly and Ellie disagreed on was religion; Ellie was agnostic on her very best days, while Milly, raised Baptist, was a committed Christian, albeit as down to earth and humane a one as Ellie could have asked to meet.

There'd been maybe a handful of conversations over the years that'd made Ellie uncomfortable, highlighting as they had the gulf between their beliefs.

Milly sniffed. "Well, you tell me what kind of person does this. Eh?"

She had a point: people believed madder or stupider things and acted on them every day. "If some cult's grabbing people to sacrifice to Satan, where are they? I mean, I get this is a great neck of the woods to move to if you wanna sacrifice goats and dance around bollock naked without anyone seeing, but I think we *would've* noticed if anyone new had moved in."

"Why's it gotta be someone new?"

"What?"

"Look." Milly leant forward, sipping her tea. "I know what you're thinking. You're thinking about a bunch of mad hippies turning up and buying an old house. Cults aren't always like that though, are they? Sometimes they're right under your nose, and no-one realises until they do something – like this."

Ellie nearly burst out laughing. "You mean people here? Barsall?"

"Why not? Think about it."

Ellie was going to speak, and then stopped. It wasn't impossible. Things went on behind closed doors all the time – abuse, addiction, relationships gone horribly sour and lethally toxic. Sometimes there were signs, clear in retrospect but meaningless or merely odd at the time. And sometimes the first you knew of it was when it was over. She remembered one of the worst cases she'd handled in Manchester. A family only a few streets away from her; she'd bumped into the dad in the corner shop a few times, waved to the mother as she did the school run with the kids. The dad had been a pleasant enough bloke – funny, friendly. A bank manager. And then one day Ellie had been sent to take a look, because neither parent had been in work for a week, nor the kids been seen at school.

It'd been summer. The car in the drive. Curtains drawn. No-one answering the door. A judgement call; Ellie had busted the patio window and gone in.

The garden had been overgrown with buddleia; that'd been a sign right there, in retrospect. It'd been left to grow wild for over a month. Buddleia was a nightmare if you let it get hold, and they had. Until she'd broken that window, all Ellie could smell was its sweet, honeyish scent; whenever she smelt that now, it made her sick. The odour that had spilled out of the shattered window had obliterated it.

The husband had had a gambling addiction, and been embezzling to cover it. Shifting money between accounts to buy himself time, needing a bigger and bigger win each time to try and fill the hole. The house had been heavily remortgaged, without the wife's knowledge. But it had all been about to come crashing down around him. Up to that point Ellie could have pitied him, but not what he did next.

There'd been no evidence of a struggle; they found cups of unfinished cocoa laced with GHB. The wife and children had been strangled: the husband had lain down beside them, then cut his throat with a Stanley knife.

That had been in a cul-de-sac, part of a row of identical new-build houses. Clean, pristine and tidy, with only the drawn curtains, that morning, to set them apart from the rest. Ellie had never been able to look at houses like that since, not without wondering what might be going on inside. Made her nineteenth-century terrace here in Barsall that much more appealing.

Oh, yes. Anything could go on behind closed doors. Barrowman Farm was another case in point.

"What about the Harpers?" said Milly. Great minds clearly thought alike. "You said yourself they've cranked up the mental."

Ellie had to laugh. "Cranked up the mental, doctor?"

Milly started laughing too. "About right though, innit?"

"True." Ellie got her chuckles under control. "Cranked up the mental," she said again. "But the way Liz was talking – didn't sound as if it was them. She kept saying 'they'll come for you tonight'."

"Maybe meant her kids. Or maybe, you know, they put on their outfits, and that's it – they're not themselves anymore. Like an alter ego. Jekyll and Hyde."

"Maybe." It was the closest thing to an explanation that made sense. Even so, her instincts were against it. But if wasn't the Harpers, then what? "Those sodding signs," she said. "They mean something."

"Well, duh." Milly rolled her eyes. "They're signs. That's the whole point." She pursed her lips. "Tell you who you should talk to."

"What's that?"

"Pastor Matt."

"Matt Williams? What for?"

"Even if *you* don't believe in the Devil, some people do. You don't believe in God, but people worship Him. So you don't have to believe in the Devil to believe in Devil-*worshippers*, do you?"

"Suppose not."

"Well, then?"

Ellie tried to picture Tom Graham's face if he overheard this conversation – *too much imagination's bad for a copper, Ellie* – but couldn't, not quite. It was already murky outside, and would soon be dark. And it was far, far easier to believe in the Devil by night.

20.

Later, much later, when Joel was quiet and sleeping in her arms, Jess put him gently in his crib and slowly, slowly inched the chest of drawers away from the doors, listening between each movement to ensure no one heard. When the door was clear she eased it open, slipped off her shoes, and padded down the landing and then the stairs in her stockinged feet to listen.

She knew the farmhouse, every creaking board of it, where to tread and where not to if she didn't want to be heard, and knew, too, the sounds her family made and what they meant. Paul was singing, a low slurred mumbling with a hint of tune in it, a noise he only made when drunk. Which at least meant he wouldn't come near her door again tonight.

The others were talking amongst themselves, voices raised over Paul's drone. Jess tiptoed down the stairs to the next landing, listening.

"…that bitch Ellie Cheetham," Mum was saying. "Could have fucking done without her."

"*They'll*'ve got her, though," Frank said. "Won't *They*?"

"Like as not, like as not. And if not tonight, tomorrow –"

"Just wish I could fucking see it," Keira said. "See her shitting herself when *They* get hold of her –"

"Yeah, yeah, all right, Keira, you fucking said. Change the fucking record, f'Christ's sake. She's a fucking pig and we all hate her, but she's finished now. Nowt to worry about anymore. It's us I'm thinking of."

"Us? What we got to worry about?" Keira sounded panicky. "Liz, you said we'd done everything we –"

"We have, you silly mare. Everything we could. Just tomorrow I'm worried about. We were gonna give *Them* the Famu-whatsit bitch and Dave Dickhead Chapple, but Ellie bastard Cheetham pissed all over that, didn't she? All we've got now's bloody pigs and sheep to give *Them*."

"We gave *Them* that before."

"That was before, Keira. *They've* been having fun all night up in Barsall, haven't *They*? Pigs and fucking sheep might not be what *They're* after anymore."

"Could always…" Keira tailed off. A long silence.

"Could always *what*, Keira Lucas?" Mum said.

"Never mind."

"Out with it."

"Well, I just thought – if you think we've got to – there's always Jess. Or better still, that kid of hers. It's all deformed and probably a fucking retard too."

There was a silence after that, but not an angry one. Jess knew the silences in this house as well as the sounds; Mum hadn't been shocked into silence, but was mulling the idea over.

She ran back up the stairs, not caring if she made any sound or not. She wasn't even waiting to hear Mum's answer, because that wasn't the worst part. No, the worst part was that when she'd even *talked* about not keeping the baby when she was pregnant she'd been knocked halfway across the room, but once she'd gone through all the agony of bearing him, not to mention bringing him up, Keira could talk about feeding Baby Joel to *Them* – not to mention Jess herself – and Mum stopped and thought about it.

Try it, you bastards, just fucking try it.

In her room, Jess shut and bolted her door, then dragged the chest of drawers back into place. She remembered something else, and pulled open one of the drawers and rooted in it till

she found what she was after: one of Tony's cartridge knives.
She opened it out and sat on the bed, resting a hand on Joel's
cradle.

For a while, she just felt numb.

And then she began to feel again.

First, anger.

Then hate.

And after that – slowly, carefully but steadily, because her
hatred had given her a clarity and a need to hurt she'd never
had before – she began to plan.

21.

Even with the heating on, the chill from outside crept into the Land Rover and Tom Graham was glad he was wrapped up against the cold. The woollen cap he'd pulled on felt pitifully thin and frankly didn't cut the mustard; pity Ellie hadn't left her KGB hat in the car.

Out on the Height the sky was dark, and the only sounds were the muffled wind and the hiss of static from his radio: still no signal, even out here. Wasn't quite dusk yet, but you wouldn't have known it; the clouds and snowfall had cut off the last of the failing light. The wind had to be gale force by now, and the snow was coming down thick and heavy, piling up against the windscreen faster than the wipers could clear it away.

Ellie'd been right about Matlock; even the thought of driving back to Barsall made Tom's palms sweat and trying to get to Barrowman Farm would've been a kamikaze job if they'd left it this long, never mind anywhere else.

They'd got the kids out of there, that was the important thing. Ellie and the others. One hole in her fur hat, and that was all the damage, although Bert Annable'd taken a pot at the front of the farmhouse, so Christ knew what would happen when the snows cleared and the Harpers went crying to any ambulance-chaser who'd give them the time of day.

Well, he'd officially been home sick and the raid was all Ellie's doing – the glory and the grief, all in one. Yet here he was, out on the Height with a radio that didn't work – he'd have more luck with a flaming carrier pigeon – doing his bit.

Probably time he jacked it in, really. He'd turned fifty-five, year before last, and so was eligible for his pension. Reduced benefits if he retired now, but better to do that and still have your health, wasn't it?

Barsall had always been a quiet beat. A simple life. Apart from the Harpers. But now they were kicking things up a gear. Nearly had a Wild West shoot-out there today. Maybe Paul Harper was cooking meth – turned people mental, that stuff, didn't it? Place was going to end up like America, nutters with machine guns everywhere you looked. No thank you, not for him. Retire and stay out of it with Thelma. Live a quiet life that way, if he still could – if any bugger still could now.

Well, he'd talk it over with the Mrs, whenever this was over with. For now, though, he was still a copper. Maybe not much of one – oh, he knew what Ellie thought of him, what everyone did, that he was just a time-server, not sticking his neck out any further than he could help – and they might be right, but this was still his job and he wasn't a shirker. He'd been out on the moors enough times, hadn't he, hunting lost hikers in weather like this? Helping bring them safely home, or retrieving their frozen corpses. And how many times had he done that last one? Every bloody winter, some poor sod ended up like that. Not even hikers all the time: even locals could come a cropper, like Tony Harper. After a while it got to you, all the death. Ate into you. Even so he wasn't a shirker, or a coward. He'd taken the Queen's shilling, signed on the dotted line. A contract. A bargain. An oath. Call it what you like.

So he'd do his part. Keep on a little longer, then head back into Barsall. See how Ellie wanted to play it then.

And back her up. He'd have to. She'd given him a way out and he'd taken it, but it'd been the coward's way out and he knew it. He'd go back and help however he could and if there was flak afterwards over Barrowman Farm, he'd take it, because that was his job. He'd take the lumps, and Ellie could have any gongs or praise that were going. She'd earned them.

Another five minutes, then he'd make his way back. He'd been out here long enough without even a whisper in reply. Call out a couple more times, then knock it on the head.

"Matlock from Sierra Four Five, urgent call, over. Matlock from Sierra Four Five, urgent call, over."

Nothing. Only the mush of static, as blurred and formless as the snow and the dark.

Sod the five minutes; he'd head back now. He turned the key in the ignition and the headlights flared on.

Something moved up ahead.

He didn't get a good look; it recoiled from the light, back into the darkness, but he got an impression of thinness and long, long limbs. Like a huge bloody spider.

Snow blurred and flurried through the headlights.

No. He'd seen nothing: shadows and snow, caught in the light. That was all. He was seeing patterns where there were none. Like Ellie. Too much imagination. That was a laugh. He could hear Thelma snorting at that: *When was that ever your problem, Tom Graham?* He could make out a silhouette in the snow, just at the edge of the light.

One of the picnic tables, that was it. But it was the wrong shape – too tall and thin. Well, the light played tricks, and the way the snow piled up on top of stuff could do the same with shapes and outlines.

But he knew the layout of the Height by now, after all these years, and there was no table directly ahead of where the car was parked now.

He'd got himself mixed up, that was it. Hadn't parked quite where he'd thought. Besides, whatever he was looking at wasn't moving. It was just standing still.

Same as it had been until he'd turned on the lights.

"Sod this," he muttered aloud. He'd been heading back

anyway, hadn't he? Well, then; if this wasn't his cue to shift his backside he didn't know what was.

He shifted into reverse, looking up to check the rearview.

The wind lifted the snow like a curtain, revealing three thin, crouching shapes at the edge of the snowed-up picnic area, beside the road.

Tom Graham was not a man given to any language stronger than "bloody hell" and "sod that" – Thelma had cured him of that habit long ago, to the extent he'd ever possessed it – but he quite distinctly heard himself utter the words "Fuck me sideways" at this point, and in a dismayingly thin and wavery tone.

They weren't moving. They were at the edge of the light. He remembered how the first thing, if he hadn't imagined it – but by now he knew he hadn't – had bolted when the headlights came on. Didn't like the light. If he reversed quickly, they might scatter from the tail lights.

Although those weren't as bright as the headlights. And maybe the first thing had only been startled by the light, rather than actually afraid of it.

Tom looked forward, through the windscreen, and could no longer deny another thin shape was indeed crouching in front of the car. Or, moments later, several others.

Reverse at full speed towards the road – that seemed the best option. Even so, he glanced left and right, out of habit, only to see there were more of them. They were much closer on either side of the car.

Tom shifted gears into reverse; as he did, something hit the rear of the Land Rover, shattering glass. When he looked back, he saw one of the tail lights was out, the darkness behind the car thicker, and that the thin things were moving.

Then something hit the front of the car, and one of the headlights went.

Looking ahead, he saw the crouched shapes stir into spiderlike motion. Tom flung the gear into reverse, but as he did so a thin limb jerked and a third blow struck the front

of the Land Rover. Glass shattered again, and the last of the
light extending ahead of the Land Rover collapsed in on itself
into snow-swirling darkness. With a blur of scuttling motion, a
horde of pale shapes engulfed the car.

22.

The Assemblies of God church was almost empty when Ellie got there, with only a few hangers-on who preferred its light and warmth to the prospect of heading home through the billowing snow. Matt was in his office upstairs, overlooking Halliwell Way, which was all to the good. If Ellie was going to start discussing Devil-worship, she'd rather do so privately.

"Hi, Ellie." He smiled and did his best to look friendly, but Ellie picked up a distinct *Oh God what now* vibe from him. For all that Milly thought the sun shone out of his backside, Ellie had never taken to Matt Williams. There'd always been something soft about him: less a lack of fire and brimstone than a more fundamental lack of substance. "Can I do for you?"

"Wanted to ask you something in confidence."

"Oh. Okay." He looked, if possible, even less enthused than before. "Cup of tea?"

"Not right now." Ellie took her phone out. "Milly reckoned I should talk to you."

"Oh?" He looked a little more perky, maybe seeing a potential new addition to his flock. "What can I –?"

"What do you know about Satanism?"

Matt blinked. "In what sense?" Maybe he thought she planned on joining the opposition and was hoping he had their contact details.

Ellie swiped through the pictures on her phone. "This is in confidence, like I said."

"Um, okay."

"There were markings at the crime scenes. Some sort of symbols I didn't recognise. Milly thought they might have some occult significance."

"Um, okay. Can I take a look?"

Ellie showed him the sign she'd found near Tony Harper's body. Matt frowned. "Hm. Er, no. Don't recognise it."

Bollocks. "How about this one?" Ellie swiped through the other images to the one above the Becks' door.

"Sorry. I can check online when we've got the internet back. Church has a few resources on this subject, and some of my colleagues are a bit more knowledgeable about this than me." Matt hesitated and bit his lip. "You know who might be able to help?"

If I did I wouldn't need to ask you, would I, you wazzock? "Who's that?"

"Reverend Lowe up at St Alkmund's."

As opposed to any other Reverend Lowes in Barsall? Ellie managed not to say that either. She was irritable as hell from the day's stress and exhaustion, but she shouldn't take it out on Matt. "Madeleine Lowe?"

"Yeah. She's very well up on the esoteric stuff. Bit of a hobby of hers. Odd one for a Christian, if you ask me –" Matt coughed as he registered that Ellie hadn't and didn't plan to.

"Thanks." Ellie put the phone in her pocket. "Cheers for your help today, Matt. It's appreciated."

"Glad to be of assistance. Any word on Joda and Barbara?"

"No. Sorry."

"I'll pray for them. How's Charlotte?"

"Dead to the world, last I saw. Milly gave her something to help her sleep."

"'Sleep that knits up the ravelled sleeve of care'," sighed Matt. "Sorry. Shakespeare. Theatre's always been something of a passion of mine. Used to want to be an actor, you know, when I was younger. I suppose some would say that this *is* theatre of a kind."

Ellie had no idea what sort of reply to that he expected, so she said nothing.

"I've been trying to decide if I should visit Charlotte. Perhaps when she's recovered. Or maybe now. Prayer can help, sometimes."

"See what Milly says." Ellie knew her friend would always put her patients first, Pastor or no Pastor. "You got your phone?"

"Of course. Not that it's much good at the moment."

"If she wakes up and starts talking while you're there, make sure you get it out and start recording. Need all the info we can get right now."

If police work taught you anything, it was that most people were creatures of habit; rituals and patterns offered comfort and continuity in a world increasingly devoid of either. Madeleine Lowe was no exception: each afternoon, she allowed herself a short break from her pastoral duties, and whatever the weather made her way to the *Grove Inn*.

Unlike the *Waggoner's Rest*, which had been taken over by Wetherspoons a few years earlier and boasted the same soulless open-plan décor of every Wetherspoons the length and breadth of the land, the *Grove* was a family pub dating back to Elizabethan times – the oldest building in Barsall, in fact. Heavy oak beams held up the low ceiling – thank God you couldn't smoke in pubs now or the air would have been suffocating – and, as in the *Bell*, there was a real log fire in the grate. Sally Cupit, the barmaid, smiled and nodded at Ellie as she walked in; no one else took much notice. The few drinkers there, mostly older men, seemed almost as somnolent as the dogs snoozing at their feet; another reason Ellie preferred it to the *Waggoner's*. She'd long been mulling getting a dog herself. God knew she'd enjoy the companionship, especially of a creature that offered unconditional affection – try getting *that* from a man – but her being single and working a copper's hours would have meant the poor beast spending most of its time alone, which didn't strike Ellie as fair.

Madeleine Lowe was also single – her husband having run off shortly before she'd come to Barsall ten years earlier – and she'd never shown any sign of wanting to replace him, despite interest from a few local men and even a couple of women. But her hours were a little more social, or at least more conducive to working from home. In one corner of the pub was a row of three booths; Madeleine was in her usual spot at the rearmost one, reading glasses perched on her nose, a glass of red wine at hand and her face buried in a paranormal romance novel.

She was a lean woman in her early forties with untidy black shoulder-length hair, a thin pale face and startlingly blue eyes; her jeans and chunky sweater gave her a girl-next-door look. It was only when you looked closely that you saw the dog-collar peeping out of the sweater neck.

A greying black Labrador – Shona, that was her name – lay dozing on the floor beside her seat, and a Jack Russell terrier – Ellie wasn't sure, but she thought he was called Snappy or Scrappy, something along those lines anyway – curled up on her lap. She was seemingly engrossed in the travails of a woman in love with a wereleopard (if the cover art was anything to go by), and the dogs didn't alert her to Ellie's presence – Shona looked rheumily up at the new arrival, blinked and then closed her eyes again – so Ellie cleared her throat and the vicar of Barsall looked up.

"Ellie! Sorry, wack, I was dead to the world. What's up?"

"Hiya, Madeleine. Was hoping you could help me with something."

"Happy to if I can. Take a pew. Oi, Reuben, budge up."

Ellie looked at the bench seat opposite Madeleine to see a Bedlington terrier lying on his back, legs akimbo and pedalling at the air as he (there was no doubt about his sex given his position) chased oneiric rabbits – at least until the second or third time Madeleine called him, at which point he sat up, blinking and suddenly awake, then scooted over to the side of the bench seat. He eyed Ellie as she sat down, sniffed at her, then licked her hand and put his head in her lap.

"He likes you," Madeleine observed.

"Is he the latest, then?"

"Yeah. Got him from a shelter in Derby. Hard to imagine anyone not wanting a little beauty like him, eh?" Madeleine dog-eared one corner of her book, put it down and took off her glasses. "So what can I do you for?"

As she took off the fur hat – if Madeleine saw the bullet gouge, she didn't mention it – and peeled off her gloves, Ellie's gaze strayed to Madeleine's glass of wine and she found herself wishing she'd ordered something for herself before sitting down. She reminded herself she was on duty. "Take it you've heard about the latest drama?"

"Which one?" Madeleine took a sip of wine and gave a crooked smile. "Sorry, I shouldn't make light. I can think of three off the top of my head, and none of them are funny."

"Wakeman Farm, the *Bell*, and –"

"And what just happened over at Barrowman? Yeah. You okay?"

"I'm fine."

Madeleine's gaze strayed to the hat, and Ellie looked too. It was the first time she'd paid proper attention to the damage – the singed, ragged black hole next to the hammer and sickle badge. The room seemed to roll and spin as the full reality of what had happened crashed in on her again.

Dimly she was aware of Madeleine talking, of footsteps and of Sally Cupit coming over and setting something down on the table. A hand touched hers. "Ellie?"

She looked up. Madeleine was leaning forward, frowning. "You okay there?"

"I'm..." She was still holding the fur hat in her hands. She put it down on the table beside her gloves. "Sorry. Bit of a senior moment there."

"Senior moment my shiny red arse," said Madeleine. "You've only got a couple of years on me, and I'm not ready for the bloody geriatrics ward just yet. Anyway –" She nodded down at the table, and Ellie saw there was a glass of whisky there "– that's a Cragganmore. Couldn't remember which was your favourite."

"I'm working, Madeleine. I can't –"

"You shouldn't still be working after the day you've had already, but here you are."

Sod it. One wouldn't hurt. "Thanks," Ellie muttered, and enjoyed a sip of the whisky. "Anyway –"

"Anyway, this is about the 'drama', I'm guessing?" Madeleine grinned. "Let me guess, it's about those marks over the door at Wakeman?"

"You heard about that?"

"Around here? Come on, people talk. Take it with a pinch of salt, obviously – all gets a bit Chinese Whispers otherwise. Inverted crosses and 'Hail Satan'."

"That what they're saying?"

"Close enough."

"All right. Well, I talked to Matt Williams, and he referred me to you."

"I swear he thinks I'm a secret pagan," muttered Madeleine.

"He just thought you might know a bit more about the occult angle, Satanism, that kind of guff."

Madeleine rolled her eyes. "Sodding Nora. Well, obviously, I will if I can."

Ellie lowered her voice. "You heard about Tony Harper as well?"

Madeleine nodded. As ever, word travelled fast.

"You heard there was a weird mark near his body too?"

Madeleine's eyebrows rose. "I did *not* know that. Same one, or different?"

"Different mark, but made the same way. Charcoal, by the look of it."

"So you want me to take a butcher's? Fire away." Madeleine dug out a notebook and pen. "Never know when I'll get an idea for a sermon," she explained. "That or remember I've run out of Jaffa Cakes."

Ellie swiped through her phone's image gallery till she found the mark above Tony's body. Frowning, Madeleine copied it into her notebook. "Okay, got that," she said. "What else?"

Ellie scrolled to the pictures from Wakeman Farm. "Looks like the same marking repeated over and over," she said. "Let me know if anything else jumps out."

Madeleine sketched the second symbol down, tapping her pen on the page as she scrolled on through the pictures from Wakeman Farm, then those from the *Bell*. Finally she put the phone down and took a sip of wine. "I don't recognise the ritual," she said, "but I recognise the signs."

"So what are they? Satanist?"

"Phoenician."

"They're what?"

"Phoenician. It's a Semitic language – it's actually the oldest written alphabet we know. Greek, Latin, Hebrew, Arabic – all their alphabets derived from it."

"Semitic? So that's what, Middle Eastern?"

"Originally, yeah. They were a seafaring society – traders, merchants. Don't think they ever got as far as Derbyshire, though." Madeleine leant back in her seat. "Lucky for you Matt Williams doesn't know his arse from his elbow. Comparative religion's my thing. I like looking at the roots of stuff – where it comes from, what different faiths have in common, how they overlap. I mean, round here that's rich pickings, cos there's a lot of pagan survivals and superstitions. But I like looking further afield, too. And if it's religion you're after, the Middle East's the place to go. Sorry." Madeleine waved her wine glass. "I get a bit carried away."

"No, it's fine." Ellie sipped her Cragganmore and did her best to savour the taste. "So none of this means anything to you?"

"Didn't say that. Like I said, there's deffo some kind of ritual going on here, just not one I know."

"So something brand new?"

"Well, that or dead, dead old," Madeleine grinned. "So do give us a heads-up if it turns out to be. Make my name with that, wouldn't I? Anyway, the symbols – I can tell you a bit about them."

"Okay."

"Phoenician letters form an alphabet, but each one on its own can also mean something, like a hieroglyph." Madeline tapped the second symbol, the one Ellie had found at Wakeman Farm and the *Bell*, "this one's called *gīml*. The shape's supposed to represent a throwing-stick or staff sling."

"So… a weapon? Someone's telling us this is a hit?"

"Maybe. It corresponds to the Hebrew character *gimel*, which in turn is related to the term *gemul*. *Gemul* means 'justified reward', which, depending on the context, can mean 'punishment'. Like when someone gets their comeuppance, people say they got their just reward? I suggest, given *this* context, that's the meaning that's supposed to apply."

"So it's revenge? For what? What could the Famuyiwas and the Becks have done?"

"Revenge, or justice – to whoever did it, I mean. As for why – well, that's your end, not mine. Maybe because both the families weren't local, originally? Moved to Barsall from elsewhere?"

"Yeah, but years ago. Like about half the village now." But that was hardly comforting, with dusk coming on up. *You'll all see. They'll come for you tonight.*

"You and me included," said Madeleine. "Cheery thought, eh?"

"What about the other one?"

"This?" The vicar tapped the one from Tony Harper's crime

scene. "That's called *hē*. It's got two meanings: 'window' and 'jubilation'."

"So, first they're celebrating, and now they're taking revenge?"

"Maybe celebrating the fact that they were about to take revenge? Or could? The whole 'window' thing, maybe? Like a window of opportunity? I dunno."

"What about Hebrew? You were saying about the other one –"

"Yeah, Hebrew's not much help to us with this one. *Hē* corresponds to the Hebrew letter *hei*. *Hei* can be a preposition, like 'the', 'that', or 'who', or if it's used as a prefix, means the statement's a question. And if it's a suffix, it means 'towards'. Having fun yet?" Madeleine chewed her lip. "Only other thing I can think of is that *Hei's* sometimes used in a religious sense, as an abbreviation for *Hashem*."

"Meaning...?"

"Literally, 'the Name'. It's used in Judaism as a way of writing 'God' without actually saying it."

"So it basically either means God, a window, or 'yee-haa!'?"

Madeleine raised her glass. "Welcome to my world."

Ellie swiped back through the pictures on the phone. "It's *their* bloody world I'm worried about, whoever they are."

And then the pub door flew open, and a voice called Ellie's name.

23.

"Ellie Cheetham. Good to see you're working hard."

Thelma Graham hadn't bothered to shut the pub door behind her; one of the drinkers got up, scowling at her safely turned back, and closed it.

"I'm consulting the Reverend Lowe about something," said Ellie, already annoyed at her need to justify herself.

Thelma looked pointedly at Ellie's whisky. "So I see."

There were a number of things Ellie could have said, but they'd have reduced the conversation to a slanging match or worse. "What can I do for you, Thelma?"

"I was just wondering if I could have my husband back at some point," she said. "He isn't well, you know – called in sick today, but you still packed him off on some fool's errand to –"

Ellie broke in on Thelma's chuntering. "Tom volunteered to go out to the Height and try to raise Matlock from there." How long ago had that been? "He's not come home?"

Thelma sighed theatrically. "Would I be here if he had?"

Ellie didn't rise to the bait. "I'll go check on him now."

Thelma sniffed and gave the whisky another pointed look. "Are you sure you're fit to drive?"

"*Quite* sure," said Ellie. "Thanks for your help, Madeleine."

"No problem. Give us a shout if you need anything else."

Ellie scooped up her phone and ruffled the Bedlington's hair, prompting a loud sigh and tut from Thelma. Madeleine rolled her eyes.

"I saw that, Reverend Lowe," said Thelma. "I would have

thought you of all people would want to uphold standards in this community. I'll be raising this issue at the next parish council meeting –"

Madeleine bowed her head over the Jack Russell, pretending to fuss over the sleeping dog. "Get out while you can, Ellie," she muttered. "Save yourself."

Ellie managed to keep her face straight as she picked up her hat and gloves and made for the door. She felt rather guilty about leaving Madeleine in the lurch, but told herself the vicar might have trained the Jack Russell to hump legs on command.

Ellie went back down the High Street as fast as she dared to the Assemblies of God building. She knocked as much crusted snow off Tom's X5 as she could, got the engine running and the wipers beating, switched on the blue light and drove past the roundabout towards Halliwell Way.

Most of the roads around Barsall, even long stretches of the North Road, were unlit. The streetlamps went some way to improving visibility, but once Ellie had passed the last of them she only had her headlights to rely on, and the world collapsed into a swirling tunnel of illuminated snow.

Ellie cut her speed to twenty miles per hour, then ten. She didn't anticipate any traffic coming the other way, with the possible exception of Tom, returning to base and the wrath of She Who Must Be Obeyed (as he occasionally referred to Thelma when safely out of earshot), but there was always the danger of ice on the road, and if she was going to encounter that she intended to do so at the lowest possible speed.

It was just under a mile from Barsall to the Height. Halliwell Way sloped down, hugging the side of the hill; there was a high wall of limestone rose to Ellie's left, while to her right there was a crash barrier, then a sheer drop. Ellie kept as close to the rock face as she dared without risking a collision, took first one and then the other hand from the wheel as she drove to wipe sweat off her palms, and fervently regretted the three sips of whisky she'd had in the pub.

Up ahead was the bend in the road. The Height was more or less round the corner, but the hillside would no longer shield her from the wind, which meant that the blizzarding snow was about to get even worse.

Not far to go, though; Ellie kept telling herself that. Not far at all.

A sudden wave of misery and loneliness hit her, pretty much from nowhere. Blindsided, she thought dizzily. She wanted to be home, and for the first time in years she dearly wished there was someone there to hold her, cook her dinner and, most importantly, to tell her all would be well. For the first time, work no longer felt like enough. Which was one hell of a piece of timing.

So easy to roll the car in this weather. To crash and freeze to death. Or worse. Ellie's hand strayed to the shotgun, remembering the knife in Tony Harper's hand, the state of the *Bell* and Wakeman Farm, and most of all Liz Harper: *You'll all see. They'll come for you tonight.*

Enough. If she was going have an identity crisis she could do it at home, with the doors locked and a whisky poured. She'd drive to the Height, find Tom, then get the pair of them back to Barsall.

But as she reached the Height and pulled slowly into the picnic area, there was no light; just the hi-vis yellow of the Land Rover's chequered "Battenberg" pattern flaring in Ellie's headlights. It looked wrong, somehow. A moment later Ellie realised why: the Land Rover was overturned and lying on its roof, the windows smashed.

"Shit," Ellie muttered, and put the headlights up to full power. The car's interior was still partly in shadow, but there was no sign of anyone inside, or any kind of movement. Nothing in the area visible in the headlights either.

Tom had always kept a heavy police-issue flashlight – one of the spares from the old station – stowed in the X5's passenger footwell; Ellie grabbed hold of it and climbed out of the BMW, pocketing the keys as she went. The X5 had a Runlock, so the engine kept running and the lights stayed on.

While the Height's position made it the best place to go when a signal was hard to come by, it also meant it caught the full blast of any passing storms, and tonight was no exception. Ellie flinched from the stinging flakes and the immediate icy chill, and went towards the Land Rover.

Snow was piling up against it, inches deep, and drifting into the interior. Ellie tried to guess how long the vehicle would have been in that position. Not too long – ten minutes? Twenty? But that could be a long time, too – if you were injured, and out in the cold.

She crouched by the rear of the upturned car and played the torchlight over it. Not only the rear window, but the tail lights had been shattered too. She crab-walked round to the passenger side, shining the torch inside, but her first impression had been right; the car was empty. All the windows were gone – not just broken, but smashed out with a thoroughness that had left only a thin rime of glass at the very edge of the frame.

"Tom?" she shouted, although with a growing sense of futility. "Tom!"

No answer. He could be lying only yards away, already half-buried in the snow. She shone the torch around, in search of any irregularity in the carpet of white. The picnic tables and litter bins were caked with snow, but there was no mistaking any of them for what they were; what she was looking for would be lower, not much more than a bump on the ground.

She found nothing. But the torch's range was limited, especially in this snow. She'd need to explore further. She'd have to be thorough, check the entire area. And quickly. Whatever had happened to Tom, hypothermia would be well on its way. If he was alive.

He's not. You already know that. He's dead as they come. Look at the state of the car, for Christ's sake. No-one's gonna do that, 'specially not to a police car, and let whoever's inside walk away.

He might have been kidnapped, like Charlotte and Dave. The Harpers, getting in some kind of revenge for earlier, maybe thinking Ellie was inside. He might be at Barrowman Farm – battered, bruised, but alive.

You don't believe that. Any more than you believe the Harpers trashed the Bell *or Wakeman Farm. This is whoever Liz Harper was shitting bricks about.* They'll come for you tonight, *remember? Fucking look around you, Ellie. It's tonight* now.

The torch-beam swept through the flurrying snow, and across something pale and huddled – like someone crouching? But when Ellie brought the beam back to bear, there was nothing. Trick of the light. Couldn't have been Tom anyway. It had looked too thin.

All right. Think. Keep it together. Work quickly. If Tom was still alive –

You know he's not, Ellie. Admit it and get out of here.

No. She didn't *know* anything, not for certain. *Assumption is the mother of all fuck ups,* her old sergeant had liked to say when she was a probationer, and it was a lesson Ellie had taken very much to heart. As she should have: he'd drummed it into her after she'd made an assumption about the scene on an industrial estate where a trio of armed robbers had ditched their getaway vehicle. The assumption had been that they were long-gone, so there was no need to check, for instance, the doorway of the industrial unit she was moving past. As it had turned out, one of the robbers had been injured and had collapsed at the scene, dragging himself into that very doorway before passing out from blood loss. As Sergeant Basra had never let her forget, she'd been bloody lucky: if he'd been conscious, it wouldn't have ended well for her.

So Ellie didn't assume. She circled the Land Rover and shone the torch around, looking for any sign of Tom.

He could be right here, in the picnic area. Just a few more yards away, beyond the range of the light. And she wouldn't know.

If just one of the radios would work, or the phones, she could get help. But as it was, she either searched the area alone or went back to Barsall for assistance. How long would that take, and how long would Tom – injured, maybe unconscious – have been out in the cold already? How much longer would he be, if she went back? And, most importantly, how long could he last?

He's already dead, Ellie. You know that. Just like Joda and Barbara, Grant and Sally and that poor lad Richard. Rick. Richard. No; this wasn't the time for that; she couldn't think about anything now but the job. *Whatever: he's dead, just like they're dead, and you know it.*

No. No assumptions. She had to –

Check the bodywork.

She found it on the driver's side, above the Battenberg markings on the inverted door. A vertical charcoal line with a shorter, diagonal one pointing down and left from the top. *Gīml.* Justified reward. Punishment. Revenge.

Punishment for what? For fucking what?

Doesn't matter, not now. What matters is that you know Tom Graham's beyond help. What matters is getting your arse back to Barsall.

There was a moment of indecision – the misery of responsibility, the dread of facing Thelma Graham – the desperate wish that someone else would take the cup from her followed by the realisation that a) that was basically how Tom had spent his whole career, and b) nobody was going to.

If this was what Liz Harper had threatened – and whatever the evidence the certainty was in Ellie like a stone in her gut – the priority now was to get back to the village and alert them. Whatever his faults, Tom had been a police officer: he'd have understood that.

Ellie crawled into the Land Rover; there was police equipment she'd have to salvage. Her first thought was the radio set, however little use it may be, but it was resting on the inverted ceiling; the casing had been battered until it buckled and cracked, the electronics removed and smashed with the same vicious, methodical thoroughness she'd seen in the Becks' kitchen.

There was equipment in the back: road signs and traffic cones, a fire-extinguisher, a life-ring. An unopened box of emergency supplies: foil blankets, energy bars, a box of road flares. Ellie dragged it free of the car and then spun round, suddenly convinced she'd find someone behind her.

No one. Just snow-covered ground lit by her headlamps, and falling flakes dancing in their glow.

Again, the question intruded – what if Tom was lying yards away, just out of sight? It was a judgement call; if she was wrong, and they found his frozen corpse tomorrow, she'd face the consequences, live with the guilt.

Ellie took a step towards the X5, and stopped.

There was something in the snow.

It was thin and narrow, a blurred grey shadow, just past the edge of the headlights' glare. It was motionless, and seemed to go in and out of focus, the white flurries alternately revealing and concealing it. Ellie had an impression of some sort of fabric flapping around it, and of long, drawn-up limbs; she remembered the shape she'd glimpsed minutes before. She shone the flashlight towards it, and it fell back into the darkness, out of sight.

Ellie's skin prickled. The flashlight shook, the beam wavering. When she turned, she saw more of the thin shapes. A line of them stretched across the picnic area and disappeared behind the wrecked Land Rover. A second line extended from the opposite side of the wreck, back towards the X5 and beyond it. Again, they recoiled and disappeared when she shone the torch directly at them, but when it passed she'd see the pale bonelike limbs and blurred thin bodies crawl back to their former positions, cutting her off from the road.

If she could just get to the car. The engine was running – so shut the doors, shift gears, hit the accelerator. The watchers, the thin things – people, they had to be people of some kind, didn't they? – surely they'd get out of the way of an oncoming vehicle.

The shotgun was in the car too. In the car and not with her.

Three seconds to reach the car. Another two, if she was lucky – she fumbled for the keys – to shut and lock the doors, not that they'd done Tom any good. And then to reverse. How fast could the watchers move in that time? How much damage could they do?

Despite the cold, sweat trickled down her back. *You'll find out any minute if you don't stop dithering. Move.*

Ellie stepped towards the car.

And the pale things attacked.

24.

Something flew past Ellie's face, missing by an inch, and she stepped reflexively back. Another object struck her wrist a moment later; she yelped, her hand opened and the flashlight fell into the snow.

The cry provoked a shower of missiles; Ellie flung up her arms to shield her face. Another projectile hit the fallen flashlight's casing. A loud crack resounded from the X5's bodywork, then another, and another.

Ellie scooped up one of the fallen missiles; it was white and hard and searingly cold even through her gloves. Snow, compacted into ice.

Glass shattered, and the blue light went out. Ellie ducked; none of the missiles came near her, but two more hit the flashlight casing. More struck the X5; a headlight cracked. But the watchers hadn't come any closer, even though they outnumbered her twenty to one.

Glass shattered, and the flashlight went out. The grey shapes shifted; maybe they'd edged forward, or simply leaned in. But it was enough; the connection was made. The power had been out at Wakeman Farm and the *Bell*. Kathleen Beck had said that the lights had failed just before the monsters broke in.

Monsters. Ellie hadn't known what to believe when she'd heard that description, but it no longer seemed so fanciful. She still couldn't see them clearly because of the snow and their keeping to the shadows, but what she could make out seemed too impossibly long and thin to be human.

Glass shattered to the X5's rear. One of the tail lights.

Costumes, she told herself. Masks. A cult, as Milly had said: a pagan survival or revival, orchestrated by the Harpers or some unknown clan of hermits. It sounded ridiculous, but what other explanation was there?

That didn't matter now. Whoever or whatever they were, her priority was escape.

A headlight shattered and went out. Darkness flooded in across the snow to her left, and the crouched figures moved – fast, scuttling, like huge spiders. Their attention seemed less on Ellie than the light itself. At least for now – once it was out, that might change.

In the car, then, and drive.

Ellie moved forward; her boot crunched in the snow. The creatures' heads swivelled towards her.

Ten feet to the BMW. But when she moved, what then? Why were they keeping back from the light? Did it hurt them, somehow, or was extinguishing it before they attacked part of a ritual? If the second, stopping Ellie getting away would likely take precedence over strict religious observance, or whatever in hell's name this was.

More glass broke at the rear of the BMW. One headlight now remained; when that was gone, they'd attack.

And then Ellie remembered, and crouched beside the box she'd hauled from the Land Rover, popping the lid. The creatures' heads shifted at the sound, and she froze. But the ice pellets kept ricocheting off the X5, and more glass broke.

If the remaining headlight went, she was finished. She reached into the box, pulled out a road flare and fumbled at its paper wrapping, fingers thick and clumsy in the gloves. She tugged one off with her teeth, tore at the paper to expose the cardboard cap.

More glass cracked, but the light held. The pellets might be breaking windows instead, or chipping the light's glass cover. But it wouldn't last. They'd only one target to aim for.

Ellie removed the cardboard cap. There was a metal striker on one end; hitting the tip of the flare with it should ignite it. Like striking a match. *Should*. Depended on the flare's age. How old were these? And she'd no lighter or matches –

But the flare caught on the second strike, and sparks and smoke erupted from it. The line of creatures wavered as the red glare spilled out across the snow; Ellie threw the flare towards them. It fizzed on impact with the ground, but continued spewing smoke and light. The thin grey shapes unfolded their long arachnid legs and scuttled backwards.

An ice pellet flew past Ellie; another caromed off the side of the BMW, but most were hitting the ground where the flare had landed, kicking up puffs of fallen snow. Ellie grabbed another flare: the second time was easier, and the flare caught on the first strike of the cap. She hooked her left arm under the box, raised the flare in her right, then ran towards the 4X4.

The shapes to her left hung back. The line to her right swayed back and forth, wanting to keep her from the car but recoiling from the flare. She reached the X5 and hesitated, trying to get a hand free to open the door. There was a scuttle of movement, and she glimpsed in her peripheral vision the creatures rushing towards her.

She turned and thrust out the flare. Two of them were coming at her; one veered away and the other recoiled. She glimpsed grey, etiolated bodies, limbs almost as long as her, with pale translucent fabric wrapped around them, and half-shrouded, eyeless faces, ending in blunt fanged muzzles. When they retreated, she threw the flare after them and wrenched open the door.

She shoved the box into the passenger footwell, scrambling across the seats. Twisted round as she went because she'd left the door ajar. Spindly white fingers reached through it, coiling round her left wrist. Their length could have been some kind of prosthetic, but the arm was impossibly, impossibly thin. Impossibly strong, too, but it was the thinness Ellie noticed first, the absolute impossibility of that arm belonging to anything approaching a normal human being. Pale translucent fabric hung in loose folds from it.

She clutched at the door. The handle. Please let her find the handle. Her fingers closed around it and she yanked the door to, hard, slamming it on the stick-thin wrist – once, then twice. The hand opened – no sound, no cry – and recoiled. Her third slam of the door caught the fingers. They stuck out of the join between door and jamb: thin white sticks. Then they twitched and were pulled back through the join. The car rocked; the door swung open.

Ellie pulled it shut again. A torn piece of pale fabric hung from the join. The keys. The keys. There could only be seconds before another attack. The flares were distracting them, but that one headlight would be so easily shattered and without it she'd be driving as blind as these things apparently were through the snow.

The passenger window splintered as a pellet struck. Ellie got the keys in the ignition, gunned the engine, then threw the X5 into reverse. It slewed backwards, and hit something: Ellie glimpsed a pale blur flung backwards through the dark and snow, limbs flailing. Again, no sound. Never a cry. Utterly silent.

She pulled the car out onto the hill road, threw it into forward gear and floored the accelerator. It surged forward; snow whirled, glowing, in the single headlight. Ellie pulled into the right-hand lane, driving on the wrong side; better to scrape the rock face than veer too far left and go through the crash barrier.

Something flickered in the light up ahead. Something pale and in motion. One of *them*.

How fast was she driving? Ellie didn't dare look: faster than she'd gone on the way down, anyway: faster than was safe. But she accelerated anyway, fumbling for her seatbelt and pulling it on. Her hat slipped over her eyes; Ellie knocked it off, into the footwell.

She had to focus on the road ahead. Had to get back to Barsall. Warn everyone. They should be safe with the lights on. The monsters could only break so many lamps. They'd be safe, unless the power failed –

Mustn't think of that. Just get back. Drive. Focus ahead. But she couldn't stop herself glancing at the rearview mirror, and saw they were still behind her. She caught glimpses, snatches, of them, scuttling up the road in pursuit.

And they were gaining on the car.

25.

The shotgun was on the backseat but Ellie might as well have left it at home, all the good it could do her now. She had to laugh at the absurdity of that thought – and did, out loud, a high jagged noise that sounded so hysterical, so utterly unlike her own voice, that she stopped as soon as she heard it.

But it *was* absurd. What would she have done? Fire one-handed through her own rear windscreen (Thelma Graham's rear windscreen, rather, and wasn't that going to be a fun discussion when or if she made it back?) while steering blind with the other? Might as well put the barrel in her mouth and have done – quicker and easier that way.

The creatures were fast, impossibly fast. How far up the road had she come? The bend, where was the bend? It was as if the road had lengthened since she'd come down it. If she missed the bend – if she was going too fast and didn't turn in time – she'd go through the crash barrier as if it was paper. A car crash might still be better than letting those things get hold of her – the sight, the very thought of them made her skin horripilate – but only if it killed her outright.

The image of being trapped, helpless, maybe paralysed, in the wrecked car while the creatures closed in on it and peeled it open to get to her, like children unwrapping a gift, was as vivid as it was appalling. And then there would be no-one to warn them in Barsall. Someone had to, and Ellie was the only person who could. She was a police officer, she reminded herself. She'd taken an oath. *I will, to the best of my power, cause the peace to be kept and preserved and prevent all offences against people and property.* She had to make it back if for no other reason for that.

And so she had to focus on the road – and, for now, to forget about the creatures. She needed to watch for the bend, or it would finish her as certainly as they would.

Ellie gritted her teeth and eased her foot off the accelerator a little, cutting speed. She didn't look at the rearview or what might be gaining – couldn't, mustn't. She leant forward, squinting through the windscreen.

They were closing in – they'd be on her any second –

And then the wind dropped, only a little but just enough. She'd reached the bend, where the hill's bulk became a partial shield against the wind, and visibility improved, showing Ellie the crash barrier rushing up to meet her.

She swung the wheel hard right and the X5 fishtailed; there was a crazy, terrifying instant where she thought the rear end would drift too far left, smash through the barrier and take her down the hill. Instead the car clipped it and rebounded, slewing right.

The front left of the BMW gouged into the barrier up ahead. It buckled but held. But there was a splintering of glass, and, finally, the surviving headlight went out.

And then the engine stalled.

Fuck.

Ellie lunged across the backseat for the shotgun, yanked it into the front and dumped it on the passenger seat, twisting the key in the ignition with the other hand. *How's that for multitasking?*

The engine caught; Ellie threw the car into reverse.

It crashed into something solid but yielding, flinging it backwards. She put the BMW into forward gear, and in the same moment the driver's window shattered.

She lurched sideways to avoid the spraying glass, but as she straightened a huge white spider unfolded its legs directly in front of her face, shot forward and clamped hold of her head.

Ellie realised she was screaming. She swung the wheel right, away from the edge, with one hand; her left clawed across the passenger seat for the shotgun. She found the safety catch and clicked it off. Now get hold of the pistol grip, quickly. There's a round in the chamber – a jolt and it could fire. Can't see. About to crash.

The shotgun was big and long and cumbersome, but she managed to blindly shove the barrel out through the shattered window. It hit something solid, and she remembered how she'd pushed its barrel into Liz Harper's stomach hours before. *I'll blow you in fucking half,* she'd threatened. And in return, Liz had promised *They'll come for you tonight. All of you.*

Ellie pulled the trigger, and the blast inside the car was as though someone had boxed her ears with a pair of cymbals. A high-pitched *eeeeeeeeeeeeeeeeeeeeee* sounded; she could feel the engine running, vibrating through the car and her body, but couldn't hear it, couldn't hear anything other than that sound. But the grip on her face was gone, and she could see and breathe again. She swung the wheel left before she ploughed into the rock face, then right before she could hit the crash barrier, dumped the gun across her lap and steadied the wheel in both hands, flooring the pedal despite the darkness.

Terrifying seconds of no light at all; only the reduced wind and resulting slight improvement in visibility enabled her to glean any hint of what was around her. But then she was all the way around the bend – so many jokes to be made there – and the lights of Barsall were in view. It was all straight going now.

Ellie accelerated up the road. In her peripheral vision, a pale shape loped alongside the X5 like an emaciated, hairless dog. Fucking greyhound from Hell. It veered towards her; her first instinct was to recoil from it, swerve left to get away, but that would all too easily send her through the crash barrier and down the hillside, and fuck that.

Besides, this creature – it and its brethren – was responsible for Tom. And for Joda and Barbara. Grant and Sally Beck. And yes, even Tony Harper, who whatever his faults hadn't deserved a lonely freezing death in the snow. So she swung the wheel right, towards the thing, and sideswiped it. A judder of impact shocked through the car, surprisingly solid despite the creature's thin, light, appearance. She heard the thump of the collision over the high shrilling noise in her ears, but if the thing made any cry as it was knocked flying, she didn't hear it. It tumbled away through the snow and was gone.

The BMW slewed left, towards the barrier. Ellie steered against instinct, into the skid, then right again. A screeching sounded over the whine in her ears, and she glimpsed sparks flying up on the left as the Beamer's wing scraped along the crash barrier. Then the X5 was clear, swerving back into the middle of the road. Speed dropping. It was going to stall. It was going to stall.

Don't fucking panic. Keep control. Don't accelerate too suddenly – you'll flood the engine and stall it for certain. There. Now, more gas. Don't look behind you. The X5 surged forward.

Something slammed into the side of the X5, making it swerve. Ellie fought for control and accelerated further. The lights were up ahead, but why the hell weren't they getting closer?

Something scratching at the driver's window, inches from her head. *Don't look.* She mustn't look.

Glass cracked inches from her ear.

She mustn't look. Focus on the road. The light. They didn't like the light. It would run away.

Unless they only *preferred* to stay out of the light. Given no other option, it mightn't stop them.

But she'd be in the High Street. There'd be people there. She wouldn't be alone.

Nor would whatever was clinging to the car.

The window burst inwards. Ellie flinched as chunks

and grains of glass sprayed across her face like ice crystals. Something clutched at her face and hair.

Ellie screamed out loud – not terror, or at least not only terror, but rage – and swung the wheel right, bracing for impact. The X5 crashed sidelong into the hillside; the shotgun flew off her lap into the footwell – she flinched, but it didn't go off – and the thin digits went limp on her face.

The engine sputtered and died.

She twisted the ignition key. The engine coughed and groaned. The lights weren't far away. But still so far. Would they have heard the crash in Barsall? What would they even do if they had?

The engine coughed and groaned again. Blows thudded against the X5's bodywork. She could hear metal screech. Things clunked and broke. They were clinging onto the car, tearing at it, trying to prise things loose and break them.

The engine caught, and Ellie floored the accelerator. The BMW lurched forward, but it struggled. Things were clinging to it. She swerved right to left and back; one of the weights fell away. The X5 shot forward, gathering speed. Something else fell loose and it raced forward now. One more creature still hung off its right wing, tilting the vehicle to the side. The first attacker, the one she'd crushed. Even in death it hung on. She risked a glance now. Its head hung limp outside the window. Then it rose. And then swivelled towards her. It was eyeless, with a snout. And at the end of the snout: long yellow incisors, like a rat's.

"Fucking *die*," she screamed at it, and bore right, grinding it against the rock face as she accelerated. The head jerked up and from side to side – and then it was slipping away. She pulled clear of the wall and did her best to force the accelerator through the floor. The X5 barrelled forward, and the pale thing fell loose.

There were more of them on the road. Another one was pacing alongside the car now – no, two of the fuckers. They were trying to get close, but Ellie focused on the lights ahead and leant on the accelerator pedal with all her weight. Black ice or slamming into some unseen obstacle weren't even considerations any longer.

The X5's engine began to knock.

"No," shouted Ellie. "No, no, fucking *no.*"

She risked a glance in the rearview. The crushed white thing lay in the road. More pale shapes flitted past it. One down, anyway; one dead. But even as she watched, it stirred and rose back onto all fours.

The BMW's engine coughed and caught and knocked. Dying. Going any second –

A pale road sign swam up out of the murk to her right: WELCOME TO BARSALL. Laughing almost hysterically, Ellie hit the car's horn as hard as she could. And then, as it blared, she sailed into the warm embrace of the first of Barsall's streetlights.

The X5's engine finally died – irony of ironies – just as she passed her own front door. The BMW didn't stop, but ploughed forward under its momentum towards the crossroads and the war memorial. Ellie hit the horn as hard as she could, fighting for control, stomping on the brake and pressing down on the clutch.

The car mounted the memorial plinth and climbed the first two or three of the conical structure's concentric steps. It seemed to rise a little further, as if battling to climb upward, then, with a sigh of dying hydraulics, it sagged backwards and came at last to rest.

There was a still, beautiful moment where all Ellie could hear was the engine hiss and tick as it cooled. Then she remembered the things and shoved the door open, grabbing for the shotgun and hauling it out after her as she stumbled clear on weak, strengthless legs, almost stumbling and falling on the memorial's uneven steps.

People were running towards the car. *Milly, where are you?*

Someone was shouting her name, but Ellie waved them aside, staring up the High Street. She half-raised the shotgun, a hand on the slide, trying to chamber another useless round. Useless, yes, because she'd seen what effect it had had on one of the attackers. None, zilch, fuck-all. And there was an army of them out there. No, not an army, that was silly. *Stick to the facts, Ellie, to what you saw.* She'd only seen between a dozen and twenty. Although if shooting the fuckers didn't kill them, or flattening them with a car, twenty of them would be more than enough.

Up the road, at the edge of the glow from the first set of streetlights, she saw a cluster of pale blurs. They weren't moving; they were still, watching. Waiting. Calculating. And then they rippled into motion, and vanished back into the dark.

"Ellie?" Plant-Pot was standing beside her, eyeing the shotgun cautiously. "Ellie, are you okay?"

"Never better, Andy," she managed through her teeth. They were chattering. She remembered something. She put the shotgun's safety catch back on, then laid the gun in the footwell before clambering back inside the X5. A hand caught at her jacket, but she shook it off.

Ellie fumbled in her pocket for an evidence bag. Several of the glassine envelopes fell out at once as she removed one. Should really have gloves for this, latex ones on both hands instead of a police uniform glove on one – the other having been removed when she'd been stripping the cover from that first flare. But fuck it. She had no idea what was taking place, but one thing she felt entitled to state as an absolute fact was that this was most definitely not a normal night on duty.

The scrap of pale material was still there, hanging from the gap between the passenger door and the jamb. She took hold of it between her gloved finger and thumb – she didn't want to touch it with her bare hand – and opened the door in order to lift it free. She was starting to shake now: delayed reaction, shock. As if the day's fun and games at Barrowman hadn't been enough.

She slid back out, swaying and wobbling, then sat down on the memorial steps. Plant-Pot stood over her, gawping down. Other familiar faces: Pastor Matt, the Robinsons, Chris Brailsford. Noel pushed through the crowd. "Ellie?"

"Gimme a minute," she said. "Evidence." The hardest part was getting the glassine envelope open. "Fuck."

Noel crouched beside her. "Let me," he said, and gently took the baggie from her grasp. He opened it and held it steady as she lowered the scrap of material inside. "The hell's that?"

"Evidence." She fumbled the baggie into her pocket, then zipped it shut. "Don't know what the hell it is, but they were covered in it."

"They?"

She gestured to the car. Something red glinted in the driver's footwell: the hammer and sickle badge on the fur hat. She fished it out, clutching it tight before it could slip from her shaking fingers.

"Let me through. Let me through." Thelma Graham pushed her way out of the crowd. "What in God's name have you done to my car?"

Sod my husband, what have you done to my car? Ellie couldn't hold in a burst of weak, hysterical laughter, which only served to outrage Thelma further still. "Are you *drunk*?" she demanded. "She's drunk! I saw her before in the pub, drinking away."

"Leave it, Thelma," said Noel.

"Oh, I'm sure you'd like me to be quiet – you and all her *friends*, you'll all rally round, won't you? I know what you thought of Tom, how you ganged up on him behind his back –" Thelma broke off, finally remembering her spouse. "And where *is* he? Ellie Cheetham, where is my bloody husband?"

"He's dead." Ellie hadn't meant to shout, but the shock had left her struggling to put a sentence together or make it audible, and when she finally overcame it the words came out in a near-roar. "I got to the Height and his car was trashed and there was no sign of him. Then –"

"How do you know he's dead, then, if he wasn't there? Why didn't you do your job and look –"

"I barely got out of there myself," Ellie shouted back. "Look." She gestured at the X5.

Thelma sniffed. "Drunk," she said again.

Ellie almost went for her then, but Noel's arm was around her shoulders. "Enough," he said. "I'm getting her to Milly. Ellie, can you walk?"

"Think so." She stood. Her legs wobbled. "Maybe not."

"We'll take my car."

"Wait." She pointed into the X5, to the box she'd salvaged from the Land Rover. "Bring that."

"Okay."

He got the box under one arm and steered her through the crowd. Thelma barred their way. Noel tried to move around her, but she moved to block him. Julie Robinson caught her arm and said something, and Thelma moved aside. What had she said? Was she supporting Ellie, or undermining her?

Couldn't think like that. As they cleared the crowd, Ellie touched Noel's arm and turned back. "Everybody should go back to their homes," she said. "Stay inside. Lock your doors. Bolt your windows. And whatever you do, make sure you keep the lights on."

"Drugs," Ellie heard Thelma say, but ignored it. She was shaking so badly now she could barely stand, and almost fell into Noel's car. He pushed her legs inside and shut the door, then got in and drove them to Hollybeck Row.

26.

Despite her advice, as Noel helped Ellie out of the car outside the surgery she saw headlights following them down Hollybeck Row. Car doors slammed as Noel helped her up the surgery steps, followed by the sound of Thelma Graham's voice.

Milly opened the door and gawped. "The actual fuck?"

"Long story," said Ellie.

"Watch out," said Noel. "The angry mob's behind us."

"Fucking perfect. Get her in the waiting room."

Ellie's stomach churned. She ran to the bathroom and shut the door behind her. Afterwards, she ran cold water over her wrists and splashed it on her face.

Fists were banging on the door. They'd got in. They were attacking. No, they weren't banging on the bathroom door. It was more distant. Outside the surgery. "Where is she?" someone shouted. Ellie knew that voice. "We want to talk to her, now! I want to know what she's done with my husband!"

Fucking Thelma. Of course. Anger flared through the numbness and exhaustion and propelled her upright. Ellie flushed the toilet and strode back through the surgery, waving Milly back from the door. She flung it open. "The fuck do you want, Thelma?"

Thelma stepped back. "I want to know what's happened to Tom."

"I told you."

"The truth!"

Ellie kept her voice level with an effort. "I got to the Height. The car was trashed. Tom wasn't there."

"Did you even look for him?" Thelma addressed the crowd. "She was in the pub, getting drunk with the vicar! Drunk!"

"Noel?"

He was at her side. "Ellie?"

"The box in the car. There's a breathalyser kit. I'll do the test right now."

"You were drinking," said Thelma.

"One whisky, Thelma. And I'd barely sipped it when you barged in. That's *after* what happened at Barrowman."

"Oh, you've an answer for everything," Thelma said. "I'm a policeman's wife, Ellie Cheetham – think I don't know how to cheat a breathalyser test?"

"Fucksake, Thelma," Milly said, "wind your fucking neck in."

"My husband's missing. I will not shut up."

Ellie ignored Thelma. A fool's game even engaging her as she had. She was a police officer; she'd authority here and had to assert it. She looked past Thelma to the crowd. "Sergeant Graham volunteered to take his vehicle to the Height earlier and attempt to contact Matlock. When he didn't return, I went to investigate. The vehicle was in the picnic area, overturned. Windows broken. No sign of the Sergeant. There is a chance he's still out there – visibility was very poor."

"Didn't even do your bloody job –" said Thelma.

"I was attacked. By whom or what, I'm still not clear."

"What do you mean, *not clear*? Who or what? What are you talking about now?"

"There were multiple attackers. From their MO I suspect they are responsible for the recent incidents at Wakeman Farm and the *Bell*." *And Tony Harper.* "For whatever reason, they're avoiding any areas that are lit. The power was cut off at the farm and the pub and they were trying to smash the lights on the car. They didn't pursue me into the village; so as long as we keep the lights on, we should be fine. I need volunteers to watch the village perimeter – by that I mean the limits of the areas we've got street lighting for. Everyone else, the best thing to do is remain indoors, and keep your lights on."

"Ridiculous," huffed Thelma, and it hurt Ellie to see doubt on certain faces in the crowd.

"I'll sort the volunteers out," Noel said, giving Milly Ellie's hat. "You get yourself seen to."

"Go get 'em, Jones," said Milly, and pushed him outside. She shut the door and steered Ellie into the waiting room. "Let's have a look."

Ellie took off her jacket and stab vest. Broken glass fell on the floor. "Shit."

"We'll sort that later."

"Milly, wait – there's –"

"Shurrup," said Milly, flashing a penlight in her eyes. "So?" she said, having found nothing more than a few minor cuts Ellie hadn't even noticed sustaining.

Ellie gave her the details. Milly shuddered, touching the gold cross she wore. "Maybe it's Judgement Day."

"Milly."

"Ellie, I know you don't believe, but – come on. You're not telling me this shit's normal."

"Not normal's one thing, Armageddon's another." Ellie remembered the evidence baggie. "Here."

Milly held it to the light, grimacing. "The fuck's this?"

"That's what I want to know. I mean – the things were wearing it. Wrapped in it, like mummies or something."

Milly bit her lip. "Do me best, but you know I'm not CSI here."

Ellie followed her into the second waiting room. Charlotte was asleep on the couch. "Dead to the world, poor kid," said Milly, pulling up a metal stand. "Probably best." Donning a pair of latex gloves, she took out the pale material with tweezers and spread it out. "Weird." She picked it up and held it to the light. "Oh God," she said at last. "*God.*"

She returned the material to the envelope and peeled off the gloves. "What is it?"

Milly motioned Ellie back into the waiting room. "God, I could murder a fag."

"And you a doctor."

"Don't act like you never get cravings too. And I don't mean for Jones' body." Milly clasped her small hands together, as if to pray. "It's skin."

"What?"

"Think it's the top layer, the epidermis. Looks as if it's been treated somehow, like a preservative. Toughened up."

"When you say *skin* –"

Milly was shaking a little. "Can't be a hundred per cent, not just by looking. But… yeah, think it's human."

Ellie sagged back in her chair. "If I ever needed to get through to Matlock…"

Milly bit her lip.

"What?"

"I dunno." She touched the gold cross again. "Just thought – maybe they've got problems of their own."

"What's that supposed to mean?"

"Why aren't the roads cleared, Ell? Council's always got a plough and a gritter going up the North Road, weather like this. Seen one today?"

"Not really noticed, Milly, what with everything."

"Bet it's not been cleared. Maybe this – you know, whatever it is – maybe it's not just happening here."

"We back on Judgement Day again? Milly, come on. Got enough to deal with right now, without you going –"

Milly folded her arms. "Without me going what?"

"Sorry. Look. Right now we've got –" Ellie made a helpless gesture "– whatever the hell's out there to deal with. Last thing I need is for you to start going off on one about the end of the world. I'm responsible for these people. Barsall. Okay? I need your help for that."

"Fine."

"Milly, I'm not having a go at your faith."

"Sounded like it."

"Look, if you're right, none of this'll matter anyway. But until I see otherwise, this is a local problem and my job's to get us through it. I don't want to lose anyone else, okay?" Saying that made her think of Tom; for all he'd done her head in, Ellie's eyes filled up. She wiped them on her sleeve. And then there was Joda. She'd liked Joda. And Barbara, who'd only wanted to die in whatever peace she could. Grant and Sally Beck. And the boy, Richard – *Rick* – whose last act had been to shove Kate Beck into the crawlspace and pull the cover over. And Tony Harper. What must that have been like? Heading home, and then those things coming out of the snow. Herding him, like dogs a sheep, across the foot of the hill. What must it have taken him to scramble up to that ledge – towards the hill road – only to find them already above him, looking down? That would've been how it happened; Ellie could see it. Tony boxed in, huddled on the ledge, knife in hand, hoping to wait them out. But they'd been waiting too, and the cold hadn't bothered them.

"All right." Milly touched her hand. "So what now?"

"Fucked if I know, frankly. Just try getting through tonight. See where we are in the morning. If the weather's any better someone can go for help. Even if it's like today, we might have to chance it."

"Think we'll be okay tonight?"

"Maybe. Whole place is lit up, so that helps. Light seems to be all that bothers them. I blasted one with a twelve-bore, point-blank, and it just got up again. Tried to fucking flatten another one against a wall and –" Ellie shook her head, all the memories from the ride back to Barsall flooding back. "Light," she said again. "Dunno if it actually hurts them, or they just prefer the dark. But all the power was out at the *Bell*. And you heard Kate Beck – same thing happened at Wakeman's before they busted in. Probably why they got attacked first – on the outskirts. Isolated. More vulnerable. Easier to – shit."

"Wouldn't have thought you'd have any problems doing that, after the night you've had." Milly grinned, but Ellie didn't. "Ell? What?"

"Bert." She stood up. Her legs, thankfully, remained steady. "He went back home."

"Shit."

"Borrow your car keys?"

"Ell, I don't think you should be driving, state you're in."

"Yeah, well."

"I'll get Jones to go check."

"No." If anything happened. If Noel didn't come back. Milly would blame Ellie, or herself, or both of them. Enough. Better Ellie went. Who'd miss her, after all? "I'll do it."

Milly looked ready to argue, then sighed and shook her head. "Fine. Any chance you can bring it back in one piece, though?"

"Do my best." There was probably a joke to be made about Milly's car insurance and Acts of God, but Ellie chose not to risk it.

Milly peered through the surgery windows' blinds at the crowd outside, then fished in her jeans pocket for her keys. "Here you go. It's in the alley out back."

"Thanks." Ellie picked up the shotgun. She hesitated, then loaded another cartridge to replace the one she'd fired. It might not be much use, but it helped. A little. She took half a dozen road flares out of the box, put her stab vest and jacket back on, and finally reached for her hat; somehow donning it felt almost like crossing herself. Then Milly opened the back door, and Ellie stepped outside.

27.

Ellie climbed into Milly's sturdy pink Audi and reversed out of the alley onto Hollybeck Row, shotgun across her lap, road flares on the passenger seat.

Before the crowd outside the surgery could react, she'd driven onto Halliwell Way, spun the wheel and guided the Audi onto Blackfield Grove. The cascade of snow had become a trickle, drifting down in the streetlights' glow. Except outside the surgery, there was no one out of doors.

She turned onto Litch Way, alongside Blackfield Park, which was in almost complete darkness. Ellie didn't look: too easy to convince herself she'd seen white things moving in the blackness, and she couldn't afford to imagine too far.

Litch Way led out of Barsall, across the top of Slapelow Hill. The houses fell away; half a dozen streetlights led up to the village boundary, and then there was only the road and the night-black, snow-white fields either side of the car.

Ellie's palms sweated on the wheel; she was out in the dark again. Grey shapes flickered at the edges of her vision, thin as greyhounds, pacing the Audi on spider-thin legs. She kept her eyes on the road, trying to dismiss them as tricks of the light.

Visibility was fucked, even without the snow. But Annable Farm was closer than the Height, and the journey there safer. The top of Slapelow Hill was broad and flat; if Ellie went off the road the worst that'd happen was the car ending up in a ditch. Although that would be bad enough, in these conditions, even without whatever was lurking in the snow.

Better still, though, Annable Farm had light. Bert had had problems with trespassers in the past, so he'd set up floodlights, security cameras and motion detectors – not cheap, but he could afford it. With all the snow blowing around, setting off the detectors, the lights would be permanently on. Unless he'd switched them off to save power, deciding no-one was mad enough to come out there in this weather.

Or unless something else put the lights out for him.

Ellie focused on her breathing: slow, steady breaths, in and out. All she could control for now: that, and keeping the car on the road.

That was all she had to do: there was just one road, and it led straight to the farm. She kept her eyes ahead; no good could come of looking at the flat, empty fields on either side.

Was that light up ahead? She dimmed her headlights. Yes. A faint, luminous haze. But then the glow seemed to dim. Was it receding? Another vehicle? She accelerated round the bend in the road: the glow became clearer.

There was Annable Farm: the centuries-old stone main building and the newer barns and silos. One of each either side of the house. But only the ones to the right of the house were still lit. The rest were in the dark.

A blown fuse, a loose wire, the motion sensors not working –

But the Audi's headlights lit up the gate, and what was clinging to it. It writhed as the light hit it and its eyeless head swivelled, pointing backwards at Ellie like an owl's. The thing dropped from the gate and bolted aside. It wasn't alone; when Ellie looked in either direction, she saw more of them perched on the fences around the property, and pale shapes darting through the shadows around the blacked-out part of the farmstead.

The floodlights illuminating the house's driveway flickered out and darkness poured across the path. Other things followed it. No doubt this time: more of the creatures, moving to surround the house.

The remaining floodlights flickered. More of the creatures were perched on the hedges or lurking beside the road, crouched catlike with arched backs, eyeless shrouded heads pointing towards her. Again it occurred to her that if they couldn't *see* the light they might *feel* it, perhaps as a source of pain.

A weapon, maybe? Although it was hard to imagine car headlights succeeding where a twelve-gauge buckshot round had failed. And her headlights hadn't the power of the floods around Annable Farm, which now were almost gone.

One last flicker, and the floods went out: only the light from the farmhouse windows remained. The creatures closed in on it. how many *were* there? At the Height Ellie had estimated between a dozen and a score of the things, but there was twice that number here, or more.

The creatures didn't move towards her. No doubt they would have under different circumstances, just as they had before, just as they'd taken Tom. They'd take anything and everything in Barsall, if they could just disable the lights. But for now, their priority was Annable Farm; if she didn't interfere, they wouldn't attack.

The farmhouse lights flickered.

This was what had happened at Wakeman Farm and the *Bell*: surrounded, blacked-out, and finally broken into. Bert was alone in there; no doubt he had his shotgun handy, for all the good it would do him. Once they were inside, it would be over in minutes, if not seconds.

Ellie's gaze shifted to the drive. How far to the farmhouse? A hundred yards? Two? She remembered the drive back from the Height. There'd be more of the creatures this time: she'd have to park up, stationary, a sitting duck for missiles aimed at her lights, while Bert ran from the house to open the car door, exposing them both to direct attack, before driving back across the top of Slapelow Hill. Hardly any distance normally, but they'd be in darkness, with the entire horde in pursuit.

The lights flickered again.

There was no chance. None at all. If she'd only been running a couple of minutes later, it would all have been over by the time she got here – nothing to do, no hard choices to make – and she could have driven back with a clear conscience.

But she hadn't, it wasn't, and she couldn't.

Do your fucking job.

But the lights would be out in seconds now; Bert would be gone before she even reached the house. And if he wasn't, what then? Again she rehearsed the mechanics of a rescue: even if Bert made it aboard, the drive back would finish them. She wouldn't get as far as the gate.

She had everyone else in Barsall to consider too, or so she told herself. But she knew the truth: *You're afraid, Ellie Cheetham, too afraid to try.*

The creatures looked away from her, as if they already sensed her choice. That almost made Ellie ram the gate and try after all, but before she could the farmhouse lights went out, and the pale silent horde rushed forward. Some clustered around the ground floor; others scuttled up the walls like lizards. Glass broke; wood cracked and split under blows.

Move. Drive. Fucking do something.

But she didn't. Couldn't. She already knew there was no chance, that Bert Annable was already dead.

A shotgun fired inside the house. The snow had stopped and the wind had died and the creatures made no noise as they moved, so the sound rang across the hilltop. A second shot, a third, then nothing more. Ellie might have heard a cry. Then there was only the faint sound of breaking things.

A few of the creatures remained perched on the fences. Another slunk into view at the gates, just outside the headlights' glow, all of them facing towards her. They didn't advance. Not yet. *Go away, little coward. Live a little longer, till we come for you as well.*

Ellie heard herself mumbling an apology to Bert as she

reversed away from the gates. She checked the rearview: the road was empty.

Reverse. Three-point turn. Accelerate away.

Behind her now, at the gate to Annable Farm, more of the pale shapes were gathered, to watch the coward go.

She wasn't a coward. She wasn't. There'd been nothing she could have done. She had to warn the village. Try and organise some kind of defence. She told herself that. It might even have been true, but part of her refused to believe it.

But that didn't matter. For now, she drove.

And in the fields on either side of Litch Way, thin white shapes loped alongside the car.

28.

The creatures followed her back across the hill, but she remained unmolested all the way to the village limits. As the Audi passed the WELCOME TO BARSALL sign into the glow of the streetlights, they fell back; when Ellie checked the rearview, she saw them crouching in the road, just outside the light, watching her go. Or whatever they did without eyes. Smelling her fear, maybe, as it receded.

She looked left as she passed Blackfield Park, but to her dismay the white shapes she'd glimpsed there didn't resolve themselves into patches of snow. There were too many of them, arranged in rows disappearing into the shadows.

She'd have liked to believe she was imagining the sight, but people were leaning out of their windows on Chapel Bank, overlooking the park, staring down at something below.

Somehow, the creatures were already in the village. How they'd managed that didn't matter for now. At least the light was keeping them back; the closest rank of the things was right up against the park railings, the tips of their long figures straying onto the pavement. No-one, thankfully, had been stupid enough to go over to that side of the road, but there were rubberneckers on the pavement opposite, gawping.

Ellie resisted the temptation to shout out of her window for everyone to go home. She had to think. She couldn't just start raving about monsters: there was no telling what Thelma Graham had been saying about her, or who might have been listening to it.

Bert. She didn't want to believe it. She tried to convince herself he might have found a hiding place, like Kate Beck, but knew that wasn't him. Besides, he'd lived alone; the creatures had surely known the house was inhabited, and wouldn't have stopped till they'd found him. And she'd heard the gun firing. No. He'd gone down fighting.

Only this morning, he'd been banging on her door and getting her out of bed. He'd been beside her at Barrowman Farm, firing both barrels at the unseen sniper. He'd been by her side, and where'd she been when he'd needed her?

There'd been nothing she could do, except get herself killed: Bert would have understood that. But she'd liked the old sod; he'd been quiet and steady, with that sarky sense of humour that always appealed to Ellie. They hadn't been close, but he'd been *there*. Solid. Part of the furniture, even the architecture. And now he was gone. The bastards had taken him and she'd done nothing to prevent it.

Well, what was that old saying? *Don't mourn, organise.* Where'd she heard that? Noel, it might have been – it was a quote from an American union activist, framed and murdered by the cops. Funny choice of inspiration for a British bobby either way. But it fitted. There was stuff to do. And she had people to convince.

She'd been driving almost on autopilot, turning back onto Blackfield Grove, then Hollybeck Row. The Audi's headlights caught the crowd still gathered outside the surgery. Christ, hadn't they fucked off yet?

She parked on Hollybeck Row, realising too late that the crowd were between her and the surgery and swarming towards the car. Thelma Graham's perm was bobbing above the crowd as if they were bearing her severed head as a trophy. *I should be so lucky.*

She thought of restarting the car and reversing back into the alley, but it was already too late; the crowd had already encircled the Audi. No way to manoeuvre it without the risk of hitting someone. She had to stay calm. Above all else, she must remember that. She had to convince people. Persuade.

Convince and persuade them they're surrounded by monsters?
Good luck with that.

A fist rapped on the driver's window. Thelma, no doubt:
Ellie could hear her shouting, but the words were blurred and
unclear; ironic, considering how the sounds from Annable
Farm had been so horribly, nightmarishly distinct.

Fuck it. She unlocked the door, put her hand on her baton –
just in case – and got out.

"Here she is," said Thelma. "Finally come out of hiding, Ellie
Cheetham?"

Ellie mustn't be drawn. She had to take charge. There was
a danger to the public. But her thoughts were a horde of cats,
resisting order. "All right. Now everybody listen –"

"Where's my husband?" Thelma's voice was ragged with
grief, her eyes red, and just then Ellie could only pity her.
"What did you do with him?"

"Sergeant Graham is missing," said Ellie, with all the
authority she could muster, "and I'm sorry, Thelma, but
we've got to assume the worst. I've reason to believe it's the
work of the same individuals responsible for the –" Attacks?
Disappearance? Murders? She mustn't hesitate, should have
rehearsed this properly before speaking "– incidents at –"

"Stop lying!" shouted Thelma. "You were getting drunk in
the pub when –"

"I was doing nothing of the sort –" Don't be drawn. Stay
focused. "I've also reason to believe the whole village is in
danger. I have to ask you all –"

"Danger? What danger?"

"To disperse –"

"What fairy stories are you telling now?"

"– and return to your homes –"

"Listen to her, for God's sake." Madeleine Lowe shouldered
through the crowd. "She's telling the truth." Madeleine turned
to Ellie. "I did a little homework after –"

"Don't listen to her," Thelma cried. "They're in it together."

"Come off it!" Julie Robinson fought to Ellie's side. "You all know Ellie. When's she ever –"

"You're another of her cronies," said Thelma. "All of you, against my Tom."

She was cracking wide open now – and, painful though it was to see, thank God, Ellie could feel the crowd's mood shift. Beyond them the surgery door inched open; in the gap she saw Milly biting her lip, weighing whether or not to intervene.

The tide was turning, and she wasn't on her own. Ellie opened her mouth to say something else, but there was a clatter of footsteps, and a dozen people, led by Ernie Stasiolek, came running down Hollybeck Row. *Fucking what now?*

"We've got trouble." Ernie held his shotgun broken over one arm. "The park's full of – I don't know what the Hell they are." The Stasioleks lived on Blackfield Way, Ellie remembered, on the far side of the park. "And there's something out on Litch Way – they're smashing all the streetlights."

It was starting. Ellie reached into the car, pulling out the shotgun and the box of flares. "Everybody listen," she shouted. "We don't know exactly what we're dealing with, but for whatever reason, we *do* know they don't like bright light of any kind. So your best protection right now's to get indoors, secure all entrances and keep all lights on." But wouldn't that give the things a target? If she only had a few minutes, just to gather herself. But she didn't. "As long as we keep the lights on, we're safe."

As if in response, all the lights on Hollybeck Row – streetlights, houselights, all of them – flickered. Ellie heard screams from Blackfield Park and Litch Way, And from the crowd around her too.

She thought of the pylons that marched across Wakeman's Edge and Fendmoor Heath. Giants, but little more than steel frameworks. All too vulnerable to a determined enough enemy; all too easy to picture one swaying and buckling, blue fire crackling around it, then toppling at last...

"Everybody get inside," Ellie shouted, pushing her voice down into its lowest register so she sounded in control and not about to panic, whatever the truth of things. "Find a light source – torches, candles, anything you can –"

The lights flickered again – for longer this time, and with longer periods of blackness in between. There were more screams, and a sound of breaking glass.

"Ellie!" There was a rattle of steel; Milly was outside the surgery, pulling the steel shutters down over the front of the building. She pulled down another over the front door as the lights stabilised again, then padlocked them both. "Come on. Round the back."

And then the lights went out.

29.

The lights went out at Barrowman Farm, and Jess gave a little cry. In the dark Keira snorted at her in disgust and Mum made a sound somewhere between a tut and a scoff. She shrank back into her corner of the kitchen.

"Frank, Paul – generator!" Mum shouted. "Now!" Torches flashed about the kitchen. "Now! Get a fucking move on!"

A torch-beam shone on the cellar door. Frank blundered over and wrenched it open. Paul shone his torch down the steps as Frank stomped down them, out of sight. Paul went to the cellar doorway, his thin beanpole shape silhouetted against the backwash of light from Frank's torch. Jess could run and shove him in the back, send him headfirst down the steps, break the bastard's neck –

But Jess couldn't be sure that'd work. Even if it *did*, what then? If she messed things up so the generator didn't come on? *They'd* come in and that'd be the end for the Harpers. She didn't care about that – Frank, Paul, Keira, Mum, they could all fuck off and quite literally die. But Dom, like her, was treated like shit and had no choice in how things went. He didn't deserve that, did he? And then there was Baby Joel – Joel, yes, *Joel*, not fucking Steven, she'd call her child what she fucking liked and fuck anyone who didn't. *They'd* have Baby Joel's skin off in seconds and the rest of him buried in salt. No; Baby Joel deserved better. So Jess stayed still, for now.

Stupid bloody Jess, they called her, Useless Jess, no good to anyone, but she wasn't bloody stupid – not as thick as they thought, anyway. She'd already begun to plan, and she'd surprise them all with it, all her shitten family – but not yet. Not just yet.

Paul clomped down the cellar steps. Joel grizzled in Jess' arms. She shushed and rocked him. He caught one of her fingers between the two digits of his cleft hand and held on tight. Down in the cellar, the generator coughed and growled; the lights flickered. It finally roared back into life, and the lights came back on.

Mum's lighter clicked, and Jess smelt fresh fag-smoke – though you could barely tell in this kitchen, the way the old bitch smoked. Bitch, yes. Bitches, Mum and Keira both. Frank was as thick as they claimed Jess was – brains of a pig – and as for Paul, brother or not, Jess'd gladly slit his throat if ever she could. She'd had enough; stupid worthless little Jess had finally fucking had enough.

"Right," said Mum. "All we need now's to keep it going till morning. Reckon we can do that."

"Sure we'll be all right, Liz?" Keira was scared too, even if she was trying to sound like she wasn't. Good.

"Fine." Mum grinned. "Listen out and you'll hear. They're keeping busy up there. If you're lucky you'll hear 'em screaming."

Ellie Cheetham screaming. Dr Emmanuel screaming. Dr Emmanuel was nice. Jess remembered her warm dark eyes and gentle voice when she was pregnant, telling Jess she could help her if she needed it – to see someone from the Housing, or get rid of the baby if she'd wanted. And Jess'd wanted to, but hadn't dared. Bring the outside world down on the family? She'd never have been forgiven for that, nor having an abortion. But if she had, she might have a flat of her own now somewhere far from here. Maybe a job, too. Definitely a life. Far from Mum, Keira, or Paul. But she'd been afraid to say anything – afraid to even think of living without the family – back then. Now, though? Now, it was different.

Then again, if she *had* got away what state'd she be in now? Maybe none: maybe this was only happening here, and she'd have been safe in Matlock or Derby. Or maybe Mum was right and this was the beginning of the end, and *They'd* be cutting off Jess' skin right now. But she'd have had a few months with a life of her own, believing she had a future. She could almost see it: for the first time in her life she could actually imagine how it could have been different, how she could have *made* it different. But now that chance was gone, and what future could she expect instead? A life spent at Barrowman Farm, shouted at by Mum, jeered at by Keira, used by Paul when there was no-one else around – and there wouldn't be anyone else, not anywhere, if all Mum's tales were true?

Jess wanted to cry, but knew she mustn't. If they thought she was scared she'd only be made a mock of, but her tears would be of anger, not fear. And if they ever knew that – knew how much she hated them and wanted to be free of them – God help her.

"I'll go up," said Keira. "The attic. Listen out." She grinned. "Maybe we'll be able to hear."

"Leave the windows shut," said Mum. "The skylight too. Don't draw them. Keep the lights on, but hidden. Remember?"

"Yeah." Keira grinned again, reciting:

"Board your window, keep on the light,
When the Tatterskin walks at night.
Hush and be still, make never a cry,
And pray the Tatterskin passes by."

"That's a girl," said Liz, and Keira grinned wider still. She was scared – Jess could practically smell it – but happy too. Excited. Because all Liz's stories were true and no one else's rules mattered now, only theirs.

Paul sat at the kitchen table, smoking and proper shaken up. He hadn't believed, not really, not till now. Whatever he'd seen at the *Bell*, all he'd really cared about was the chance to get hold of Charlotte Famuyiwa.

Jess knew she'd pay for him losing his chance. And when she did, Mum'd blame Ellie Cheetham for coming down and messing things up, or Charlotte for getting Paul all turned-on, but any time Jess might have believed that was long gone.

I hate you all, she said silently, then hugged Baby Joel close. *Not you, sweetheart.* Maybe not Dom, either. But the rest? Mum and Paul, Keira and Frank? Fuck them all. Funny: with everything else being torn apart, this should've been the time she clung to her family above all. But if the alternative was spending the rest of her life alone with them, she'd rather be dead – rather find Ellie Cheetham, who'd always played fair with her, and Dr Emmanuel, who'd always been kind, who might have been the only one who ever had been, and die with them. If they weren't already dead.

She wasn't that brave, though. Go out in that night, with her baby? Being a Harper wouldn't keep her safe: *They* hadn't spared Tony, had they?

There was a chance, though, wasn't there? A chance tonight wouldn't be the end for everyone else. Mum'd said there'd be another day after this; then tomorrow night, the Dance. So maybe *They* wouldn't get everybody; *They* might even spare a few for now, like cats tormenting mice. And if there were people left in Barsall tomorrow, Ellie Cheetham would be one of them. And if so...

...if so, Jess would have something for her.

Because Jess had an idea.

Paul puffed on his fag, fingers trembling. Keira went up the stairs, Frank beside her. Mum sat down and began smoking too, not looking at Paul. Dom huddled in a corner, arms around his dogs, muttering to them. He'd be happy there, and feel safe. So that just left Jess.

She slipped down the hall to the front room. Baby Joel grizzled and she unfastened her shirt, offering a breast; he latched on and fell quiet. Could she hear noises through the cracked and boarded window, drifting across the valley from Slapelow Hill? She told herself she didn't. Jess sat on the sofa and nursed her child, and reviewed the plans she'd made for the morning.

30.

They didn't even flicker: there was light one moment, blackness the next. The first screams were of confusion and shock. Then, from the direction of Blackfield Park, came a fresh outbreak of screams, and these were of terror and pain. They became a wave, and they got louder. Closer. Something was coming.

Milly caught Ellie's arm. "Come on."

"I –"

"Ellie, now!" Milly dragged her to the alleyway. "Can't save anyone else if –"

"This way!" Ellie shouted. Madeleine was beside her, but Ernie Stasiolek stood frozen: his family were back the way he'd come, but no-one could have willingly gone towards sounds like that. "Ernie!" He turned, blinking at her. "Ernie, this way! Julie! Phil!" Milly didn't look happy and Ellie saw her point – last thing they needed was a stampede in the alley – but she'd left Bert to his fate and couldn't do that again, if she could help it. "Thelma!"

But Thelma Graham stood motionless, and if Ellie didn't stop she'd still be shouting names when the monsters came. And so she let Milly drag her down the alleyway, and she didn't look back to see who did or didn't follow.

As they fled down the ginnel behind the surgery, Ellie heard Thelma scream.

Milly padlocked and bolted the back gate, although Ellie suspected it would only hold for seconds, then ran across the yard to the surgery's back door. "Coming through," yelled Milly, and the others scattered from her path.

Screams from the street and further afield seemed to hit Ellie from all sides, dizzying her. They were coming from all over Barsall.

"Come on, come on!" Phil Robinson, panic in his voice. "Get it open –"

"Quiet," Ellie hissed over her shoulder, and stepped towards the gate. Had there been movement, out in the alley? She couldn't tell, not with all the screams, the sounds of breaking wood and glass, tearing metal, shattered stone. The only sounds, she realised, were coming from people or things they owned or lived in, being broken and torn apart. The creatures themselves were silent.

The back door opened. "In," Milly whispered. "You too, Ell."

Ellie backed towards the door. Her heel caught on a loose paving-stone; Milly steadied her, then backed across the threshold too.

Milly had taken over the Hollybeck Row Practice when Dr Da Silva, an elderly Indian GP, had retired six years earlier. Before that, badly shaken by an attempted break-in at the surgery – one of the few remotely serious crimes in Barsall's recent history *not* committed by one of the Harpers – Da Silva had invested in tighter security, including steel shutters at the front and back. When Milly'd joined the practice as his junior partner, he'd drummed the necessity of locking up for the night into her, and she'd kept the deeply ingrained habit up. Luckily.

The windows of the kitchenette at the practice's rear were already shuttered as usual – a lot of effort otherwise to view an unprepossessing backyard – so once inside Milly only had to pull down the shutter over the back door. As she padlocked it and then shut the door, something began slamming itself against the gate in the yard. Ellie put the flares and shotgun down and helped Milly lock and bolt the door.

"What's happening?" cried a panicked voice from a

consulting room. Phil Robinson muffled a startled cry, and Julie muttered "Fuck."

"Everybody quiet," Ernie said. Milly bustled past him towards the consulting rooms; Ellie followed, activating the torch on her phone. One of the doors opened and a blurred shape reached out for her.

Her torch lit Charlotte Famuyiwa's face; the girl opened her mouth to cry out, but Ellie clamped a hand over it. "It's me. Charlotte, it's Ellie Cheetham. Keep quiet. Whatever you do, you've got to keep quiet."

Milly emerged from the other consulting room with Kate Beck and pointed out front, towards the waiting area. Ellie nodded, motioned Charlotte to follow Milly and Kate, then went to get the others.

31.

Milly found candles and a pair of electric lanterns, which she set in the middle of the waiting-room floor. The eight survivors sat around them, listening to the screams and sounds of breaking things from the street outside and through the surgery walls: the creatures must be forcing their way into other houses along the row.

At last those sounds died away, and only the ever more distant shrieks from outside remained. The heating had failed along with the lights; the surgery grew progressively colder. Kate's teeth chattered; Ellie's, too.

Milly got up. Ellie opened her mouth to speak, but Milly put a finger to her lips and disappeared into the kitchenette. There was a faint clicking sound, and a few seconds later Milly came back through.

"Soz," she whispered. "Just checking to see if the hob worked."

Ellie stared at her. "You were gonna brew up, in the middle of this?"

Milly shrugged. "Dunno if you noticed, Ell, but it's fucking brassic in here, and we've got people in shock."

Fair point. And, admittedly, a strong cup of tea was suddenly very appealing. Or coffee with a quarter pound of sugar in it. "*Was* the hob on?"

Milly shook her head. "Gas is out too."

Ellie nodded. Made sense. Gas meant both heat or light, and the attackers would deprive their intended victims of both if they could. Milly patted her shoulder. "Don't worry. Got an idea."

She slipped into a consulting room, emerging with an armful of blankets. The survivors wrapped themselves as tightly as they could in them and huddled closer around the waning, warmthless lanterns. Shared body heat was better than nothing; besides, there were worse dangers than the cold tonight.

Charlotte was still in her underwear, but the surgery ran a charity collection for unwanted clothing and Milly found jeans, heavy boots, a t-shirt and a sweater for her. Very *infra dig* compared to what Charlotte normally wore, but she seemed happy enough to wear them tonight.

The sounds from outside ebbed and flowed; whenever Ellie thought they were going to fade out completely, they rose again. And she just sat, as Barsall died around her, her neighbours, her friends. She was a police officer; it was her duty to keep order.

Well, go on out then. You know you won't. You know you're staying put.

Ellie tried to think of an alternative, but found none. Instead, she opened the box and began counting the flares. There were twenty: she began peeling off the paper wrapping, so they could be deployed more quickly if needed. She stuffed wads of shredded paper in her jacket pockets: it'd burn quickly. If light was the creatures' enemy, fire was her friend.

She tried to think of nothing as she worked, or find a good memory to focus on. But her mind wouldn't settle. She'd made some memories in Barsall, among the quiet of the Peaks, but the present poisoned them. Before that, she'd made memories with Stan, with Richard; she tried to dwell only on the good times with them, while they'd lasted, but there too her focus was dragged inevitably forward to the ending.

She'd finished a long shift to find her phone full of missed calls and messages: school first, then Stan. Richard had collapsed in the playground. They'd tried to get Ellie but couldn't. Stan was at the hospital. Richard was in intensive care. And then the other voice messages:

Ellie, where are you?

Ellie, call me.

Ellie, call me as soon as you get this.

And finally: *Ellie, it's Stan*; then a long silence, and: *call me back*. Nothing else, because you didn't tell your wife your child and hers was dead in an answerphone message. And worst of all there was no-one to blame. An aneurysm, caused by a birth defect: no-one's action or inaction had played a part, no-one's malice or error. No negligence on the school's part, the paramedics', or the hospital's. Nothing anyone could have done would have changed the final outcome in the slightest.

Nobody to blame, unless you believed in God. Milly had never pushed her faith on Ellie, so they'd rarely discussed the topic, but late one night when very drunk Ellie had challenged Milly to justify a God who allowed a child to die at the age of seven from a time-bomb planted in his skull at conception. What was the point of that? What purpose did it serve? Why allow so vicious an absurdity to take place? And Milly had looked back at her, eyes full of sorrow and compassion, and said *It's a fallen world, Ellie, love*. A fallen world. As good an explanation as any, or none at all.

Ellie looked at her phone: two hours had passed. She was almost surprised the things were taking so long to work their way through Barsall's population. Weapons were useless against them; only light seemed to deter them. Maybe a few people still had light sources, forcing the attackers to find ways to extinguish them, or to wait till candles burned out and batteries were drained. Or perhaps they were toying with their prey, like cats with mice: making them suffer, drawing out their game.

Fire was a possible defence, even a weapon, but what good was that to them here, hiding indoors? For now they would just have to wait.

Another hour went by. The Robinsons huddled together, hands clasped; Ernie Stasiolek, thumping his fist against his thigh, eyed the door longingly. Some men would already have run outside, attempting to get back to Chapel Bank, heedless of the danger to themselves or others: Ernie at least was clear-headed enough to recognise he couldn't help his family dead. Marzena Stasiolek was every inch as tough and level-headed as her husband, and would if necessary die to protect their children. The best course was to get through the night and hopefully find them whenever it was safe. Even so, it could only be a torment to wait helplessly while his neighbours screamed outside – screamed, and eventually fell silent.

And he wasn't the only one: Milly was silent too, hands over her mouth, but her eyes were brimming and Ellie knew better than to approach her now; Milly was holding things together by the thinnest and most tenuous of threads with Noel out there in the night, quite possibly adding his screams to the rest.

Kate Beck, meanwhile, rocked back and forth, fist in mouth so as not to cry out, doubtless reliving the events of the previous night. Charlotte sat motionless, still looking dazed, having only just woken from her sedated sleep into this.

Madeleine Lowe, for her own part, prayed quietly into her clasped hands. At last she finished and opened her mouth to speak, but then the shutters over the back door rattled and she only gasped.

Ellie hadn't heard the back gate break down; the things must have climbed over the back wall. She picked up her shotgun; Ernie Stasiolek, face pale and set, loaded two cartridges into his own weapon.

The shutters rattled again. Ellie knelt and took aim at the back door, sweat trickling down her back. The sound wasn't repeated, but she stayed there until her arms ached; finally she lowered the shotgun and sat back down.

Julie Robinson laughed weakly; it rose, close to hysteria, then stopped. She muttered something to herself.

Madeleine looked up. "What was that?"

Julie shook her head. "Nothing."

"Was that a rhyme? I thought I..."

After a moment, Julie shrugged. "Just something my great-gran used to say."

"How did it go?"

Julie looked uncomfortable at the prospect of public performance, but finally whispered: "*Board your window, keep on your light, when the Tatterskin walks at night.*"

"Interesting."

"Really?" said Milly. "Right now?"

"Came across something like it when I was going through some of the bumph back at the Vicarage," Madeleine said. "That's why I came here."

"Because of an old rhyme?" whispered Phil.

Madeleine shook her head. "I was looking through the parish records for anything like the stuff Ellie showed me."

"The Phoenician stuff?" said Ellie.

"Yeah. Or to see if anything like this'd happened before."

Kate Beck flinched at a particularly loud scream from outside and glanced towards the shuttered front window. "I think we'd remember. This isn't something you'd skip over if you were keeping a diary."

"The Tatterskin," Ellie said, almost to herself, remembering what she'd glimpsed back at the Height, the arm caught in the X5's door; that piece of pale fabric, and what Milly had said it resembled. When she looked at Milly in the dim lantern-light, she saw the same thought there.

Madeleine shook her head. "Not on this scale, no, and not in anything like modern times. But on a smaller scale −"

Something crashed against the shuttered front door.

"Sh," breathed Ellie. *Ignore them and they'll go away*: the bullshit advice teachers gave you about playground bullies, and it never worked on them. Fuckers like that battened on pain like leeches, or found their prey's joy so intolerable they had to extinguish it at all costs. Either way, they kept at you until they drew blood and the only real way to be rid of them was to kick the shit out of the bastards so they were afraid to come after you, or put them in a state where they could never hurt anyone again. Both of which seemed impossible with an enemy like this.

Milly fumbled for the candles, and blew them out one by one. Another blow crashed against the front door shutter; now the one over the front window began to rattle too. The creatures had always known Ellie and the others were here, she realised. They'd just gone for the easier pickings first.

Everyone was looking at her, eyes glistening in the lamplight. *What do we do now, Constable? Tell us. Show us. Do something. Please.*

The shutters in the kitchenette rattled louder and louder. Then one of them crashed like a cymbal, and the noise rang through the house. Kate cried out, then put a hand to her mouth. The shutters became still; long slow icy seconds ticked by. And then the shutters at the front crashed and shivered, and the front window cracked across as the metal covering it buckled.

"Oh fuck," said Julie.

Glass shattered in the kitchenette. The shutter panels there were buckling too. More of the things forcing their way in, like leeches after blood. The front window burst inwards, showering them with glass. Kate bit her lips to keep from crying out again. Milly made a strangled noise. Thin white fingers wormed through the crumpled steel panels, groping for a hold.

Ellie flipped open the box of flares. "Everybody, take two of these. Quickly!" the others rooted and fumbled in the box. "Now, upstairs. Do it!"

"Ellie –"

"It's okay, Mill. Know what I'm doing." She hoped. "Get 'em in the loft." Milly frowned back at her. *Thinks I've lost it.* "Go on. Quickly."

Still Milly hesitated, but the others were already at the stairs. Sound like you know what you're doing and people will do as you say: one of the first lessons she'd learned as a copper. In their fear no one gave a moment's thought to stealth, and the sound of footsteps thundering up the staircase made the creatures tear and wrench at the shutters all the harder. Milly stepped back. "Move," Ellie mouthed, and Milly darted into the hallway and up the stairs as the front door cracked from top to bottom.

Four flares left in the box; Ellie stuck three through her belt, uncapped the fourth, safetied her shotgun and slung it across her back. Then she grabbed two blankets from the floor and ran for the stairs.

She'd almost reached them when the cracked door split open and a white arm lunged into the hallway, and seized her with a thin white steely hand.

32.

Ellie screamed, in revulsion as much as out of fright or pain. The creature's claws sank through the blankets over her shoulder and her jacket; only her stab vest prevented the talons from piercing her skin.

The creature forced its upper body through the gap, its blind muzzled face swivelling to and fro in its cowl of stolen skin till it pointed directly at hers. *Tatterskin.* At the end of the blunt, bullet-like muzzle, the yellow rat-like incisors glistened and gnashed. Ellie fought towards the stairs, against the pull of that arm, and began striking the metal cap against the tip of the flare.

The shutters in the front room had split apart – she could see that much in the dying glow of the electric lanterns before they flickered out, and the long thin body of another creature was writhing through, tearing at the carpet tiles.

In the kitchenette, the back door splintered and broke. Ellie kept striking the tip of the flare.

Ellie's attacker forced its other arm through the door, tearing at the wall as it pulled itself towards her. Behind it, more thin white shapes swarmed in to surround the surgery.

The flare caught, erupting in smoke, sparks, and red, glaring light. The creature recoiled; its grip on her weakened. Ellie lunged forward before it could pull back through the shattered door, and thrust the flare into its face.

Until then, the creatures had been absolutely silent, making no sound even when shot or crushed, but now this one screamed, loud and shrill, an amalgam of wounded child and furious beast, nails on blackboards and forks on steel, and let go of her arm. Ellie ducked as it flailed with its claws, but then it dragged itself back outside, in pain, terror or both.

The one that had climbed in through the front room window crawled backwards, away from her and the stairs. And for a moment, Ellie realised, the house was *still*; the sounds of splintering wood and buckling metal had stopped.

Ellie pulled a blanket from her shoulder and touched the fabric to the fizzing, spewing flare. At first, nothing happened. She backed up the stairs; it wouldn't take them long to resume the attack, if they hadn't already – the monstrosities could already be in the kitchenette, crawling silently down the hallway. But the fabric smouldered: embers caught and glowed in it, tiny grains of light that blossomed into flames.

Fire licked up the hanging folds of the blanket. A flame touched Ellie's hand and she gasped in pain, almost dropping it. Instead she swung it against the wall beside the stairs until the wallpaper ignited, then tossed the blanket over the banister into the hallway. As she climbed the stairs, smoke billowed up around her. She coughed and choked, eyes streaming, but there was a fire now, down in the hallway. And as she reached the landing, another of those screams – viciously loud and piercing, as though someone was shrieking directly into each of her ears – rang out from below.

The fire was spreading fast. Downstairs, metal clanged and clattered again, but this time Ellie felt certain it was a retreat rather than an advance. The air on the landing was already thick with smoke: she could barely see, and every breath made her cough. "Milly?" she shouted.

"Up here!"

When Milly lowered the ladder from the ceiling hatch it almost caught Ellie in the head. She'd pulled it up after her. Sensible. No point making things easy for the creatures. Ellie climbed up into the dark cramped loft. Ernie pulled her clear of the hatch, then helped Milly pull the ladder back up and drag the hatch cover back into place as Ellie coughed and wiped her eyes.

The air was clearer here, at least; enough that her coughing fit subsided. It wouldn't last, though; the crackle of flames was getting louder and smoke was seeping up between the loft-floor joists.

"Fuck sake, Ellie," Milly said. "What'd you do?"

"Turns out –" Ellie spat out phlegm. "Turns out they don't like fire."

"No shit."

The fire got louder. Ellie studied the others in the flare-light; Charlotte and Kate were shaking, and Phil Robinson looked little better off. Julie and Madeleine seemed more composed; Ernie remained expressionless.

"So now what?" Milly said.

"The roof," said Ernie, before Ellie could. "Nowhere else to go. Move along the row." He nodded to himself, something like a smile on his lips. "The fire will keep them back."

"We'll freeze," said Kate Beck. "It was bad enough in the crawlspace last night, we'll be exposed, and –"

"We'll have some heat," said Ernie. "It'll buy us time, anyway. More than we'd have otherwise."

"He's right." Madeleine dragged the ladder across the loft, peering up at the roof's interior. "A little help?"

Ellie picked her way over the joists, holding up the flare. They braced the ladder against a joist and propped it up to reach the ceiling: Ellie held it steady while Madeleine ripped away handfuls of lagging, then gouged and battered the lathing with Ellie's baton. Ellie winced as the first slate clattered down the side of the roof into the street, but the blackness outside was full of firelight, which should keep the creatures back, even while the flames ate the building below them away. Ernie moved to Ellie's side, reaching up to pull away the slates, widening the hole until it was on either side of the roof's central beam.

"Getting fucking hot in here," said Charlotte.

It was, too; Ellie was already sweating, and Ernie's and Madeleine's faces glistened. Julie gripped Phil's hand to steady him.

"Want any help?" said Milly.

Ernie shook his head. "Anyone else will get in the way." He grunted, knocking more slates loose. "Just move when you're told to."

Ernie focused on one side of the central beam, Madeleine the other. Ellie dragged her sleeve across her forehead: the loft was baking hot now and the smoke was pouring up between the joists ever more thickly. Ellie's eyes smarted. Charlotte began coughing; then Phil, then Kate.

"Think we're ready," Ernie called. He handed Ellie his shotgun, then climbed up and poked his head out through the hole before worming his upper body through. His shoulders flexed, back muscles rippling, and he levered himself out. His boots caught the edge of the gap, kicking another two slates loose, then vanished upwards. After a few seconds, his face reappeared, now upside-down. "Okay. Let's go."

"Charlotte," said Ellie: of all the survivors in the loft, the smoke was affecting her the worst. She helped the girl to the ladder; Madeleine guided her up and Ernie reached out to take her arms. For the first time since the attack, the big Pole smiled. "It's going to be all right," he said; Ellie couldn't hear what he said after that, but it was clearly meant to soothe and apparently succeeded.

Charlotte climbed up through the hole, then crawled backwards over it, clutching at the central roof-beam with her arms and legs, so that she was on the opposite side to Ernie. "Next," he called.

Ellie held up a hand. "Julie, next. Then Milly, then Madeleine. Then you, Phil, and then Kate. You go across after her, Ernie. She'll need helping. I'll go last."

Julie Robinson took a deep breath and climbed, wincing as

the ladder creaked under her weight. She was the least agile of the group, but made it onto the roof without incident. Milly muttered to herself non-stop as she climbed the ladder; Ellie was fairly certain it was a prayer.

"Better let me have that," said Madeleine, reaching for Ernie's shotgun. "You'll need at least one hand free."

Ellie had almost forgotten she was still gripping both the shotgun and the flare. "Right. Go on."

By now she, Phil and Kate were coughing badly, and could barely see for the smoke. The loft floor was hot underfoot; the lagging had started smouldering. Ellie squeezed Phil's arm; he breathed out and forced a smile. Kate stared upwards at the gap, face almost serenely calm in between coughing fits.

Overhead, Ernie handed the shotgun back to Madeleine so he'd have both hands free. "Phil?" said Ellie. "Go."

Phil obeyed, grunting and mumbling "Oh shit, oh shit," as he went. Ellie turned to Kate. "All right, love?" Kate coughed, almost delicately, then. "Off you go, then."

Ellie steadied the ladder for her, smoke streaming out through the hole in the roof above. The flare cast its livid glow across the loft's interior, but now so did the dull orange light of the fire. The thick smoke glowed dully, and Ellie couldn't breathe properly. She put a foot on the rungs. She had to move now, wherever Kate was; she wouldn't last another half-minute.

Ellie shut her eyes and climbed, till finally her head emerged from the gap; she leant out to the side, clear of the smoke, and gulped the cold night air.

"Ellie! Come on. There's no time."

Ernie was right. She could hear things cracking below. Ellie dropped the flare into the loft and pushed her torso up through the hole, clutching the roof-slates and central beam. Ernie gripped her upper arms and steadied her, then helped her climb the rest of the way out. "Everybody just keep going backwards," he called. "I'll tell you if anything's in the way."

As they cleared the surgery roof, timbers cracked and gave way, sending a column of flames and sparks shooting up into the sky.

Straddling the roof-ridge, they dragged themselves along: the slates were too slippery with ice and snow for anything else. There was no way around the chimney pots except to grip the stonework in a clumsy embrace, like an unwilling dancing partner, and shuffle round until you resumed your former position on the other side. They went slowly; better that way.

Ellie didn't dare look left or right yet. She didn't want to see what was waiting at ground level. Or what had become of her village. She could still smell smoke, but couldn't tell if it was from the fire or her own clothes and hair.

"We'll stop at the next roof," called Ernie. "Catch our breath. Watch for the drop behind you."

Ellie craned her neck to see over the rest of the group, and saw why he'd picked the next roof to stop at. One of Hollybeck Row's residents, Stanley Riggott – always a rum turkey – had begun a loft conversion on his home but expanded it into a full third storey, complete with a flat roof. That had been the fruit of a year-long running battle over planning permission, and a good deal of dissatisfaction from his neighbours about the inconvenience, not to mention the appearance of what had been locally dubbed "Riggott's Folly". (The words *Bloody eyesore* had been uttered more than once.)

Ellie had seen their point and struggled to see Stanley Riggott's – why anyone would want their house to look like a flat-topped stone box was beyond her – but tonight she felt deeply grateful for him for giving their little group a much-needed respite. The "drop" Ernie had warned about was only a couple of feet, the flat being only just below the level of a normal roof's apex. She climbed down, then straightened up, wincing as her back protested.

Flames poured upwards from the surgery, where the roof had completely fallen in; Ellie couldn't tell if or how far the fire had spread, but the firelight shone widely enough to illuminate the immediate surroundings, including the roof of Riggott's Folly, and most of Hollybeck Row. The far side of the road was in shadow, and in it those now-familiar shapes crouched motionlessly, watching. Or whatever they did, having no eyes.

Ellie crouched beside the others. "We need to keep as quiet as we can," she said, thinking of how those eyeless heads had swivelled at the softest crunch of her boots in the snow. Her voice was hoarse from the smoke. "Far as I can tell, they hunt by sound. So with any luck, they don't know where we are yet."

No one spoke; the only responses were dull, dispirited nods. Ellie could still hear people screaming, but they were growing fewer and fewer in number, dying out in the night. The fire gnawed and crackled. And in the shadows at the edge of the flames those pale, tattered shapes waited, patiently, for them to die down.

33.

No moon, no stars. The section of Hollybeck Row lit by the fire was an island in a black and teeming sea. Three other fires – one already waning and shrinking down – were the only other objects in that gulf. Ellie tried to guess their positions, but in the total darkness it was hard to be sure.

Other than them she couldn't see a single light, even in the distance: the creatures had obviously knocked the power out somehow, but over how wide an area? As Milly had pointed out, no-one had cleared the North Road that morning; maybe the Becks and Famuyiwas hadn't been last night's only victims, or Barsall the only place under attack.

It could be all over the county. The country. The world, for all she knew.

Ellie took a deep breath; her throat was raw and the cold air made her cough. She covered her mouth to muffle it. For now, it didn't matter what was happening in Matlock, or Manchester, or Mombasa. That could wait till tomorrow. What mattered was surviving the night. Hopefully the things would go when the sun rose: they hated light, after all. But living things were adaptable; maybe they could tolerate it, given time. But if daylight brought a respite, however brief, there'd be time to make better sense of the situation and develop a strategy beyond immediate bare survival, assuming anyone was left alive in Barsall come morning, or indeed anywhere else.

Survive the night. That was what mattered, for now.

The flames sounded like bones being gnawed.

"What now?" said Ernie. "We can't stay here."

He was right. Already the roof was growing hot from underneath. At least the things had cut the gas off as well as the power. Suddenly Ellie was no longer either numb or tired, and sat up straight. "Okay. We need somewhere to hole up till dawn. And light. Or even better, fire."

"Definitely fire," said Milly. "Or if those things don't get us, this lovely little thing called hypothermia will."

Madeleine got to her feet. "What d'you think they did? Knocked out one of the pylons?"

Ernie shrugged. "Sounds about right."

"No heat, no light," said Madeleine. "Just like that. This time of year – long, cold nights. And we're helpless against both enemies. The cold and... them." She turned to Ellie. "Which reminds me."

"Yeah?"

"Like I said, I was going through parish records before – looking for anything that rang a bell with any of this. Found a few things –"

A loud, alarming crack, a muffled bang, and sparks billowed up into the sky. The house beside the surgery had caught fire.

"No offence, Mad, but it's gonna have to wait. We need to move."

"All right. But hang on. Here."

Madeleine lifted her sweater and pulled a wad of papers in a clear plastic wallet from her waistband. "Managed to print this stuff off before I came out. So, anything happens to me –"

"Got it." Ellie stowed the wallet in an inside pocket and zipped her jacket up. She could feel the waves of heat from the flames. "We need heat and light," she said. "Since the power's out, most of the buildings here are liabilities, not assets. We need a big fucking fire that'll stop us freezing and keep those things back. Can't do that inside a house. Suffocate if we tried. Our best chance'll actually be in the open. Build a fire there."

"That'll take time," said Ernie.

"We've got the flares," Charlotte chipped in. "They don't like light. Right? So the flares'll keep them back for a bit."

"For a bit," said Phil.

Julie squeezed his hand. "Just have to hope it's long enough. Where we going then? Holly Beck Woods?"

The edge of the woods lay twenty or so yards beyond the end of the row, a long way in this darkness – and then they'd have to ward the things off with flares and torches building a fire from sodden deadfall. "I'll bet at least one house along here has a fire-pit," said Ellie. "In which case what we need, fuel and everything, we might find a little closer to home."

"How do we find out, though?" said Ernie. "Climb down and check every garden shed?"

"Everything tonight's a gamble." Ellie dug out her phone.

"Still no signal," Milly said. "Checked before."

"It's the time I'm after. Nearly eleven. When's sunrise? 'Bout eight?"

"Yeah."

"Nine hours, then." And while there was darkness, it would be inhabited. Ellie shook her head. Think too far ahead and she'd be paralysed; Tom Graham had always said too much imagination was bad for a copper: he might, for once, actually have had a point. A muffled bang sounded a few houses away. "Head for the end of the row. All still got your flares, right? When I give the word, light them up. But not before."

Milly's eyes were reddened – from the smoke, from mourning Noel however hard she tried not to think of him – but her face was set. "Ready when you are."

Grunting, Ellie climbed up onto the rooftop beside Riggott's Folly, trying not to wonder where Stanley Riggott might be now. Milly dragged herself after her. Grunting and puffing, Charlotte and the Robinsons followed, and then Kate Beck.

"Shit," Kate said, a frightened, wavery edge in her voice: Ellie looked back to see she'd climbed up behind Phil Robinson, but slipped sideways a little. Ernie Stasiolek steadied her and helped right her balance; Kate saw Ellie looking and forced a smile. "It's okay," she said. "I'm okay." She started moving forward; when there was enough space, Ernie climbed up after her.

"All accounted for," he called.

Milly prodded Ellie in the ribs. "Come on, you. Mush."

Ellie laughed weakly, then kept pulling herself along the roof. There was another chimney up ahead, still inside the charmed circle of firelight. For now she focused on that. Beyond the rooftops, the pale things made no sound.

Some found traversing the rooftops easier than others. Madeleine was long-limbed and wiry, monkey-nimble in negotiating the chimneys, while poor Milly, with her short legs, found each one a nightmarish and potentially fatal struggle and Kate had to be helped by those on either side of her to make up for her unusable arm.

Ellie only looked down once: the vague, blurred impression of thin shapes clinging spiderlike to the side of the house below was more than enough to prevent her doing so again. Her thighs and arms already ached; they'd need another break before too long.

She managed, just about, to get around the third chimney and pull herself about halfway along the roof-ridge, then stopped. It wasn't only from tiredness, although that played its part. The firelight, already weak, shone no more than another six feet along the slates ahead of her. And white things moved in the dark beyond, their yellow rat's-teeth bared.

34.

The creatures kept to the shadows as ever, making any head-count chancy at best, but Ellie guessed there were a dozen at least on the rakes and ridges of the roofs ahead. She held up an arm to halt the others. "Two minutes. Catch your breath."

She looked down, and saw more creatures clinging to the walls below her, one even hanging off the guttering. She looked to the other side: it was the same story there. "When I give the word, light the flares – *not* before. Then we carry on, same as we have been. They can last up to an hour, and we've all got spares, so nobody panic or rush. That's more dangerous than anything right now. The light'll keep them back."

There was a muffled explosion behind them; Ellie clutched the ridge for support. The fire flared brighter, and the pale shapes on the next roof scattered from it.

Kate almost lost her balance; Ernie steadied her in time. "Fuck," she said, with her usual clear, cut-glass precision. It made her sound far calmer than she probably was. "Fuck."

"You're all right," said Ernie. "I've got you."

"We need to move," said Phil. "Whole bloody row could go up."

"That would have already happened, if it was going to," said Ernie. "They cut off the gas as well as the lecky, remember?"

Phil nodded, licking his lips. "Yeah. Sorry, guys." Ellie heard the shame in his voice; everybody hoped to be the hero if a crisis came, but feared they'd be the coward, the one whose panic endangered everyone else.

"Phil, mate, it's okay," said Ellie. "We're all freaking out here. Like I said, gives us a bit more light so we won't have to break the flares out just yet – see?"

She gestured round. The light from the burning houses now lit both sides of Hollybeck Row so that it was clear of the creatures – except at the very end, which remained dark. It also lit the houses' extensive back gardens. The house they were crawling along now had a conservatory out back, and a trimmed lawn no doubt used for garden parties in the summer and in the winter for –

"Down there!" Ellie pointed. "Milly, you see what I'm seeing? Ernie?"

"What am I supposed to see? A garden? There's a shed. There's –"

"No!" said Milly. "Ernie, look. Near the shed, on the lawn."

"What is it? Some kind of hole?"

"Firepit," said Ellie. "Sunk in the middle of the lawn. What were we just saying?"

"You think there'll be wood in the shed?"

"Got to be," Ellie said. "Got to be something we can use."

Unless the owners had used up their stocks of fuel, or stopped using the firepit. But it was so much closer than the woods. If – *if* – there were wood and firelighters in the shed, they could keep a fire going till morning.

But what about the house itself, if the fire kept spreading along the row? Ellie tried to gauge the distance between building and pit, which stood near the far end of the lawn, where a row of pines grew. "This place might do it," she said. "All depends what's in that shed."

The glow dimmed; clouds of black smoke were shrouding the flames. The fire must have reached something that burned poorly. The lawn began fading from view, and pale shapes that the light had driven back began edging across the grass.

"So what do we do?" called Julie.

***

The flare hissed into life, spilling smoke and red light. Ellie leant outward, practising the throw: too far and she'd miss the conservatory roof; not far enough and the flare would fall down the rake into the plastic guttering.

She let it drop; it spun, bouncing off the slates. Ellie's breath caught, but it landed inches from the conservatory roof's edge, the red glow pooling around it.

"Okay," Ellie muttered. "Here we go."

She'd no idea whether or not the flare would damage the glass of the roof, or how long she'd have before it did. At the same time, she couldn't rush her next move, or *she* might miss the conservatory roof and land in the back garden, where the things were waiting.

Ellie brought her leg over the ridge, gripping onto it with both hands. She thought she saw smoke escaping from the eaves of the neighbouring house – that was how fires spread along a terrace, from roofspace to roofspace – but couldn't be sure. She let her weight drop, sliding feet-first down towards the conservatory, keeping flat against the rake as she slithered down it. A couple of tiles clipped her cheek. Her boots caught in the guttering, halting her descent. She rocked, almost overbalancing, but thankfully settled flat against the rake again.

The gap between the guttering and the conservatory roof was less than a foot; Ellie stepped down, swaying, then held the flare out over the edge of the conservatory so it illuminated the lawn. The creatures were there, waiting in the shadows. The flare-light licked the firepit's edges, filling its snow-clogged interior with flickering shadows, and reached past it to the shed.

The shed, upon which all our hopes depend…

No easy way to climb down; Ellie couldn't trust the guttering with her full weight. Instead she crouched, then jumped, bending her knees as she hit the ground. The impact shocked through her, but she rolled and came to her feet in an unsteady crouch.

Done it; she'd done it.

Wait.

The flare – where was the flare?

It smouldered in the snow and grass a few feet away. Two pallid spider-shapes scuttled towards her; she snatched up the flare, and they halted.

Behind you; don't forget to check behind you.

Ellie swung round, sweeping the flare in an arc. White shapes crouched all over the lawn, but only the two nearest her, as far as she could tell, had moved. So far. And none, thankfully, barred her path to the shed.

And if the shed's empty, if there's nothing you can use? What then, Ellie? How do you get back to the others?

She wouldn't think about that. They'd work out something.

Or they'll leave you behind. Less risk that way.

"Fuck off," she muttered aloud.

The white things remained still. The two that had advanced towards her had assumed those familiar crouching postures again.

Ellie took a deep breath, then dashed for the shed.

She didn't see or hear the creatures behind her move, but knew they had. Up ahead, those on either side made no move to block her way, but their long fingers splayed outwards through the snow, then curled in tightly, balling into fists. One raised a hand.

Ellie understood, an instant before a projectile launched from behind her flew past her ear. Another struck her shoulder, hard and stinging; she stumbled as a third clipped the back of her head. The creature up ahead of her wound its arm back and threw; the chunk of ice struck her in the shoulder, her hand opened and she dropped the flare. When she dived to grab it, more ice-chunks hit her. One glanced off her cheek;

another skimmed her forehead. Were they going for her eyes? In her peripheral vision, she saw them closing in. She shut her eyes, pawing for the flare.

Loose snow sprayed into her face as she scrabbled. Like dogs digging, they were trying to throw it over the flare, put it out so they could get at her. She pulled another flare from her belt, took off the cap and struck it; it caught, thank God, first time. Brandishing it, Ellie made for the shed, head down and tucked behind her raised left forearm.

The only surprise, really, was that they hadn't tried this before. The terrace was a source of light as it burned; blind as they were, could the creatures differentiate between that and the flare's smaller glow, sensing light only by the pain it caused? Would they be directing their attention towards the roofs now, if they realised Ellie had come from there? If so, Milly and the rest could expect a similar bombardment to this. And they were in the dark already, completely exposed to attack and unable to manoeuvre; if they dropped the flares when they were pelted with ice the pale swarm would be on them in seconds.

Which made finding fuel, here and now, no longer a hope but a necessity. The shed was only feet away; Ellie crashed almost headlong into the door and fumbled at it left-handed, ice-chunks thudding into her back. *Please God, let it be on a catch and not a lock. A catch and not a lock. A catch and not a lock –*

It was a catch; a simple swivelling wooden catch with a hole below it. Ellie pushed the catch, hooked a finger into the hole and pulled the door wide. More ice hit her, but she got in through the door and pulled it shut. And the flare was still burning.

There was a small Perspex window. One of the creatures was gnawing at it, incisors scoring furrows in the plastic. Ellie thrust the flare at it, and it retreated. For now.

How will you get out? How do we get out? How do I get out?

The shed. Check the shed.

Ellie turned, the flare held high, and began to laugh.

The back of the shed was filled with stacked, neatly chopped wood and boxes of firelighters. There was a can of kerosene, too, and a heavy-duty flashlight. Enough for a fire, and an extra light source to boot.

"There's fuel!" she shouted. "We've got fuel –"

The shed lurched as something crashed into it from the side. Wood cracked. The flimsy structure tilted. One of the creatures was trying to tip it over.

The door flew open. Long hands groped inwards, reaching for her. She swept the flare in an arc across their path, and they were snatched back out of sight. A fanged eyeless muzzle lunged into the gap and she jabbed the flare towards it. The prospect of victory had made the creature overconfident: Ellie felt the flare hit something solid and the thing recoiled, almost deafening her with its infantine, bestial scream.

Not done yet, you bastards; still fucking here. But the thin wooden boards were splitting and cracking. The shed wasn't a heavy structure, but if it collapsed the things could blot the light out, pile on and crush her.

Ellie swung the flare from door to window, then thrust it at the thin white fingers squirming between two boards. The joke might be on them if they did bring the shed down; if the kerosene can split and the fuel ignited, the bastards would get a hell of a surprise.

Still won't do you any good, though.

The shed lurched on its base; the walls tilted. Closing in, falling flat. Ellie couldn't hold back a cry, and that seemed to be the signal for the things to rush the shed. They rammed into the side of it and the whole structure tipped sideways. Wood splintered, the far wall toppled towards her and the roof fell in; Ellie tried to stay upright, but her balance went and as the shed collapsed she fell. And the things piled onto the wreckage to claim her.

35.

Their weight was on her; it lessened for an instant, then a second impact smashed into Ellie through the splintered boards, driving breath from her lungs. The bastards were jumping up and down on her.

The flare. Where was the flare? All she could see was darkness. Her right fist was empty. The flare was either extinguished or hidden under debris; it certainly wasn't doing anything to deter the creatures now. Ellie clawed at the ground; the weight crashed down on her again but no long hands clutched her. Of course the creatures weren't attempting to pull aside the wreckage: why risk being exposed to the light if the flare was still lit? To them it was like killing a venomous spider: they wanted her dead but didn't want to touch her. Instead they'd stamp her out.

The weight crashed down on Ellie again: her upper torso this time instead of her lower body. They were working their way up; the next one would land directly on her head. Ellie kicked and thrashed and struggled, grabbing any solid object she could find – a spanner, a hammer, a splintered board – and throwing them aside. Even if she couldn't find the flare, even if she only fought her way into the open to be pulled apart, better that than being stomped to death.

Dimly she heard shouting: the others, up on the roof. Did they realise they were next, that the creatures would be pelting them with missiles once Ellie was dead? Or perhaps the things had already begun; it wouldn't take many of them to finish her now.

But the final skull-crushing blow didn't fall, and then the weight came off her. Ellie kicked and struggled, shoving aside pieces of tar-papered roof and squirming out from under the boards.

"Get back!" someone shouted.

The flare. Where was the flare? Ellie still couldn't see it as she forced her head and shoulders into the open again. Probably trampled out: maybe better if it had, if that can of kerosene had split open. Although even burning would be better than the creatures.

Another flare was burning on the conservatory roof, but the glow was faint, almost extinct. They were supposed to last longer. Perhaps it was a dud. The pale things crept away from Ellie, towards the dimming glow.

"Begone! In the name of the Lord Jesus Christ, I command you!"

Ellie had never thought Madeleine Lowe to be any kind of zealot, but that was definitely the vicar's Wolverhampton accent she could hear, which added a hint of absurdity to the proceedings. *Hell of a time to go all Praise-Jesus and try to exorcise the fuckers, Mad.*

Ellie fumbled in her belt for another flare and twisted off the cap. The creatures had fanned out into a rough semicircle around Madeleine; they'd forgotten Ellie for now. Madeleine held a wooden crucifix ahead of her, her long face pale and determined. Overhead on the roof, red flare-light illuminated the others as they stared down, seemingly paralysed.

Ellie struck the metal cap against her flare. Nothing happened. The second time she got a single spark; the third produced the same again, together with a curl of smoke. *Come the fuck on.*

"In the Name of the Father, and of the Son, and of the Holy Spirit, I command you to be gone." Madeleine was no longer shouting; her voice was low and steady, very level.

For a moment Ellie almost believed. The creatures seemed

to be held at bay, if not on the verge of retreat, by that slight figure and its faith. But at most it had been curiosity, and that curiosity was quickly sated; as Madeleine opened her mouth to speak again, the things rushed forward.

"Oh shit," said Madeleine, and then they were on her.

Ellie struck the cap against the flare again and finally it caught, erupting in a vivid blaze of light as she ran forward. The pale things closest to it recoiled, the ones hunched over Madeleine – she was screaming, Ellie could hear her screaming – twisting round towards this new source of pain. She thought she could see Madeleine, crumpled under the scrawny leprous shapes, and Ellie threw the flare directly at her.

On their third or fourth date, she and Stan gone ten-pin bowling. It had been a good evening. They'd been in love; neither had yet dared use the word, but she'd already known she felt something new and different for him, and later he'd admitted it had been the same for him. So much possibility lay ahead of her, the way he'd looked at her had made her feel beautiful, the belle of the ball, and the cherry atop the sundae, proof positive that she was skilled and brilliant and could achieve whatever she aimed at, had been how that evening she'd bowled ten-strike after ten-strike, knocking every single pin flying almost every time. It had been a good feeling, one long lost to her under a fog of time and grieving and antidepressants, and she'd almost forgotten ever having had it. For the briefest of split-seconds, though, Ellie felt that triumph all over again as the flare landed among the clustered creatures and sent them scattering across the lawn.

Madeleine lay face-down in the snow beside the still-burning flare, blood soaking into the spindrift around her. Flurries of white powder landed on her back. The creatures were flinging snow at the flare, trying to smother it.

Ellie ran forward – towards her friend, towards the light. Beyond that, she had no plan. Missiles glanced off her as she dived, landing beside Madeleine, and clawed for the flare, snatching it up and standing over the vicar, the flare held out ahead of her just as Madeleine had held out the crucifix.

Madeleine moaned in pain, and her legs moved feebly in the snow. Still alive, at least for now. But then the creatures moved to encircle Ellie, cutting her off from both conservatory and shed. Two of them were already plucking at the shed's remains. She'd no idea how intelligent they were, whether they understood how fire was made or if they knew what the smell of kerosene meant. No doubt they'd scatter or destroy anything that could be used against them, if they recognised it as such.

A stalemate for now, but the flare would only burn so long. The creatures were crouching, waiting silently. That was all they had to do. Just as they no doubt had with Tony Harper, only they wouldn't wait for Ellie to die of the cold. And already the flare seemed dimmer.

"Come on!" someone bellowed. Ellie turned to see Ernie Stasiolek jump from the conservatory roof, flare in hand, slashing at the creatures with it. Julie and Phil Robinson careered down the rake of the roof behind him, one after the other; they were both still clambering down when Charlotte Famuyiwa landed on the conservatory, then leapt from it like a dancer to land in a crouch a few feet from Ernie. "Have that, you bastards!" she screamed, laying about her with her flare. "Come get it! Not so fucking hard now, are you?"

The combined glow from the flares now lit most of the lawn, forcing the creatures back. Ernie and Julie ran to the ruined shed; Phil knelt by the firepit, clawing out handfuls of snow.

"Charlotte," Ellie called, ducking as yet another missile flew past her head. "Charlotte! You watch that side. I'll take this one. Keep the fuckers back."

The girl nodded. "Right."

Up on the roof-ridge, Milly and Kate Beck shuffled forward so they were above the conservatory; Milly manoeuvred herself around to face Kate.

Phil ran to join Ernie and Julie. The firepit was now clear. A projectile glanced off Ellie's shoulder; not ice this time, but a piece of wood. Even the fire mightn't save them, she realised; the things could just pelt them with anything that came to hand. But they could have done that before, at the Height – there'd been heavier objects that could have killed and maimed Ellie outright – and hadn't.

Maybe they wanted you alive and whole. Remember what they're wearing.

The fabric swaddling the creatures flapped in the wind. Ellie felt sick.

Kate tossed her flare onto the conservatory roof, and Milly steadied the girl as she awkwardly dismounted the ridge. Then Kate slid clumsily down the rake.

A fragment of brick narrowly missed Ellie's head. Phil and Ernie now crouched beside the firepit, layering wood and firelighters. Julie had run back to the shed, where she'd left a flare burning, stuck in the ground; she came back with two armfuls of wood and the kerosene.

"Here we go," said Phil. Smoke was rising from the nest of split logs, and the first flickers of flame.

"Ernie," Ellie said. He looked up. "Take over from me." She sprinted over to the conservatory, where Milly was trying to climb down from the roof, short legs swinging in the air. "Hang on, Mill. I'm here." She dropped the flare to the ground and helped her friend down. The two of them reached up to assist Kate.

With a loud *whoosh* and a bright orange glow, the fire shot up. It dwindled quickly, but now the flames had taken hold. Julie grinned weakly, and put down the kerosene.

The rain of missiles abated; they couldn't do anything to put the lights out now. Ellie picked her flare back up; then she and Milly helped Kate over to the fire.

36.

They huddled around the fire: with no blankets, it would be all they had tonight to stop them freezing. Ellie eyed the split logs and broken boards Julie had retrieved, hoping they'd last till morning.

"Let's have a look at this." Milly folded up her puffa jacket as a pillow for Madeleine, then peeled off the vicar's torn jacket and sweater. "Oh God."

Surprisingly Madeleine had only sustained one major wound – the rest were scratches – but that single wound was appalling, a deep cut that ran from the nape of her neck to the small of her back, exposing bone.

"Gotta work fast here," Milly said. "Madeleine? Hun? Can you hear me?"

Madeleine made a faint sound; Ellie leant down, their faces almost touching. Madeleine was white with shock, face slack, eyes unfocused. "Mad? How you doing?" Stupid question. "Madeleine?"

Madeleine focused blearily. "Dogs."

Ellie found her hand, squeezed it.

"Madeleine?" said Milly. "Can you hear me, love?"

Madeleine nodded weakly. "She can hear you," Ellie said.

"You've got a bad cut here, sweetheart," said Milly. "It's gonna need cleaning and stitching. Gonna give you something for the pain now, okay?"

"Please do," said Madeleine faintly.

Milly unzipped a bum-bag fastened around her waist. She

always kept one around the surgery, packed with medical supplies in case of emergencies. She injected lignocaine along the length of the wound, then poured spirit on a handful of cotton swabs and began cleaning it. Madeleine groaned faintly; either the lignocaine had deadened what would otherwise have been sheer agony, or she was too weak to scream. Her eyes closed.

Milly didn't look up. "Keep an eye on her, Ell. Anyone else injured?"

"Nothing new," said Kate Beck, wincing as she shifted nearer the fire.

"All good," said Ernie. "Charlotte?"

The girl nodded.

"We're okay," said Phil. He and Julie huddled together, holding hands.

"Ell?"

"Just bruises from those things using me as a fucking trampoline. Anything I can do?"

"Hold Mad steady for me. Don't want any sudden moves when I'm stitching her. And swab away some of the blood so I can see what the fuck I'm doing. Deep wound like this'll need closing in layers."

Madeleine made a faint noise in her throat as Milly pushed a suture back through the skin beside the wound; by the time Milly had finished she'd passed out, which was probably for the best. Milly cut and tied the thread, gave the wound a final swabbing, then taped dressings over it. "Cover her up and keep her warm."

"She be okay?" said Charlotte.

"Fine, love," Milly called. "Touch and go," she whispered to Ellie. "Lost a lot of blood."

Madeleine lifted her head weakly. "Ellie," she whispered.

Ellie leant down. "The fuck were you trying to do there? Commit suicide?"

"Testing theory."

"About what? How to get yourself killed? Congratulations, you nearly managed."

A weak smile. "Had to try. I mean. If those things aren't demons, what are they? Eh?" Her eyes closed, then reopened. "Ellie – notes I gave you. Read them."

"I will. Promise."

"Help you." Madeleine's eyes closed again, and she slept.

Despite her promise, Ellie didn't pull out Madeleine's notes: she felt close to passing out herself. Twice she actually dozed off, waking both times to find her head on Ernie Stasiolek's shoulder, having lolled against him. He didn't seem to even register Ellie's presence: he was looking into the fire, no doubt brooding on Marzena and the kids.

Julie and Phil sat in silence, glad of one another's presence but not wanting to call attention to it while among so many others separated from their loved ones. Charlotte and Kate, with their shared losses, talked together quietly; Milly occupied herself with Madeleine. And what did Ellie have? At least having no significant other meant she wasn't sick with worry about them, although *that* wasn't much of a boast.

She had her job, and... that was it, really. Protect and serve, as the Americans said. And she couldn't do much of *that* just now, other than keep the fire burning till sunrise. Dawn would end this. Hopefully.

Till tomorrow night.

Help would come by then.

It should've come today.

Help would come. It had to.

Over the crackling flames Ellie heard screaming, far away and fading.

Might be the last people in Barsall, except you eight. Maybe seven, soon.

Milly covered Madeleine with the remains of her jacket and

pullover, got up and trudged towards the remains of the shed, which now lay comfortably within the firelight. She rooted among the debris and dragged some plastic sheeting back, draping one piece over Madeleine. "Not much," she said. "But it's something."

Whatever that "something" counted for. Even if Madeleine survived, there was still the coming day to get through until help came. Which it might not. The day would be spent gathering the resources to survive another night in case it didn't. And so on each day after that, till they'd burned all there was to burn and there was nothing left to hold the monsters back.

Ellie shook her head. She of all people couldn't think like that. They were safe for now, comparatively at least. She had a job to do. A duty to perform. Not to any monarch or state, but to whoever remained to depend on her.

"You okay, Ell?" Milly asked.

"Just tired."

Tom Graham might have been on to something when he'd talked about the dangers of imagination. Ellie certainly couldn't afford it now. Too many grey areas, too many blank spots: filling them with speculation only made things worse. She had to focus on what was known, and on the immediate future. Getting through the night. And in the cold light of day – cold in every sense; how many people might have escaped the creatures only to freeze to death? – she could review whatever facts there were and draw what conclusions she could. She'd do whatever she could, whatever she must, for whoever was left. Tomorrow, in the sun.

But for now: survive the night.

"What's on your mind?" Milly said.

"Nothing."

Milly just looked at her. Ellie glanced around. Julie and Phil were wrapped up in one another; Kate Beck's good arm was around Charlotte, who was crying on her shoulder. Ernie Stasiolek glowered at the things in the surrounding darkness, cold rage in his face. What did he see? Did he imagine them taunting him somehow? Maybe his own conscience was, for not going to his family. Without Ernie's help, Ellie doubted they'd have lasted this long. If the others saw him crack up, it would be like tearing a building's foundations away. And they mustn't fall. She lowered her voice to a whisper. "Just occurred to me – you know how we're always saying there's at least one poor sod turns up frozen to death out here, every bloody winter?"

"Like Tony Harper?"

"Yeah. Never wondered how our stats'd compare to the rest of the area."

"Those markings are new, though."

"Yeah. Or very old." Milly frowned, and Ellie shook her head. "Sorry. Trying not to let my imagination run riot. Or to think too far ahead."

"I get that," Milly's eyes filled up. "Trying not to think about Jones. He's out there – or he was, I mean, and...."

Her voice cracked. And what could Ellie say? *Don't worry? I'm sure he's fine?* Only an idiot could offer such platitudes now. There was nothing *to* say; better, sometimes, to recognise that. She took Milly's hand, and squeezed it. Milly squeezed back, trying to smile. Ellie went to hug her, but Milly shook her head. "Don't, Ell. I'll be in fucking bits."

Sparks flew up from the fire. The creatures hung in the shadows. Their cloaks of human skin rustled; Ellie thought of that single precise cut along the length of Madeleine's spine and hoped Kate and Charlotte hadn't drawn the same conclusions.

She thought of looking at her phone; didn't. She was afraid to see how far away first light still was.

"Dogs," said Madeleine faintly.

Milly leant over her. "What's up, love?"

"Dogs." Madeleine looked up at Ellie. "My dogs. I left them. At the Vicarage. Only thought I'd be out for a few minutes."

Ellie squeezed her arm. Madeleine blinked up at her.

"Anything happens. To me I mean. Tomorrow. Can you go there Ellie? Please. Make sure that they're okay. All I've got." Her gaze shifted to Milly. "Sorry."

"What for, love?"

"I know. Noel out there. And me worrying about dogs. Stupid. Sorry."

Milly took Madeleine's hand. "Not stupid at all, love."

"I'll pray for him."

"I'll check," Ellie said. "Promise."

Madeleine's eyes closed. Her lips moved; a prayer, maybe.

The fire crackled. There was no other sound; the screams had stopped. A relief in some ways, but how alone did that silence mean they were?

That suddenly seemed a very abstract concern, though; one Ellie couldn't really care about. Whatever energy had got her through the night so far was gone. She could barely keep her eyes open, let alone move.

She had to stay awake. The creatures might still attack. She couldn't drop her guard. But her eyes wouldn't stay open. So tired. Exhausted. She could rest them for a minute; that couldn't hurt, could it? So Ellie closed her eyes.

PART III
A wrathful moon

21st December
Sunrise: 0818 hrs
Sunset: 1550 hrs
7 hours, 32 minutes and 18 seconds of daylight
Midwinter's Eve: the longest night of the year

37.

Jess wasn't stupid, whatever Mum or Keira reckoned. She'd planned things carefully, and all inside her head. Writing them down might have made it easier, but it'd have been a risk: Paul would be on the prowl in search of new secrets to hold over her, and there was no telling what Keira might do out of pure spite.

Her plan was complicated enough, and vulnerable in a dozen places to the wrong person looking the wrong way at the wrong moment. She mightn't be the fool they thought her, but even when she'd got herself and Baby Joel away from Barrowman Farm she'd have a long way to go in foul conditions; dangerous enough at the best of times. So many things to get past. So many hurdles where she could fall.

By rights, she should leave Baby Joel behind. Going out in the cold like this, it was so easy to meet with an accident, or simply underestimate the cold's deadly, killing strength. A baby would be so vulnerable to that, and would slow her down. Might be safer to leave him: let Paul change his nappies. That almost made Jess laugh, the image of Paul trying not to spew up all over the kitchen while he tried to change a pair of shitty Pampers.

But he wouldn't. Would anybody? Mum? Keira? They'd been talking about giving Joel to *Them* only last night. Might as well drop her child in a crocodile tank. No. He mightn't freeze, but leaving him here'd be far crueller. Better to take the risk.

Jess had a mobile phone – an ancient Nokia, heavy as a half-brick – with an alarm function; she'd stowed it beneath her pillow, directly under her head, so she'd hear it but (hopefully) no-one else would. In the event, she'd been lying awake for over an hour before it began to bleep.

She shut it off immediately. Joel grizzled in his cot; Jess went over and shushed him, then parted the curtains and peeped through the window boards. She saw thin grey light, brightened to a glare by the thick snow in the yard: daybreak, if only just.

Movement from downstairs. Jess stayed at the window, peering out into the yard, listening too for footsteps on the stairs and eyeing the barricaded door.

The back door slammed, and Mum moved across the snow. She passed out of sight, but Jess kept watching and after a few minutes Liz came back, stick in one hand, a trussed lamb kicking under her other arm. So for now, at least, she'd decided against Keira' s plan.

Liz walked off, towards Thursdale. Once she was out of sight, Jess moved.

She'd dressed during the night. Sweater, trousers: plenty of layers. Under the bed were her coat, boots, a woollen bobble-hat, a bag of baby things and a backpack.

A last look at Joel in his crib. Then she moved the chest of drawers and tiptoed onto the landing, to the room at the end.

It wasn't locked. There *was* a lock, but Mum never used it. Everyone understood: that was Mum's office, and you didn't go in.

But now, Jess did.

Inside, on an old kitchen table, stood an old desktop computer, the ledgers where Mum kept the accounts, a few scuffed and battered books, and the Family Bible.

It was a huge thing, dauntingly so; Jess almost changed her mind, at the thought of lugging it all the way to Barsall. But she thought of Paul and Mum and Keira, how she hated them all; and then, most of all, of Joel.

If Joel grew up here, who'd teach her little sweet boy to be a man? At best, Frank. At worst, Paul. Even Jess knew all men weren't like those in her family; Joel certainly wasn't. Not yet. But if he grew up here, they'd poison him.

It had probably been the sharpest insight of her young life; funnily enough, it had led her to consider, at last, that maybe she deserved better too.

They might all be dead up in Barsall, Mum'd said. But they might not. Ellie Cheetham might still be alive, and Dr Emmanuel. She hoped so. Dr Emmanuel was nice, and Ellie was tough. Brave. She'd make sure Baby Joel was safe.

If he and Jess survived the trek.

But first things first. Jess picked up the Bible: its covers were heavy wooden boards with metal corners. Huge and thick; worn gold edging on the pages. She forced it into the backpack; it was a struggle, but in the end it fitted. She zipped the backpack shut, then tiptoed back into her room.

Jess hadn't timed how long Mum had been away from the house yesterday morning, but knew where she was going, so she could guess. Jess had time; she had a chance. She only needed a little luck, if she left now.

She pulled on her boots and laced them tight, then took out the plastic bag. First thing she took out was the baby carrier, fastening it over her sweater. She'd worn it often enough – baby or no, she'd still had chores to do. Then she dressed Joel – a woollen cap, a thick woolly romper – before fastening him in. Next, her coat – she'd deliberately picked one several sizes too big, so she could zip it up to leave only Joel's head exposed, so he could breathe.

When she pulled on the backpack the weight of it all nearly pulled her over, and her crooked back complained. She'd be in agony when – if – *when* – she reached Barsall. But that was for later.

Jess went onto the landing, biting her lip. Mum'd told them to keep watch in shifts through the night, like last time. But come the dawn, they could rest: they'd earned it. No need to go out clearing roads like yesterday – no-one left to clear them for, and no-one left to convince about the stuff from the Family Bible. They all knew now; all believed. They could take it easier today. Save their strength for tonight.

Still, it was a farm and everyone here was used to early rising. Jess crept along the landing – slow, steady, taking care once more to avoid any loose boards. Dom had been sharing the shift with Mum, but even from the landing above Jess could hear him snoring. She padded down the stairs, steadying herself on the banister as the weights on her back and her front fought to pull her off-balance.

When she reached the hallway, she eyed the front door, wishing she could drive. Everyone else, even Dom, had learned while they were still in short trousers, but not her, and there wasn't time to learn now. If she cocked up, she'd be hurt or dead. Joel, too. And her plan to get away would be ruined. No. Better to go on foot.

Dom lay on the couch in the front room, head back. Dead to the world. He might come with her, if Jess asked. Or not. Hard to tell. She couldn't take the risk. *Sorry, bruv.* She tiptoed on down the hall.

The kitchen was empty. Steam still rose from a mug on the table; a pencil-line of smoke hung above the ashtray where Mum hadn't put her fag out properly.

Jess stroked Joel's head. Her little boy, having to breathe that in, along with the damp in the air and the whole rotten stale shitty smell of the place. She was angry suddenly. She remembered the surgery on Hollybeck Row, and Dr Emmanuel. That had smelt clean. She hadn't realised how bad the air here was until she'd come back to it. Clean air was like the boys in her scrapbook. It was lovely, but it wasn't meant for someone like her.

Well, she didn't know about the boys, but she was leaving home at last, telling Mum and the rest to fuck off, and it was a new world anyway, one where anything could happen. But the air was different. Even if she didn't deserve clean air, Joel did.

Dull black metal gleamed on the table. The pistol lay there, beside a full spare magazine and a box of bullets.

She hesitated. How long before they bothered themselves to wonder where useless Jess was, or Mum decided to check the Family Bible again? Jess didn't know. Or how much sooner either of those things might happen if the gun wasn't there.

But if she had the gun, she could stop them taking her back. One way or the other. If she had to.

Could she, though? Shoot at her own family? Her mother, her brothers – even Keira? Or turn the gun on herself so they couldn't take her back? And what about Joel? Would she leave him alone with them, or –?

Jess shook her head. No. It would've been easy to put the gun in her coat pocket, but there was more danger than safety in it, and she was carrying enough extra weight around already.

She opened the back door; it wasn't locked now. Mum wouldn't have bothered: no-one to keep out now, not until dark.

Cold wind blew into her face, and flecks of snow.

Jess stepped outside and eased the door shut behind her. Joel grizzled again as the cold nipped at him. "Hush baba," she said, rocking him. "Hush." The cry building in his tiny throat ebbed away.

Jess followed Mum's tracks through the backyard till she was clear of the farm buildings. They led across the narrowing fields: Mum'd already crossed the big one behind the house and shut the gate behind her, heading over the next. All across Thursdale, towards Barrow Woods.

Jess considered waiting till Mum was out of sight among the trees; one look back and she might see her daughter running away. But Mum wouldn't be at the Hollows long, and might realise Jess was gone the second she walked in. Jess would be walking through heavy snow, and they had tractors to follow her in.

She was insane to try this. She should have grabbed the pistol. But it was too late now. She turned to her right, and crossed the fields towards the copse below Slapelow Hill. By the time she was over the drystone wall and trudging up through the trees her back was throbbing, but she gritted her teeth; with her short legs she was always getting left behind, so walking at a fast clip and pushing on through discomfort were second nature to her.

Tattered incident tape flickered from the trees beside the path; this must be where they'd found Tony. She looked up towards the road, the ledge below the crash barrier. She could see the mark there: one black upright stroke, three to the side.

The bastards had killed her brother. The only one she'd cared about. 'Cept maybe Dom, sort of. *Sorry bruv*, she thought again. Then she turned left, towards the end of the boundary path and the winding, sloping one leading up to the Height.

38.

Even after sheer exhaustion overrode everyone else's fear, till one-by-one sleep claimed them, Milly Emmanuel sat gazing into the fire. Feeding it, too: that was important. It mustn't go out. The dark had to be kept back.

Ellie zonked out first, followed by Charlotte and Kate – the two girls, sisters in grief, spooned together for warmth – and finally Phil and Julie. Ernie Stasiolek, like Milly, stayed awake as the night wore on, only looking up occasionally from the flames, until eventually sleep claimed him. No doubt he saw Marzena and the kids there, just as Milly saw Noel.

She wondered if Ernie believed in God. She'd never seen him at her church, but there were two others in Barsall. Or he might be Catholic, in which case Lord knew where he worshipped.

Well, the Lord *would* know, of course.

If Ernie *did* believe, how well had his faith sustained him tonight? Milly had prayed, of course – what else was there, when you'd done all else you could? – but for the first time in her life, she hadn't felt as though anyone heard. And that had never happened before. She'd always *known* she was seen, accepted and loved – sins, imperfections and all. But tonight, that familiar feeling wasn't there.

She told herself it was shock – she was dazed and numbed from it – and the fear that she'd lost Noel. She didn't want to accept that was possible, wanted to tell herself that God wouldn't allow it, but terrible things happened every day, like

261

Ellie's little boy dying. Because it was, as she'd told Ellie, a fallen world.

Her faith was being tested. That was how she had to think of it. The fallen world was harsh; life was cruel. Faith didn't exempt you from it. Other people had endured the same loss, or worse. So she had to endure, too. Endure. Hope. Believe. And live her faith: do good, and treat others with love.

She told herself that, but a horrible guilty fear nagged her: that she couldn't feel God's presence because it wasn't there to be felt.

Not that the atheists were right – she'd never believe that – but in its way this fear was worse. It was the fear that God was no longer present, because the world had been given over to something else. That either God had turned away and permitted the world, or this part of it, to become the plaything of demons – because what else could those creatures be? – or, worse still, that the power of evil could actually overcome His.

To believe that was blasphemy. Milly didn't believe it; she insisted to herself she didn't. But it was what she feared.

Even so she continued to pray, in hope of answer, through all that terrible, lonely night. To pray, and feed the fire, keeping its light strong. Because only the light kept the monsters back. The cross couldn't: Milly had seen Madeleine try that, and fail. Had her faith been weak? Or had God abandoned or been driven away from them?

She knew what Ellie would say: the creatures, however horrible and unnatural they seemed, were nonetheless things of flesh and blood, in which case a cross and Jesus' name would no more keep them back than they would a hungry wolf. But, by the same token, they could be fought, and killed. For once, Milly hoped Ellie was right and she was wrong.

She didn't know, but for the time being, that didn't matter. She realised that in the darkest watches of the night, when even Ernie was asleep. She looked up and saw the creatures, massed on the lawn. They'd crept close, to very edge of the firelight: shoulder to skeletal shoulder, row on row. Dozens of them, or scores. There might even have been hundreds.

In the morning, in the sun, she'd practice who and what she was on whoever was left alive. She'd see what was to be done, and do it. Till then, she'd protect the people who slept around this fire. Her friends; her neighbours.

So she gazed into the fire and not at the things gathered around it, and she prayed, more uncertain than ever in her life whether those prayers were heard.

From time to time she checked on Madeleine Lowe, but she'd done all her skills and limited resources allowed. The battle was now between Madeleine and shock trauma, blood loss and the cold. If she got through that, her chances were good, barring infection; hopefully the antiseptics Milly had applied would be enough.

"Milly?"

She looked up, blinking; she'd almost fallen asleep. Ernie Stasiolek sat up, rubbing his eyes. He looked at his wristwatch. "You been up all this time? Get your head down. I'll take over."

She almost argued. Earlier she'd half-convinced herself that God would let Noel live if she stayed awake till dawn, but God didn't make bargains. Everything was according to His will. Or if it no longer was, she wouldn't make bargains with whatever had replaced Him.

"Thanks," she told Ernie, and lay down to sleep.

She was the first to wake, in the cold grey morning. The fire was embers now, smouldering and orange.

The bare empty lawn glittered: the snow had melted, then refrozen as ice. But the creatures were gone, at least for now.

The house had burned in the night. She vaguely remembered the heat from it, the stink. But the smoke had poured away, straight up into the air. Small mercies. The windows were blackened, the conservatory a charred skeleton straddling a heap of ashes and melted plastic. The fire had ended there; the last two houses on Hollybeck Row were unburnt, though the windows and doors were smashed in. Milly doubted anyone would be left inside, but there might at least be food or medical supplies.

She stacked two fresh pieces of wood carefully over the embers – they still needed the heat, if not the light – and crawled over to Madeleine, checking her temperature and throat pulse: weak, but steady.

Milly considered waking the others, but decided against it. Let them rest; she'd enjoy the quiet while she could. She'd always liked that. She was usually up well before Noel: she'd sit around the house and read, or slip outside for a walk. Blackfield Park and Holly Beck Woods were always nice. Or had been.

Stiff from the cold and sleeping on the ground, she walked on the spot for a minute and stretched, then made her way into the last-but-one house on the Row. "Hello?" she called, neither expecting nor receiving a reply. She found spots of blood on the living room carpet, beside an overturned mug and a half-dried coffee spill, and murmured a brief prayer for the occupants, wherever they might be now, before turning her attention to practicalities. She collected all the bedding and blankets she could find and stacked them in the kitchen. She also found tea, coffee, sugar, dried milk and – best of all – a hob kettle. Trying the kitchen tap, she was surprised to discover the water still worked. But then, cutting it off wouldn't have been much use to the creatures. If they meant to come back tonight no one in Barsall was likely to live long enough for thirst to be an issue.

Milly brought the blankets outside, draped them over the others, set the kettle among the embers to boil and went back into the house for mugs and teabags. Brewing up at the end of the world. Absurd. But what else could she do?

When she came back, Ellie was sitting up and rubbing her eyes. "Hey."

"Morning, cock. Brew?"

The couple who'd lived in the last house had been regulars at the surgery, both with long-term medical conditions. There was no sign of them, not even blood, but Milly knew they'd have been at home, and wouldn't have stood a chance when the things had smashed their way in.

The husband had had a knee injury that flared up and subsided intermittently; she found the codeine pills he took for the pain and the wheelchair he used to get around when it was bad, both of which would be useful for Madeleine. Best of all, there was a woodburner in the living room, so the group could move inside the house. With the shattered door and windows it was still bitterly cold, but less exposed than the lawn.

Ernie gulped his tea gratefully, then picked up his shotgun. "I have to go."

Milly knew where, of course. "D'you want any of us to come with?"

Ernie shook his head.

"I hope they're okay, love."

Ernie nodded, then went into the hallway and out through the smashed front door.

"What's the plan now, then?" Charlotte asked.

For a moment Ellie seemed off-guard – helpless, lost – but then rallied. "We search the village. Look for survivors. Once we've done that –" She stopped and considered. "Two things," she said at last. "Because as I see it there's two possibilities. One, whatever's happening here's localised, which means there's help out there if we can just get hold of it. Two –"

"We're on our own," said Kate. Charlotte squeezed her hand.

"Yeah. Which means we'll have to look to ourselves. Mainly we're gonna need food and fuel."

"And stuff like this." Charlotte tugged the blanket round her shoulders.

"We won't be short of it," Milly said. "God knows if there's even anyone else left." She had to stop thinking like that. They couldn't be the only ones. There had to be others. Noel. She couldn't even remember the last thing she'd said to him. Something flippant and off-the-cuff, no doubt. Not even *take care*, much less *I love you*.

"Most important thing," said Ellie. "We need to be ready for nightfall. Dunno about you lot, but I'm pretty sure they'll be back."

"Oh, they will," said Kate Beck. "They're nothing if not persistent."

"Right, then." Milly stood. "Better get moving, hadn't we? See who else's made it."

And, she thought – despite her best efforts – who hadn't.

39.

A lamb this time; a little variety couldn't hurt, since she couldn't give *Them* a human offering as originally planned. Ellie bloody Cheetham's doing again, with her bloody interfering; with any luck, at least, *she* wouldn't be a problem anymore.

Liz took the left-hand path through Barrow Woods, stopping occasionally to check on the lamb. It wasn't struggling like the piglet had yesterday, and if it died on her she'd have to trek all the way back to the farm. Although she already wondered if that mightn't be a good idea – bring a few animals this time, to be sure she kept *Them* happy.

But *They*'d have fed well last night, and on their favourite meat; any amount of pork or lamb came a poor second to that. It was what the sacrifice *meant* that mattered: *we remember you, and pay you tribute*. She hoped it'd be enough. Maybe a trip to Barsall was called for – round up a survivor or two. None of them would get through the coming night, anyway: they were food for *Them* whatever happened.

Or if all else failed, there was always Keira's idea from last night. Liz had vetoed it at the time, but if it looked as though *They* wanted more than pig or lamb, the baby would do, if there was no other alternative. Jess was young enough to breed more.

At the Hollows, when she stepped through the gap in the broken embankment, Liz could already see the markings on the pink stone had changed: the second of the vertical lines had been rubbed out, leaving only a blurred black smudge.

Another of the nights had passed. The last day, today: tonight there'd be the Dance. And after that...

Well. After that, they'd see. Hopefully, the family had earned their reward: survival. That was their goal, always.

As she approached the hole the lamb finally stirred, bleating and kicking its trussed legs. Still alive, then. Liz lifted it above her head, said the words, then threw it down, turning away from the sounds that echoed up the shaft.

She smelled cooking bacon as she crossed the backyard, but this time there were no raised voices: a better start to the day than yesterday, at least. Her stomach growled; hearing the lamb being torn apart alive would've put many people off their food, farmers or no, but Liz was tougher than that.

Keira was at the kitchen range, with the rest of the family – bar Jess and her brat – around the table; Paul was in Liz's usual place. Keira managed a grin, but under the bandages on her face she looked sallow and drawn. "Brew and a cob, Liz?"

Liz nodded. "Thanks, lass." Keira had done as well as any of her boys, and better than Jess. Did no harm to show Liz valued that.

A pack of bacon stood open by the stove, more sizzled in the pan. Keira prepared a pair of cobs and handed them to Liz on a sideplate, then tossed some fresh rashers into the fat before refilling the kettle. Liz kicked Paul's ankle. He blinked at her, then got up, scowling, and moved to the side. Liz sat down and bit into a cob. "Everyone sleep well?" she said through bread and meat.

"No," said Paul.

"Good," said Keira. She and Frank laughed; he touched her hand. *Them* or no *Them*, someone'd had their oats last night. Whatever got them through, Liz supposed. She'd not judge them for that.

Dom gave a weak smile and a dull laugh, then looked down at his plate as Keira's gaze shifted towards him.

"No Jess?" Liz asked.

"Still in bed," said Keira. "Shouted up before, but nothing. Sulking, I 'spect."

Liz grunted. Time of month, maybe. She considered chivvying the girl or sending someone up to do it – Keira'd jump at the chance – but decided against it. Jess was worthless at the best of times. Better keeping her out of the way. Some rest would make her what little use she was again.

Liz finished the first bacon cob and began on the second as Keira set a mug of tea beside her. "Here you go," the girl said, and Liz felt a rush of genuine affection for her. The daughter she should have had.

"Ta, love," she said, smiling as a contented flush spread across Keira's sallow cheeks, then waved the cob at her. "Now get us another of these." Couldn't let herself get too soft. She took a gulp of tea, and then another bite, as Keira bustled back to the range.

40.

They left Madeleine, Charlotte and Kate huddled around the woodburner. Madeleine had fallen asleep, Kate's arm was giving her pain and taking care of them took Charlotte's mind off her own losses.

What they were doing now, Ellie guessed, was much the same for Milly. If Noel had been caught outside by the creatures, there'd be no trace of him, no way of knowing how he'd died, or even if – for all they knew, the creatures' victims were dragged away to torment at leisure. Although having seen what they'd done to Madeleine, Ellie doubted anyone would survive their attentions long.

A couple of burned-out houses still smouldered, among them Riggott's Folly, whose unusual construction hadn't spared it from the blaze. The skies, for now, had cleared to a bright duck-egg blue discoloured by smuts of smoke from the remains of fires. And perhaps from some new ones, too. Ellie hoped so: it would mean others had survived.

Milly's Audi lay overturned at the alley entrance, lights and windows shattered, panels battered and crumpled. The car had been almost flattened, the creatures wreaking their full fury on it. There was a sharp smell of petrol.

Other wrecked cars dotted the road or pavement. The unburnt houses on Hollybeck Row looked as empty as the rest, the symbol Madeleine had called *gīml* charcoaled over each empty doorway. "Hello?" called Ellie. "Anyone there? Hello?"

No answer. Nonetheless they went door to door to make

sure, checking the houses in pairs. When they reached Halliwell Way, every house in sight was the same: broken doors and windows, that mark above the lintels. A light wind blew; Ellie hardly felt the chill, but it rattled bits of debris in the street – broken glass, pieces of metal or plastic. The detritus. What remained. The noise was the most desolate thing she'd ever heard, and something teetered in Ellie, as if she was on the edge of a pit. *Might as well give up. What can you do? Everyone's gone. They're all dead. The world's empty. You're all that's left, and that's only till tonight, when those things come back.*

She shook her head.

Milly touched her arm. "Ell?"

Ellie squeezed her friend's hand. "I'm all right, hun. Just..." She gestured around. Milly nodded. She understood: of course she did.

A deep breath. Easy to give in, but Ellie wouldn't. Step back from the pit's edge. Continue. Work. A job to do. "Okay. First step, find out who's left."

The wind rattled the creatures' leavings, like the shaking of dry dead bones. A kind of mockery. *This is all you'll find.*

"Where do we even start?" Phil sounded small and hopeless, almost childlike.

Ellie thought for a second. Practicalities. Better that than the creeping formless dread of what the world had become, and would again tonight. "You and Julie, head that way," she said, pointing up along Blackfield Grove. "See if you can find anyone. Ernie'll be around somewhere." Though God alone knew in what state; Ellie realised she'd been waiting to hear a gunshot ever since he'd gone to look for Marzena and the kids. She hadn't yet, but there were no other sounds from that direction, either: none of the laughter and relief, however weary and muted, you'd expect if he'd found them safe. And there were other, quieter ways to die. "Check the Grove and all around the Park, then Smithy Lane. We'll do the Way and the High Street. Meet up at Church Street."

"And if we *do* find anyone?"

Ellie squinted down Halliwell Way, trying to guess the sources of the smoke. "If they can move, tell them to head for the Assemblies church, or whatever the nearest thing standing is." She looked at Milly. "Do whatever we can to treat people there, yeah?"

Milly nodded and gave a weak, wan smile. "If they can't walk, note down where they are and I'll come find them. If anyone's in a bad way – like they need seeing right now or they'll die – come get me. Yeah?"

Ellie took her phone out, and dialled Julie's. "Might as well give this a try," she said. NO SIGNAL. She sighed, and stuffed it back in her pocket. "Well, goodbye to that idea. Let's get started, then."

It was slow, grim work, going from door to door, calling out and checking each room to find the same spectacle she'd seen yesterday at Wakeman Farm and the *Bell*. But as Ellie turned to leave one devastated kitchen, a faint whimpering came from a cupboard under the sink. Inside it was a little boy, maybe six or seven years old. She picked him up and carried him.

"Where are Mum and Dad?" he asked.

"I don't know, love. We'll find them. Don't worry."

"They told me to hide and keep quiet. Someone was trying to break in."

His voice cracked; Ellie rocked him. "We'll find them, love. We'll find them." What else could she tell him, at least for now? The truth could – would have to – wait.

They found eight survivors along Halliwell Way; given how desolate the village now looked that seemed a vast number until Ellie remembered how tiny a fraction of the population they made up. There were – or had been – over seven hundred souls in Barsall, and only these were left.

Ellie heard their stories as they walked. Four of the survivors were an entire family, the Coopers – Mum, Dad, big brother, little sister – who'd climbed up into their loft conversion, bolted the door and huddled in silence all through the night while the creatures had moved through their house below.

Josh Pidcock, a thirtyish man who lived alone, had been playing computer games in his box room when the power went, and looked out of the window to see the creatures in his garden. When he heard them breaking in he'd bolted the bedroom door and hidden in a corner under blankets; one of the things had smashed the window and crept around the room, stopping only inches away from him before apparently losing interest and crawling back outside. He, too, had managed to remain silent, which had no doubt saved him: Ellie guessed his visitor had been afraid it was wasting its time and missing out on the fun to be had elsewhere.

An elderly couple, John and Victoria Kennard, had surrounded themselves with several Tilley lamps in their kitchen, and sat in barely controlled terror – John Kennard had been convinced his heart was finally about to fail – while a dozen creatures swarmed down their hallway and gathered at the kitchen door, held back only by the light. They hadn't tried to break the lamps, although they could have easily enough, only crouched there for nearly an hour before crawling away. "Maybe we were too old and stringy for 'em," Victoria Kennard said. For all Ellie knew, she was right.

By the time they reached the war memorial, Ellie felt exhausted; there was something uniquely draining about seeing the village she'd made her home so desolate and empty. The blue sky and bright winter sun, after all the storm and snow, only underlined the emptiness. "Quick break?" she said.

Milly nodded. She looked just as weary, and the survivors were in no better shape. She looked up the High Street towards the Assemblies of God building, took a step forward and stopped. "No," she said, and went back to the memorial and sat on one of its concentric steps.

Following her gaze, Ellie saw the Assemblies church was in the same state as the other buildings they'd passed, down to the charcoal sign above the door. Not that Milly could have had any illusions, since last night, about religious symbols having any power over the creatures, but even so Ellie could only imagine the gut punch it must have dealt her. The Trinity that underpinned Milly's life were her faith, her work and – for all she ragged him – Noel: one was almost certainly gone, the other teetering. At least she still had her work, though she wouldn't have much to treat except shock and hypothermia. Madeleine had been lucky; Ellie doubted anyone else the creatures had got hold of last night would have escaped.

Ellie put her arm around Milly's shoulders as her friend cried. One by one, the other survivors sat around the memorial. Tom Graham's X5 had been flung away from the monument and onto its side, half-on and half-off the pavement. The Coopers were looking after the boy from under the sink; the Kennards held hands; Josh Pidcock stared around the village with a lost look on his face, then sat down too.

Milly was crying too hard to speak, face buried in her hands. Ellie could think of nothing to say and hugged her close, looking at what had been Barsall, trying to process it. So many people she'd never see again. They were just – gone.

"Milly?" said a voice.

Ellie yelped in alarm at the sudden noise; it had come from the High Street, along which three figures – one very familiar – were approaching the memorial.

"Milly." Ellie shook her. "Look. Look!"

Milly wiped her eyes and focused on the approaching trio. "Jones?" She jumped to her feet and broke into a run.

Noel and Milly hugged tightly; his companions were Amy and Kevin Lee, who ran the Chinese chippy.

"Hey," Ellie said.

"Hello, Ellie," Amy said, managing a smile. Kevin raised his hand in a silent wave.

"I was bloody lucky," said Noel. "Was round here when it all broke loose." He shook his head. "They were all over the High Street in seconds. Most people didn't stand a chance –" He rubbed his mouth. "I was near enough to the chippy though. Amy and Kevin got me inside. There's a meat locker in the back. Steel door. Shut ourselves in for the duration." He kissed the top of Milly's head, looking around. "Bloody lucky," he said again.

"Jones?" she mumbled into his chest.

"Yes, love?"

"Shut up."

Noel chuckled weakly, met Ellie's eyes and winked. "Yes, love."

41.

As if at a secret signal, more survivors began emerging along the length of the High Street, far more than there'd been along Halliwell Way. Maybe all the store rooms in the shops had helped.

Ellie was relieved to see familiar faces like the Brailsfords, and Laura and Tara Caddick. Laura carried her shotgun over her arm; not much use against the creatures, but it heartened Ellie to see her. Laura was steady and tough; God knew they could use that now. And at least she'd be spared a repetition of the slow grim house-to-house search she'd had to carry out on Halliwell Way.

Several people had fallen and injured themselves in the rush to find a hiding place and one woman, pressed against the woodburner whose light had kept the creatures back for hours, had suffered severe burns. It was enough to keep Milly occupied for a little while. Ellie wasn't as worried for her friend as before given Noel's survival.

They set up an impromptu clinic in the Assemblies church: the creatures had destroyed everything even vaguely technological they could find, smashed Pastor Matt's lectern to splinters and scattered the chairs hither and yon, but otherwise there was no real damage. Matt Williams, too, was among the missing. Had he tried to use his faith as a shield, like Madeleine? Privately, Ellie doubted the thought had even occurred to him, but didn't say so to Milly and never would.

The creatures had left the now-familiar charcoal symbols on

the walls, which Milly pressed a couple of survivors into scrubbing off – hard going with only cold water available, but it was Milly's church, and she wanted all signs of the things removed – as she set about organising her makeshift hospital, rounding up volunteers to act as nurses. Some tended the injured; others combed the village with a shopping list of supplies.

Seeing that small, determined figure about its work, Ellie felt a wave of affection and pride. *That's my friend, that.* She shook her head. *Good job no one knows what a mard-arse you are under it all.* But there was good in the world: remembering that was always important.

Going house-to-house along the High Street looking for any survivors they'd missed, Laura Caddick ran into the Robinsons, Ernie Stasiolek, and the survivors they'd found along Blackfield Grove and Smithy Lane. Ernie trudged on to the church alone, shoulders bowed, eyes hollow and red. Ellie wished to God there was something she could say, or indeed that she believed in God. Sometimes she found the idea of one terrifying and at others comforting; this morning fell decidedly into the second category. Although like Richard's death it raised the question of why this had been allowed to happen. And the only answer was Milly's: *It's a fallen world, Ellie, love. A fallen world.*

Ellie squeezed Ernie's shoulder; a wave of sudden emotion threatened to make her weep, but thankfully passed. She still had work to do. "I'm sorry, mate."

"I got home," said Ernie. "All the doors and windows broken. Those signs everywhere. Maz, the kids..." He gestured, helplessly. "Just gone."

"Ernie, I'm so sorry."

His face crumpled, then straightened with an effort. "Whatever you need, to fight them. You tell me, right?"

Ellie nodded, glancing around the church. "We need to be ready for tonight."

"We'll need a fire, then. Fires, plural. Big ones, to last the night."

"And to keep everyone warm. Safety in numbers." Ellie looked around the church, wondering how many survivors they'd find on Church Street. Which reminded her. "I'll catch you up."

"Where you going?"

"Got a promise to keep."

The houses on Church Street tended to be larger properties, more widely spaced out. One had burned down; nearly all the rest were empty. Ellie found one family of three who'd been lucky and quick, and a woman near-catatonic with shock, worse than Kate Beck had been when Ellie and Bert Annable found her. Ellie tried not to think of Bert.

She put the traumatised woman in the family's care, directed them to the Assemblies church and carried on. Two more empty houses, then there was St Alkmund's and the Vicarage.

Opening the lychgate, Ellie went through the churchyard, trying not to notice how many gravestones had been broken or overturned, or the condition of the church; she wanted to enjoy a few moments' peace and stillness.

She'd married Stan in a church very like St Alkmund's, and on a very similar day, all flawless sky and brilliant sun. A winter wedding: she'd have been happy with a quiet registry office do, but Stan's mother had wanted the full works, and his family had been paying. It had been a good day, anyway, and she'd been happy, even if she'd looked like a bloody meringue in the wedding dress – all frills and lace, what in Hell's name had she been thinking? Richard had already been growing in her, although she hadn't known it then. She always wondered if the flaw in his brain, the ticking time-bomb, had already taken shape as well. It had been a good day, but Richard's death had tainted the memory in retrospect. Like film footage of a laughing child you knew would, seconds later, be blown apart by a landmine.

Ellie sat down on a bench by the path, surprised how tired she suddenly felt. She dry-washed her face, craving another cigarette. Hell of a time to fall off that particular wagon. Should have kept her eyes open in one of the empty houses; might have found a spare packet. Grave-robber thinking, she knew, and she was supposed to be a police officer, but with others rooting through houses in search of medical supplies and gathering anything flammable they could find for the bonfires a packet of B&H was hardly obscene.

Ellie's eyelids drooped; she was in danger of falling asleep here on the bench. Couldn't do that. Mustn't. So much to be done – but the desire to take a moment to herself and just *rest*, however briefly, was near-irresistible. Resist she must, though: everyone in Barsall was in the same boat, and she had a job to do.

Ellie stood up and started towards the church. The windows, of course, had all been shattered, and the heavy main doors torn off: one lay in the grass by the steps. The now familiar *gīml* marking had been etched above the doorway, along with the symbol she'd found beside Tony Harper: *hē*, or *jubilation*.

While Madeleine's faith hadn't stopped the creatures, blind or not they'd had no trouble recognising its temple and taken great pleasure trashing it: there were divots and cracks in the church's stonework where gravestones had been uprooted and smashed against it. Ellie had seen less inviting sights than the building's dim interior, but not many: later she might check it out, but only if time permitted – there was enough work to do already, and only so many hours of daylight. But first she'd keep her promise to Madeleine Lowe.

From the outside, the Vicarage was in a better state than the church, the only damage being the now-familiar pattern of missing doors and windows and the *gīml* marking. Inside, though, the destruction was greater. As Ellie had expected, anything of a vaguely technological nature lay smashed and heaped up in the living room, but also every book the creatures could find downstairs had been torn to pieces. Some were cheap paperbacks, the kind Madeleine devoured, but the majority were religious in tone or related to local history and folklore. If Ellie remembered rightly, though, most of Madeleine's books were in her study.

She searched the ground floor of the Vicarage, calling for the dogs but hearing no response, then went upstairs. On the half-landing where the staircase angled round lay a dark heap: Shona, the big Labrador. The old girl's eyes were open and glazed; Ellie sat beside her and rested her hand on her head, stroking the cold neck and withers. All she could think of was how grey Shona's muzzle was. Madeleine had had the Labrador as long as Ellie could remember, but all the vicar's dogs were rescues. No telling how long it had taken Shona to find a home.

It wasn't right to leave her on the stairs. Ellie gathered Shona up in her arms. She couldn't see any wounds, but the bitch's head lolled with a horrible limpness. A broken neck, most likely: hopefully quick and painless, though there was no saying what the preceding minutes had been like as the creatures had swarmed into the house.

Ellie laid Shona down on the landing; she'd decide what to do about her later. Stupid, really, with so many people gone. But this was the only corpse she'd seen the attackers leave. And whatever you'd seen, there was always something about cruelty to animals.

Ellie called out again, aware she sounded choked. She thought she heard a whimper from Madeleine's study. It did no harm to look.

The study had been devastated. Madeleine's laptop lay in flinders, half-buried beneath a carpet of shredded paper, torn leather binding and broken boards. Had the destruction been inspired by religious hatred, or the fear that something in the room might yield information? She'd have to talk to Madeleine when the vicar was up to the conversation. Then

Ellie remembered the papers in her jacket's inner pocket, and realised she mightn't have to.

There was another faint whimper.

"Hello?" Ellie looked around the room. The ruined shelves, the battered desk. There was an old cupboard in the corner. She put a hand to her baton, just in case, then opened the door.

She jumped back, fumbling for the weapon, as the little Bedlington unleashed a volley of barks at her, crouching with his back arched, head down and teeth bared.

"Reuben?" Ellie took her hand from the baton. "Reuben? Hey, Reuben." He growled, but less fiercely, and Ellie extended her other hand towards him. Maybe he'd recognise her scent, if she didn't stink too badly of smoke. *He likes you*, Madeleine had said, yesterday afternoon and an eternity ago.

Reuben's snarls subsided, either because he recognised Ellie or just realised she wasn't one of the creatures – although from what Madeleine had said the human species in general hadn't given the dog much reason to like them either. He nosed forward, sniffed at Ellie's hand, then licked her fingers. She knelt and petted him.

A white and tan bundle lay in the corner of the cupboard. Ellie leant past Reuben to touch its short, smooth fur and cold pelt, then lifted the small shape out. It was the little Jack Russell: Snappy, Scrappy, whatever he'd been called. His head lolled, like the Labrador's; this time the skull was misshapen too, obviously crushed. Ellie couldn't look at it; it made her feel sick.

She carried the Jack Russell out to the landing and laid him beside Shona on his left side, concealing the worst of the damage to his head. She should go back into the study and look for clues, but couldn't: the weariness she'd felt in the churchyard, the sorrow she'd experienced on finding Shona, they all came back, harder than before, and she sank down at the top of the stairs. She looked at the two dogs. One so big; one so small. *Bastards*. Ellie realised she was crying.

Not just for the dogs, although that was bad enough: for Tom
Graham, and yes, for Thelma too; for Bert Annable; Marzena
Stasiolek and her children; Pastor Matt; Joda and Barbara;
Grant and Sally; Richard, for whom she had no second name.
Maybe her own Richard, too; she'd cried for him often enough
in the past but there were always more to shed. And so many
others.

The Bedlington licked Ellie's face; she put her arm around
him. *He likes you.* She stroked his fur and he nuzzled her; after
a little while, he put his head in her lap and shut his eyes.
"Yeah," she muttered. "You get your head down, little fella.
One of us should."

She still felt choked, but the worst of the crying jag had
passed. Ellie wiped her eyes on her sleeve and breathed out:
she'd kept her promise. She'd have to decide what to do about
Shona and the Jack Russell. The ground was frozen, it would
take time to bury them, and she still had the living to consider
and she'd have to attend to them. But not just yet.

Remembering the printouts, she unzipped her jacket. They'd
been folded in half and pressed flat; smoothing them out and
keeping them smoothed was something of an operation, but
she managed. In her lap, Reuben stirred, then settled again.
Ellie took a deep breath, and began to read.

42.

The owners of the High Street's corner shop – which wasn't on any actual corner, despite the name – were missing, but Plant-Pot and his family had survived and had got to work sourcing whatever supplies Milly needed. The corner shop had stayed in business, even with the Co-Op a couple of doors down, by being a well-stocked general store and contained extensive winter supplies, blankets and hot water bottles in particular: a good job from Milly's point of view, as cold and shock were her biggest enemies just now.

They also yielded camping stoves and hob kettles – a godsend as the Assemblies church's tea urns were electric and therefore useless – and a wide range of beverages, a detail Milly found borderline hilarious: *It's probably the end of the world; do you want tea, coffee, hot chocolate or cup-a-soup? We've got chicken, oxtail, country veg or minestrone. No, I've no fucking idea if the country veg is suitable for vegans. Or gluten-free.*

They'd need proper heating soon, though. And proper, solid hot food. Dried noodles would be the best they could manage for now; the kettles would be melting at this rate. Or, more likely, camping stoves would run out of gas.

Well, one thing at a time. Treat everyone who needed it. Feed and shelter everyone, best she could. Then work out what came next. Talk to Ellie, whenever she showed up again – *let it be soon, Lord, I can use the help.*

"Milly?" Chris Brailsford nudged her. "Thought you might want these."

A packet of John Player Specials and a disposable lighter. "Get thee behind me, Satan," Milly muttered, but took them anyway. "Ta, cock."

She looked around the church. Things seemed on an even keel: half a dozen volunteers were now helping out, and nobody was left waiting in line. She could, Milly decided, allow herself the quickest of breaks.

There were benches all along the High Street, including one almost directly outside the church; Milly sat, peeled the wrapper off the fag packet and stuffed it in her jacket pocket. She'd never been a litterbug and didn't see much point starting now. Again, she nearly laughed: *It's Armageddon, please dispose of your litter carefully.* But the small things mattered, even now. She was who she was, and she'd hold fast to that whatever happened.

She lit a cigarette. Her fingers shook and she was tired: the head-rush from the fag rocked her back on the bench. She smoked for a few minutes, then pinched the cigarette out half-smoked and returned it to the packet. She folded her hands in her lap, bowed her head and tried to pray.

What to ask for? If this *was* the end, it was likely past time for praying. But she shook her head. Again, she'd go on as she always had: if that wasn't good enough for God, it was too late to change it. And she didn't know for sure this *was* the end of the world. There'd been nothing about those creatures in the Book of Revelations, and Madeleine Lowe's cross hadn't protected her against them. For now, at least, she'd act as if the creatures were a natural disaster like a flood or earthquake. Help whomever she could, however she could, and pray: for the strength to get through it, and for mercy on the living and the dead.

So she prayed for those things, then leant back on the bench and relit her half-smoked cigarette. *Finish this, then go back in.*

The High Street was mostly empty. Laura Caddick was smoking outside the church, slouching wearily back against the wall; a man drank from a tin cup on a nearby bench. On another bench, a woman rocked back and forth, face in hands. Milly trod out her cigarette, got up, and started towards her.

"The fuck?" said Laura Caddick.

Milly turned. Laura now stood bolt-upright, leaning forward like a hunting dog and staring towards the war memorial, beyond which a tiny figure – very small, very thin – was tramping determinedly past Ellie Cheetham's house, wrapped in bulky, ill-fitting clothes and carrying a heavy backpack. Under a luridly-coloured bobble-hat was a small white face, taut with pain: Jess Harper.

"The fuck's she doing here?" said Laura, striding forward. The man on the bench got up, too.

Shit. Milly glanced back at the rocking woman; she'd have to wait for now. Milly went across the street at a fast clip, aiming to reach Jess before the others.

"What the fuck do you want?" Laura shouted as Jess reached the memorial. "The fuck do you want here?"

"Whoa, whoa, whoa." Milly broke into a short run. "Take it easy. Jess?"

The girl blinked, then focused on her. "Dr Emmanuel?"

"Easy?" Laura Caddick rounded on Milly. "She's a fucking Harper. They're the ones who –"

"It's Jess Harper," snapped Milly, and as the poor girl staggered closer, face beaded with sweat, she saw how the front of the girl's coat bulged, saw another woollen cap and a hint of pale skin showing and realised she'd brought her child with her. "What the fuck do you think she's been through, living in that house? How the fuck do you think she got that baby? Think she wanted it? That she had a choice? Eh? Who do you think the father is?"

"It wasn't him!" Jess screamed it, and they all stepped back, even Laura. The girl was crying. "It wasn't Paul. It wasn't. It wasn't him."

The anger on Laura's face faltered and faded. Jess was

shivering with cold and exhaustion. God knew what state the baby must be in; Milly prayed the poor mite was still alive. "It's all right, love," she said. "Let's get you seen to."

After a moment, Laura Caddick moved to join them. She plucked at the backpack's strap. "Want me to get that?"

Jess shook her head.

"Okay." Laura took Jess' free arm instead. "Come on, kiddo," she said at last, and the pair of them steered the girl towards the church.

43.

Madeleine's printouts were extracts from the journals of four former vicars of St Alkmund's.

Three mentioned disappearances in the area, particularly outlying homes that had been found unpopulated. Some had simply become unworkable, others abandoned by owners fleeing their debts, but several showed signs of foul play. One minister referred to "pagan and devilish symbols" scrawled on one empty building's wall – Ellie could guess what *they'd* been – while another had collapsed into a sinkhole that had opened underneath it.

So the things had been active before, if never like this.

The fourth set of extracts, more substantial, dated back to the tenure of the Reverend Dr Bayliss, who'd been Barsall's vicar in the early to mid 1860s. He'd been well-educated, with a degree from Oxford; maybe he'd annoyed someone influential to have ended up in Barsall, or maybe it had been his choice. Not everyone was ambitious; some found contentment in other, smaller ways.

Bayliss certainly hadn't lacked energy or drive: he was an enthusiastic preacher who organised practical relief for poorer villagers and patiently taught members of his flock to read or write. He also had a keen interest in folklore and archaeology, especially regarding the roots of Christianity in his parish, and the older religions it had displaced.

A cynic might have wondered if Bayliss' various good works had merely been intended to win the locals' confidence, but whatever the truth, he'd improved numerous lives while gaining material for a series of (sadly mostly unpublished) monographs.

Most of the material was commonplace stuff to a modern reader; nothing Ellie couldn't have found with a five-minute Google search, had the internet been working: folk rituals to find out the boy or girl you'd marry, like eating an apple at midnight on Halloween and looking in a mirror, or sleeping with a sprig of rosemary and a crooked sixpence under your pillow. And the ghost stories, of course: the headless woman who walked at a three-lane-ends between Dronfield and Cold Aston, or the murdered one who appeared by night in a house near Stony Middleton, poking holes in the bread.

But there were the other, darker tales: the little people; the cannibals of the woods near the Dane Valley, or the lost town of Kirk Flockton that had once stood on Fendmoor Heath and had sunk into it overnight "either – depending upon which account one takes heed of – due to tremors of the earth, flooding that made the Heath so marshy and dangerous a place, or due to being claimed by the Devil for the wickedness of its inhabitants". Or that old Derbyshire staple, Hob Hirst – "from *hob of the hirst*", Bayliss wrote, "although it may also derive from the Anglo-Saxon *thurs* or *thyrs*, meaning giant or monster".

Thurs, Ellie noted: *Thursdale?*

"The current Church is not the original", Bayliss noted, "having been built scarce fifty years ago. The original St Alkmund's was on the far side of Barsall Village, where Blackfield Meadow now lies. Thus far I cannot determine the old church's fate, or why it was not rebuilt upon the original site.

"Blackfield Meadow itself will, no doubt, repay further investigation: it is the site of the so-called 'holy well' – as elsewhere in the region, Barsall folk 'dress the well' each year, decking the well or spring in flowers to propitiate its native spirits – or, perhaps, the 'little people' who dwell beneath it. For in the legendry of Derbyshire we find, again and again, tales of hobs and sprites dwelling underground or in deep caves.

"The educated reader will of course be aware that many Christian churches were erected on sites once sacred to older, pagan faiths. Doing so both demonstrated the new faith's superiority to the old, while subsuming the old faith into the new. I believe the old St Alkmund's Church to have been one such case. I believe the name of the farmstead it stands beside – Grove Lea – to refer to one of the pagans' sacred groves.

"More intriguingly, there are hints from certain old tales (I must gain my parishioners' confidence to a higher degree, in order to glean more information!) that Blackfield Meadow may once have been the site of a long barrow. Old Fred Annable showed me a flint arrowhead he'd found in the meadow as a boy. These ancient burial-chambers were sometimes holy sites in themselves, so the location may have been a place of worship from the earliest days of this region's habitation, even before the days of the Druids and their ilk. There may even be a *second* barrow in the vicinity of Slapelow Hill; indeed, there's a coppice in nearby Thursdale called *Barrow Woods*! But Martha Woodthorpe of Barrowman Farm (note also the name of the farmstead!) is a most unsocial and cantankerous sort, unwelcoming even to men of God…"

Blackfield Meadow, Blackfield Park. Which had been teeming with the creatures the night before. And Thursdale, and Barrowman Farm. Not the Harpers – but then, Harper hadn't been Liz's maiden name, had it? From what Ellie had heard, it'd always been the women who ruled the roost at Barrowman Farm. So surnames could change easily from one generation to the next, while the family stayed the same…

"I *must* gain access to Barrow Woods", read what was near enough the final entry in Bayliss' journal, "be it by hook or by crook. I've no doubt there are discoveries of importance to be made".

According to a note Madeleine had appended, the Reverend Dr Bayliss had drowned in a nearby river not long after, or so it had been assumed from belongings found lying on the bank: his body was never recovered.

"Great," muttered Ellie. "Fucking Harpers." She'd hoped, at least, to put off any further dealings with *them* till later (for she'd no doubt they were all still very much alive). But another visit to Barrowman Farm seemed increasingly in order, assuming she could gather enough local support for the attempt.

Ernie might be up for it, she supposed, and Laura Caddick, hopefully Noel as well. Bert Annable would have come too, if he was still alive – but Bert was gone. She could have saved him, but she'd run away.

You'd no choice. You'd never have made it. You had to get back and warn the others. What would have happened if you hadn't been there?

They might have figured it out for themselves; none of them were stupid. If she hadn't come back to the village, Ernie Stasiolek might have been with his family when the lights went out.

And what good would that have done? He'd just have died with Marzena and the kids.

Or found a way to keep them alive –

Ellie shook her head. Reuben stirred, lifting his head and blinking up at her. She ruffled his hair, then stuffed the printouts into her inside pocket. A few new clues, but ultimately little she hadn't known this morning: there were monsters, they'd be back tonight, and the Harpers knew more about them than they were willing to tell.

"Come on," she told Reuben. "Stuff to do."

She wrapped Shona and Snappy-or-Scrappy in a blanket and carried them both downstairs, then found a lead for Reuben.

Almost as an afterthought, she tried Madeleine's landline, her own mobile and her AirWave handset – she'd almost forgotten she was still carrying that – but as she'd expected, there was nothing.

Ellie packed any supplies she thought might be of use – food, blankets, fuel – into an old rucksack she found under the Vicarage stairs, shrugged it onto her back, took Reuben's lead and set off up Church Street again.

44.

At Barrowman Farm the chores had been neglected, for today was unlike any day Liz had known before. *They'd* shown themselves and made themselves known as *They* hadn't in hundreds, even thousands of years.

Things weren't done yet, of course – there was the Dance to come tonight, before the last and greatest changes took place – but the morning sun had already risen on a world utterly unlike yesterday's or any other in living memory. Barsall would be in ruins now. All the pretty-pretty shopfronts smashed; all those who'd looked down their noses on her family, gone.

Well, maybe not *all*. Not *yet*.

She sat at the kitchen table, the last bacon cob eaten, the last cup of tea drunk; no room for another drop nor morsel. Dom huddled in the corner with his precious bloody dogs; Paul snored in a chair at the table's other end – asleep, and it wasn't even midday, the lazy sod. Still, the last two nights had been trying, and tonight wouldn't be any easier. Whatever the family did to ingratiate themselves with *Them*, one slip, one mistake, one moment's lack of attention, and God help them.

Which God wouldn't, because He wasn't there. If He ever had been, His time was past. That smooth little sod Matt Williams, that cow Madeleine Lowe – oh, Liz would've *loved* to have seen *their* faces when they saw what'd come for them. Prayers, crosses and Bibles wouldn't help anyone now. Not the Bibles they had, anyway; only one Bible would help, and it belonged to Liz.

Dom in his corner. Paul asleep at the table. Keira and Frank had slipped off to the front room together – or had Liz (for admittedly she'd dozed a little herself) heard their footsteps creaking up the stairs? Testing the suspension on the bed again, no doubt. Liz chuckled. No harm if they did; might get another baby started. If there was a future for anyone other than *Them*, it belonged to the Harpers now.

Still no sign of Jess, the silly cow. Upstairs feeling sorry for herself, no doubt. She'd always been useless. But Liz didn't mind today. Today was for resting up, to prepare for the final night, which was coming soon enough: today was the solstice, the shortest day and longest night. What better night for the Dance? Let Jess keep to her room, then; it kept the silly chit out of Liz's and everyone else's way.

What time *was* it? Liz consulted her wristwatch and grunted to herself. Past eleven, already. The sun would be down by four o'clock; by half-past at the latest it'd be full dark; sooner if there was more snow and heavy cloud. They'd best be ready.

Not much to do, of course. There shouldn't be anything left to take care of. But best to be certain. Best consult the Bible.

Liz reached for her stick, rose grunting to her feet. Paul blinked at her, half awake, spittle on his lips. She shook her head and waved to indicate there was nothing of concern. His eyes closed again.

She limped down the hall. No Frank and Keira in the front room, so she'd been right about the footsteps on the stairs. No creaking from above; no doubt they'd done whatever they'd had in mind and fallen asleep.

On the top floor, Liz paused for a second outside Jess' bedroom. No sound came from behind the closed door, and the girl normally snored like a pig with her crooked back. The brat wasn't normally so silent either. Maybe it'd died in the night. Might be a blessing if it had. Or not. Even if it turned out as weak as its mother they'd need all the new blood they could get, to inherit whatever earth remained. Or to offer *Them* a sacrifice, if it came to that.

But Liz had more important things to concern herself with now. She went past Jess' room and opened her office door.

Where'd she put the damned Bible? She'd thought it was on her desk, but it wasn't now. Must have put it on a shelf. Or under the desk, perhaps? No, she'd never do anything so stupid – too easy for mice to get at. The Family Bible was far too valuable for that.

Liz gripped the stick tighter. No, she'd no doubt in her mind: she'd left the Family Bible on the desk. And no one in the family – no one – would *dare* go in the office without her say-so. None of them.

Yet someone had. Who, and why? Frank hadn't the brains for a move like that. Keira might – not out of any planned treachery, but in order to know what to do, should anything happen to Liz. But that didn't ring true either: Keira would have asked first, or at least said something to Liz's face. Dom couldn't even fucking read, and Paul had no interest in anything he couldn't fuck. So who did that leave? The dogs?

Liz stepped out onto the landing, drew breath to shout, then stopped.

To her left was Jess' door.

And the room beyond was so unusually silent. Not even a snore, or a baby's cry.

The little bitch couldn't have. She wouldn't dare. But –

Liz threw the door open.

An empty bed, an empty cradle, an empty room.

Liz stood blinking at the sight. She could hear herself breathing, in and out through her nose: a hoarse, ragged sound. Her heart had begun pounding. Palpitations. She leant on her stick to steady herself. A heart attack would be all she needed now. Calm. Calm. But the sight before her didn't change.

Liz turned and stamped across the landing, then down the stairs. If she'd dared – the little bitch. The little bitch.

"Frank! Keira! Paul! All of you, on your fucking feet *now*!"

The bitch, the traitorous little bitch. "Jess!" It came out as a scream. "Jess Harper, show your face fucking *now*!"

But that call, at least, went unanswered.

They searched the farmhouse, but found nothing, and her coat and a rucksack were missing.

"Where could she even fucking go?" Frank demanded.

Keira came back into the kitchen from the backyard. "Where else? Little cunt's run off to Barsall, that's where. Ellie fucking Cheetham and that do-gooding bitch Milly Emmanuel."

"She wouldn't." But Frank didn't sound certain.

"She fucking *did*," said Keira. "I looked outside. She went out the back. Saw her footprints – she went over the fields to the hill road."

Good thinking on Keira's part. This was the daughter Liz should've had.

"What do you wanna do, Liz?" Keira asked. "She's no fucking loss."

"No," said Liz, "but that Family Bible is. I want that back, and before dark." She pulled open one of the kitchen drawers; inside was a police stab vest. Tony had come home with it one night – claimed he'd nicked it from the old station, though more likely he'd bought it off some bloke in the pub while hammered. She put the vest on under her sweater, went to the kitchen table and pulled on her coat, then shoved the target pistol into a pocket and picked up her shotgun. "Tool up," she said. "We're going to Barsall."

45.

When Ellie first got Reuben out of the Vicarage, she had to drag him by his lead, eventually giving up and carrying him. Halfway up Church Street – thankfully, as it was an uphill climb – he began to squirm in her arms, so she set him down and he practically towed her up the slope.

As she plodded down the High Street he kept stopping and tensing; he'd sniff the ground and shy away, no doubt having caught a whiff of the creatures' scent, but as they approached the war memorial Reuben began pulling on the lead, claws scrabbling on the pavement. Charlotte Famuyiwa and Kate Beck were outside the Assemblies church, Charlotte pushing a wheelchair in which a familiar figure huddled.

"Hey," said Ellie. "Madeleine."

Madeleine looked up at her and managed a weak wan smile. She was pale. Sweat on her forehead; shivering. "Ell. Reuben."

The dog pulled forward and set his front paws in her lap; Madeleine stroked his head. "Shona?" she said at last. "Snapper?"

Snapper: *that* had been the Jack Russell's name. Ellie shook her head; Madeleine closed her eyes in pain, then winced as she leant back in her chair, sheer exhaustion in her face. "God almighty," said Ellie. "Get her inside."

Kate nodded to the lead. "Want me to take him?"

"Please. Can you take this too?" Ellie shrugged off the rucksack. "Hope you don't mind, Mad – pillaged your cupboards a bit."

"Pass it here," Madeleine held out her arms. "Meant to suggest it before." She hugged the rucksack to her chest. Her head sank forward and her eyebrows drooped.

Ellie looked up at the girls. "Seen Ernie anywhere?"

"Groveley Meadow, I think," said Charlotte.

Ellie squeezed Madeleine's shoulder. "Take care, mate. I'll catch you up."

Madeleine nodded tiredly. Charlotte wheeled her into the church; Kate followed with the dog. God knew what Milly would say to that, but Ellie wasn't staying to find out. She carried on, now with a lighter faster step, up Halliwell Way.

A footpath led off Halliwell Way just before the bridge across Groveley Beck, which snaked down through the fields from the Holy Well in Blackfield Park. Ellie trudged over Groveley Meadow, which took up most of the space inside the trapezoid formed by Barsall's four main roads – Blackfield Grove, the High Street, Smithy Lane and Halliwell Way

Groveley Farm, standing in one corner of the meadow, had belonged to a cantankerous old sod called Eric Lorne, who'd been constantly threatening to take a pot at hikers and tourists taking the footpath across his land. Ellie had had words with him about that more than once, although looking at the blackened shell of the farmhouse, she doubted she ever would again: it must have been the site of one of the fires they'd seen last night. The burned-out house on Church Street had been another; the third, Ellie guessed was somewhere on Smithy Lane.

Beyond the farmhouse, more or less dead centre in the meadow, was a sprawling heap of wood. People were traipsing over the trodden, muddy grass carrying armfuls of wood and other flammables to add to it, mostly smashed-up furniture; half a dozen others were sorting the heap into smaller, neater piles. Overseeing it all, smoking a cigarette, was Ernie Stasiolek.

"Ernie," Ellie called; he turned and waved, then held out a packet of Lucky Strike as she approached. "Since when?" she said; she'd never seen Ernie smoke.

He shrugged, not meeting her eyes. Ellie realised he'd given up for Maz and the kids. "Thanks," she said quickly, to cover her embarrassment, and took one. He gave her a light; Ellie coughed as the smoke caught the back of her throat.

"You're welcome." A grim half-smile touched Ernie's lips. "Think a lot of us gave up giving up this morning."

This morning: it was nearly afternoon now, and how long till it was dark again? Three hours, four; five at the absolute maximum. Ellie nodded at the woodpiles. "Picked the spot, then?"

"Yeah. Well away from the beck, so it's pretty dry here. Plus the stream-bed's pretty deep. High banks – get very dark down there at night, even with a fire. So I thought we'd best keep clear of it." He drew on his cigarette. "Need to make sure we've got plenty of water," he added, absently. "Bottled, I mean. Don't think I'd trust the stream water for drinking."

Ellie had no idea how much bottled water was left in Barsall, but suspected a shortage of that was the least of their problems. "Think it'll be big enough?"

"I think so. There's sixty, maybe seventy of us left, I heard."

Ninety percent of Barsall's population, wiped out in a single night. And another night to come. "We'll be ready for them this time," Ellie told him.

"If you say so." Ernie looked far from certain. Ellie couldn't say she was either.

"Hey, Ellie." Laura Caddick tramped, a bundle of chair- and table-legs and broken-up furniture panels lashed to her back. "Heard about our visitor?"

"Visitor?" Ellie looked at Ernie, who shrugged.

"The Harper girl."

"Jess?"

Laura nodded. "Gave her a hard time when she first showed

her face. Shouldn't have. Poor little scrap. If half I've heard's true –"

"She's here?"

"Back at the Assemblies. Half-frozen, poor kid, and that little one of hers." Laura accepted a cigarette from Ernie. Ellie couldn't remember if she'd always smoked, or if she was another one who'd started afresh today. "She was asking for you."

"Yeah?"

"Said she had to talk to you. Wouldn't speak to anyone else, even Milly."

The hits just kept rolling on. "Better go and –"

Ellie stopped; Laura and Ernie had frozen too, looking up and past her. The same stillness spread across the field, the men and women who'd been gathering wood growing motionless and silent. And in that stillness, the noise they'd heard grew louder: a distant sound of engines.

46.

Jess never slept deep, never had, even before Paul had done what he had. There was never any telling, in their house, when there might be shouting, sounds of violence – that, or Mum kicking down the bedroom door and dragging Jess out of bed for fucking up this or that household chore. No wonder she was always tired.

When she'd got to the village, she'd been close to falling down and near-frozen, unable to even feel her fingers. She'd been scared at first, too, when Mrs Caddick came marching out to meet her: Jess knew her by sight, knew she hated all Harpers and why. She'd shrunk from the look on Mrs Caddick's face. But then Dr Emmanuel had been there, and she'd said something and Jess had seen Mrs Caddick's expression change. Seen the pity in it. Better than being hated, anyway.

The pair of them had marched her into the church, through the huddled, shivering, wild-eyed survivors, to a corner at the back. Away from the rest. She wasn't one of them, never would be. But at least she'd be left alone.

"Let's get that off you." Dr Emmanuel had helped Jess free of the rucksack. "Fuck me sideways. Weighs a ton. The fuck you got in here?"

She swore nearly as much as Keira, but it wasn't the same. Keira's words were sharp as glass, hard as rock or pebble, and she flung them at people – Jess especially – like things meant to hit and hurt. Dr Emmanuel's had no cruelty or spite in them. They were like the bits of coloured paper people threw at the weddings Jess'd seen in films. Keira's swearing made her flinch and shrink; this just made her smile. "Bible," she said.

"Bible?"

"Family Bible." Jess took the doctor's arm. "Got to show Ellie. She needs to see it. It'll help." If anything could.

"All right. Settle down." Dr Emmanuel wrapped blankets round her. "Joel," said Jess, realising that at some point the child had been taken from her. "Baby Joel –"

"He's fine, love." Dr Emmanuel stroked her hair. "You kept him good and warm. We're looking after him. You need to look after yourself right now."

He was okay. Dr Emmanuel said he was okay. Someone came over, handed Dr Emmanuel something. A mug. "Here, love. Get this down your neck."

Tea. Hot. Sweet. Scalding. "Dr Emmanuel."

"Told you before, love, it's Milly."

"Milly."

"Yeah?"

"The Bible," Jess said again.

"I heard you, sweetheart. I'll show her, soon as I see her face."

"Okay."

Someone had called out; Dr Emmanuel – Milly – looked round and grimaced. "Duty calls," she muttered. "Tara?"

A young girl came over: about Jess' age, give or take. A bit taller, but nearly as thin. A different thinness, though: lean, wiry, tough. She looked familiar, somehow. What was it about her face?

"Just keep an eye on her for me, okay?" said Milly. "Any changes, give us a shout."

"Will do." The girl looked at Jess, face unreadable. That face – it looked like –

"Cheers, Tara." Milly got up. "See you in a bit, Jess, love."

Tara; the second time she heard the name, Jess made the connection. The face was like Mrs Caddick's – younger, softer, but this was still Laura Caddick's girl, looking at Jess with no expression and eyes she couldn't read. What was Jess supposed to say? *I'm sorry? I know what it's like; it happened to me too?*

In the end, she said nothing, and it turned out she didn't need to. "You'll be all right," Tara Caddick said. "Get your head down. I'll keep an eye out. No one's gonna hurt you."

"Thanks," Jess whispered, wanting to cry. Mum'd drummed into her over the years how everyone outside the family hated every Harper. *We're all scum to them, cos of who we are. All you've got's your family, Jess Harper, and don't you forget it. All them out there, they'd knife you soon's look at you.* But not everyone did. Jess supposed, as she closed her eyes, that it could be all a trick, that Tara would slit her throat as she slept, but she didn't believe that, not really. She was too tired to stay awake, anyway. She closed her eyes and settled herself as best her crooked back would let her. Her lips moved as she tried to pray, to any god that might listen to the likes of her, that she wouldn't dream.

She didn't, but she didn't sleep long either. She blinked awake in her cocoon of blankets to the sound of engines. Voices, too. People in the church. Muttering: puzzled, hopeful, worried.

The engines were getting nearer, and one had a particular coughing note Jess knew very well.

Liz put the tractor in neutral and killed the motor. Villagers stood gawping in the street outside the Assemblies church, which was in the same state as everywhere else – trashed, ransacked, the Sign marked above the door. All the God-bothering shit proven worthless: when *They* came in the night, Jesus and prayers did nothing.

Liz climbed down from the cab, reached back in and took the shotgun from under her seat. Keira got down too, unslung her rifle and slipped off the safety, nearly panting with excitement.

There'd been, Liz reckoned, one last shred of unbelief left in the girl, right up until the ride up to Barsall. Then she'd seen the pigs' Landy at the Height, flipped over on its back, battered and crumpled like tinfoil, glass everywhere. And the gap in the ranks of marching pylons on Fendmoor, the wires hanging limply down to the fallen one's wreckage. Keira had whooped then, in pure glee; even Liz'd had to smile at that. Girl must feel like the queen of all the world today.

Behind them, the second tractor halted with a squeak of brakes. Its engine cut out, too, and there was silence.

Noel Jones had run to the upstairs office as soon as he'd heard the tractors, rifle bouncing against his back. Army training: take the high ground. Mightn't be trouble, but you never assumed: assumption was the mother of all fuck-ups. Ellie's old sergeant used to say that, she'd told him. So had Noel's.

He'd not been in the army long. He'd been young enough that it'd seemed a good idea at the time, but old enough to soon realise what kind of man he'd become, and to know he didn't want that.

He'd been considered one of the bright ones. Comms and IT had been his forte; he'd taken that training back into civvy street and built the business he now ran from home. But he'd always been good with a rifle, too: best shot in the company, the colour-sergeant had crowed, maybe even the regiment. Not something he was particularly proud of, but it had its uses out here, if you were after some small game for the pot.

Noel had never taken a human life; he'd come under fire once in his Army days, but that was all. Most of the time he'd been well away from the main action, and he thanked his Methodist-Chapel God for that. But he still had the training, and the skill.

He recognised the battered tractors the second he saw them, even before Liz Harper clambered down. He opened the office window, swept the papers off a small side-table and picked it up; exactly what he needed.

***

The people of Barsall: look at them now. Stuck-up bastards who'd treated Liz and hers like shit, with their nice clothes all dirty and torn. Wild hair and grey faces. No hot-water showers for any of these this morning. No expensive moisturiser for the ladies or muesli for the men. They'd slept little and badly, woken rough and cold and shaking into a new world where they just didn't *matter* anymore. Now they looked at her family with fear instead of contempt – fear, and, finally, at long fucking last, respect.

"We're looking for my daughter," Liz said. "She stole something of ours. We want it back." *It*, not *her*; she emphasised that for Keira's benefit: all that mattered was getting back what'd been stolen. There was no coming back from what Jess had done. The girl was nothing now except a traitor to be punished – and who better to carry that sentence out than the one true daughter of Barrowman Farm? But first, the Bible.

"We know she's come this way," Liz said. "Saw her footprints in the snow. So where is she?"

Everyone just stared at them, not answering. "Oi," Keira shouted, "dickheads. You were asked a fucking question. Where is she?"

Someone shifted their weight from one foot to the other, but no one spoke.

Jess sat up. They'd come after her, or rather after the Bible. The Bible, and maybe Joel, to raise themselves or feed to *Them*. As for Jess herself, Keira'd be straining at the fucking leash to finally get rid, and Mum might let her now. Probably give Joel to Frank and Keira to raise, if they let him live.

That thought made Jess shake with rage. She wriggled out of the blankets, unsteady on her feet.

"Whoa." Tara stood, reaching out. "Take it easy."

"It's them. They've come after me."

No, not her. The Bible. The Bible and Joel.

Outside, she heard Keira's voice, harsh and grating.

"Same old shit," Keira said. "None of these'll give us the steam off their piss. They think they're better." Her grin widened, savage and hot. "Don't worry, Momma Bear. I've got this."

Keira stepped forward and looked from face to face, till she reached Sally Cupit, the barmaid from the Grove Inn. Liz seemed to remember she'd got Keira barred from there. "Right, then," Keira said, then brought the rifle to her shoulder and fired. Didn't even need to aim at that range; she was the best shot at Barrowman Farm. Sally Cupit's permed hair flapped as if in a gust of wind; a fine red spray blew out behind her; solid matter fell to the road surface with wet slaps; and she dropped, like a coat falling off a hanger. She flopped onto her back, mouth open and one eye missing, the other staring up. Keira worked the bolt. Click, clack. An empty cartridge clinked on the ground. She shoved the bolt forward again. Another bullet chambered.

Even Liz hadn't expected that. But this was a new world, with new rules, and they were its masters: so, why not? They could do as they pleased now, especially to get what was theirs.

Grinning, Keira shouldered the gun again. "Next!" she called.

47.

Ellie heard the shot as they reached the bridge over Groveley Beck and broke into a sprint down Halliwell Way, Laura and Ernie keeping pace as she unslung the shotgun and held the weapon across her chest. She skidded on ice, yelping in shock, but kept her balance and pelted on. The safety catch was still on – be all she needed to fall and blow her own face off – but her thumb was on it, ready to flick it off. She'd need the gun ready to fire any second, because there were no prizes for guessing who this was. Bastard Harpers; of course they'd survived. They knew what this was, or at least more than the rest of them did.

Noel heard the shot as he reached the window. *Christ!* He ran to look but the deed was done; Sally Cupit lay in the High Street, blood pooling around her head. Even Liz Harper looked shocked. He heard a rifle bolt being worked, crisp and clear in the cold shocked air, then Keira Lucas' voice.

But he couldn't see her, only the barrel of the rifle; the tractor's snowplough was in the way.

Noel set down the table, then dragged up a chair. He sat, resting his elbows and upper body on the table top. Didn't even need to poke the barrel out of the window; he could get them in his sights from here –

Or at least he could get Liz: telescopic sight or no, Keira was still shielded by the snowplough's blade.

***

"Hide the book," Jess told Tara. She felt calm now. It was Joel, that was part of it, but it wasn't just about love: it was hatred too. They'd treated her like shit for so long, like she was worthless. Now she'd pay them back. "The Bible. Don't let 'em find it. Or my baby. Tell 'em I took 'em with me."

"What do you mean?"

"There's a back door, right?"

Tara nodded.

"Show us."

Keira moved the rifle barrel from face to face. Smoke still trickled from the muzzle and breech, clear and sulphur-sharp in the clear winter air. She was still grinning, and Liz heard her murmur: "Eeny, meeny, miney..."

"She's in there," said one of the shopkeepers from the High Street, pointing to the Assemblies church. His face was the colour of cottage cheese, which was no surprise to Liz; he'd barred Keira from his shop too.

"Paul," said Liz. "Frank."

But as the boys sprinted towards the church, other running footsteps sounded, coming down the street. Liz looked past the crowd to see Ellie Cheetham running towards them, the Caddick bitch and Ernie Stasiolek beside her. Keira was already aiming the rifle as Liz raised the shotgun to fire.

There was a garden behind the Assemblies church, with weeping willows, rockery, benches and a pond. Jess had sat out here on a couple of occasions when she'd been allowed to come to Barsall with the rest of the family and been able to slip away. It was a pretty place, even in winter.

She'd prayed here, which was, according to Pastor Matt, what the place was for: prayer, meditation, guidance. She'd tried that when she was carrying Baby Joel, but if God'd had any answers, they'd been too quiet for her to hear.

She crossed the garden now at a fast clip, to the wrought-iron gate at the far end. Thankfully, it wasn't locked: just a bolt you pulled back. Jess slipped out, shut the gate behind her and shot the bolt back into place. Maybe they wouldn't realise she'd come this way.

Except they would, of course. Where else could she have gone? But that wasn't the point: the point was to give Baby Joel a chance – the Bible, too, to keep that away from them, but Baby Joel most of all.

Jess heard gunfire.

Noel saw Paul and Frank Harper run to the church's front door and heard it crash open; there were shouts from downstairs. *Milly*. Should he move, go and deal with that threat? But now Ellie ran into view, Laura and Ernie behind her. She dived, they all did, and the rifle fired again.

Liz Harper opened fire with her shotgun, then ducked back, cursing, as Laura Caddick fired back at her. She ducked behind the snowplough, but was on the side exposed to Noel.

"Everybody down," Ellie shouted, and dived for the tarmac; she landed hard and lost her grip on the shotgun. Heard the gunshot a second later, although the bullet'd probably passed over her already.

Keira worked the rifle's bolt. Ellie reached for the shotgun, but the deer rifle was already pointing at her. Behind the telescopic sight, Keira's sticking-plastered face grinned. It had been her trying to kill Ellie at Barrowman Farm yesterday; course it had. Would've succeeded too if not for Bert Annable, but Bert was gone and at this range Keira could hardly miss.

Liz Harper's shotgun boomed, three times, fast: the cut-down one with the big magazine she'd had yesterday at the farm. *Should've taken it with you, Ellie, not left her with that kind of firepower*. But it wasn't Liz about to kill her now. Ellie hawked and spat at Keira, even though she knew it'd never reach her.

A rifle fired, a single whiplash crack.

48.

Noel had been about to shift the rifle's crosshairs onto Liz Harper – he could deal with her at least – but then Keira had moved forward. Not much: he still couldn't see her properly, but the gun was fully visible, and at that range, with this rifle, Noel could hit that easily enough. He sighted on the wooden forestock, and squeezed the trigger.

Wood splintered; Keira's gun flew out of her grip and clattered across the road. She fell, face bloody, clutching her eye and screaming. Noel pulled back the bolt, but Liz spun and fired up at the window. Glass and splinters. He ducked, then straightened, pushing the bolt forward and looking through the sight again, glimpsing Liz run towards the building, disappearing out of view under his window.

He'd have to lean out to get her, and she'd take his head off before he could fire. He could hear the shouts and cries from the church below. Liz could be in there now, and if she wasn't her boys were.

Milly.

Noel ran for the stairs. Out in the street, shotguns boomed.

Liz had fired first at Ellie, then at Ernie and Laura; now she aimed at Ellie again, but as she did the brickwork by her head exploded into dust as Laura squeezed off a shot. Liz whirled towards the new threat and Ellie raised her shotgun. Liz saw her and hesitated for a second, and that was all it took. Ernie

310

fired both barrels of his gun, and Laura Caddick emptied her own weapon, pumping the slide fast as she could. Liz's tatty coat exploded into blood and scraps; she slammed back against the church wall and slid down, painting it red.

Ernie broke open his shotgun to reload; Laura stood, slotting fresh cartridges into her weapon. The three of them started towards the church.

As Laura and Ernie reached the door Ellie heard a boot scuff tarmac and spun. Keira Lucas was aiming a shotgun – sawn-off, barrels cut practically to stubs – across the snowplough at her. Her teeth were bared; one eye was a bloody ragged wound, the other wild with hate. Ellie dived again, landing on her side as the first barrel discharged. She pulled her own gun's trigger in reply, and Keira recoiled behind the snowplough again, sparks flying from blade and bodywork where pellets hit.

"Ellie?" Ernie yelled. "Are you –"

"Get after Paul and Frank," she shouted back. From the ground she could see under the tractor. She saw Keira's legs: the girl was moving towards the back of the vehicle. Circling around, towards the church.

The church, and Liz. Liz and her guns.

Ellie moved to intercept her; as Ernie and Laura vanished inside the church, Keira came round the back of the tractor and ran towards Liz.

Noel reached the last flight of stairs to see Laura Caddick and Ernie Stasiolek coming past. Ernie looked up and nodded in his direction. The pair of them were moving slowly, spreading out. Noel reached the foot of the stairs, then peered round the corner.

Paul and Frank Harper were edging back towards the kitchen at the rear of the church; Paul held Tara Caddick against him by the throat, as a shield. Laura was silent, jaw clenched.

The rifle was cocked and loaded; Noel aimed around the corner, sighting on Paul's head.

Ellie raised the shotgun, but ducked back as Keira fired the sawn-off's second barrel at her. Ellie swung back round to take aim, but Keira was kneeling, grinning, by Liz, the big Ithaca pump-action cradled in her hands.

Keira's grin became a laugh, and she pulled the trigger, but the shotgun only clicked. She screamed in rage, pulled the slide back – an empty cartridge spun out – and shoved it forward, then, before Ellie could fully raise her own gun, pulled the trigger again.

Ellie leapt back behind the snowplough as the Ithaca boomed, shot spattering the bodywork. She poked her gun around the side of the tractor and fired back, but only heard the crack of pellets smacking into the wall. Keira racked the Ithaca's slide, fired, racked the slide again.

Ellie kept still, waiting. Over the whining in her ears she heard Keira wheezing and panting, the sounds of objects clattering on the ground. *Reloading.*

Ellie never knew what made her move, but she broke left, around the far side of the tractor, in the same second Keira fired under the vehicle. Shot clattered off the tarmac and something hit Ellie's right ankle; she stumbled, almost lost her balance, but managed to stay on her feet.

She heard the shotgun being racked again; another blast was coming. Ellie jumped for the cab. The Ithaca boomed; another blast sprayed under the tractor. Ellie pulled herself into the cab and saw Keira and her bloody one-eyed face crouched beside Liz. She screamed something at Ellie, pumped the slide, and fired again.

Noel must have moved a little too suddenly, because Paul Harper saw him with the rifle and pulled Tara up onto tiptoes, hunching down so Noel couldn't get a clear shot.

"Stop fannying around and come on!" Frank called. Paul back-pedalled towards the kitchen; when he reached the door, he shoved Tara forward and ran after his brother.

Laura sprinted forward, shouting her daughter's name. Ernie charged for the kitchen, shotgun in his hands. Noel slipped the rifle's safety catch back on and followed.

Laura knelt by her daughter. "Sweetheart?"

"I'm okay, Mum. I'm okay." There were gunshots from the back of the building. "Jess," said Tara.

Laura nodded and stood. Noel followed her through the kitchen, in time to see the Harper brothers vanish through the gate at the end of the garden. Ernie reloaded his shotgun, snapped the barrels closed and nodded to Noel. Laura brushed past him, cutting through the garden. Once again, Noel followed.

Ellie flung herself forward across the seats. Glass exploded around her, raining down; something flicked the fur hat from her head. *Fire back. Fire fucking back.* She thrust her own gun forward two-handed: a clumsy grip, a wild shot. She pulled the trigger as Keira pumped the slide.

The blast hit Keira in the chest, knocking her back into the wall. The Ithaca clattered away; Keira slid down, coughing bloody froth from wounded lungs.

Ellie clambered through the cab and dropped back down onto the road. Keira wheezed and fought for air, face darkening, pawing at her chest and stomach. Breathlessness, Ellie thought – but then Keira's hand reached her waistband and pulled a pistol out.

Ellie fell sideways to one knee, racking her slide. The pistol fired, and something plucked the shoulder of her jacket. The pistol arced towards her; she racked her weapon's slide and pulled the trigger again. The side of Keira's face burst and splattered up the wall; the pistol in her hand fired wild, bullets spanging off tarmac and bodywork.

Keira fell sideways. Bubbling, wheezing sounds came from her: she was still breathing. As Ellie moved towards her, she grunted and tried to raise the pistol, but couldn't get it more than an inch off the ground. Not that it would have helped if she had: the bolt was locked back, the gun empty.

A last breath rattled in her throat; blood bubbled on Keira's lips. Her eye stopped blinking and grew fixed. She was still.

Her shattered skull steamed. Red and white and pinkish grey: blood and bone and brain.

Ellie gagged but fought it down. She wouldn't vomit on a corpse, even this one. For all the times she'd thought of smashing Keira's face in, she felt no triumph.

Ellie pulled the pistol from Keira's hand. Beside the dead woman, Liz Harper lay slumped against the wall, eyes closed; her mouth hung open, as if to bellow in outrage at her fate.

"What can I tell you, girls?" Ellie said aloud. "Things are tough all over."

She was starting to shake. A packet of tailor-mades, somehow undamaged, stuck out of Liz's pocket. Ellie took it. *To the victor the spoils.* She sank down on the church's step, put a cigarette in her mouth, then realised she hadn't got a light and began to laugh and cry all at once.

"Love." Milly put an arm around Ellie's shoulders, then lit her cigarette with a plastic lighter. "Here."

Ellie leant against her friend. The street stirred back into life and the living emerged, to gather round the dead.

49.

Jess backed away from the gate, then turned around.

There wasn't much to see. More fields, white with snow, canted down the side of Slapelow Hill, towards Fendmoor. The pylons stood straight against the white ground and blue sky, except the one that lay in a tangle of buckled steel. All open ground nowhere to hide.

Jess ran along the path behind the houses. The yards and gardens were fenced and gated, to keep animals out. None of the gates budged when she rattled them.

Noise and shouting came from the direction of the church. Jess had to find somewhere, quickly. If Keira or Mum were behind her, they'd shoot her in the back without thinking twice. Keira would jump at the chance. Frank might hesitate, though in the end he'd do as Mum told him: he'd stuck up for her when they were younger but hadn't done for years, not even against Paul. Only Tony had done that. Dom'd tried a few times, only to get bitch-slapped till he cried, so he didn't bother any more.

Her vision was blurred as she fought for breath. She no longer bothered trying the gates. Most of them were solid wood; she just struck at them as she blundered past. None budged.

Paul wouldn't kill her if he could help it. He'd want her alive, for one last bit of fun before the end. That thought gave Jess extra impetus, pushing her faster and further than she'd thought herself capable of, especially after the morning's exertions.

Passing a particularly high stone wall topped with broken glass, she slapped weakly at the heavy wooden gate. By now she was so exhausted she didn't even realise it had swung open till she staggered past.

Jess halted and stumbled back to the gate; it yawned open to show a littered back yard and a house with shattered windows. The back doorway lay open, a black charcoal mark above it. Jess shoved the gate closed behind her, but the bolt was gone: *They* must have smashed the gate open to get at the house, rather than climb the glass-topped walls.

Jess ran to the back doorway and through the kitchen. Her back was agony; she could hardly breathe.

The brothers ran behind the houses, and Ernie and Laura went out after them. Mistake, thought Noel; they could have fired on the bastards from the cover of the garden entrance. He could provide covering fire from there, at least; his rifle easily had the range.

Ernie fired at the brothers; Paul fired back with his rifle and Laura dived to the ground. Ernie cursed, ducked down and fired his twelve-bore's second barrel in response. The brothers disappeared through a back gate up ahead; as Ernie broke the shotgun open to reload, a gun barrel poked out into view.

"Ernie! Get down!" Noel shouted.

A shotgun boomed twice; Ernie fell with a cry. Noel ducked back inside the garden's entryway as pellets smacked into the stonework, then peered out again as the shotgun boomed a third time, to see snow explode from the ground inches from Laura Caddick.

Ernie lay curled up on the path, groaning. Blood on the snow. Up ahead, a bulky figure, a baseball cap on its bald head, was aiming around a wooden gatepost.

As Laura fired back with her shotgun, Noel moved out onto the path and lay down in the snow, tucking the rifle stock into his shoulder and adjusting the sight until a pink blur resolved itself into Frank Harper's face. Frank's shotgun flashed and boomed; shot whistled over Noel's head. Laura fired again and Frank let off a wild blast that tore up another strip of snow, then pulled back out of view.

Laura went forward in a low, crouching run. As Noel got the gateway into sharp focus, Frank leant back out, raising the shotgun.

A headshot would be more certain, but that was a smaller target, easier to miss. Noel shifted the crosshairs to the centre of Frank Harper's chest, crooked his finger around the trigger and squeezed.

The rifle drove back against his shoulder; the crack of the shot rang and echoed down the flank of Slapelow Hill and out across Fendmoor. Frank Harper was driven back against the post behind him. There was no pain on his face, only confusion and surprise. He stood up straight, stepping out of the gateway, then dropped his shotgun, fell face-down in the snow and began crawling painfully across the path.

Noel worked the rifle bolt on a kind of autopilot, his body seemingly divorced from the rest of him. His fingers shook. Laura ran to the gate, jumping over Frank, and was lost to view.

Noel knelt by Ernie. The tall man was grimacing in pain, clutching his left thigh, but seemed otherwise uninjured. "I'm all right," he said. "I'm all right." He nodded towards the gate. "Go on!"

Noel obeyed, reaching the gate in time to see Laura disappear inside the house. Frank Harper had stopped crawling and lay still. His blood surrounded him, a deep red sun in the snow.

"Oh Jessie?"

Paul's voice was only feet away; Jess could see his shadow on the littered floor.

Even huddled behind the end of the sofa, she could see the High Street through the shattered front-room window. She'd thought of jumping out – she'd run through the house to find the front door still in place, and worse still locked – but what if Mum and Keira were outside? So she'd chosen to hide, as she'd always done, and that had never worked with Paul.

He'd be on her in a second, and she'd have no chance. She never had, not against him.

But that'd been before. She wouldn't have dared defend herself properly, with a knife or gun. Mum would've always taken his side. But now it was different.

The cartridge knife was slippery with sweat. It felt tiny, a straw, against Paul's gun. Nonetheless Jess transferred the knife to her other hand and wiped her palm on her trousers.

Paul stepped into view, grinning down at her. "Jessie," he cooed, and reached for her left-handed, his right aiming the rifle in her general direction.

The knife by chance was hidden in her left hand, and that gave her an advantage; he'd have seen it otherwise and made her let it go. She switched it to her right hand so it jutted point-down from her fist as he seized her shoulder; when he tried to pull her towards him, she threw herself forward, screaming. The rifle fired past her into the wall, and she stabbed at his face. The first blow ripped a furrow in his cheek; the second tore through his lips, cracking teeth. It stuck for a moment; she thought the blade would snap, but then it came free.

Paul, screaming, grabbed her hair. Jess brought the knife down again and he let go, staggering back across the room. When she wiped her streaming eyes, she saw the green cartridge case sticking out of Paul's chest. His eyes were mad with pain and wrath; he raised the gun.

"Harper!" someone shouted.

Paul turned. A shotgun fired, the crash of it deafening in the confined space. He cannoned into the wall, all long thrashing bony spider-limbs, then staggered forward, firing the rifle. The side of his neck and shoulder were stripped of flesh; half his face hung off the bone. Then Laura Caddick shot him in the groin, and he doubled up screaming.

Laura Caddick pumped the shotgun's slide again, face pale. There was blood on her jacket and Jess realised she'd been shot as well, but she didn't look angry, scared or even in pain: she looked very calm and steady as she stood over Paul and aimed at his head. Determined. She looked as if she were about to unblock a toilet or kill a trapped rat: something unpleasant, but necessary.

When she pulled the trigger, Jess looked away. Something wet splashed her face; when she looked again, it was splattered all up the front room's green and gold wallpaper.

Laura Caddick slumped into an armchair beside the window. "That's him sorted," she said.

Jess' ears were still humming from the gunshots. A dog barked somewhere. A woman was speaking outside on the High Street, through the shattered front room window. Otherwise, silence.

Dr Emmanuel's boyfriend came into the front room and stared around him – at the blood, at Paul, at Laura. As he opened his mouth to speak, Jess shut her eyes.

50.

Ellie smoked three or four cigarettes, one after the other. By then poor Sally Cupit had been moved into the Co-Op's freezer and laid beside Tony Harper. His corpse had escaped last night's depredations, either because the door had defeated the creatures or because they only liked live prey. The other Harpers' bodies were left where they'd fallen: someone flung plastic sheeting over Liz and Keira, not wanting to waste the blankets. The sheets clung to the bodies, sticky and red.

Paul Harper had shot Laura Caddick in the chest, but the small-calibre bullet had only embedded itself in a rib, leaving her in discomfort and even grumpier than usual, but otherwise unimpaired. Ernie Stasiolek had collected a couple of pellets in the meat of his leg and, once they were removed, stayed on his makeshift bed with a very bad grace: Ellie suspected he'd be up and about the moment Milly turned her back. The Robinsons and Brailsfords had taken over setting up the fires in Groveley Meadow and gathering supplies for the night, with Chris Brailsford breaking into the pharmacy on the High Street in search of a shopping list of stuff for Milly.

Ellie found Noel in the Assemblies church kitchen, smoking. Everyone seemed to be doing that lately. "Hey," she said.

"Hi."

"You okay?"

"Not really." He gave a shaky laugh. "Five years in the Army, and I never killed anybody."

"I know, mate. Same here. I mean, not the Army but..." she trailed off.

"I just keep seeing it. Frank Harper, I mean. The way it knocked him back. How he was trying to crawl away."

"Yeah," Ellie said again, recalling Keira's last seconds – for all she'd loathed the girl in life, it was hard to keep it up when you saw someone dying. Even if they *had* died trying to shoot you with an empty gun. She kept seeing Keira's face: half her head all blood and bone and exposed brain. Ellie felt a moment's sickness; then it passed and she thought *Good riddance to the bitch*, before feeling sick again at having done so. She wasn't sure if she was being callous or honest, lacked something or was merely human. *Feel guilty on your own time, Ellie. There's stuff to do now.*

Except that she wasn't sure what. Things had moved on, and left her at a loose end. She felt more tired than she'd been in months. "I'm gonna go upstairs," she said. "Crash out for a few minutes."

Noel nodded. Ellie felt guilty, as though she should say something more to him. *You're a copper, not a social worker,* she thought, and smiled to herself at the cliché.

"What's so funny?"

What *had* been? Already she'd forgotten. She was so tired. "I don't know. Anyway. If anyone's after me –"

"You'll be upstairs."

"Yeah."

Ellie turned to go.

Screams and shouts from outside, and then an engine roared.

Liz woke with a sudden shocked wheeze, as if from a nightmare. Probably had. Just couldn't remember it. That was how it went, most of the time.

She was in agony, but her head was clear. She'd always

woken quickly: fast asleep one moment, awake and alert the next. No foggy middle ground, and a good thing too.

She was under a musty-smelling plastic sheet, with Keira slumped against her. Stupid sods hadn't even made sure she was dead. Then again, she was practically swimming in blood: she could feel it, hot and horribly sticky under the shredded stab vest, soaking her trousers. Her upper left arm and her right thigh throbbed.

But she was alive under the plastic sheet, and Keira was dead, her head half-gone.

Boys?

She could hear voices nearby. Not Frank's, or Paul's. Maybe they'd got the Bible and fucked off; seen Liz and thought her dead. If so she'd have words when she got back to the farm, and with Paul especially – it'd have been his idea.

But Frank, Frank would've checked. Nothing would've stopped him making sure. So why hadn't he?

Cold dread fingered her belly.

"Pete's sake, Laura, just lie down."

"I'm fine."

"Laura, you just got shot in the chest." Milly Emmanuel's voice. Liz gritted her teeth and clenched her fists; she'd like to paste that holier-than-thou little cow one. But this wasn't the time.

"It was just a crap little .22." And that was Laura Caddick, that sour-faced old boot with her slapper of a daughter. "He was always posing with that thing like he was Rambo, but it wouldn't stop an angry squirrel."

Paul. She meant Paul, with his silly little rifle. And *was*. That meant Paul was gone. Well, he'd been her son, but he'd always been a liability, sneaky little shit that he was. And he couldn't be left alone with anything that had a cunt.

"A bullet's a fucking bullet, Laura."

"You said me rib stopped it."

"Well, yeah. But –"

"We've got worse than cracked ribs to worry about, eh?"

Milly Emmanuel sighed. "Fine."

Frank. What about Frank?

"Least we don't have to worry about those scumbags any more," said Laura. A pausc. "Sorry."

"S'all right," said a small thin high voice.

Jess.

Fucking traitor, thought Liz, *fucking Judas bitch.* And then what Laura had said sank in. Not just Paul: Frank, too. She wanted to howl but stayed still. She wasn't armed: they'd taken her guns.

Footsteps came closer. "Wanna look?" said Laura Caddick.

A long pause, then a faint sigh. "No," said Jess. The footsteps moved away.

Judas. Judas Jess.

Liz waited till she was as sure as she could be they'd gone away, then eased a hand into her pocket and fumbled for her keys. She pulled them out – they were sticky with blood – then peered down in search of the one that started the tractor. When she'd found it she gripped it tight. She'd have one chance and would have to be fast. She shifted her legs slightly. There was pain, but thcy moved.

Deep breaths.

Then count to three and –

Liz flung back the sheet left-armed, biting back a yell as the wound in her arm sent a bolt of white pain up her neck and into her eye, then shoved her feet down against the pavement, boosting herself up the wall. A woman screamed – some stuck-up cow shitting her pants thinking they had the living dead to deal with now too – and Liz made a staggering run for the tractor, clawing at the doorframe. Her boots crunched in broken glass – it pricked her thighs and arse as she collapsed into the seat.

"Get her," someone yelled. Liz shoved the key into the ignition. "Stop her!"

A man tried to climb up into the cab as the engine roared into life. Liz screamed her rage at him – her dead sons, her traitorous bitch of a daughter, her dead daughter-in-law Keira, worth ten of Judas Jess – and smashed her fist into his eye like a hammer. He fell and hit the pavement with a crack; Liz hoped she'd killed him.

She rammed the tractor forward, still screaming. The people in the High Street scattered, screaming too. Fucking sheep. As she hit reverse Ellie fucking bastard bitch Cheetham came running out of the Assemblies church holding – insult of fucking insults – Liz's own Ithaca shotgun. Liz screamed her rage at the pig over the bellowing engine and would've driven straight at her, run her down like roadkill, but she stopped herself. Even if she succeeded, she'd be dead seconds later, and she wouldn't give them that victory. Besides, there were others she owed, like Judas fucking Jess for instance.

Liz turned the tractor about, the snowplough tearing open a shopfront, then floored the accelerator. She swerved to avoid the war memorial, then barrelled down Halliwell Way. No fucker followed her, and that was good. Wounded or not – the stab vest had saved her life but the shotgun blast had torn and punctured her in several places nonetheless – for her dead children she'd have killed anyone coming after her, bare-handed.

She only had vengeance left now. Ensure the Dance went on, the Sleepers woke, the old world was thrown over.

But with the hate Liz felt now – as vast and terrible as any love she'd known – that would be enough.

51.

Liz Harper had got away, and there was nothing to be done about it. There'd be worse things to deal with soon enough. In the meantime Ellie's exhaustion was still bone deep, so she turned and went back into the Assemblies church, creaking wearily up the staircase.

What time was it now? She'd forgotten to look at the wall clock, assuming it'd survived. Well, she only needed to glance at her phone – even without a signal it could give still her the time. But she didn't bother. Hadn't the energy. *You're a copper, not a social worker.*

That was why she'd smiled. She'd tell Noel later. If she remembered.

Upstairs, she found a box room with no windows. She couldn't believe how exhausted she felt. Reaction, maybe, to both the shootings and to last night. Ellie sat down and leant back against the wall. She just needed a few minutes' rest –

The creature crawled towards her, lifting its tattered cowl. This one had a face, instead of a white eyeless muzzle. Or half a face, at least: Keira Lucas', half-blown off and bloody. *You're a copper, not a social worker*, it whispered, and reached for her. Its hand closed on her arm; Ellie yelled, lashing out.

"Whoa! Fucksake, Ellie."

"Milly?" Ellie blinked: her surroundings swam into focus as the dream bled away. The box room at the church. Milly sitting back against the wall, staring at her. And everything else. The creatures. Last night. Keira Lucas with half her head blown off, pathetic and somehow even pitiable. "Oh shit," she said. "Jesus Christ."

"Oi." Milly prodded Ellie with her toe. "Language. You okay?"

Ellie wasn't, but she nodded. "Had better days," she said at last. "Sorry. Just needed to crash."

"Not surprised. Bit of an adrenaline rush there, eh?"

"Huh." Ellie managed a weak smile. "How long –?"

"Half an hour, if that. Soz, Ell. No peace for the wicked. Anyway, thought you'd wanna be up." Milly nodded towards the landing. Jess Harper was standing there, looking very solemn, arms wrapped around a huge leather-bound Bible that looked almost as big as her. Beside her, leaning on Charlotte and Kate, was Madeleine Lowe.

A scuffling sound made Ellie jump; a grey furry shape squirmed between the other women's legs, ran over to her and began licking her face. "Gerroff," she grunted. Reuben blinked, panting happily. Ellie sighed, ruffled his fur and looked up at the others. "The baby?"

"Downstairs," said Jess.

"Tara's looking after him," Milly said. "Now, budge up."

Keeping the blanket around her, Ellie wriggled back across the box room floor till she was up against the wall. Reuben put his head in her lap. Milly sat beside Ellie, cross-legged, and the two younger women lowered Madeleine into a sitting position. Kate Beck seemed be functioning quite well one-armed, but Madeleine wasn't looking well at all. Her face was pale and beaded with sweat. Ellie hoped Chris Brailsford had found Milly some good painkillers. "You okay?" she asked.

"Held together by blood and guts and piano wire, wack," Madeleine grunted. "Lucky Dr Feelgood here's sorting me out. Still won't give me the good drugs, though."

Milly rolled her eyes. "Got her on paracetamol and dihydrocodeine," she told Ellie. "Got some tramadol too, but

I'm holding back on that in case it fucks up her breathing. Mind you, at least that might stop her whinging."

Madeleine blew a weak raspberry.

"So what's all this?" Ellie asked.

"This." Jess held out the heavy Bible. "That's what they came after me for. Wouldn't have been arsed if it'd been me on my own, or even Joel."

"It's the Family Bible," Milly explained. "So it's not just your normal book."

"I've been going through it," Madeleine said, "and I think it's exactly what we've needed to put the pieces together. It's full of old papers, parchments – our friend Dr Bayliss would've given his back teeth for it. Maybe that's why he got 'drowned'."

"Dr who?" said Charlotte.

"No," said Madeleine, "Dr Bayliss."

"Fuck's sake," Milly groaned, and threw a crumpled tissue at her.

"Long story," said Ellie. "So this is, what?"

"The secret history," Jess said. "What Mum used to call it." Her eyes were dry. If she'd shed any tears for her brothers or sister-in-law, Ellie saw no evidence of them. "She kept it in her office. After Tony died –" and now there was a hitch in her voice "– she made me get it down. Read all through it. I mean, she already knew about it – her Nan'd told her. That's what she said. Don't think she believed it, though, till what happened to Tony. Could've sold it and made a mint, she said one time, only some things meant more than money." She sniffed. "First time she ever said that."

Madeleine was leafing through it. "So?" said Ellie. "What've we got?"

Everyone looked to Madeleine. The vicar shifted position, hissing as her stitches pulled taut. "Sorry," she said. "Okay. Here goes. A lot of it seems to mesh with old legends. Saxon and Norse, mostly. But it goes back even before them. There's the barrows, for a start."

"As in Barrowman Farm?" said Ellie. "And Barrow Woods?"

Madeleine nodded. "And the one under the old St Alkmund's Church, in Blackfield Park. Bayliss was dying to do a proper dig at either site. But the locals weren't big on it. The Killers –"

"The *who*?"

Reuben stirred, blinked at Ellie again, then settled again.

"Family who owned Groveley Farm," Madeleine said. "Way back before the Lornes, this'd be–"

"The *Killers*?"

"Yup. That was actually their name."

"Bet nobody messed with them," muttered Charlotte.

"Anyway," said Madeleine, "they owned Groveley Farm and Blackfield – bought it off the Church when it turned out Blackfield was no good for the new St Alkmund's. I forget why. Bayliss wanted to dig there, but they wouldn't let him." A weak, thin smile. "Agricultural reasons, maybe, or superstitious ones. Could've been either, could've been both. Anyway, Bayliss was sure there'd been a long barrow on the site. How much does everyone know about them?"

"Some sort of burial mound?" said Kate.

"Kind of. Pretty much the earliest kind of formal burial we know about. Goes back to the Neolithic Period – the back end of the Stone Age to thee and me. Usually for chieftains, respected warriors, priests. People like that. But sometimes they were sites of worship, too. So they might build them on a particular site."

"Blackfield Park was full of those things last night." Milly touched the cross at her throat. "What was the barrow supposed to do – stop 'em getting out?"

"Think so," said Madeleine. "Thing is, Bayliss thought there was another barrow, a newer one, down in Thursdale."

"Which I'm guessing became the main one," Ellie said. "That, or those things stopped using Blackfield because the barrow there was working."

"One or the other." Madeleine leafed through the Bible.

"Love to know where they got some of this stuff from. The old St Alkmund's, maybe, before it burned down. It's a treasure trove, anyway. There's a piece here – mediaeval, looks like. Says a group of Danes – Vikings – came and tried to plunder the Thursdale barrow. Only one of them came back, and he'd gone half-mad. Said the giants were sleeping underground and the Fimbulwinter'd begin there."

"The what?" Charlotte again.

"The Fimbulwinter." Everyone looked at Kate. "In Norse myths, it's the great winter, heralds the end of the world. The giants wake up and..." She coughed and shrugged. "Had a Norwegian boyfriend in my first year. He was into all that stuff."

Charlotte shook her head. "Giants? I mean, seriously?"

"'The Dane, by name Floki,'" Madeleine quoted from the book, "'pleaded to straightway be baptised a Christian; this being granted, he settled on Redheath to watch over the accursed place, and built a church there.' You know, 'Kirk' is Old Norse for 'church', and 'Flockton' – well, 'ton' means homestead or estate, and 'Flock' –"

"Could be Floki," said Kate Beck. "And I suppose Rudheath would have been the old name for Fendmoor?"

"Before Kirk Flockton sank into it," said Ellie.

"Pretty much." Madeleine sniffed, still leafing back and forth through the book. "Pity this is all we've got from those days. I'd love to know what they had to say about the Bad Winter."

"The what?" said Jess.

"There was one winter where nearly everyone in the village died," said Ellie.

"Starved or froze, supposedly," said Madeleine. "At least, I'd always assumed that. But you've got to wonder, haven't you? If maybe something like this happened before?"

Whatever else they've got down there, underground seems to be where they all come from. Makes sense when you think about it. No light."

"Okay, but... giants?"

"The Saxon word *thyrs* can mean giant, but it can mean monster, too, or demon. Thing is, the *thyrs* were supposed to be able to change size as well as shape."

"*Thyrs*?" said Milly. "Like Thursdale?"

"Might be. Anyway, far as I can tell, all this got taken pretty seriously well into the Middle Ages, maybe beyond. And they seemed to be more worried about Thursdale – looks like the Blackfield barrow was considered safe by then. Must have been, really – village is practically built around it."

"Maybe the village started as a place to keep watch," said Kate.

"Could have," agreed Madeleine. "But if it did, over time attention shifted to the new barrow in Thursdale. Apparently they kept watch on it for years, and gave the farmstead in the valley to the bravest warriors, because they'd be the first to fight and the ones to give warning. Hence, Barrowman Farm."

"That's what Mum told us," said Jess. "She said it was the women who mattered. They were the ones who kept the farm and the family going, even if the name changed."

"Makes sense," said Madeleine. "From this, it looks like there was a pretty high mortality rate. Didn't leave many men to carry on their family names. Looks like the farm had to be restocked a few times, too. Then, after the Norman Conquest, things changed. Most of the old Saxon nobles were replaced by Normans after the invasion. New lord of the manor probably thought it was all crap, and wasn't going to waste good soldiers on Thursdale. So that's how the job went from being an honour to a sort of punishment duty. They gave the farm to people who'd be exiled or executed otherwise – outcasts."

"Disposable," said Jess. For the first time since her family's death, there were tears in her eyes. "Trash. That's what Mum called the people round here. But she always said that was what we were to them."

And she'd been right; God knew that was how Ellie had

thought of the Harpers. It was only now she wondered how much of it had been a self-fulfilling prophecy. Too late to do any good. "Everyone expected them to spend their lives protecting the village," she said. "Probably hardly saw anyone from Barsall, and when they did –"

"Treated like shit," said Jess in a tiny voice.

Milly squeezed her hand. "I'm sorry, love. But you're gonna be all right."

"Am I, though?" And Jess began to cry.

It was sinking in now, how alone she was. Not that she hated Mum and the others any less, Paul especially – but she'd seen the looks she got, even here. Not just Laura Caddick – although she'd softened, despite what Paul'd done, and Tara was nice. Dr Emmanuel was lovely, too, and Ellie – but the others, so many of the others –

Same as the looks they'd used to get when the few times they'd come into Barsall: cold, judging. *Scum. Vermin.* And what'd she done? 'Cept be born a Harper? Mum'd always gone on about what stuck-up bastards they were here, how they'd get their comeuppance one day. And maybe she'd been right, cos Jess got those looks even now, when she'd run away and come to help. *Vermin. Scum.* From people who didn't even know her. She'd never hurt anyone here, had she? Worst she'd done was shoplift from the Co-Op once and get caught, and that'd only been to please Mum. Hadn't worked, cos she'd got a smacking off Mum for it – not the stealing but the getting caught, cos that'd got the whole family barred from the Co-Op for months after. Didn't mean they could look at her like that.

She hated Mum. Still did. Paul and Keira too. Didn't want to think about Frank or Dom. But where was she gonna end up now, among all these poshos with their money and nice houses and good jobs? Stupid. She'd been so stupid. She was no one now.

So now she was crying, and angry with herself for it cos it made her look weak and thick, like they all thought she was. Maybe they even thought she was sorry about Paul and Mum and Keira and she wasn't, she wasn't. She was crying because she'd been fucking stupid. Maybe Mum'd thought about doing what Jess'd done once, but had come up against the same thing: how everyone thought you were tainted, if you were a Harper.

If she'd gone further – another town, another county – it might've been different. Or maybe it was like a brand you carried wherever you went, that everyone else could see.

Jess wiped her eyes. She wasn't going anywhere anyway. No one was till this was over, if it ever was. And she couldn't go back now. She was in it with Ellie and the rest, no matter what they thought of her. And some of them were all right. They didn't all hate her. Maybe that'd be enough. She squeezed Milly's hand back, tight.

The vicar was still talking. "Probably spent more time dealing with those things than with actual people, going off all this. Sounds like the creatures were still active, even after the Normans turned up. Took a long time to get on their right side."

"That's what Mum said," Jess said. "She told us about it. Like for bedtime stories. About winning *Their* trust, being clever, making gifts to *Them*. Animals. People."

"Sacrifices," Charlotte said. "Like they wanted to do with me and Dave." She put a hand to her mouth. "Oh fuck. Dave – Dave and his Dad – no one's seen them, have they? I mean, if they had, we'd've..."

It was Ellie who finally spoke. "They lived on Church Street, didn't they?"

Charlotte shook her head. "His Dad did. Dave's got a flat on Smithy Lane."

"He went home with his Dad, love," said Milly gently. *Lord Chapple of Dogdickington*, Jess remembered her calling Ron Chapple; she bit her lip so she didn't laugh. "They'd have been on Church Street."

Charlotte looked to Ellie, eyes pleading.

Ellie shook her head. "I only found three survivors on Church Street. I'm sorry."

Charlotte's face crumpled. Her family gone, and now her fella too. Jess thought of taking her hand, but was afraid to. "I'm sorry," she said at last.

Charlotte gave her a look she couldn't read, then looked down again.

"Not even thought of him," Charlotte said. "Not all day."

Ellie looked at Madeleine, willing her to press on. Madeleine caught her eye and nodded.

"So," she said, "looks like they developed rituals and whatnot to keep the creatures onside, if not happy – make sure they'd be safe even if no one else was. And at some point, they started writing stuff down. Or someone did it for them. They'd have to be able to, really, cos we know the farm had to be completely repopulated at least twice. They couldn't rely completely on an oral tradition. Anyway, that's the background."

Madeleine looked tired and pale, off-colour. Well, she'd been badly injured, had lost blood. Even so, Ellie would have to talk to Milly later. "Anyway, that's the potatoes, now for the meat. According to this, those things aren't the real danger. They're just... servants of something else."

"Of what?"

"The sleepers," said Jess. "That's what Mum called them. The sleepers under the hill. There was a poem she used to read us." She screwed up her face. *"Beneath the hill the sleepers lie/ They do not live, but will not die..."*

"That's here somewhere." Madeleine turned a couple of pages. "Yeah:

"Beneath the hill the sleepers lie,
They do not live, yet will not die

They slumb'ring wait beneath the ground
Till their time once more comes around.

Men called them gods in bygone years,
And prayed to them in awe and fear;
Like ants round them their servants crawl,
Until once again they rule us all.

In winter nights their servants go,
To drag unwary folk below;
And seek for sign on dale or fend,
Of when their masters' sleep will end.

Board your window, keep on your light,
When the Tatterskin walks at night.
Hush and be still, make never a cry,
And pray the Tatterskin walks on by.

And should you see their charcoal brand,
Scored on hearthstone, wall or land,
The White-Christ's time it will be past,
And ancient gods restored at last.

The Tatterskins, from lairs deep,
Will cleanse the earth of Christian sheep,
O'er two night's span; on the third, the Dance
Will wake the sleepers from their trance.

And on that day, the last of all,
Old night will forever fall,
The sleepers rise to rule once more
And those who've kept the faith restored."

Milly gripped her cross in the ensuing silence, her knuckles
white. "Jesus."

Kate laughed, shakily. "Not exactly Sylvia Plath."

"Two nights, and then the Dance," said Jess. "That's what Mum kept saying."

"Meaning what?" said Charlotte. Madeleine frowned and turned a few more pages in the Bible.

"The first night – was that Tony?" said Ellie.

"No," said Jess. "That was when it started. They made their sign. See –" She was frowning, trying to remember. "Mum said *They'd* come out some nights – and go hunting. But it wasn't just for food or skins, it was – they were looking for signs."

"In how their victims died," said Madeleine. "Some sort of divination. That's what Tony was to them."

"Like you reckoned, Ell," Milly said. "'Member? Bet you're right. Bet if we checked how many hypothermia deaths we got out here – Thursdale, Wakeman's Edge, Fendmoor, Slapelow – betcha it'd be *well* above the rate for anywhere else in miles."

"A few of them wake up each winter," said Madeleine. "Come up to the surface, hunt somebody down and watch them freeze to death. Look for some kind of sign. And this year they found it."

"And took our families." Kate's voice was brittle. She looked at Charlotte.

"Started at the fringes," Charlotte said. "Places that weren't in the village proper. Warming up. Right?"

"Okay, so *that* was the first night," Ellie said. "Last night was the second. Tonight –"

"The third," said Jess. "The night of the Dance. That's what Mum said. When the giants wake up."

"So how do we stop it?" Charlotte said. "I mean, we *can* stop it, right?"

No one answered her.

"I'll keep looking," said Madeleine. "But it's not like this lot had any interest in stopping it once it started. For them it'd be like Judgement Day and the Second Coming for me or Milly."

She grimaced. "Not that I ever fancied still being around for that one."

Ellie rubbed her eyes. "If we're gonna do anything, it'll have to be before it's dark again. Mad, does it say anything else about the... creatures? Any way to hurt them? Fight them?"

Madeleine grimaced. "The folk who wrote all this were more interested in being their best mates. But they'd have to be able to protect themselves to get the chance to do that. So you can bet they did their homework there. But pretty much the only thing that seems to hurt the fuckers was light. Fire, sun, whatever. Which makes sense. Creatures of the night and all that. Trolls were supposed to turn to stone in daylight, weren't they?"

"Trolls?" Charlotte demanded.

"Trolls, goblins, little people," Madeleine said. "Maybe this is where all the stories come from, eh? Some of them, anyway. But yeah, light's the big one as far as I can tell."

"Nothing we didn't already know, then."

"Better than nothing at all."

"Can light kill them?" said Ellie.

"Don't see why not. If they're alive, they can die, right?"

"Let's bloody hope so." Wincing, Ellie got to her feet; Reuben stretched and rubbed against her leg. "And let's try and get ourselves ready."

52.

"Watch what you're doing. Fucking retard."

"Sorry Mum."

"Stop fussing. Now give us that and piss off. And stop gawping at my tits."

"I wasn't –"

"Yeah, right. Men. All the same. Now go on, buzz off. And take that with you! Pour it down the sink."

Dom slunk out with the bowl of bloody water; refastening her bra, Liz studied herself in the bathroom mirror. Gauze and surgical tape criss-crossed her torso, marking where the pellets had hit. Only seven, all told, including those in her left arm and right leg. She'd hardly call it a lucky number, but she'd been surprised it had been so few. It'd certainly felt worse. She picked up her tweezers and nudged the pellets: they lay on an old sideplate, stale toast crumbs sticking to the blood on them.

The wounds still hurt like hell, despite the co-codamol and ibuprofen she'd taken – they had proper codeine pills but those always knocked Liz out, and she couldn't afford that now.

She went into the bedroom in her grimy underwear and rummaged through a chest of drawers. Corduroy trousers, a cleanish shirt, new sweater. Her old clothes and the shredded stab vest lay in a heap in the corner. Burn them later. For now, she'd work to do.

Downstairs, she donned a new coat and inspected the remaining guns. There was a pump-action shotgun, but one of the legal ones that only held three rounds, even with one in the chamber. She took it nonetheless, and a sawn-off, then stuffed her jacket pockets with cartridges. She took a waterproof ground sheet and a foil blanket from a cubby-hole and tucked them, folded tight, under one arm, then found her walking stick and went through to the kitchen.

Dom was huddled there with two of his dogs. "Lock up after me," said Liz. "And keep the lights on."

"Yes, Mum."

Liz crunched across the farmyard, breath billowing in the air. It would be dark soon, and *They'd* be out again – and God help Ellie bloody Cheetham, Milly Emmanuel, the Caddicks and all the other scum *then*. God help Jess, too – that treacherous little whore, that fucking Judas. But for now, she'd one last service to perform.

She'd no idea what *They* could give her now that she'd want. Her kids were all gone except worthless Dom and Judas Jess, and she was too old for more. But she'd see, afterwards, if whatever life she still had could be made worth the living. If not, she could end it easily enough. That didn't matter now. What mattered was ensuring the Dance took place, and the Sleepers woke. That'd be her revenge on Jess, on Cheetham and the others, on the bastard world. Anything else would be a bonus.

So she'd make her way out to Barrow Woods – but by a longer, different route that wouldn't leave an obvious trail. She'd watch till it was nearly dark, before she got her arse home and locked up for the night. And then she'd see what the new day – if there was one – brought.

53.

In Groveley Meadow, they'd gathered every scrap of food and fuel – every stick of wood, every drop of petrol – tents, bedding, and all the drugs and dressings they could salvage from the pharmacy. Small fires had been started to provide warmth; the big ones would be lit after dark.

Noel, rifle slung across his back, walked with Ellie along the perimeter. Reuben trotted at her heels. Neither spoke; perhaps Noel was still brooding on what he'd done. Or perhaps not: despite her initial reaction to Keira's death, Ellie barely thought of her now.

Then again, she'd more pressing concerns: people looked to her for answers. They expected Milly to take care of them, but Ellie to know what to do. Which was fair enough. It was her job, her responsibility, and she was glad of it: often she felt horribly empty, a shell, as if all that'd happened had hollowed her out. She was – she almost laughed at the simile – like a balloon: a limp, empty shell that would collapse if she didn't keep it inflated with some sort of purpose.

And she had no family, no faith. Nothing but her job. Not even a dog – then again, Reuben seemed to have adopted her. *He likes you*, Madeleine had said. The little bugger seemed more interested in Ellie than Madeleine now. Ellie glanced back towards the camp, but couldn't make Madeleine out in the crowd; the only recognisable form was Milly, bustling from tent to tent in her bright pink jacket.

Maybe Reuben smelled the things' traces on Madeleine: she

was still in agony from her wounds, with Milly keeping her doped up. The creatures had marked her too, in a way. All the other injuries had been from shock, hypothermia, or accident: once the creatures got hold of you that was usually that.

After going through the Harpers' Family Bible, the vicar had lost all energy. Most likely simple exhaustion from her injuries and the previous night's events, but Ellie wondered if it mightn't be something worse. Milly had given Madeleine as many oral antibiotics as she dared, but they hadn't helped so far.

Ellie and Noel finished circling the camp. A crowd had gathered around Madeleine's wheelchair: pale and sick, the vicar offered her flock what hope she could. Seeing Milly in the crowd, Ellie moved to her side.

"God hasn't forgotten us," Madeleine said. "He's still there; still watching. I don't pretend to know His will, why this has happened, or if this is the end. We might still be spared. But we've got to have faith. I don't mean fundamentalism. Last thing we need now is to turn on each other and start rooting out imaginary sinners. We're *all* sinners, remember? But we're also loved by God. *That's* the faith we've got to have. In one another, as well as in Him. That we're not abandoned. That things aren't hopeless. That if we give each other strength and comfort, protect one another, we can come through."

She was paler than ever: there was sweat on her brow. "How's she doing?" Ellie whispered.

Milly shrugged. "Running a fever. Keeping up with the paracetamol for that, and the dihydrocodeine for the pain. Need to check those dressings once she's wrapped her little sermon here up." Milly bit her lip. "It's that cut I'm worried about."

"Infected?"

"Might be. Fuck knows what those things've had their claws in, down where they've been. Not sure the antibiotics are doing any good."

There was a mutter from the crowd: Madeleine was swaying

in her chair. "Drawn up from deep places," she said. Her eyes had rolled up, white. "In the deep, they sleep. The dark is their ark. The year dies; will the sun rise? The final solstice. The ancient dark, the old deep dark. Ginnungagap. Tohu va-bohu. Abyss. Void. The Chasm. The Yawning. In the old deep dark Tiamat rises, calling Abzu back to life. Her children: Erebos, Nyx. At their heels Leviathan, Behemoth, Jagannath crouch for employment. Ancient night. Ancient night. What hope is there? What hope is there? The light of the world. The light of the world –"

Her arms swept wildly upwards; her chair teetered and toppled. There were cries of alarm, and people rushed forward.

"Fuck," said Milly.

They moved Madeleine into a dome tent: she was dripping sweat, brow almost scalding hot. Milly shooed everyone out of the tent except for Ellie and Kate Beck, eased Madeleine's jacket off and removed the sweater.

Madeleine's eyes were rolled up, she wasn't unconscious, but she was unresponsive and hardly seemed aware of anything around her, other than the pain. Something was soaking through the back of Madeleine's shirt. There was an unpleasant smell, which worsened when Milly peeled away the material. The dressings on the vicar's back were wet and discoloured; thick yellow and brown fluid had seeped out from under them.

"Shit," said Milly. "This ain't good."

When she removed the dressings the stench worsened. The skin around the wound was livid scarlet, raised thin threads following the veins, and the cut itself had risen up into a ridge, as if she was transforming into something reptilian. Ellie shook her head; the situation was bad enough without adding that into the mix, and anything seemed possible now.

The stitches had pulled tight, gummed and crusted with pus. "Infected?" said Ellie.

"The fuck d'you think, Ell? Kate, can you fetch me backpack? And some hot water?"

"What can we do for her?" Ellie said. "Anything?"

Milly shook her head. "Antibiotics, pain relief, plenty of fluid and keep her warm. And then pray. This is nasty shit and it's worked bloody fast."

Kate brought the backpack; Milly rummaged through it and took out a packet of pills. "Bout the strongest we've got, here." She surveyed Madeleine's wound dolefully. "And I thought it was the new bugs we had to worry about."

"Eh?"

"Antibiotic resistance," said Milly. "We've been seeing more and more antibiotic-resistant germ strains, and we haven't developed any new antibiotics in years. One of the big worries, that – one of those starting an epidemic. Whatever germs they've given her, though, I'm guessing they're bloody old ones. Just as bad, by the look of it." She put the pack aside.

Kate came back with Noel, who carried a steaming Pyrex jug. Milly squirted sanitiser gel onto her hands. "Here we go."

She washed and cleaned Madeleine's wound: the vicar moaned at her touch, sweating more fiercely than ever, webs of hair glued to her cheek and forehead. Even cleaned, the wound looked little better, still horribly ridged and swollen and red. Milly applied ointment, then a new set of dressings. "Sit her up," she said.

Noel propped Madeline upright, wrapping a blanket round her. Madeleine shivered, eyes half-open, rolled back in her head. "Mad? Just need you to swallow something for me." Milly half-grinned. "Like the bishop said to the actress. Mad?"

Madeleine blinked, then finally focused on her.

"That's my girl. Okay. We've got painkillers and antibiotics. Need to get them down you, okay?"

"Fiat lux," said Madeleine.

"Eh? Madeleine, can you understand me?"

"Uh. Yeah. Milly?"

"Yeah. Okay, painkillers first."

Milly had put a couple of canned drinks in the backpack as well; Ellie didn't know if they were for her or her patients. She popped one open. "Hope you like Cherry Coke."

"Fucking hate it," Madeleine said.

Ellie had to laugh.

"Well, think of it as medicine, cock. 'Sides, it's sugar. You need the fuel. Here."

Once Madeleine had forced down the pills, Milly helped her lie down on her side. "How you feeling now?"

Madeleine shivered, teeth chattering. "Fucking wretched."

Milly tucked a blanket around her, then found another. "There's hot water bottles around here somewhere," she told Kate. "Fill a couple up for me." She looked at Ellie and shrugged. "Done pretty much all we can."

"De profundis," whispered Madeleine. Her eyes had rolled white again. "De profundis, domine. Fiat lux. Fiat lux."

"What's she on about?" said Ellie.

"I'd say speaking in tongues," said Milly, "but I think that's Latin."

"Sounds like it." Noel leant forward. He opened his mouth, but before he could speak Madeleine started talking again, more loudly.

"Down in the dark, in the old deep dark. Down in the Yawning, I see them stir. The giants. *Thyrs*. They rise! They rise! From Ginnungagap, from the corpse-shore Nastrond, Ymir and his spawn, Vörnir and Surt, Vosud and Hyrrokkin, wade the Black River in search of hated light. They rise! They rise! In Dubnos, from the House of Donn, come Ysbaddaden and Canthrig Bwt, with the Bendith y Mamau and the dread Coraniaid in their train! From Ganzir and Irkalla come Abzu, Tiamat, Erebos and Nyx with their hosts of Aqrabuamelu whose very glance is death! Tohu va-bohu. Tohu va-bohu. Down in the Yawning's jaws, Apep, Typhon, Eurymedon, Aigaion scent the final death of the sun! From the Abyss, Czernobog, Whiro,

Lotan, Tlaltecuhtli climb! In the old deep dark are Unhcegila, Tunnanu, Falak, Illuyanka too! From ancient night Vritra, Amatsu-Mikaboshi, Batara Kala, Nirgali, Ravan all come, and the legions of the Kravyad march. They rise! They rise! The old gods wake, the sun dies. Earth and waters perish as night comes forever more. De profundis, domine! De profundis! Fiat lux! Fiat lux!"

Her eyes closed. She slept.

"The Hell was that?" demanded Ellie.

"Buggered if I know," said Noel. "That last bit was Latin, and I thought I heard some Welsh somewhere in the middle there, but the rest..."

No one spoke for a while. There was nothing to say.

As she left the tent, Ellie smelt bacon cooking. Despite the lingering sickbed smell from Madeleine's wound her stomach growled; she couldn't remember when she'd last eaten anything of substance. She traced the smell to its source, a row of battered barbecues that Plant-Pot had set up. *Eat, drink and be merry, for tonight we die.*

Plant-Pot stuffed a half-baguette with bacon for her, and Ellie wandered through the camp, munching it. The bread was stale, the bacon nowhere near as crisp as she usually liked, but just now it was the food of the gods. Not to mention the last bacon sandwich she might ever eat: after this cook-out there was only canned and dried food. Assuming anyone lived long enough to be hungry again.

There was movement at her feet, and she looked down to see Reuben gazing soulfully up at her with the air of an early Christian ascetic starving himself to death for the faith. He rather spoiled the effect by licking his chops a couple of times.

"Probably scavenged half your bodyweight in bacon already, you little sod," muttered Ellie, but tore a piece off the baguette for him anyway. Reuben wagged his tail and trotted after her.

"Ellie?"

It was Jess Harper, carrying her baby in its sling. She hung back, as though she were braced for an order to go away. "All right, love," said Ellie.

Love: Jess' face brightened at that. "Hiya," she said. "You okay?"

"Been worse," said Ellie.

Jess nodded. She was silent for a moment, then spoke. "Vicar's awake."

"Eh?"

"Dr Emmanuel – Milly I mean – she said to tell you. She's awake and lucid."

"Lucid?"

"Yeah. Lucid. Wants to talk to you."

"Milly?"

"The vicar. Says it's important."

Ellie was craving another cigarette, and had only just remembered the ones in her pocket. That would have to wait. She sighed. "All right. Lead on, Macduff."

Jess frowned at that, not getting the reference, but gave a *bitches-be-crazy* shrug and strode towards Madeleine's tent. Ellie rubbed her gritty eyes, and followed.

54.

Jess unzipped the dome tent door and went through, barely stooping. Ellie hunched down and followed her. Inside, a warm fug of air greeted her, and an unpleasant smell. Years before, when she'd visited her grandmother in hospital during her last illness, the old woman in the neighbouring bed had had bedsores or something similar, with dressings that required regular changing. The stench released whenever that was done had been very like the one greeting Ellie now – infection and decay, with death close by and waiting – but this smell had a particular, alien bitterness all its own.

Jess' baby began grizzling again. "Gimme a sec," she said, and went back out.

Milly had propped Madeleine up in a sitting position against some pillows and old seat cushions; the vicar's face was the colour of curdled milk, but there were faint spots of colour in her cheeks and she wasn't sweating any more. She managed a smile. "Hey, mate."

"Morning."

"Don't suppose you've got a fag?"

"Oi," said Milly.

"Come on, doc. Not like it's gonna make much difference."

Milly looked down. Madeleine rolled her eyes. "Bloody killjoy." She turned back to Ellie. "Anyway. While I'm still compos mentis, we need to talk."

"Okay."

Madeleine opened her mouth to speak, then hesitated. "Reuben?"

"He's fine. Just stole half me bacon roll."

Madeleine chuckled. "He does do a pretty good starving-orphan impression."

Jess came back in. "Tara's looking after Joel for a bit."

"All right," said Madeleine. "So, what was I coming out with before?"

"How do you mean?"

"Milly says I was a bit away with the fairies. Coming out with all sorts."

"Yeah."

"I remember bits," said Madeleine. "I was – I dreamt it, I suppose. I was under the hill. With *them*. Saw where they lived. Where they slept, and – all of that."

Ellie shifted, uncomfortable. "Like you said, you were dreaming."

"Yeah. But it mightn't've been *just* a dream. *Felt* bloody real, I can tell you."

"What?" Ellie was suddenly annoyed. "You're having visions now? That's where we're at?"

"Ellie." Milly frowned. "Just listen. Can't do any harm, can it?"

Ellie knew what she was going to suggest – that God might be trying to save them, sending visions to His representative on earth to show them the way. It pissed her off, frankly. What next? Sacrifice chickens and read the entrails? Throw animal bones and look for meaning in the patterns? But Milly and Mad were friends. And they'd been worth listening to before. What was there to lose from listening again? "All right," she said. "Go on, then."

"There were tunnels," said Madeleine. "Caves. Full of cobwebs. There were lots of little alcoves there. That's where they slept, and waited. And way, *way* down, there was a big cavern. Huge. That was where the Dance was happening. And when it finished, the sleepers woke up."

"What were they like?"

"Gods and monsters," said Madeleine. "Wish I could be a bit more specific than that, but… you know how sometimes you can't remember something properly, because it was that bad your brain blanks it out? I've just got bits. Impressions."

She looked woozy again for a moment. "Ugh. Anyway. Look, what did I say while I was out of it?"

"You were speaking in tongues," said Milly.

"In tongues?"

"Not in tongues." At least, Ellie didn't think so. "Latin."

"Latin?"

"That's what Noel reckoned."

"Where's Noel now?"

"Fast asleep," said Milly. "I suppose I could wake him –"

"Let the poor sod kip," said Ellie. "I can remember it. There were two main bits in Latin."

"What was the Latin?"

"*De profundis, domine*," said Ellie. A copper needed a good memory. "*De profundis, domine*, and *fiat lux*."

Madeleine laughed weakly. "Of course."

"Wanna share the joke?"

"130th Psalm. *De profundis clamavi ad te, Domine*: out of the depths I have cried to thee, O Lord." Madeleine smiled grimly. "It's a supplication to God for mercy and forgiveness. In Judaism, it's traditionally recited in times of 'communal distress'."

"Well, this would qualify."

"*De profundis*: out of the depths. And what was the other one again?"

"*Fiat lux*," said Ellie. "Thought you meant your new car for a minute."

"Ha." Madeleine rolled her eyes; Ellie was afraid she was going to collapse again, but it was just an expression of annoyance. "*Fiat lux*. Well, that one's easy too. It's from Genesis. 'In the beginning, God created the Heaven and the Earth. And the Earth was without form, and void; and darkness was upon the face of the deep. And the Spirit of God moved on the face of the waters.' And then, Verse Three: 'And God said, let there be light.' That's what *fiat lux* means: let there be light. Out of the depths, and let there be light. What about the other stuff I was saying?"

"I only made out bits," Ellie said. "Something about old gods. And old night – *ancient* night. 'The old deep dark', you kept saying. And stuff about the Abyss. The Chasm. Something called the Yawning."

"You said the sun would die," said Milly. "There'd be a night that'd go on forever. The earth and sea, they'd die too."

"The poem," said Jess. "From the Family Bible. Remember it?" She recited:

"And on that day, the last of all,
Old night will forever fall,
The sleepers rise to rule once more
And those who've kept the faith restored."

"The Chasm," Madeleine said at last. "The Abyss. They're all names for the primal chaos. What existed before God said *fiat lux*. A lot of pre-Christian legends talk about the world being created by a war with the chaos gods. Usually sea-gods or chthonic deities –"

"Usually *what?*"

"Chthonic. Underground, subterranean. They had to be defeated before the world could come into existence."

"So that's what the 'old night' bit means?" said Jess.

Madeleine nodded.

"Right then." Jess nodded too, her small pale face set. "Know what we've gotta do then, right?"

"Do we?" Ellie was buggered if she did.

"They're sleeping under the hill, yeah? Underground? That's right, isn't it? C-thonk-ic or whatever you call 'em?"

"Chthonic," said Madeleine.

"Whatevs." Jess pulled a face. "Point is, they're underground, and those things are gonna wake 'em up. And when they do, the sun goes out, right? Cos what do we know they hate?"

"Light," said Milly. "Just – light."

"Right," said Jess. "So? *Out of the depths. Let there be light.* That's what it's gotta mean. We go down there and we turn the lights on. Start a fire or something. *Let there be light.* They can't do the Dance if they're dead, can they?" She looked from one of them to the other, face eager, eyes button-bright. "Put the knockers on it all, then and there."

None of them spoke for a few seconds. Jess' smile began to fade – afraid she'd got it wrong, made a fool of herself. But finally, Madeleine smiled.

"And a little child shall lead them," she said.

55.

A search of the wrecked police station had turned up an old flare pistol – Second World War vintage if it was a day, but still in working order and – more importantly – with a large supply of cartridges which could be fired from a twelve-bore shotgun if its chokes were removed. That had meant taking a hacksaw to the barrel of Ellie's gun, but she could live with that. Liz Harper's Ithaca was already cut down, so Ellie gave her weapon to Charlotte and took that.

Charlotte had insisted on coming, as soon as she heard about the plan. Ellie divided half the flare cartridges between the two of them, with the remainder split between Noel, Ernie Stasiolek and Laura Caddick, who were staying to defend the camp.

Ellie, Charlotte and Jess each donned a heavy pack containing a ten-kilo propane cylinder. Madeleine couldn't wear one due to the wounds on her back, but insisted on accompanying them nonetheless. They all wore as many layers of clothing as they could get away with without hampering their mobility: tonight would be a cold one.

Even Milly wasn't sure what was keeping the vicar upright. "Dunno what it is she's got," she'd told Ellie, puffing on her cigarette, "but it makes MRSA look like a sore throat. It's eating her alive."

"What about the antibiotics you gave her?"

Milly shook her head. "She's not gonna make it, Ell." Her voice had cracked. "I can give her stuff for the pain, but that's it. Girl shouldn't be fucking walking, but she is."

"Does she know?"

Milly nodded. "Started to tell her, but she stopped me. She'd already worked it out for herself."

"You can't be sure. I mean, she seems fine."

"That's the bit I can't get." Milly's eyes were red, and Ellie felt the same dull ache of grief. "Maybe God's keeping her going."

"What, like her faith?"

"I mean God, Ell. Can't think of another explanation."

Ellie hadn't responded to that. At best conversations like this only reminded her of the gulf between her beliefs and Milly's; at worst they left her with questions to which there was no clearer answer than the one Milly had given years before: *It's a fallen world, Ellie, love; a fallen world.*

Well, she'd no time to ponder such things now, anyway. They'd wait till afterwards, assuming there was one.

For now there were only the depths, and the fire.

"You don't mind?" Jess said.

"Nah." Tara touched Joel's cheek. "He's lovely."

She might feel differently if she had to look after him twenty-four-seven, but Jess didn't say so out loud. Hard work or not, Joel was her child. And without him, she might not be here.

"You really going down there?" said Tara.

"Got to," said Jess. "Only chance we've got." For Joel. For Tara. For herself, too, if she hoped to have anything like the life she wanted, should anything remain of the once-familiar world. Or indeed, any life at all.

Tara bit her lip. "Be careful, then," she said, then surprised Jess – and quite possibly herself – by pulling her into a clumsy, one-armed hug.

Jess patted her back, not knowing what else to do. "You as well."

They separated awkwardly. Jess went off without looking back.

***

They set off much later than Ellie would have liked, close to three o'clock. Today was the 21st of December: the Winter Solstice, the longest night. The things under the hills would never be stronger than tonight; of course this would be the occasion of their Dance. With a little over an hour before the sun went down, they had to reach Barrow Woods.

Ellie and the others walked out of the village, into the shadows of the winter dusk. A few people nodded to them and called out "good luck" or similar sentiments; Laura Caddick raised a hand in a gesture half-wave and half-salute as they passed, met Ellie's eyes and had given a stern nod, all the while somehow conveying the sentiment that she wished she was going with her and bloody well would be if not for that annoying chest wound – not that it seemed to be incapacitating her at all. Behind Laura, Tara, still cradling the baby, waved to Jess as they passed. Jess smiled and waved back, and they carried on.

The last of Milly's patients had been helped or carried to Groveley Meadow. A sorry parade of the halt and lame by any standards; God knew how many of them would last the night, with or without the creatures.

The Harpers' second tractor – pretty much the only functional motor vehicle they had left – had been moved there too; if they were still alive in the morning, maybe someone could use it to go and look for help. Its headlights were intact, too: any light source was precious.

Laura and Tara Caddick – Tara with Jess Harper's baby on her back like a papoose, which Milly was still struggling to get used to – helped Noel and the Brailsfords organise what defences they still had. Shotguns loaded with flare cartridges, the fires they'd built, and one other weapon. They'd decanted petrol into bottles to make Molotov cocktails – mixed with liquid soap so it would stick to whatever it spilled on.

Napalm. God. Milly had seen pictures of what that stuff had done to kids in Vietnam. Vile, evil stuff: the Devil's own. Fitting enough, though, for those things of ancient night.

It was very dim now, with grey and black clouds overhead. The air was icy and the grey dusk filled it, leaching colour from grass and snow, clothes and faces. Everything faded to grey; outlines lost their definition and began to blur. Torches were switched on and the campfires were lit – small ones marking the boundary, larger ones in the centre – to push the shadows back with their warm yellow and orange glow. Light and heat to get them through the cold night and all that inhabited it.

For now, Milly was calm. All that could be done had been. And she was who she was: Millicent Abigail Emmanuel, healer. That was all that mattered now; all she could still control. Her skills would be in demand soon enough, for all the good they'd do. She could only pray now: for help, for grace, for mercy, whether or not anyone was listening, whether or not it did any good. And when the enemy came and the fighting began, she'd care for the wounded until she no longer could. Whether it proved futile or not; whether or not the sun rose.

56.

They marched stiffly down the hill road, Jess leading the way. It was iced over in places, treacherous to walk on; the snow-covered ground of the Height and the fields of Barrowman Farm, rock-hard and uneven though they'd be, would be safer.

Ellie dug her phone out as they came off the road onto the Height; the others paused, knocking snow off the picnic tables, to sit and rest for a minute or two, but she pressed on to the safety railings at the edge.

The fields were white, and the road; shrouds of snow half-hid the gutted shells of the *Bell* and Wakeman Farm. Thursdale was pale and silent in the cradling embrace of Slapelow Hill, Spear Bank and Wakeman's Edge, tapering up towards the path to Fendmoor. The blotched grey clouds were infinite and empty; pale rags of sun peered through gaps in the western sky. Ellie waited, listening for a car, an aircraft, but there was nothing but the wind.

Her phone's screen was dim; in the top right-hand corner, a lone exclamation mark warned the battery was almost dead. Even if she could make a call, the thing would die on her almost as soon as anyone answered the phone. But there were no signal bars anyway. She'd expected as much, but she'd had to try.

Ellie was tempted to toss the phone away, but stuffed it in her pocket instead. One last link with the world she'd known until last night.

Will we ever have power again? Electricity? Phones? Ever have news of anything outside walking distance? It came back again to the unanswered, for now unanswerable, question of whether this madness was confined to Barsall or if it was a wider, even global, phenomenon. Although the very absence of outside help suggested the latter. Better not to think about it: doing so was pointless and unhelpful. All she knew or had influence over was here. So now she'd do what she could.

She found herself thinking, of all things, of Reuben. There was little chance of survival; assuming the world didn't end, who'd take care of him if both she and Madeleine were dead? Milly, maybe. Ellie should have asked her before setting off.

One last look across the still deadness of the valley and the empty sky; she turned to go back, then stopped and looked again. A thin black line of chimney-smoke hung above the stack of Barrowman Farm, and the battered second tractor was parked in the farmyard. She was still wondering whether or not to tell Jess when the girl leant on the railings beside her, looked towards the farm and nodded. "Looks like Mum's okay, then," she said.

"Yeah." Ellie watched Jess' face for a reaction, but there wasn't one.

"Hope Dom's all right," the girl said. "He wasn't so bad. Not like Paul." She spat over the ledge; it was hard and precise, full of dismissal and contempt for her dead brother. Ellie was still used to seeing Jess as a scared little waif, helpless and pitiable, but the last twenty-four hours had shown there was flint and steel in the girl. That shouldn't really have come as a surprise; she couldn't have survived that mares' nest without some inner resources. "Frank might've been all right if he'd had more of a mind of his own," Jess went on. "But he couldn't fucking shit unless someone told him how. Mum, or Keira." She spat again; then her face softened. "Tony, though, he was the best of 'em. He's the one I miss."

She snorted, breathed out, shook her head. "Anyway. Best get on." She nodded upwards at the dimming sky, the rags of sun which were shifting from cold white to the colour of dull fire. "Be dark soon."

She'd dragged her backpack to the railing with her: grunting and wincing, she pulled it up onto her crooked back again, then went past Ellie towards the footpath in a firm, straight-legged stride that gave her the earnest, comical appearance of a child playing soldiers. Playing at being a grown-up. Or a child forced to grow up, far too soon.

The footpath down was long and winding, the incline gentle to avoid too punishing a journey. Ellie would normally be glad of that, especially with the propane bottle on her back, but today it only served to extend their journey time. She was sure the sky above was considerably darker, the last light at the horizon a duller, more ember-like red, by the time they finally reached the bottom.

She didn't want to guess how little time remained before the things came out again. Would they only wake when it was full dark, or were they already watching the weak dying light in their tunnel entrances and waiting for the last of it to fade?

If they weren't already awake, they would be soon enough. There was little chance of success, less still of survival, but what was the alternative? Wait for the axe to fall at the camp? Or for the Dance to take place and –

You don't seriously fucking believe this, do you, Ell? Scrawlings in an old Bible by a bunch of inbreds? A dying vicar's fever-dreams? What sort of evidence is that? How Tom Graham would've rolled his eyes. *Too much imagination, Ellie. Last thing a copper needs.*

Well, she'd have preferred not to believe it, but disbelief was a luxury she didn't dare avail herself of. Dance or no Dance, the survivors' best chance was to attack the menace at its source. So either way, she was going down.

They followed Jess across the field in single file. From time-to-time Ellie stole glances at the low grim hulk of Barrowman

Farm, the blind erased eyes of its shuttered windows and that thin black line of chimney-smoke, searching for any sign of movement or threat, but saw none. With any luck, Liz Harper was in no shape to cause Ellie any further trouble.

The only sound was the crunch of boots in snow as they made their way across the untrodden fields towards the bare black thicketing woods that filled the bottleneck at the end of the valley, crawling up the slopes to Fendmoor like huge, blackened spiders in the gloom. Barrow Woods.

Tiny though she was, Jess Harper pulled ahead of the group with her fierce determined march; Ellie jogged to catch up, steam puffing from her mouth; the cold air seared her lungs. A dully glowing line of blood-coloured light marked the join between the sky and land.

The woods thickened in the dusk, colour and definition fading out of the landscape so even the distinction between the white snow and the narrow black naked trees blurred. For all that, Jess negotiated the narrow paths without a torch; neither Ellie nor the others, following her, reached for their own lights. This was a territory Jess understood better than any of them – except Madeleine, perhaps, if her fever-visions approached anything like true knowledge. Best to follow her lead; besides, given the creatures' sensitivity to light it seemed best to conserve theirs until the last moment.

The path was overgrown and treacherous; Ellie winced at every snap of brittle wood or undergrowth. Charlotte gasped and cursed; Ellie hissed "Ssh," pausing as she did to search the trees for movement. But they remained still.

"We'll be okay," Jess whispered over her shoulder. "They won't come out till it's full dark."

The bare trees rustled overhead. Ellie glanced up several times, but could see nothing.

"Here we are," said Jess at last.

They stepped out of the trees into the day's last light. In front of them was the earth bank, with its single gap. Jess led them through.

Half a dozen holes of various sizes dotted the ground between them and the second earth bank. Two gleamed with ice. Ellie shone her torch down another; it was only a few feet deep, choked with soil and grass. When she looked around she saw the two parallel earth banks were linked by another, shorter pair lying perpendicular to them, creating an enclosed space broken only by the gap they'd entered through.

"This is it," said Madeleine. "Bayliss was right. Another long barrow, or what's left of one."

"Here," whispered Jess.

She pointed to the hole that lay beneath the slab of rock set into the far embankment. Madeleine shone her torch on it, revealing its pinkish colour. "Rhyolite," she said.

"You're a geologist now?" whispered Charlotte.

"What can I tell you, wack? Far too much free time. 'Sides, you never know where you'll get a good idea for a sermon. Gotta keep the punters interested somehow."

Charlotte's laugh was short and faint.

"Rhyolite," said Madeleine again. "You don't normally find that in the Peaks." She shone the torch over the charcoal marks. The angular, reversed D; the smudged smeared marks below it.

"Those –" Jess reached out to the smudged marks, letting her hand drop before her fingers could touch them, "– Mum told me about them. There were three to start with. *They* rubbed one out for each night."

"Two nights and then the Dance," said Charlotte. "That was how it went, right? So the first night..." She fell silent; Ellie could almost see Joda and Barbara, standing at her side.

Ellie indicated the triangular mark. "What about this?"

"Dunno," said Jess.

"Mad?"

"I think it's *dālet*," the vicar said.

"Phoenician again?"

"Yeah. It can mean 'God', same as *gīml* or *hē*. It also means 'door'."

Ellie peered into the hole beneath the slab, but hesitated to shine her torch down. "So I'm guessing here's the way in."

"And out," said Charlotte. "Maybe not just for them either. Maybe this is where their god comes out into the world. When they're done, I mean."

"That's probably the whole valley," said Madeleine. "Maybe the hill as well. Or more. We don't know how big, how many..."

"All right." Jess pushed past them, a coil of rope over her shoulder. "Let's not overthink it, eh? We've work to do. And not much time."

Ellie hammered a piton into the ground to hold the rope in place; Jess tossed the rope down the sinkhole. There was a clink and clatter of loose, hard, light objects; the echoes faded, and there was silence.

57.

"Who's going first, then?" said Charlotte. Bravado, thin and brittle as eggshell.

No one answered. Ellie lit a road flare and tossed it down the shaft. Its scarlet glow washed out to illuminate a cavern strewn with pale rubble, and the smell of it mingled with odours of decay.

The whole cavern floor – what they could see of it in the flare-light – was carpeted in bones, which rose up into a hummock directly underneath the shaft. Some were white, others yellow or brown with age; some human, some animal. Ellie glimpsed the long beaky skull of a horse or cow, and a human one too small to be an adult's. The flare kept burning; the only movement was the flickering of the light.

"Right," Ellie sighed. "Here we go." She gripped the rope and leant back at the edge of the shaft, letting it take her weight, then began climbing down.

The rope creaked and swayed. Suddenly the physical effort involved in the descent was daunting. There was surely no way Madeleine could manage it. Or Jess. Could Charlotte, even? The rope rocked and swayed with her weight and that of her rucksack; she tried not to think of the piton anchoring it in place. But at last her feet touched the hummock; Ellie steadied herself, then climbed down to floor level, swaying on the loose, sliding scree of bones. Ribs and scapulae cracked and clattered to the stone floor.

Unslinging the Ithaca, she swept the barrel around the cavern as the others climbed down, one by one. The cavern was roughly dome-shaped, its grey limestone walls almost entirely black with charcoal. Most of the markings were the now familiar *hē* and *gīml*; in places they'd been scored into the rock, too.

On one side of the cavern other colours peeped through the black. Ellie went closer, and saw most of the wall was covered in a crude picture, drawn in chalk and red ochre. She saw what looked like hills, and looming over them a shape. It was hard to make out its details – the charcoal layers grew ever thicker further up the wall – but it was clearly massive in relation to the landscape. At its feet (if they *were* feet) countless tiny stick-men lay prone amid stains of red, some of them broken in pieces. The few who still remained alive seemed to be abasing themselves before the figure.

The tattered creatures couldn't have drawn that; they were blind. Men and women had created the image on the wall, as a memorial, history or warning. Or as instructions to their descendants: *this is how you survive. Kneel before them, worship, and you might be spared.* As the Harpers had ultimately done.

Charlotte and Jess had both climbed down, and now steadied the rope for Madeleine Lowe. Ellie continued surveying the cavern. There were three entrances; all were blind black holes.

Madeleine climbed surprisingly well; the "walking ghost" stage of her sickness, if that was what it was, seemed to be still in effect. She swayed when she released the rope, but steadied herself and picked her way down to the floor.

"Which way now?" Charlotte whispered. "Jess?"

Jess looked as lost as any of them. It wasn't as though any of the Harpers would have cause to come down here. There might be something in the Family Bible, but Jess hadn't seen its contents till today; only Liz Harper would know its secrets cover to cover, and she wouldn't have helped them even if she'd been there.

***

Among the thick dead brambles above the rhyolite slab, Liz Harper crawled out from under her foil blanket, cursing through her teeth.

Stupid. Weak. She'd fallen asleep – *asleep* – while lying in wait. Fucking hell's sake. Almost missed Judas Jess and her scumbag friends, and would've died of hypothermia if the noise of them below hadn't startled her awake. Died of hypothermia if she was lucky, that is: after all, when *They* came swarming out, *They'd* hardly distinguish between one human and another.

And it was near dark now. If she ran, she might make Barrowman Farm before *They* came out of the Hollows. Or not. And while she wanted to believe Ellie Cheetham could do nothing to stop the Dance and what came after, even *They* weren't invulnerable. Judas Jess had given them the Family Bible, the bitch: it wasn't impossible Ellie Cheetham would find a way.

If she was quick, if she hurried, she could deal with Ellie Cheetham and her friends, then scramble up and run like hell for home. There were minutes of daylight left still: they might just be enough.

Liz climbed down into the barrow, to the rope hanging from its piton, peered down and listened. She nodded to herself, and slung her shotgun across her back.

Madeleine limped towards the rightmost entrance. "This way."

"How d'you know?" whispered Charlotte.

"Cobwebs."

"Huh?"

Madeleine pointed. "There's still a load of 'em hanging down over that entrance. Other ones've been swept clear."

Ellie saw she was right. Ragged scraps of webbing clung to the edges of the other entrances; over the third, a thick curtain still hung down to the floor.

"And...?" said Charlotte.

"The tunnel's not in use," said Ellie. "Which is good, as we don't want to run into any more company than we have to. Long as the thing actually goes somewhere."

"It does," said Madeleine. "It will." She moved to the entrance, stooped with a pained grunt, lifted the webbing – which Ellie saw, her stomach rolling queasily, was several inches thick – and disappeared under it.

"Great," muttered Ellie, then picked up the sputtering road flare and followed. The web was filled with desiccated insects, and then with scuttling movement as tiny white spiders raced away from the intruders on spindly legs like long pale hairs. For a moment Ellie thought she was seeing tiny, embryonic versions of the monsters. She shook her head, dipped under the curtain and went into the darkness, holding the flare.

She almost cried out at what it showed her. The tunnel was perfectly round, with ribbed walls, as if a huge earthworm had slid and burrowed through the rock as its small, common cousins did through soil. Neither that nor the row of arched niches cut into the walls on either side every two feet had almost shocked a cry from her: that had been caused by the thin white things folded up inside every niche, each shrouded in a pallid cloak and with a hood hanging down over its face.

They didn't move or even breathe that Ellie could see, but showed no sign of either mummification or decay. Other than their additional shrouds of cobweb, it was all too easy to imagine them stirring into sudden life.

"Budge up," whispered Jess, bumping into Ellie from behind, then added "Fucking hell."

"Yeah." Ellie hadn't moved since seeing the creatures; Madeleine had gone forward, almost out of sight. She went after her friend, Jess behind her.

"Lights out!" Charlotte whispered, behind Jess. "They're coming."

Runnels of water glistened on the stone floor; Ellie dropped the flare into one and ground it out with her boot. If the creatures sensed the pain-giving light even for an instant, they'd know there were intruders. Cold clammy blackness closed around them like a fist, and Ellie felt a sudden deep awareness of the yards of stone above them, the ancient structure the tunnel had bored through; how many more like it must there be? She visualised Thursdale and Slapelow Hill like an enormous chunk of Swiss cheese, so riddled with hollows it might collapse like a playing-card house at a single nudge or jolt.

She didn't know how Charlotte had realised the creatures were on the move, given their silence. Even now, listening in the dark, she heard nothing – but, perhaps as Charlotte had – she felt it, as though a horde of the spiders in the web were crawling over her exposed skin. Everyone else was still, too; she didn't think they even dared to breathe. The tiniest sound might bring the creatures running.

From the direction of the main cavern came the clink and rattle of loose bone – isolated sounds at first, but rising to a rapid, intense clattering as the creatures swarmed (Ellie saw it with absolute clarity, not doubting for a second it matched the reality exactly) over the hummock of bones, then up the shaft. They were going up into the Hollows, and then they'd be racing through Barrow Woods and over Thursdale, crawling up the hillside like spiders up a wall, surging down Halliwell Way towards the meadow and the last of the living. They'd encircle the camp; who could stop them, after all? Only the fires would keep them back; the dark around the camp would belong to them.

Bone sang and clattered, clinked and fell, rang on the cavern floor.

Then, at last, silence.

And only the cold and breathing dark remained.

58.

"What are we looking for?"

"Bloody hell, Ernie, go lie down. You're hobbling around like Long John Silver."

Ernie Stasiolek put weight on his bad leg and grunted. "I'm fine. What are we looking for?"

"Think we'll know when we find it," Noel said. "Bloody things must have come out here somewhere. Maybe where the old church was?"

"Makes sense."

Noel crossed the grass, probing ahead of him with the torch, rifle slung across his back. Best to keep himself busy; easier not to think of Frank Harper that way, trying to crawl away from the pain like a child. Besides, people needed someone to look to right now. Milly would care for them, but it was Ellie who'd always known what to do. Fair enough, it being her job. But she wasn't here now, so he, Ernie and Laura had to fill the gap as best they could.

The three of them followed the glistening stream of Holly Beck to Blackfield Park. Overlooking it was Chapel Bank, but if seeing his old home affected Ernie, he didn't show it. The beck led to the well, beyond which was a reconstruction of the old church's lychgate, and a laminated sign with a diagram of the original church.

Nothing about a long barrow, but even in Dr Bayliss' day there wouldn't have been much left. A team of archaeologists might find something, given a few days, but they had one night, if that. No need to dig down, anyway, not with those things digging their way up.

They went through the lychgate – silly, really, as it stood surrounded by empty space – and shone their torches around. "Lads?" called Laura, shining her light at a spot ahead of her. There was a ragged, circular cut in the turf, marking off an area big as a manhole cover. The cut was an inch wide, and Noel easily dug his fingers in. The turf's edges crumbled, but it rose in one piece; below it a burrow, a little wider than Noel's own shoulder-breadth, led down and away.

On the underside of the turf a latticework of what looked like pale sticks, bound with thin rubbery cords, was fixed in place. Which meant the things could use tools, at least to some degree. Not comforting.

Also, Noel realised, the sticks weren't sticks. He told himself the bones were too thin to be human. The cords were probably sinew. Efficient. Waste no part of the animal. Narrow grooves scored the inside of the burrow; Noel pictured those long thin fingers scrabbling, raking handfuls of earth away.

"So that's how." Ernie looked up towards Chapel Bank above, then along the ruins to his old home. He stood for a moment, then stepped away and swept his torch around. "There's another here."

Laura studied the inside of the burrow. "Looks pretty fresh."

"Must have kept clear of this spot for a while," said Noel. Whatever had been done centuries earlier, either by Christians, barrow-builders, Saxon pagans or Norse, it had worked, at least till now. Had they known about something else these things hated as much as light? Or had the creatures just abandoned the exit after being driven back time after time?

"See if there are any more," he said. "Then let's figure out what to do when the bastards pop up."

"I like that idea," Ernie said.

***

They found four turf "hatches" in all; Laura and Ernie set eight jerrycans of petrol at intervals around them, while Noel, having found the optimum spot inside the perimeter; lay on a piece of tarp peering through his rifle's telescopic sight, adjusting it as he sighted on the cans. The protective firelight crept across the melting snow towards them, fading a few yards short of Laura and Ernie.

"Laura," Ernie hissed; when she looked up, he pointed to the nearest hatchway, hand cupped to his ear. Then Noel heard it too: a faint scuffling, growing louder.

Laura sprinted towards the camp, Ernie hobbling after her. Someone threw kerosene on some of the fires and bright orange flames soared up into the sky; sparks flew up and danced. Noel felt their heat on his face, felt it parch his throat when he gulped for breath. A shelter of light, that only deepened the dark around it.

First Laura, then Ernie, made it across the boundary into the lighted area. They were safe, or as safe as anyone could be tonight.

Someone shouted, and Noel looked towards the church grounds, but there was nothing there yet. Hands pointed instead towards Halliwell Way, where pale, ragged forms crouched on the parapet of the bridge over Groveley Beck. A moment later, white, spidery shapes began crawling from the road, across the meadow.

Liz Harper, heart hammering, gulped for breath.

The last thin white ragged shapes scuttled across the cavern floor, then up the shaft to the Hollows. Several had passed within inches of her hiding-place in the tunnel entrance; she'd wanted to retreat deeper into the tunnel away from them, but hadn't dared lest the movement draw attention to her.

Besides, Judas Jess and her new friends couldn't be far ahead, and with her luck Liz would've walked straight into them, because if they had a morsel of sense they'd be keeping still too.

When the last of *Them* were gone, she listened, and soon there were new sounds. Voices, whispering. Liz turned and peered into the darkened tunnel.

"Okay." A click, and a glimmer of torchlight. "Now, everyone take it easy."

Licking her lips, Liz unslung the shotgun and removed the safety.

"Tunnel's full of them, but they're either dead or asleep." As soon as she'd said it, Ellie felt as though she'd tempted fate. "Lights on, and keep it together, people. Okay, Madeleine –"

There was no answer; Ellie shone the torch around in search of her. "Madeleine!"

"I'm here. Calm your jets."

Ellie's torch-beam wavered back and forth across the tunnel. Curled-up, shrouded monsters leapt out of the shadows at its touch, till finally it fastened on Madeleine's face. "This way," the vicar said.

She'd kept on going in the darkness, while the others had stood frozen, waiting for the swarm to exit the caves. What was steering her? Faith, fever or some other sense that couldn't be readily computed? Whatever it was, it hadn't guided her badly thus far.

Jess and Charlotte followed Ellie in single file, Charlotte throwing glances of mingled hate and terror at the wall-niches. Finally the narrow tunnel opened out into another dome-shaped chamber.

It was similar to the one beneath the Hollows, but not identical. First, and most obvious, there was no entrance in the ceiling, which was an unbroken grey hemisphere of rock. Second, the only other exit from the chamber was another tunnel, situated directly ahead. Third were the alcoves in the walls: as in the tunnel, each was occupied by a dead or hibernating creature.

The fourth difference –

"Oh, no," Charlotte said. "Oh my fucking God, no."

On either side of the thin path leading to the opposite entrance, the chamber's floor was strewn with pits, each two or three feet across. One was empty and, Ellie saw when she shone her torch into it, between fifteen and twenty feet deep. Another was partly filled with bones – femurs, tibias, tangles of ribs and undeniably human skulls. All bore teeth marks where they'd been gnawed, and had been cracked open, presumably for the marrow and brains. Ellie felt sick.

The other two pits were filled to the top with a white crystalline powder: snow, she thought at first. But red stains had soaked through it in places, and none of the powder had melted. She picked up a little and let it fall. Hard crystals. "Salt."

"Salt," said Jess, "to preserve the – fuck, Charlotte, no, get away from –"

"Let me go. Let me g –"

Charlotte fell silent; when Ellie looked she saw the girl had stuffed her own hand into her mouth. When she took it away her lips were bloody and she was crying silently. She turned away, head bowed.

Ellie went to the pit. In the middle of the white surface was a bloom of red and black where Charlotte had scraped the salt away. It was a face, or had been when there'd been skin on it. The meat was still on the bone. Even the eyes.

Salt, to preserve the meat.

Charlotte knelt to study one of the shrouded figures, nudging aside the webs to touch the hem of its garment before Ellie could stop her. The thing didn't stir; its sleep was too deep for so minor an intrusion to disturb it.

The cloak was ragged and irregular in colour and shape; when Ellie came closer, she saw the individual pieces of skin, stitched together however many decades or centuries ago, yet still supple somehow. One piece had a nipple; another had eyelids, nostrils and mouth, all stitched closed. *We waste no part of the animal.*

Ellie reached out for Charlotte, but the girl twisted away. "I'm fine," she said, wiping her mouth. "I'm fine."

"We've got to go," said Madeleine, standing by the entry to the far tunnel. Despite her gaunt face and fever-bright eyes, she somehow looked serene, like a picture Ellie had once seen of an Eastern Orthodox religious icon. "We haven't long."

No one needed any encouragement to get out of the chamber; in fact, there was a brief bottleneck as Charlotte and Ellie tried to do so at the same time. Charlotte motioned Ellie ahead of her: "Age before beauty," she said.

"Piss off," said Ellie, but went first anyway.

When the last of them had moved on into the tunnel Liz Harper cat-footed after them, barely glancing at the bone- and salt-pits. The unchosen. That was what her family had been to these people for so long: outcasts, scum, disposable. *How does it feel, suckers?*

She knew what was in their backpacks now. Judas Jess' hadn't been fastened properly, so Liz had seen the neck of the propane bottle. So that was their plan. Liz bit her lip. There was a chance that it might work. Fire and light might be enough, in the right place. It was *Their* only real vulnerability, but a potentially lethal one. It was why *They* had to strike using surprise and overwhelming force. Deprive their prey of light, then wipe them out before they could learn how to defend themselves.

Liz couldn't be sure if a shotgun blast would detonate the propane bottle. An explosion here wouldn't stop the Dance, but if didn't kill Liz outright, it might wake the creatures slumbering in the wall niches. And if it did –

Well, if it did she could turn the gun upon herself. If it came

to that. Better than the alternative. And at least she'd know
that she'd had the last victory, that her children were avenged.

Liz went into the tunnel, towards the torches' distant glow.

"Madeleine?" Ellie whispered. "Do you know where we need
to go? How to get there?"

Madeleine didn't answer or even turn around. In the
moment before her friend stopped walking, Ellie realised
this tunnel, unlike the previous one, had no alcoves in the
walls, and that the walls weren't made of rock: it was just a
circular burrow in the earth. Soil; nothing more. And as she
realised that there was a rumble, and a hiss of falling earth.
Soil peppered her face, dropping from above in dusty streams.

"Shit!" Jess shouted. "Back! Back – oh fuck –"

There was a rumbling crash behind them; Ellie spun, raising
the torch. Clouds of dust billowed towards her; Jess blundered
back through it, coughing and spluttering. Another crash came
from ahead and Madeleine vanished in a fog of dust, but as
it cleared and settled – leaving them all coated in powder,
resembling ancient ghosts – Ellie saw her standing exactly as
she had, motionless in front of a solid wall of fallen earth.

An earth tunnel, built to collapse: a trap. *They wanted us
down here. Any more fucking bright ideas, Mad?* Had the visions
sent to guide her only done so in order to dispose of a potential
threat? Or had Madeleine, in those moments, been on *their*
side at all?

Liz buried her face in her coat-sleeve and bit down on it,
simultaneously experiencing both terror and the urge to
hysterically laugh.

They'd known. Of course *They'd* known – *They*, or *Their*
masters. Ridiculous to think an enemy could intrude here
undetected, or that *They'd* have no defences prepared. And so

now Judas Jess, Ellie fucking Cheetham and the others were trapped, and if they were lucky the four of them would only suffocate or starve. If not, *They'd* come – *Them*, or something worse.

Or Liz could do it, as she was trapped there too, hidden in the shadows at the end of their little tomb, hidden by the darkness and still-settling dust.

She could end things for herself now, if she wanted: a quick death, guaranteed, and leave the rest to her gods. But Ellie Cheetham was a cunning, dangerous enemy, and besides, Liz wasn't about to let her traitor child outlive her, not when the little whore had already outlived so many loyal ones. Keira: if only Keira had been her blood child, not Jess.

Besides, mightn't Liz's gods show her mercy for this one last service? It wasn't impossible she might find her way out of here, not if she dealt with Cheetham and her crew.

Who knew? *They* might even give her good children back to her. They were gods, after all. What couldn't gods do?

Liz itched to kill Jess first. She was the traitor, the one Liz hated most of all now (and it had taken some doing to outstrip Ellie Cheetham in *that* regard). And what greater loyalty could she show *Them* than to sacrifice her child? But Ellie was the most dangerous. Kill her first. Then – assuming the propane tank didn't blow them all to hell – Liz would deal with Judas Jess.

Liz hunched down and took aim at Ellie Cheetham's back.

Madeleine turned and smiled; a pretty ghastly sight, as the dust had caked so thickly on her face it resembled a cracked ceremonial mask, through which only her fevered eyes and yellowed teeth showed. Oh Christ, had she snapped? Or had something else taken possession of her?

Ellie could believe anything now; rationality crumbled away in this ancient dark, especially when you already knew the old tales of giants, goblins and gods were true, when you looked to dying women's visions for guidance. No great stretch to imagine that, if Madeleine's mind could seek out things hidden in the depths, what lay hidden in the depths might seek her out in return.

"It's all right, wack," said Madeleine, and coughed, wafting the loose dust away. "It's still me. It's okay, Ell. Everybody. This was meant to happen. We're gonna be –"

"Ellie," screamed Jess.

Something – some*one* – slammed into Ellie and knocked her sideways into the tunnel wall. Then there was a flash and a sound of thunder and Jess flew backwards, her chest and face splashed red.

Shotgun, Ellie realised, and flashed her torch down the tunnel to see Liz Harper rising to her feet, teeth bared, screaming as she worked her gun's slide to fire again. The weapon was already aimed at Ellie. She fumbled for the Ithaca, knowing already she was too slow, too late.

But then the ground rumbled again, louder by far than before, and the tiny section of unblocked tunnel vibrated like a tuning fork. Dust and rocks and old roots showered down on them; Liz stumbled sideways, her gun firing wild into the ceiling.

The vibration, Ellie realised, sickness in her guts, was from below. The ground underfoot was not only shaking: it was sagging. Bowing. Giving way.

A moment of silence came, when she dared to hope it'd stopped.

"We're gonna be okay," said Madeleine Lowe, calmly, clearly and with the fullest conviction imaginable.

And then Liz Harper screamed "Fucking *die*", and racked her shotgun's slide once more.

And then the floor collapsed, and Ellie was screaming like everyone else as they fell into an empty blackness, seemingly without end.

59.

Reuben growled, then began to bark. To Noel's left, Ernie Stasiolek fitted Ellie's shotgun to his shoulder; to his right, Laura Caddick aimed her own gun. Then the dog stopped barking and the camp was silent. With a soft thump, the first turf hatch flew open. Even in the gloom Noel saw the scrawny white limbs groping out.

Another dull thump; another. More long, grublike forms emerged. In seconds they'd be swarming in earnest, and the jerrycans would be obscured by their shapes.

Noel aimed at the nearest can and squeezed the trigger. He heard a clanging thud as the bullet hit its mark, before the boom of Laura's shotgun blotted it out. Another can jumped and spun, torn open and glugging its contents onto the ground.

Ernie held his fire while Noel and Laura methodically blasted the canisters. With the chokes removed, Laura's gun fired wide sprays of shot, and one of the blurred white shapes spun backwards, before climbing back onto all fours and creeping forward again.

"Ernie!" Laura shouted.

"On it," he said.

The white, ragged horde rushed forward. Ernie fired, and a single red point of light shot upwards on a thin pointing finger of smoke. It shone for a moment like a low red star, then dropped back down, fading; by the time it fell among the wriggling white shapes onto the petrol-sodden ground it was a dully glowing ember, but that was enough.

There was a sudden brilliant flash and a warm wet breath on Noel's face as snow evaporated with a sound like a gasp. And then the screaming started.

The screams made Noel recall the legend that a mandrake had roots resembling a man and screamed, when plucked, so terribly it killed whoever heard it. Maybe the creatures – thin and pale as roots – were the source of that myth too, as well as those of trolls and goblins.

Appalling though they were, the screams meant victory, however temporary. Thin shapes writhed and fell amidst the flames, and the smell rolled out over the camp, sour and acrid and foul; it scorched Noel's throat, scalded his eyes, and made him want to retch.

He looked away from the fire, back across the field towards Halliwell Way. At first his eyes were too dazzled to see anything, but at last he could make out the blurred pallid forms of the creatures that had been advancing across the meadow. They'd halted, at least for now.

It was the same story when he looked towards the High Street to the west, or south at Smithy Lane. More of the creatures had been advancing from each of those – he guessed they'd poured up the hill road from Thursdale and spread out to encircle the camp – all of whom had now stopped in their tracks.

Noel would have said they were watching, but they couldn't do that; instead he guessed they were listening, or maybe scenting. God knew the reek from the fire was hard to miss.

The screams died down. Mercifully, the appalling stench from the fire also abated – that, or its sheer awfulness had killed Noel's sense of smell.

The pale things kept still. As far as Milly could make out their shapes, they'd all subsided into their crouching postures. Maybe they'd had enough, now they'd seen the villagers could fight back.

What was the Harpers' Family Bible, anyway? Not God's Word, like the Bible Milly knew: just so many rumours, half-truths and speculations. Sleepers under the hill, prophecies, the Dance, the Fimbulwinter – myths, no truer than Goldilocks and the Three Bears or Jack and the Beanstalk. Whatever grains of truth they might have, it didn't make them Scripture –

But even as Milly seized the hope, it broke like rotten straw. The creatures had begun moving again. They came from Halliwell Way, like a low but inexorable pallid wave; from Smithy Lane and the High Street too. Rolling slowly and steadily in towards the camp.

Ellie caught a brief glimpse of Charlotte's terrified face in a stray flash of torchlight, and then there was only the blackness around them, which seemed endless. They'd been tossed like a handful of dust into an infinite void, scattering so far out through it that the others' cries were barely audible. They'd fall and fall and be lost forever –

Bullet time, they called it: those long, stretched-out moments that come in crisis or combat where time slows to a crawl for everything other than your own racing mind and reflexes, so that split-second decisions and actions are reached and unfold at an almost leisurely pace. Except there was nothing any of them could do.

Although the fall seemed unending, they couldn't have dropped any great distance or the landing would have killed or maimed them all. As it was, the impact knocked the wind from Ellie's lungs.

What had she fallen on? It felt sharp and brittle, like dead wood, although there seemed to be fallen earth there too. A heavy thump and a yelp of pain sounded nearby; someone else landed beside her.

There was a sound like sawing wood; Ellie realised it was

breathing. Her own, that of others. But there was also light. It glowed a couple of feet away – one of the torches, half-buried in the pile or heap they'd landed on.

A pile or heap. Groping for the torch, she realised what had broken their fall. It was dead all right, but it wasn't wood. It wasn't wood at all.

Ellie picked the torch up, hand shaking. "Is everybody all right?" she said, and shone the torch around.

They were still alive.

A few yards from the gaping hole where the ground had opened under Ellie and the others, Liz Harper lay blinking in the dust, wiping her coat-sleeve across her mouth.

"Is everyone okay?" she heard Ellie Cheetham say again. "Charlotte? Mad? Jess?"

Liz had thought the shaft bottomless, or at least deep enough to kill them on impact, but the voices sounded as though they came from no more than twenty feet below.

There was still a round in the shotgun's chamber; Liz loaded two more into the magazine. She'd got Judas Jess at least, blown her scraggy little chest apart; she'd seen it. That left three to kill.

Ellie shone the torch over the scattered remains. The shaft was seven or eight feet wide, with a floor of impacted bones and soil. Other remnants were scattered here and there – a miner's lamp, a hiker's boot, a broken, rusted sword. *You're not the first to come down here, for whatever reason. And none of these poor bastards got out either.*

Madeleine lay groaning on her side, face grey. Charlotte helped her sit upright. "It's all right," the vicar said. "It's all right." There was a rank smell in the shaft, fresher and fouler than anything that could have emanated from the bones:

the smell from the dying woman in the hospital again, only worse. "Think some of me stitches broke."

Ellie, Charlotte, Madeleine – "Jess?" said Ellie.

"Jess?" Charlotte, half-turning. "You – oh *fuck*."

Jess lay crumpled on the far side of the shaft, eyes glassy, mouth agape, red froth on her lips. Her chest was bloody and shattered, and now all Ellie could hear was her breathing – a tortured, wheezing noise.

"Oh fuck." Charlotte was crying. "Oh fuck, no."

"Shit. Jess. Jess." Ellie moved to the girl's side, wiping blood from her face with her sleeve. She should prop her up – help her breathe if her lungs were injured – but what else might be damaged, and made worse if the girl were moved?

She heard movement overhead a second before Charlotte yelled a warning, and threw herself sideways. The shotgun roared a second later; the bone-heap's surface erupted in a hail of splinters. Above her, Liz Harper worked the slide of her gun, screaming "Fucking *die*." Ellie fumbled for the Ithaca, but it was the tunnel all over again: she was too slow, too off-guard.

A dazzle of red light erupted in the pit, then streaked upwards with a *whoosh*. Liz screeched and dropped the shotgun, clawing at the air. Fire and smoke spewed out of her left eye; her face was a red-glowing, screaming mask. Then she dropped over the edge of the pit and landed with a crash among the scattered bones.

Jess slumped backwards; the flare pistol still locked in one small hand. Ellie was afraid she'd died, till she saw that fresh blood was still bubbling on the girl's lips. Charlotte crawled to her side.

"Charlotte, give me a hand," Madeleine said. Ellie heard a clink and clatter of bones.

"What?" Charlotte turned towards the vicar. "Help us!"

"We can't stay here," Madeleine said. "Got to get out and *fast*."

"What?"

"This isn't the bottom of the shaft," said Madeleine. She was pulling skeins of cobweb from the wall, revealing the mouth of another tunnel. "It's a blockage. Too many people fell down here over the years. Something got wedged and the rest piled up on top. This shaft goes a *lot* further down."

Ellie was afraid to ask how she knew, just as she was now afraid to look down at the bones and earth she was crouched on, in case doing so broke whatever spell held them in place. Madeleine passed her torch to Charlotte, who shunted it into the tunnel mouth to light her way. "Come on," the vicar said. "Before –" She left the sentence unfinished.

"Jess," said Charlotte.

Ellie hesitated. A hard and ruthless part of her wanted to say nothing could be done, that the girl was already dead or good as, that they had neither time nor strength to carry someone in such a state. But if the bone floor gave way, Jess would fall down into the depths and be lost there forever. And she deserved better than that. "Get her up," said Ellie.

Charlotte unfastened Jess' backpack, then lifted her into the tunnel entrance and Madeleine's arms. The floor shifted and cracked, and there was a trickle of dust. "Move," said Ellie. "Now."

First Charlotte, then Ellie climbed up into the tunnel. Ellie looked back towards Jess' backpack, the only thing they'd left behind. Losing it meant one less weapon against the creatures, but even if going back hadn't been suicidal, none of them could have carried two of the things. Ellie turned away, but something seized her ankle and pulled.

She screamed and kicked out. One of the creatures – one of the creatures was awake, and attacking her. But as she rolled onto her back, Ellie saw that it was Liz Harper, one side of her face a black and red ruin, a gaping socket for an eye, snarling through gritted teeth as she tried to drag Ellie out of the tunnel and herself in. Ellie kicked at the scorched face, but Liz's grip refused to break, and the sound of dust trickling was joined by the clatter of bones as the bone floor sagged in the middle, then gave way, Jess' pack tumbled into the hole and vanished into blackness. In the same moment, Liz's full weight fell on Ellie's leg, and she was being dragged back out of the tunnel.

Charlotte lunged past Ellie, driving the butt of her shotgun into the crown of Liz's head, into the ruined face, till Ellie heard things crack. Liz's grip slackened, and gravity did the rest. Liz clawed and scrabbled for a handhold, but it was too late, especially when Ellie kicked out wildly with both legs. Liz Harper fell backwards into space and was gone, leaving only a scream that might have been terror or rage.

About half the blockage remained in place, anchored by the dried, packed earth. Then it, too, cracked and fell away. A few chunks of bone and earth clung to the shaft's edges, but otherwise there was only blackness. When Ellie shone her torch down the shaft, she saw only a long stone throat seemingly without an end.

"Jesus Christ," muttered Charlotte.

"Got to go," said Madeleine. "Haven't much time left."

She was already moving down the tunnel, shining her torch ahead. The walls were lined with those now-familiar web-shrouded alcoves, occupied like the others they'd passed. The creatures they'd fought so far could only be a fraction of the army asleep down here. And these were just the advance troops, the attack dogs. The real enemy, the big guns – those were sleeping down here too, waiting to be woken up.

Charlotte looked at Jess, then Madeleine. "Go on," said Ellie. "I'll look after her."

Jess was still breathing, however tormentedly. She looked tiny, and ridiculously young, even more so than she was. Her eyes were closed. There was blood smeared on her cheeks where Charlotte had wiped away the froth, but more of it was accumulating on her lips. Ellie pulled off one of her own sweatshirts and tore it into strips to bandage the chest wound, then picked her up. The poor kid felt so light.

Cradling Jess in her arms, Ellie followed the others along the tunnel, between the alcoves of the still unwoken dead.

Liz Harper tried to move, but every attempt brought crippling shocks of pain.

Her face was a white fire of anguish, with a spike of it drilling through the ruined socket of her eye. Her spine wasn't broken, at least. Almost a pity, as it might be the only bone in her body that wasn't. Arms, legs, ribs: she'd caromed off the shaft walls as she fell, which had grown more jagged as she went. A protruding rock had shattered her pelvis like an old china sink, but the final impact had somehow failed to kill her. Her fumbling fingers (not just her spine that was unbroken, then), encountered fragments of ancient, brittle bone that crumbled at her touch. Maybe that had cushioned her fall.

At least Judas Jess was dead. Had to be. Liz had got the treacherous little cow in the chest. She'd managed that if nothing else. But Ellie Cheetham and the rest were still alive, and had escaped the trap they'd fallen in.

They wouldn't succeed, though. Liz had to believe they wouldn't. *They* would take care of Ellie Cheetham and her friends –

Something moved in the darkness.

Several somethings.

More than several.

Not her. Not her. She'd served *Them*. She'd –

But they were all around her, scuttling insect-like in the dark.

This wasn't fair, she thought. This wasn't fucking *fair*.

But thin, clawed fingers were plucking at her, and robes of tattered skin brushed her face.

60.

Fabric flapped and rustled. Milly looked around: all but a tiny handful of folk had retreated inside their tents. What else could they do, after all, other than huddle down and hope to live till sunrise?

Reuben slunk out of hiding and licked Milly's fingers. Milly moved between Ernie and Noel, who stood with their guns at the ready. She could still feel the flames' heat, but it was fading. Once the fire in Blackfield Park burned out, they'd be surrounded on that side too.

The creatures crept towards them, silent. Oh God, how many this time? Milly couldn't count them. For a moment she thought they'd keep coming, light or no – rolling through the camp, smothering the fires with their bodies so the rest of the horde could fall on the survivors in the dark. But the creatures halted at the firelight's edge and settled back into their waiting crouches; shadows danced and rippled in the folds and hollows of their cowls. The flames bowed and wavered in a gust of wind; their robes and hoods of skin billowed. Otherwise they were still as stone.

The creatures were ranked six or seven deep; if not for the fires they'd engulf the camp in seconds. But so far, they held back.

Wind. The roar and gutter of flames. Milly was afraid the fires would be blown out, but the wind dropped and they brightened again. Still the monsters didn't move.

The heat on the side of her face faded. Milly dared a glance towards the old church grounds: except for a few dully glowing

383

embers, the fire had burned out. More pallid shapes flowed in from either side, closing the gap.

They have now compassed us in our steps: they have set their eyes bowing down to the earth; like as a lion that is greedy of his prey. Milly waited: while they couldn't venture directly into the firelight, they weren't short of tricks, but the creatures remained crouching, motionless. She dared hope they might, if capable, be experiencing a glimmer of fear.

The flames dimmed and flared under fresh gusts of wind. Nothing else moved.

Then the things began to moan. It came, at first, from the blackness behind Milly; then the creatures on either side of the camp picked it up, finally those dead ahead.

The sound, neither human nor animal, rose and fell, its pitch shifting apparently at random. It was the howl of lost and wounded things; it was the groaning of things dying, frightened, alone and far from God. It was the wind keening in rocks and trees; it was the grief of all the dead. It was a terrible sound: Milly wanted to flee from it, to cut it off and kill it, but could do neither. Only listen.

The creatures looked different, somehow: Milly moved forwards, closer to the edge of the light.

"Milly –"

"Shurrup, Jones," she whispered.

The monsters didn't react. As she reached the perimeter of the lighted area, Milly saw their heads were thrown back, the twin pairs of incisors inside their muzzles splayed outwards as if on hinges. They didn't pause or even, seemingly, breathe: it was as though they were conduits for a sound that came up from somewhere else – the depths below the peaks and dales, or another, deeper Pit.

Milly was about six feet from the nearest creature, the closest she'd been to one without trying to either escape or fight it. It didn't seem aware of her; it just crouched and sent its weird call skywards.

The sound vibrated in her belly, sending a wave of nausea through her, and worse. Milly experienced sudden, overwhelming fear: her heart began pounding and she struggled to breathe. This must be how Ellie felt during an anxiety attack, but Milly knew this dread had a single, very specific cause. One which, if she continued listening, she'd clearly perceive.

Part of her wanted that to happen – better to know the worst and face it – and she found herself swaying closer to the edge of the firelight. But then she recoiled, certain suddenly that whatever it was would be too much to bear.

Maybe she'd see the giants – because what could the Harpers' "giants" be but devils? – and the sight of them might strike her dead or drive her mad. Or perhaps, perhaps, it would show her what they were dealing with, and how to defeat it –

"Milly!" Noel grabbed her arm; Milly stumbled backwards. She'd been only two or three feet from the nearest creature: another step would have taken her out into the darkness with them.

"Fuck," she said at last. "Thanks, Jones."

"*Christ*, Milly. Do *not* do that to me again."

"Soz."

"You okay?"

"Think so."

They moved back, joining Laura and Ernie in the middle of the camp. Ernie eyed the monsters, pale-faced, sweat on his forehead. Milly touched his shoulder. "You okay?"

He looked away from the things, wiping his mouth. "Think so. That sound they make. Does something to your brain."

"Great," said Laura. "I mean, this is new, isn't it? No one else ran into this last night?"

Noel shook her head. "Don't think so. Not like they needed any secret weapons last night, though, was it? Having a whale of a time, they were."

"Looks like they're cranking up the pressure," Milly said.

"Better go round the camp," said Ernie. "Check on everyone. Last thing we need's –"

Someone screamed. There were cries of alarm, shouts, running footsteps. Someone shouted "Hold him," and a man ran screaming towards Milly and the others. He didn't see them; his eyes were fixed on the creatures beyond. It was Plant-Pot, though Milly barely recognised him in his terror and rage, charging madly at his tormentors to punch or choke those horrible moans into silence because there was no escaping them and he couldn't endure them for another moment, even though he'd be killed in seconds. Which was what the beasts wanted, of course: to drive or lure the survivors out of the light.

Phil Robinson got there first, though. Plant-Pot was the bigger of the two, but Phil, while shorter, was heavier. He stepped into Plant-Pot's path, crouched and turned to catch the running man in the stomach with his shoulder. Plant-Pot doubled up and flew over Phil's back onto the ground; Phil pivoted and fell on top of him, grabbing his arms and pinning him flat. Plant-Pot struggled hard, but more people ran in and helped hold him steady. Someone clapped Phil on the shoulder. "S'all right, mate. We got him."

Phil climbed off, shaking, then stumbled away before anyone could speak. Milly saw Julie hug him tightly, and then the Robinsons disappeared inside their tent.

Chris Brailsford and his Mum helped Plant-Pot away. Poor sod, but it wasn't hard to understand. Good work from Phil, there, and a surprise; Milly had been afraid he'd crack if anyone did.

Although he still might, with that moaning still going on, causing hallucinations, dread and panic. Andy Brailsford would just be the first, unless –

Milly began to sing. She'd a decent voice, thank God; she'd sung in Pastor Matt's choir. Now her voice rose above the camp:

"Abide with me, fast falls the eventide,
The darkness deepens, Lord, with me abide;
When other helpers fail, and comforts flee,
Help of the helpless, Lord, abide with me..."

Kate Beck joined in, to Milly's surprise; she hadn't thought
the girl was the religious sort. Then again, she was a drama
student, so any chance to perform. But that wasn't a kind
thought, whether or not there was any truth in it; besides, it
didn't matter.

"Swift to its close ebbs out life's little day;
Earth's joys grow dim, its glories pass away;
Change and decay in all around I see..."
Now other voices joined in:
"Oh, Thou who changest not, abide with me."
Noel began singing too.
"I need Thy presence every passing hour,
What but Thy grace can foil the Tempter's power?"
Milly could barely hear the creatures' moaning now.
"Who, like Thyself, my guide and stay can be?
Through cloud and sunshine, Lord, abide with me."

By now everyone had joined in. Half were singing the bits they
could remember and humming the rest, but that didn't matter:

"I fear no foe, with Thee at hand to bless;
Ills have no weight, and tears no bitterness;
Where is death's sting? Where, grave, thy victory?
I triumph still, if Thou abide with me."
The moaning had died away.
"Hold Thou Thy cross before my closing eyes;
Shine through the gloom and point me to the skies;
Heaven's morning breaks, and Earth's vain shadows flee;
In life, in death, Oh Lord, abide with me."

The song died away; once again, the only sound came from the fires. The beasts remained in the shadows. The blackness beyond them, around the camp, seemed absolute; Milly felt a swirl of dizziness and vertigo, suddenly convinced that they were floating like a raft on an ink-black sea. Fragile, leaky, so easily overturned by a wave or swamped by a storm. And the sea full of sharks and other, more terrible things. Monsters of the deep.

Someone else began singing: Tara Caddick, Jess' baby in her arms, looking shyly down but belting out the lines with all her lungpower. Milly bit back hysterical laughter when she realised it was a Katy Perry song. But Laura joined in, and then the rest. Noel caught Milly's eye and grinned. It wasn't even about the words now; it was about music, solidarity, a refusal to give in. Spiting the bastards with communion and joy.

The moaning began again at some point, but Milly barely noticed. As Tara's song faded somebody else weighed in; after he was done, there were a few moments of silence before someone else began. Noel sang an old Welsh hymn called "Calon Lân". Milly barely understood a word of it, but knew it was beautiful. He sang alone, of course; after him old John Kennard, who'd been a miner once upon a time, remembered the '84 strike all too well and probably thought he'd had quite enough religion for one evening, began belting out:

"You can't get me cos I'm part of the Union,
You can't get me cos I'm part of the Union,
You can't get me cos I'm part of the Union,
Till the day I die..."

And so it went on, until at some point they realised the moaning had stopped. Silence returned, and they waited for whatever came next.

The next attack would involve no games; Milly knew that

in her bowels. When it came, it would be unrelenting, and wouldn't end until the light was gone and the dark supreme.

She tried to pray, to beg forgiveness of her faults before the end, but nothing came.

Ancient night. Ancient night. That'd been what Madeleine had said. *The old gods wake, the sun dies, and earth and waters perish as night comes forever more.* Sitting on her crate, looking out into the dark, Milly touched the cross at her throat. To even talk about old gods was blasphemy; there was only one. Everything else was the Devil. But who or what had spoken through Madeleine, then?

Reuben whined and licked her hand. Milly ruffled his hair. None of that mattered now. This was as simple as could be. Black and white: a relief, almost, in a life so full of greys. No complexity here, no negotiation, no difficult questions – just standing steady and defying the old deep dark.

Which was all dead grand and heroic, but Milly wasn't the heroic sort. Given the choice, she'd sooner keep her head down and muddle through life's tangles and complexities as best she could, her faith the dim torch that lit her way. But life didn't offer such choices. The first Christians, in Rome – their choice, too, had been black and white. Bow down and lose their souls, or keep their faith even if it meant their lives.

They were all fucked anyway, unless Ellie pulled off a miracle. Milly wasn't even sure if she should hope or pray she did – if this *was* Judgement Day, surely that was God's will and to suggest a man or woman could stop it was blasphemy.

But, again, this resembled nothing she'd read of in Revelations. And the Bible wasn't always to be taken literally. Well, then. *Whomever is righteous, let him be righteous still; whomever is wicked, let him be wicked still.* She was who she was, and who she'd carry on being: Millicent Abigail Emmanuel, doctor, healer, Christian. Her whole life, everything she stood for, was about loving kindness to others. Didn't matter whether God rewarded her for it, or even saw her right now. She was who she was, and she'd continue to be.

61.

Jess's ragged, painful breathing faded as Ellie carried her along the tunnel; finally it stopped, and the small shape lay still and quiet in her arms. She made no move to put the girl down; apart from anything else, there was no space to do so. The narrow tunnel didn't branch or bend. Besides, Ellie wouldn't lay Jess down in a place like this, under the monsters' eyeless gaze.

She didn't want to lay Jess down at all; didn't want to admit what the absence of breath now told her. She didn't know why this one death should seem so wrong, so unjust, but it did. Whenever she closed her eyes, she saw that small figure, tiny but somehow indomitable, striding determinedly on through the snow. Jesus, she was blubbering, skriking away like a little kid, now, as she walked.

And she couldn't do that. Mustn't. Out of everyone here, she had to keep it together. But it was so fucking unfair. Shot by that bitch of a mother she'd fought so hard to escape. The casual, absurd cruelty of it, like a final spit in the face.

Ellie shook her head and kept going. She didn't know how long they walked. Felt like hours; might have been minutes. Maybe it was both; maybe time worked differently, down here, to the outside world. All those legends of men and women who spent a day with the hidden folk, only to come home and find their loved ones grown old or dead. Even if they got out of here alive, there was no guessing what they'd find when they did.

You had to stop asking questions in the end, or go mad from it all. No point, anyway. Ellie wasn't in charge. Madeleine was leading the way, and that was fine. It was good to lay her burden down. The metaphorical one, anyway, of leadership and responsibility. The one in her arms was very real and she'd be carrying it a while yet.

But for now, she could only follow. One foot in front of the other, between the ranks of sleeping monsters. *The sleep of reason brings forth monsters*: what was that from? A painting, wasn't it? Goya. That was it. What then did the sleep of monsters bring?

"All right," said Madeleine. Ellie registered vaguely that their surroundings were no longer quite so claustrophobic: the tunnel had widened into another of the dome-shaped chambers, although this one appeared disused, the wall alcoves empty, and the floor pits –

Salt and bones crunched underfoot. Some of the pits were empty, heaps of gritty rock salt strewn everywhere, while others were filled with cracked gnawed bones: some old and yellowed, others freshly stripped of meat. Torn-down cobwebs strewed the floor around the empty alcoves' mouths. *Salt. To preserve the meat*. The things that had slept here had woken and fed.

"Ellie." Charlotte touched her arm. "*Ellie*. You can put her down now."

She wasn't sure she could at first; she'd been carrying Jess so long the girl felt like a part of her, and to lay her down would almost be to mutilate herself. But then she was crouching, lowering the body – lowering *Jess*, she couldn't, wouldn't, think of her as *a body* and nothing else, not yet – to the floor. And then she was kneeling, and she was crying, and she couldn't stop. But she had to stop. She had a job to do.

"Easy." Charlotte beside her, an arm around her shoulders. "Ellie, I know." Her eyes were red and full of pain; there were tears on her cheeks, too. "I know. But we've no time. We have to end this."

"Yes." It came out as a croak; Ellie tried again. "Yes." She somehow stood. Felt the propane cylinder's weight on her back. Breathed out. She was still crying, but dragged her sleeve across her eyes and made herself stay upright. *Richard.* Oh Christ, why was she thinking of him, now? She mustn't weaken. Not so close to the end. There'd be time to grieve afterwards. Unless the Dance woke the giants; no time then for anyone to cry. Only scream.

Ellie shook her head, breathed out again, and tried to perform the steadiness she wanted to feel. "Right," she said, and made herself look down at Jess, who lay on her back, head turned to one side, resembling a discarded doll. Ellie crouched and lifted her.

"Ellie –" said Charlotte.

Ellie propped Jess against the wall, in a sitting position. The girl's head drooped, chin on her chest. Her short legs stuck out; tufts of newspaper protruded from her boots, packed in to make them fit. "Right," Ellie said again. Jess was still clutching the flare pistol; Ellie prised it from her grip, reloaded it and stuck it through her waistband. "Sorry. Let's crack on, eh?"

There was a soft murmuring. Madeleine, Ellie realised: she'd been praying quietly all the while. "Amen," the vicar said, then turned, swaying slightly, and looked around the cavern. There were two entrances; unlike the first chamber, neither looked overgrown or disused. "This way, I think," said Madeleine, pointing to the left-hand one.

"You think?" demanded Charlotte. But Madeleine had already entered the tunnel. Charlotte turned to Ellie. "You sure we should –"

"Got any better ideas?"

Charlotte looked at Jess. "Last time we followed her –"

Madeleine's voice floated out of the tunnel. "We went the right way," she said. "We're on a lower level now. Closer to them."

Charlotte gave Ellie a mute, pleading look. But she'd been right before: there was no more time. Ellie followed Madeleine.

"Ellie?" Charlotte called after her. "Oh, fuck it. Wait up." And she followed too, boots crunching in the salt and bones.

62.

"Want one?" said Kate Beck.

Milly blinked; she hadn't even heard the girl sit down beside her on the upturned plastic crate. Kate had Reuben on a makeshift lead; the dog jumped up and put his muddy paws on Milly's leg. "Gerroff," she said. "Sorry, love?"

"Cigarette?" Kate was holding out a packet of Silk Cut. Weak-ass smokes, but the packet of B&H Chris Brailsford had given Milly was long gone. Her throat was raw from smoking, but she'd have plenty of time to quit, if there actually was a tomorrow.

"Ta, cock." Milly accepted the cigarette and the proffered light. Kate tucked the lighter back inside the cigarette packet and the packet back inside her sling, smiling her enigmatic smile and staring into the thickening dusk. Already Halliwell Way was barely visible.

Milly honestly couldn't read the girl; other than just after they'd found her in her parents' crawlspace Kate Beck had maintained a kind of chilly calm, like deep water frozen over and crusted white with snow, hiding everything underneath. She was polite, even funny, but it was all surface; everything real was hidden. Perhaps unfairly on Milly's part, she never felt she could wholly trust or like her, even though she'd done nothing wrong.

Now, though, the mask seemed to briefly drop. "Not long now," Kate said. Milly heard a hint of fear – she wouldn't be human otherwise – but other emotions, too, harder to decipher. Anger, hate, resignation, even acceptance; Milly glimpsed them all, but only for a moment. Then Kate turned and smiled at her, the mask back in place. "Well, just have to do our best. Anything you need doing?"

"Not right now." All that could be done had been; only the waiting remained.

"Fair enough," Kate nodded. "Let's just enjoy our cigarettes, then."

"Yeah."

They sat, and smoked, and waited.

Ellie had no idea how deep they were now, or how long they'd been walking. The new tunnel sloped down, more steeply than the first, and began winding – a slow, descending spiral – before finally branching out. And then branching again. And again.

There were constant forks, and endless side-tunnels leading off from the main, but Madeleine, moving at a fast clip, took turning after turning without a moment's pause, as if following an invisible rope. Like Theseus in the labyrinth, following Ariadne's thread, except this was leading them into peril and not away. Ellie had already completely lost track of the way they'd come: she'd have to hope Madeleine could retrace their steps, assuming they lived to try, and that Madeleine's God gave a toss about them once they'd served their purpose. Or that He was playing any part in this. Perhaps Madeleine's visions were just a kind of immune response on reality's part, designed to protect it from the chaos the ragged things embodied. Either way, having served their function, their survival might be of no more interest to whatever was guiding them than that of a few white blood cells would be to Ellie herself.

They passed through endless warrens with alcoves in the walls – some empty, some occupied – and two more of the dome-shaped caverns in quick succession, before the space opened up around them, so massively that Ellie felt dizzy. Far above, just within the torchlight's reach, she saw the tips of stalactites.

"Bloody *hell*," said Charlotte.

They were on a flat stone ledge that extended about twenty yards ahead of their current position, then dropped away into nothingness. A hundred feet beyond *that*, another ledge faced them; it too was at the top of a sheer face that led down, and down.

Ellie went to the edge and shone her torch downwards, but the thin ray of light couldn't reach the bottom; the chasm likewise extended as far as she could see in either direction. She tried to calculate its scale and couldn't. It was impossible; there was no way all this could exist beneath Slapelow Hill and Thursdale. Perhaps they were under Fendmoor now, or Wakeman's Edge, or beyond. Or perhaps they'd fallen into some other, parallel realm that could extend for countless miles, perhaps even into infinity.

It didn't matter. They were here.

"We need to cross here," said Madeleine.

"How, exactly?" demanded Charlotte.

Madeleine strode towards the edge. Ellie opened her mouth to call her back, but the vicar shone her torch directly ahead, and it gleamed on stone.

It looked like a bridge, although it was so caked in precipitated limestone – dripping with stalactites, studded with stalagmites – that for all Ellie knew it was a natural feature. In any case it led across the chasm. Madeleine stepped forward; she hesitated as she set foot on the bridge, then swayed and gripped the parapet for support.

"Mad?"

"I'm okay." The vicar stood up straight with an effort and smiled at Ellie. She looked appalling: pale, sweaty and gaunt, as if she'd lost a substantial amount of weight since going underground, her sickness burning her up from within. "Just dying. But we already knew that, eh, Ell?"

The only sound was the drip of water. No one spoke. There was nothing to say. Madeleine sighed. "Anyway," she said, and set off over the bridge.

Ellie followed, keeping to the centre; it wasn't particularly wide, and the parapet was no more than hip-high, which felt like scant protection given the depth of the drop on either side.

Gusts of cold, rank-smelling wind blew up from the depths. Looking down felt positively insane, but nonetheless Ellie did. The abyss called out, sometimes.

The chasm's edges were jagged and put her in mind of teeth, as though they were walking across an open, hungry mouth. What had Madeleine said? *Down in the dark, in the old deep dark. Down in the Yawning, I see them stir.* And indeed something *did* seem to be stirring down there, lighter than the blackness. Ellie couldn't make it out clearly and was reluctant to shine the torch directly at it, but eventually she made to aim it down.

"Don't, Ell." Madeleine hadn't turned round. "You don't want to see. 'Sides, they're not far off waking as it is."

Ellie shone her torch ahead again. She'd glimpsed something. She wasn't sure what – a horn, a claw – but it had been frighteningly big. She did her best to convince herself it had only been a formation of oddly-coloured rock.

"Good call," said Mad. "They're a long way from the worst things down here."

She didn't elaborate, and Ellie didn't ask. Especially not when she realised how regular the gusts of wind from the chasm were; how like breath.

"Tea?" said Kate Beck. She was carrying two steaming tin mugs by the handles with her one good hand, God alone knew how; when Milly took one from her, it was so hot she nearly dropped it. The girl sat beside her, firelight lapping her white profile.

Reuben began barking at the shadows, pulling at the lead. "Easy. Easy," Milly said, pulling him back by the collar. "Shh, now. *Quiet.*"

The dog fell silent; Milly and Kate peered into the shadows. Kate half-stood and cocked her head. "Listen. Can you hear...?"

Milly was about to say no, but then she heard a clank and scrape of metal, the faint clunk and clonk of brick and stone. It grew louder: a series of heavy, clunking blows, then the grind and scrape and screech of metal again. Metal being pulled apart. "The fuck?" she said. But the question answered itself: "Ammunition." All the wrecked cars; all the ruined buildings. Metal parts. Brickwork.

The noises were distant, coming from Halliwell Way and the surrounding roads. But when she squinted into the darkness, she could see white shapes, crawling closer.

"Shit." Kate stood up. "Everyone watch out," she shouted. "They're going to –"

But they'd already started, and that was what finished her. Milly actually glimpsed what did it: a car's engine block, sailing down with almost leisurely slowness, the instant before it smashed into Kate Beck's face and swept her aside like a broken doll. And then Milly was diving for non-existent cover, scrabbling across the muddy ground as another missile crashed down onto an outlying fire, flattening it out of existence, and the thin white swarm rolled forward to claim the dark that fell.

63.

The bridge seemed unending, but finally they reached the other side, as if emerging from a black sea onto an empty beach. Their feet crunched in loose scree, stone chips and fragmented bone.

The sheer rock face ahead of them stretched up until lost to sight. At floor level, punched into it at regular intervals, was a series of circular entrances, each about fifteen feet across. Madeleine swept her torch's beam across them.

"Where now?" Ellie whispered. Quiet in the stone cathedral.

"Shh." Madeleine held up a hand. "Hear that?"

As Ellie listened, she began to: a faint, rhythmic sound. An underground river, maybe? No, not that: it was sharper, solider, more regular. Almost like –

"Is that a drum?" said Charlotte.

Madeleine nodded, then shone her torch across the entrances again. "This one," she said at last, and strode forward. "I think."

Ellie hoped that was a joke on Madeleine's part.

The new tunnel, at least, was less claustrophobic than the ones before it. Ellie tried not to contemplate what sort of creature it had been built to accommodate. The drumming was louder: at least two instruments, she guessed. She could hear another noise, too: a kind of whistling or piping, like a flute or recorder. A tune of sorts, but atonal and discordant. Something about it seemed to seep into Ellie's bones, chill as liquid nitrogen.

Madeleine stopped and raised a hand. "Here."

The tunnel opened into a low cavern containing three other entrances. How had Madeleine led them down here? Some heightened awareness brought on by the hallucinatory intensity of her fever? Had the knowledge been passed on by the germs or poison that were slowly killing her? Or was her God guiding her? If so, had it been only accident they'd walked so quickly into a trap, when otherwise they'd been guided, as far as Ellie could tell, clear of danger?

Or, given how quickly Madeleine had led them from the blocked shaft to here, had it been intentional, to provide a short cut? In which case, what had Jess been? Bad luck? Collateral damage? A sacrifice? Maybe she hadn't mattered to Madeleine's God, being tainted by association with her family.

Ellie reminded herself she didn't believe in Madeleine's God. Still: even dead, Jess couldn't catch a break. For her body to be left down here, too, after so long fighting to get clear of Barrowman Farm's gravity well, seemed like injustice piled on injustice, cruelty piled on cruelty. Not that there'd been any real alternative to leaving her behind. Even so, if they somehow made it back out and passed the way they'd come, Ellie would bring her back to the surface. Get her away from Thursdale in death at least.

"Turn your lights off," Madeleine said.

"What?"

"Just do it. Trust me."

Ellie clicked off her torch, expecting the blackness to fall in on them with the density and force of collapsing earth. Instead, there was light: a cold, silvery glow, unlike any light she remembered seeing. It limned the walls of one tunnel, shining up from around a bend where it angled down.

Madeleine switched her torch back on; Ellie and the others did the same. "Nearly there," said Madeleine. "Get ready."

She made for the tunnel entrance. Charlotte unslung her shotgun and took off the safety catch. Ellie did the same, then stepped forward and caught Madeleine's arm. "I should probably go first, mate."

"Your choice, Ell. It's just a straight run from here, I think. But I might make a better human shield. I'm dying anyway."

Again, it disturbed Ellie to hear Madeleine acknowledge her death so lightly. Maybe it was a side effect of whatever delirium or heightened consciousness drove her. Ellie wondered if Madeleine's God had prompted her to take on the monsters armed only with her crucifix, so she'd be infected with the means to truly fight back? More collateral damage, the Light sacrificing its pawns to gain advantage against the Ancient Dark?

"I'll go ahead," said Ellie. "Just in case there's any surprises."

Besides which, she doubted they could find their way back without Madeleine's help – always assuming Madeleine's God had any interest in their doing so once they'd served its purpose. And always assuming that they could: for all Ellie knew, trying to prevent the creatures reaching their apotheosis at this point might be as futile as trying to halt a runaway train with her outstretched hands.

Ellie's torch was on a sling; she hung it over her shoulder, steadied the Ithaca in both hands, then started down the tunnel's winding slope.

The weird, pale light grew stronger and stronger, the discordant, arrhythmic drumming and piping louder and louder, as they went. Soon the glow was very bright, and Ellie switched the torch off. One by one, the others following did the same.

The chill silver glow lit the tunnel clearly as the morning, coming from around a final bend up ahead. The piping and drumming had by now risen to a nigh-unbearable volume. Madeleine's face was inscrutably calm, almost masklike, its sheen of sweat the only clue to her suffering. Charlotte held her shotgun pointing down and to the side. For a moment they stood, silent.

"Right," said Ellie. "Off we go, then."

The tunnel opened out onto a ledge in another sheer, high

rock wall. Thirty or forty feet below was a stone floor; the ceiling was hundreds of feet overhead. It was hard to gauge how many, even though the silver light reached all the way up: it was another huge, impossible space.

Directly opposite them was the source of the silver light, and of that strange and terrible tune. For a moment they looked on it; finally Charlotte said, in tones of absolute despair: "Oh Jesus Christ."

And even Madeleine Lowe had no response to that.

The blackness rolled in like a wave, with the swarm atop it like a poisoned surf. Milly stumbled back from it, passing Kate Beck as she did. All she could see of the poor girl was her lower body; the engine block had driven the rest of her into the mud like a tent-peg. There was no sign of the dog; he'd vanished into the crowd.

Something flew down towards her, missing Milly by inches before it crashed into the ground, bounced, rose, fell and careered on. The back wheel off a tractor, launched and hurled.

Milly ducked and ran as more missiles flew. She heard her feet thudding on the wet soil and remembered: the monsters were blind, they couldn't see. Something else came sailing through the air – big, heavy – and she dived for the ground, her torch spinning away from her to land yards away.

All around her, screams.

A wheel off a car flew overhead to smash directly into another campfire, and the light began to fade. Milly began to get up out of the mud to make for her flashlight, but then froze, crouching, as she found herself facing a hunched white shape no more than fifteen feet away, at the edge of a patch of firelight.

Move. She had to move. It couldn't see her. But perhaps it smelt her. And it would hear her when she ran, and then it would come after her, and she knew she couldn't outrun it.

A clump of bricks flew in. There was a thud, and the patch of firelight dimmed and faded, shrinking. The blackness spread towards her, and the creature shuffled a little closer. Something else sailed through the air and came down on her fallen torch. Glass shattered, and the light went out. Milly had to put her hand over her mouth so as not to erupt in hysterical laughter when she saw the stainless-steel item that had done the damage: the creatures were, quite literally, even throwing the kitchen sink at them now.

The missiles were comparatively few in number, Milly realised, but big, heavy and precisely targeted: the odd one flew into the crowd, aimed where the screaming and the panic were thickest – Milly rose and crouched, keeping silent and still – but the bulk of them were aimed at the remaining sources of light.

And wherever the lights went out, the creatures rushed in. There were screams, terrible screams; when she looked around, away from the creature facing her, and saw the few firelit areas that remained on the meadow, she saw the white things scuttle and leap like monstrous insects, and glimpsed people, faces she knew, dragged screaming into the darkness, where the screams grew worse and were accompanied by other sounds; sounds like wallpaper ripping. But it wasn't paper being torn.

On the cavern floor near the far wall lay an enormous slab of the same pinkish stone set into the embankment above the shaft in Barrow Woods. This, though, was heptagonal in shape, the edges rough and ragged where they'd been chipped away by crude stone tools. Similar instruments had hollowed its centre into a rough stone bowl, in which a pale, lambent fire unlike any Ellie had seen before burned.

It had a cheerless silver glow and she couldn't feel the slightest suggestion of heat from it, even though it reached halfway to the ceiling and the hollow it burned in was easily twenty feet across. If anything, the cavern was colder than anywhere else they'd been; Ellie felt a searing chill on her face that sank through her clothes and into her body, making her shiver, as if waves of cold, near-frozen air emanated from the fire, in defiance of all laws of physics. But the creatures in the cavern not only seemed to feel no ill effects but actively drew closer to it, gathering round it as humans would for warmth.

A dozen of the ragged things, risen to their full height, formed a circle around the fire, their terrible arms reaching up, pipe-cleaner bodies swaying and rocking to the rhythm of the pipe and the drums. And within that circle were the drummers, and the pipers.

There were two of each: four, in all. Each stood twice as tall as one of the ordinary creatures: the other beasts' upraised hands reached no higher than the musicians' waists. Their robes and cowls of human skin were coloured in red ochre, white chalk and the black, black charcoal with which the creatures had so often marked their passing, and their faces were hidden behind hard, woodlike masks with twin eyeholes and downturned, grimacing mouths. Eyeholes, for eyeless creatures? Or did they differ from the other creatures in that as well as size?

They commanded here, she could see that much; they were the High Priests who oversaw this rite. As for the rite itself –

"The Dance," said Madeleine. "It's begun."

The High Priests piped and drummed. Ellie saw the pipes were made of hollowed-out bones – femurs of some kind, but surely too huge to be human, for a man with bones like that would have stood as high as the Priests themselves. Some ancient beast, extinct since the last Ice Age, perhaps – cave bear, mammoth, woolly rhino, Irish elk? The bones that beat the drums might have been human, but she'd no clue what creatures' bones formed the drum-frames and whose hides the skin. Whatever their composition, the pipes and drums raised an ever-louder clamour that reverberated in the cave.

"The Dance?" Ellie mouthed. Madeleine nodded. "So, if we stop this – if we can stop it, I mean –"

"That's the big *if*." Madeleine sank against the nearest wall, face grey. "But if we can – then maybe, yeah."

Ellie looked again across the cavern – to the Dancers and the High Priests, the silver flame and heptagon – then back to Charlotte. "Up for it?"

"What you thinking?"

"Simple enough." Ellie motioned towards the heptagonal altar. "Get a cylinder over there and blow it."

"That's it?" Charlotte raised her eyebrows. "Well, it is definitely simple, no arguments there."

"Should work, though." Ellie looked at Madeleine. "Right?"

Madeleine shrugged, eyes half-closed. She looked even sicker than she had seconds before; whatever strength she'd regained seemed to be fading. "Think so," she said thickly. "Light. Fire. If anything'll do it, it's that. *Fiat lux*, remember?"

"*Fiat lux*." Ellie handed Madeleine the flare-pistol. "Case you need it." Madeleine nodded; her eyes were barely open at all by now, but she took it nonetheless. If she collapsed or died on them, how could they hope to find their way back? But that could wait, for now.

Ellie peered over the ledge they were on. There was a very slight slope, thickened by a scree of fallen rock and gnawed bones. She looked towards the swaying figures around the Heptagon and turned towards Charlotte, but the girl had already taken off her backpack and pushed it down the slope. Bones clicked and rattled; Ellie watched the creatures closely, but if they registered the sound they took no account of it. With luck they were deep in reverie, sunk into the ritual trance that would complete their work.

Wake the sleepers, thought Ellie. And what would happen then? She remembered the things she'd glimpsed in the chasm. *Down in the Yawning I see them stir*. Best not thinking on that.

She unfastened her own backpack. "Leave this with you," she told Madeleine. "If we don't make it – do what you can."

Madeleine nodded feebly. Ellie climbed down, swaying to keep her balance. Charlotte wove ahead of her, arms outspread, then slipped and slid. A skull bounced down the slope and, brittle with age, shattered like a teacup on the cavern floor.

Charlotte stared up at Ellie, eyes and mouth wide. But the Dancers carried on as before. She breathed out, nodded to the girl, and they continued.

They didn't look back; Madeleine was as far away now as Milly, Noel and the rest, and as such beyond Ellie's immediate help.

At the bottom of the slope they retrieved the backpack. Ellie unslung the Ithaca, shrugged the pack on and cinched the straps tight: she'd take the risks, and give Charlotte the best chance possible of escape.

Ready? Charlotte mouthed.

I should be asking that, Ellie thought. She was tempted to shake her head and mouth *no*, not least because, of course, she wasn't. Who would be? How did anyone make ready for this? But that was life: a fusillade of shocks, changes and curveballs, good and bad, that you'd no way to prepare for. This was just the latest.

And so she nodded. Then she took the safety off her gun, and she and Charlotte began creeping towards the column of silver fire.

Another scream and Milly turned. Phil Robinson was cradling Julie in his arms as she bucked and heaved. Something long and thin protruded from her chest. A metal rod; the creatures had flung it into the camp and it'd skewered Julie like a javelin.

Bastards –

Another heavy projectile smashed into the ground a yard from Milly's shoulder. People were screaming in panic, which would only tell the monsters where to aim. The more damage they caused, the more panic; the more panic, the more noise, which would help them cause more damage – and so on, and on, till –

Something sailed down and smashed into a bonfire. Burning logs and sticks flew: the light ahead of Milly dimmed, and the white shapes, no longer still, swarmed closer.

A chunk of burning wood lay a few feet from Milly. She wriggled towards it through the mud and grabbed the end that wasn't still alight. It was hot to the touch, but not unbearably. She got up, then ran towards the encroaching white shapes. She lunged, stabbed, swung: they fell back, but not far, spreading out to try and encircle her. Any second, another missile would come down, or one of the things would outflank her. Were they getting bolder? Maybe willing to suffer pain in exchange for getting hold of someone?

There was a cold wind at her back. Was no one trying to relight the fire the things had hit? And how long before more projectiles hit the remaining fires, trying to crush them out and scatter them? Their safe haven had become a killing ground. But Milly didn't turn. Didn't dare. The fire in her hand might be all that held them back.

"Milly, look out!"

She ducked without turning, fell to one knee in the mud. Something sailed over her head, but it came from behind her this time, and was flying towards the creatures. It was on fire, and shone like glass – a bottle of some kind. A bottle filled with –

When the projectile fell among the creatures, there was a bright flash and a billow of flame. A wave of sound smashed into Milly – that horrible drilling screech of theirs, multiplied a dozen or more times – and the white swarm scattered, and Nocl ran towards the damaged fire with a plastic jerrycan. Ernie and Laura followed; each lit and flung another Molotov cocktail into the pale, tattered ranks.

The creatures scattered from the firebombs, but quickly regrouped, launching fresh fusillades of brick and concrete and metal. Something whistled over Milly's head to land with a dull thud; a second later, another source of light faded, and shadows fell across her.

For an insane moment she felt safe, some old primordial instinct kicking in about hiding from danger in the darkness. But the darkness *was* the danger; she had to get to whatever light still remained. But she couldn't; she was frozen.

Oh shit, oh fuck, oh Lord –

The white things crawled towards her through the shadows, like huge white spiders with yellow fangs. The one leading the charge would be upon her in seconds.

Milly managed to stand up straight. If she could just break the paralysis she could make a bolt for it. Not much of a chance, but better than waiting for the end. *Help me, God.* But not only could she not feel His presence, for the first time in her life, she felt uncertain of His very existence: she felt a terrible aloneness as the creatures closed in.

Too late, anyway; when she turned to look for the nearest fire she saw they'd surrounded her. Crouching, and now inching inwards.

The closest one was almost on her now. At the end of its muzzle, gnashing relentlessly like machine parts, were those teeth –

Milly Emmanuel tried to find her God. Milly Emmanuel tried to pray.

And then there was a shot, and fire and smoke exploded in the creature's eyeless face. With that awful drilling howl it reared up, flailing, and fell back. Another shot: another creature was hit, flames erupting from its side, and behind it stood Noel, pumping his shotgun to chamber another round.

"Milly," he shouted. She ran towards him, weaving sideways to keep out of his line of fire. He pulled the trigger again: another red signal flare screamed past her, towing a banner of smoke, and another monster shrieked. Noel let the shotgun drop, hanging on its sling. He crouched; when he stood up there was another Molotov cocktail in his hands. As Milly reached him, he flung it overarm at the creatures, then turned and fled with her, reloading the shotgun as he went.

The meadow was almost completely dark by now. Scattered, fading fires marked the use of other petrol bombs. One large bonfire was still burning, the furthest back. Shotguns fired. Another petrol bomb exploded. They were holding, but how long for? *Always outnumbered, always outgunned.*

One of the creatures rushed at them, cannoning into Noel and knocking him down. Milly screamed – for him, for her, for all of them – but the shotgun fired and the thing reared back and fell away, screeching and burning. Noel racked the slide and blasted it in the head, then caught Milly's arm and they ran.

A shotgun boomed – two flares, one after the other – as they staggered into the last fire's glow. Laura Caddick handed her weapon to Tara, who passed her another gun and began reloading the first; strapped to Tara's back, Jess' baby howled and screamed, his little red face screwed up. *Woman, behold thy daughter; behold thy mother.* There was a cut on Laura's forehead, leaking blood, and she looked a little paler than normal as she shouldered the gun, but otherwise she was unharmed. Ernie Stasiolek fired into the advancing creatures, calmly and methodically, until his gun was empty, then reloaded.

Milly slumped to her knees on the churned ground, and finally managed to wheeze "Thanks."

"Mention it," said Laura through her teeth.

Ernie raised his shotgun and fired again. Beside Milly, Noel slotted fresh cartridges into the pump-action. There was blood on his face. She thought of the wounds the creatures' claws had inflicted on Madeleine Lowe, and the unstoppable, slow-killing infection that had followed. "Jones?" she said. "That thing, when it had you, did it –?"

Not Jones, Lord. Not Jones on top of everything else, after last night when she'd thought she'd lost him –

"No." He dabbed the cut on his forehead. "Something they threw, love. Just a graze. I'm fine." He looked down at his torn, punctured jacket. "Think so, anyway."

The dark teemed with deadly white as Noel investigated the rips to ensure no blood had been drawn. The ones closest to the last fire crouched with their weight braced now on their hind legs; in their forelimbs they cradled chunks of masonry and steel.

Surrounded like this, there'd be no chance. The fire would be battered out within seconds, and anyone left alive would be flayed and torn apart by the monsters. Nowhere left to go. Nothing left to do. Milly tried to remember the words of a single prayer, and couldn't. *My God, my God, why have you forsaken me*?

"All clear," Noel said. "Not that it matters now."

He put the shotgun to his shoulder. Laura and Ernie moved to other points of the final circle, guns aimed outward, and Milly waited for the axe to fall.

64.

The cavern floor was dust and gravel of pulverised bone; with partial skeletons protruding in places from the mass. With the propane tank's weight on her back seemingly growing heavier with every step, Ellie's boots sank shin-deep into the dust, slowing her progress to a maddening trudging crawl.

At least the dust muffled their footsteps, although with the clamour of the pipes and drums – growing ever louder – Ellie doubted they'd have been audible if they'd been clomping across bare stone in hobnailed boots. In any case, the Priests and Dancers were deep in their reverie, entranced in the final steps of their ritual.

They were about fifteen yards from the altar when the piping faded; Ellie froze, holding out a hand to halt Charlotte too. But the drummers continued drumming, the Dancers to dance.

One Piper turned to face the fire, then bent forward. Its face descended, seemingly towards Ellie's, with only the veil of silver flame between them. The mask was now so close she could see the crude stitching that held its segments together. It wasn't wood: on closer inspection it resembled perished leather, or dried meat. Skin, of course: a mask of skin. At least there was only pallid white flesh behind the eyeholes: the thing couldn't see her. She held her breath, in case it heard her exhale.

The Piper lowered its bone flute into the silver flame; the yellow-white bone blackened and charred. The second Piper stood behind it, waiting. The Drummers beat out their rhythm. The Dancers swayed.

The Piper straightened up and turned. Ellie breathed out; her head pounded from holding her breath so long. She glanced across at Charlotte, and they crept forward again.

The first Piper knelt, offering the bone-flute in both hands. The second Piper took it, turned towards the wall, then slowly, carefully scored a symbol onto the rock with the blackened end of the flute. Triangular, like a sort of backward-facing capital D: *dālet*, Madeleine had called it. *Door.*

The Piper scored another symbol as Ellie and Charlotte crawled through dust and bones. *On thy belly shalt thou go, and dust shalt thou eat...* Not the best time for Ellie to recollect her long-ago Sunday School classes. The dust caught at the back of her throat. Bones. People. She fought the urge to retch or cough. Beside her, Charlotte let out a muffled sneeze. Ellie glanced sideways; Charlotte's hand was over her mouth, her eyes wide, but when Ellie looked towards the creatures, they were still engrossed in their ritual.

The Piper completed the second symbol, then began drawing a third. The second mark was the most familiar of all: a vertical line with a diagonal pointing down and to the left. *Gīml.* Justified repayment; reward and punishment.

They were four or five yards from the fire now; Ellie began fumbling with the clasp securing the backpack's straps across her chest.

The Piper had finished the third symbol, which Ellie saw with no surprise was *hē*, the vertical line with three horizontal ones sloping off to the left. *Jubilation.* The one they'd found where Tony Harper had died; the one that had begun it all.

And would end it, too. The circle was closing. But the backpack's clasps refused to budge, seemingly determined to stop her doing what she must –

The Piper pressed the charred flute to the cavern wall under the first symbol, scored a long horizontal line across the stone and cast the flute's remains into the fire. The other Piper began to play again. Ellie felt the tune vibrate inside her, in her guts and bones. The floor began shivering, little ghosts of dust spiralling up from it as thin trails of it spidered down from the ceiling overhead. Another Bible quote came back to her: *The earth will shake, rattle and roll.*

The back wall of the cavern began to crack along the charcoal line the Piper had scored. But the crack spread out further in both directions, then widened. Chunks of limestone fell away.

"Oh *fuck*," Charlotte moaned – might even have screamed, but Ellie barely heard it and so the creatures, in their ecstasy, were unlikely to have either. More of the wall crumbled and dust boiled up, filling the cavern like smoke. Ellie choked and coughed; for long seconds she was blind, but then the silver glow shone through it.

The dust was settling. The silver flame was a brilliant column now that touched the ceiling. The Dancers knelt, facing the wall; the Pipers and the Drummers too, the Drummers continuing to beat out their rhythm.

Almost the entire cavern wall had fallen away, to reveal another wall behind it. Something it had concealed – or, perhaps, given how pieces of it still clung to the new surface – had formed a crust over. It was a dull, stonelike colour, but was neither stone nor metal. What was it, then?

Ellie had time to note a kind of seam running across the second wall, at about the same level as the Piper's charcoal line, but only just. Because now it too began to split.

The split widened and widened; the material of the second wall crumpled and peeled away from the glistening surface that lay beneath. There was a hint of white, but most of it was a bright, vaguely luminescent gold. And, in the centre of the gold, a thick horizontal line of black.

Like the pupil of a sheep's eye, or a goat's –

The split closed, then opened again, even wider than before. As its lid rose, the huge caprine eye gazed into Ellie – *through* her – and the Piper's tune rose to the ceiling in ecstatic triumph. In jubilation, as the first of the Sleepers woke.

***

A roar, thud and crash, then an explosion of light. The wedge of a snowplough blade ploughed into the creatures encircling Milly's group. Some were knocked flying; the rest ran screeching from the headlights' glare.

"Follow me!" someone shouted overhead. "Follow me!" It was Phil Robinson, Milly realised dazedly, leaning out of the tractor's cabin. The Harper's second tractor. He turned the vehicle around and accelerated across the meadow, rear lights blazing too.

The survivors staggered after him. He wasn't going particularly fast: Milly realised he was trying to keep her and the others inside the protective glow from its lights. But he couldn't go too slowly either, or the creatures would smash the lights. And Milly's legs were only short; already it was pulling too far ahead of her.

Noel caught her round the waist, lifted her off her feet, and ran, teeth gritted; when they were level with the tractor, he caught hold of the doorframe. "Climb up!"

Milly wasn't sure how, but somehow she managed. Phil, intent over the wheel, barely glanced at her as she slumped into the passenger seat. She turned, looking for Noel, but he let go of the doorframe and tumbled back into the crowd.

"Jones!" she shouted. "Jones!"

Someone else scrambled up into the cab. Milly twisted round, hoping, but it was Ernie Stasiolek, shotgun in hand. "Budge up," he told her; numbly, she obeyed. Something caromed off the windscreen and Ernie fired back into the dark. Something howled in pain.

"Thought you might need a hand," Ernie told Phil. Fire erupted behind them: more Molotov cocktails, covering their retreat.

Phil didn't answer; he was muttering and mumbling to himself. He seemed to be talking to somebody just outside the driver's window, but there was no one there. "I'm on it, Jules," Milly thought he heard him say; then he shouted, "Hold on", and floored the accelerator.

The tractor lurched and rolled across the drainage ditch at the edge of Groveley Meadow; the plough blade caught the barbed-wire fence and tore it out of the ground. The tractor rocked as it mounted the roadway. Milly thought it would topple over, but it regained its balance and surged forward, the intersection of the High Street, Church Street and Smithy Lane. She grabbed Ernie's belt as the vehicle lurched, or he'd have been hurled from the cabin.

She heard the screaming out in the darkness, glimpsed the crowd's scattered frightened faces and the thin white shapes racing after the tractor. Josh Pidcock stumbled and fell; the instant he slipped out of the light the things in their tattered skin-cloaks fell on him. Ernie fired a flare at them, but it was no use. Josh and his screams were lost in the dark.

Phil swerved, circling, then shifted into reverse, so that the tractor and its headlights faced the field. Buying time, if only seconds.

Sounds came from the field. Screams and tearing skin. The ones like Josh Pidcock who hadn't been fast or lucky enough; the ones who'd fallen behind. But some people had made it. Only a handful, though. So few of them. *Is this all that's left?* Milly thought she saw Noel – or maybe just wanted it to be him. She couldn't be sure.

"The church!" Phil shouted. "Get to the church."

The remaining survivors ran past the tractor. The creatures shrank back from the headlights, but a brick smashed into the windscreen, starring it white. "Fuck," muttered Ernie, reloading his gun.

Nothing Milly could do now; only wait and hope and pray. She touched the cross at her throat, but no words would come. The tractor reversed down Church Street, as slowly as Phil dared, covering the survivors' retreat.

***

Dust swirled thick about the cave. Charlotte lay coughing and choking, trying to clear her streaming eyes, and Madeleine could have seen nothing from her position. So only Ellie saw that giant, goatish eye, shining a terrible gold, gazing through the dust.

She fumbled with straps and clips, and somehow managed to get the pack off. "Charlotte." She grabbed the girl's arm. "Charlotte!"

The girl looked up, still coughing; then she looked past Ellie at the cavern wall and her mouth sagged open. Ellie jerked on her arm. "Charlotte!" The girl focused on her, blinking. Ellie pointed at the backpack. "Help. Quick."

The Dancers and the rest were still rapt in their worship, backs turned. And they were blind. But if they heard one sound over their drumming and piping and the earth's shuddering, or if the Eye perceived the threat and somehow alerted its worshippers, neither Ellie nor Charlotte would have a chance.

They had only seconds.

"Into the fire," Ellie shouted in Charlotte's ear. She took one set of the backpack's straps, half-lifting it from the ground. After a moment, Charlotte grabbed the other straps and they began to swing it back and forth.

"When I say," shouted Ellie, staring up at the impassive Eye – did it see them? Did it see? "When I say." Charlotte was shaking, white with dust. Did Ellie like look that? Probably. Two ghosts, in a cavern full of monsters.

"Now," Ellie shouted.

And they let go.

Milly saw another brick hit the tractor's windscreen. Now everything in front was a blur. But that didn't matter when you were going backwards. Beyond the windscreen, though, the headlights' bright glare had dimmed: one had been smashed. Phil pressed the accelerator down. Then the other headlight smashed, and there was only the monsters and the dark. Ernie Stasiolek fired his shotgun empty, ducked back cursing as a stone flew past his head. "We're there! Out! Quickly!"

He dragged Milly from the cab, then Phil, who stumbled like a zombie, blank-eyed. Ernie pushed them both through the lychgate, then turned and flung a Molotov cocktail overarm at the tractor. It smashed against the machine; fire engulfed it. "Go!" he shouted.

Milly caught Phil's arm and shepherded him through the churchyard. Ernie followed, reloading as he went, while behind them the monsters' outraged, anguished shrieks climbed the black sky.

Milly fell to her knees on the church floor, heaving for breath. She heard a voice she knew: *Noel*. She looked up and saw his face, soot-blackened and sweating but alive. He reached out a hand, and Milly scrambled over to him.

Between him and an equally exhausted-looking Laura Caddick lay Tara and Baby Joel; they must have practically carried the pair of them down the last stretch of Church Street. But they'd made it; they were here. For all the good it would do.

The church's doors were gone. The windows too, and there was no light, other than a few torches in the survivors' hands and some candles from the altar, which were frantically being lit. Wouldn't do any good.

Something small and white burst in through the doorway, and someone screamed, but it was only Reuben, his torn lead still trailing behind him. He ran over to Milly and she hugged him close to her and Jones.

Ernie backed through the shattered doorway, firing his shotgun till it was empty. He retreated into the church, fumbling in his pockets for fresh cartridges. He had none left.

Phil Robinson sank down into a heap and hugged his knees to his chest, muttering to himself and rocking back and forth. Tara Caddick was crying, holding Jess' baby close and mumbling to him. He wasn't crying. Was he dead? Might be lucky if he was. Better than the creatures getting their claws on him.

Milly shook, exhausted. Her throat felt scorched and parched and cracked: she wondered if there was enough time left for a sip of communion wine, assuming there was any around. Funny the places your mind went, at the last.

Reuben chased his tail a couple of times, then darted towards the windows and halted a few yards away, barking furiously. Laura and Noel shouldered their guns, although they were only gestures; Ernie reversed his empty shotgun and held it like a club, then yelped and dropped it; the barrel was too hot to hold. He pulled his sleeves down over his hands and picked it up again.

A pale, spidery shape climbed into one of the empty window frames. Then another, and then another still. Something crawled into the empty doorway and crouched there.

Finished, thought Milly; *finished*.

And she'd neither breath nor words with which to pray.

The pack sailed towards the altar. For a moment it looked as though it would land directly in the silver fire, but it fell short and landed at the very edge, hitting the stone with a splitting thud that rang out even over the piping and the drumming and the thunder in the earth.

The music stopped. The Dancers and Priests began to swivel slowly towards the source of the noise. The earth groaned and growled; dust fell from above.

Surely the canister must have buckled from the impact, but if any gas was leaking, the silver flame didn't ignite it, even though the canvas pack had begun to blacken and crumble.

"Go." Ellie gave Charlotte a push. The girl stared. "Go! Run!"

The Dancers crawled to the edge of the altar. The Priests stood silent, in their masks of buckled skin. And the backpack lay blackening beside the fire.

The earth creaked and groaned; otherwise, the only sound was the thud of Charlotte's feet in the dust as she ran. Ellie stepped slowly backwards, holding the Ithaca at hip level, hands wet with a paste of sweat and dust. *Pull the trigger. Pull the bloody trigger.* But the shot would draw the creatures straight to her. A treacherous, coward's thought: if she didn't move, made no sound, they'd go after Charlotte instead of her.

Pull the trigger, Ellie. But her finger wouldn't move. One of the things leapt down from the altar and scuttled across the cavern floor homing in on the prints Charlotte had left.

Do it. Do it.

Couldn't. It was suicide. Had to. Didn't dare. She let out a frustrated grunt, and that did it; the creature slowed its scuttling crawl and its head, machine-like, swivelled towards Ellie. Everything in her seemed to recoil from the sight and maybe that was why her trigger finger finally moved; in any case the Ithaca bucked in her hands with a dull boom, and a flare shot towards the backpack.

Her aim was good despite the cut-down barrel; the flare smacked into the rucksack and Ellie threw herself down into the dust, braced for the explosion. But there was no sound or flash, and then she opened her eyes to see the monster's fanged proboscis rushing up towards her.

Her scream was a visceral response, a reflex she could have no more stopped than she could have willed her heart not to beat, but even as she made the sound she knew it had doomed her. She squirmed backwards through the dirt, wrenching at the shotgun's slide as the first creature came at her. Behind it she saw the other Dancers leaping off the altar and scuttling in her direction. Behind them the Priests stood motionless and the Eye gazed down from the wall; whether it saw her, or even understood what she was, Ellie had no clue.

But the Ithaca's slide went back, and the fired cartridge was ejected from the breech. She shoved the slide forward, and a fresh one was chambered. And as the monstrosity's claws reached for her, she thrust the gun towards that hated face and pulled the trigger. The shotgun boomed and kicked: there was a flash, then fire, and the creature fell backwards, taloned limbs thrashing, raising whirlwinds of dust; Ellie rolled backwards to avoid those claws. Through the dust she saw the other Dancers rushing in, horribly fast.

Fight or run: she was dead either way, but now she was also calm, her earlier panic gone. Ellie worked the slide, fired at another of the creatures, pivoted and fired again. Both her targets fell, thrashing and scrabbling and shrieking in pain. There was dust everywhere now; she coughed and choked on it, pulling the scarf around her throat up to cover her mouth and nose.

The silver flame was a pale narrow light through the fog of powdered bones. If she could calculate the backpack's position, perhaps she could try another shot. But the other Dancers were coming, and how many rounds had she left? How many had there been to begin with? Six? Seven? Plus one in the chamber?

As Ellie turned to run, knowing already she wouldn't make it, something snagged her coat-collar.

And the cylinder exploded.

65.

So this was it, thought Milly: the last of Barsall, and of her, too. All she'd hoped or dreamt of, ending here, along with humanity and the world. *Millicent Abigail Emmanuel, this is your death.*

Maybe twenty or thirty of them remained. Noel was there, and Laura Caddick; her gun laid down beside her, hugging Tara and the baby close and crying without sound: Milly saw her tears in the candlelight. Reuben was silent now, too; the dog hunched, lowered down onto his front paws, braced to attack the first intruder to enter the building.

She could see Amy and Kevin Lee from the Chinese, who'd sheltered Noel during that first terrible attack. Chris Brailsford was there too, but not his parents; nor were John and Victoria Kennard anywhere in sight. If the missiles hadn't killed them, they'd been taken trying to flee Groveley Meadow. They'd had to move quickly, and the bastard things were relentless in bringing down stragglers.

Milly wanted to weep; she'd heard people screaming as they were taken, people begging for help, and been able to do nothing. The same with the others. All they'd been able to do was keep running. What else could she do? Yes, they'd been afraid. Course they fucking had. But worse, there'd been no chance. Nothing Milly or anyone else could do. No one. Nothing. You ran and left people behind because you wanted to live, and tried not to think about the people you couldn't help.

No sign of the Cooper family either, not even the little boy they'd taken in. She hoped she might have missed them in the crowd, but as she stared around the church she knew she hadn't. That was every survivor from Halliwell Way gone, unless Ellie made it.

Phil Robinson was there, but, Milly was almost certain, in body only. He sat in silence now, gazing ahead; occasionally he smiled, but not in answer to anything around him.

And meanwhile, the creatures crawled.

This was it, the end of things; they'd have no chance against the next attack. Their lights would be put out in seconds, and after that the things from the hill would reap one last harvest of skin and flesh: hides to wear and meat to shred with those yellow rat's teeth.

She'd seen what they'd done to Madeleine Lowe; heard the sounds like wallpaper being ripped from a wall, as they peeled men and women – even children – like fruit, sounds almost drowned out by the screaming. Milly tried to imagine the pain and couldn't. It was the kind of thing you'd expect in Hell.

St Bartholomew had died like that, flayed alive, but Milly doubted she'd the strength to face it. She was crying, too, she realised – like Laura, in silence. Or trying to. But a loud, racking sob escaped her.

"Mill." Noel drew her close. She clung to him, but inside she was empty; she was alone. *Father, into Thy hands I commend my spirit.*

Where are you, God? Where are you, Jesus? Where are you, Lord? She'd never needed her faith so much, and now it chose to tremble. Why should that be a surprise? Of course the times that threatened to prove your faith to be madness or a lie would be the ones you needed it most.

The agony that was to come. Seconds or minutes of Hell. Easy to say things of this life were temporary and soon gone, that what came after it was what mattered, but faced with those claws ripping the skin off your back – and then whatever other tortures followed, which Milly's imagination busily supplied – it was harder to be so calm.

Would God understand if she took her own life, or begged Noel to? He had his shotgun and rifle: one bullet and she'd be beyond the Tatterskins' reach. Would that make her a suicide or him a murderer, or both? Which of them would pay the price, or would God forgive them both?

If she was going to ask, it had to be now.

"I love you," he said.

"I love you too." And that made things simpler. Those should be your last words to your beloved, shouldn't they? Not *now kill me*?

But even so, the pain that was about to come –

Milly tried to decide, but before she could ask or not ask, the screams began.

There was a whining in Ellie's ears, and she was covered in dust.

She opened her eyes. Dust stung her throat. There was fire – but real fire, *normal* fire – on the altar. The silver flame was gone.

The Dancers lay in heaps, burning, weakly thrashing. Two Priests had fallen; the two still standing were also aflame. One collapsed, like an exhausted wooden tower; the other took shambling, swaying steps towards Ellie, then crashed down into the dust, which billowed up around it.

Fiat lux. Fiat fucking *lux.* It had ended the Dance, at least. Whether it had done so in time was another matter, because the Eye still remained – huge and golden, occupying the entire cavern wall.

Ellie tried and failed to imagine the scale of the creature it belonged to, and of the other things that slept in the chasm. *Down in the Yawning I see them stir.* They could shift size, as well as shape: how many multitudes, under the hill?

Elie stood. Her legs trembled. The Eye glowed, but the great, heavy, leathery lid seemed to be drooping. She was afraid to believe it, but little by little it sank; Ellie, still choking on the dust of long-ground bones, began to laugh.

This time, the Eye seemed to register her presence. It shifted position only slightly, but enough that Ellie, for an instant, felt its full scrutiny: a tiny fraction of time in which she knew it, and it her. And then the lid sank down, the terrible gold faded, and the Eye was gone.

Ellie fell to her knees in the dust; would have toppled face-first into it if someone hadn't grabbed her arm. Someone shouted in her ear. And then the screaming began, blotting out all other sound. It was distant, but composed of countless voices, none of them human, and it seemed to come from everywhere at once. It was the creatures: screaming not in agony, as when burned or caught in light, but rage – a terrible cheated fury. And with it, no doubt, a thirst for vengeance.

"Ellie!"

She heard the shout, just, over the din, and turned towards it as she was pulled to her feet. There was a face: a clown-mask, white with dust, hair stiff with it, eyes red. The sight seemed so alien she almost recoiled from it, but the mouth was shouting her name and she heard a hint of a Manchester accent in the dim, almost inaudible voice. Charlotte. Charlotte pulled her arm, and Ellie let herself be dragged across the cavern floor. The Ithaca was gone, but that didn't matter now. She shut her eyes and let Charlotte drag her along, while the screaming of those countless voices rang and echoed in the pits beneath the world.

On the ledge above the cavern, Madeleine Lowe's awareness had shifted to another level, in which she saw the things that slept beneath the hill stirring, rising towards wakefulness. Until, half-risen, they began to sink again, down into the darkness. Back into the Yawning, where they'd stir no more.

She'd expected that to be the end for her – her job done, her purpose served – but like a receding tide, her pain and nausea faded, strength flowing back into her. A last rallying. A touch of grace: *well done, thou good and faithful servant.* Or perhaps a gift: the strength and clarity to save the others.

Like so many other good and faithful servants, Madeleine suspected it would be her lot to guide others to safety but not find it herself. But that was fine. She could – haha – live with that. She was tired; she'd done her bit, and was content. Only a little further, now, to go.

She put on her backpack. The dreadful weight of it settled on her ruined back, but there was no pain, only clarity. Bones and rocks clattered below her; Ellie and Charlotte, both covered in dust, came scrambling up the slope.

"Come on," said Madeleine. Howls echoed through the tunnels: the things knew anguish, and rage. "Not much time to get out."

Ellie stared back at her with red, harrowed eyes. What had she seen? What did she know? Madeleine would have liked to talk with her, give her what reassurance she could, but there wasn't time. "Come on," she said again, and led them back through the tunnels.

Going back seemed faster than going forward, but Ellie, still reeling, numb and dazed from the cavern, was barely present for much of it. She was aware of it only in glimpses: rushing back along the big tunnel; stumbling back over the stone bridge across the chasm; gazing down into the blackness into which the pale shapes she'd glimpsed before had all sunk back down. Then squeezing through those endless, narrower tunnels beneath the hill.

And then the blurred, flurried impressions resolved themselves, slowing down into something resembling time and reality as Ellie once had known them, in a domed chamber with pits full of jointed meat, floor carpeted in salt and bones. The creatures were still motionless in their alcoves, swaddled in their capes of ragged skin, but their heads were raised and flung back now, those blunt muzzles flared open, the teeth splayed, as they howled their grief. The sound was dreadful; Ellie clutched at her ears, and was vaguely surprised when they didn't come away coated in blood. And then, at the other end of the chamber, she saw a small, familiar figure huddled against a wall, dark rat's-tailed hair hanging down over its face, short legs sticking stiffly out.

Ellie wrenched her arm from Charlotte's grip and fell to her knees beside Jess Harper. Charlotte tried to pull her up. "Ellie. Ellie!"

"One second." Ellie slid her arms under Jess, braced herself and lifted. The girl stayed in that stiff, sat-upright position – the same as Tony, Ellie realised, when she'd found him lying frozen in the coppice.

"Ellie, she's –"

"I know." She shouldered past Charlotte, after Madeleine. "A promise is a promise."

Charlotte didn't ask to whom Ellie had promised what; there was no time, and up ahead Madeleine had broken into a run. Ellie chased after her, between the alcoves holding those other pale, ragged sleepers, screaming their wrath and anguish at being cheated of their grand triumph – but mercifully, it seemed, unaware of what was right in front of them.

And then she looked back, in time to see the first of them moving. Slowly, stiffly, like some rusting old machine, with none of the terrible speed and grace the Tatterskins normally showed. But its long limbs unfurled, its skin-cape flapping around it, and its head swivelled jerkily towards Ellie, still emitting that howl.

"Oh fuck," she heard Charlotte say; the girl had stopped too – no doubt to drag Ellie after her – and looked back. More of the things were stirring, lurching out into the chamber. "Move," she screamed into Ellie's ear, and that broke the spell, and the two of them ran.

Ellie followed Madeleine. The creatures' howling grew louder; she glanced back the way they'd come, but all she saw was Charlotte, face wide-eyed and slack-jawed with fright and exhaustion. Then Charlotte looked back, too, turned and raised the shotgun.

One of the creatures was barrelling down the tunnel towards them. It still moved stiffly and jerkily, being newly awake, otherwise it would already have been upon them. Charlotte fitted the shotgun to her shoulder and fired: the flare lit up the Tatterskin's eyeless face and yellow teeth, then smashed into the creature, which flailed backwards, screeching even more loudly. The flames spread; in seconds its cloak was ablaze, and the long flailing limbs. But there were more of the things behind it, although currently flinching and recoiling from the hated light.

Charlotte fired again, and then again, before starting to reload. Ellie screamed her name, but the girl shook her head, then raised the shotgun and fired again. The air grew thick with foul, acrid smoke. Charlotte tried to reload once more, but there were no more cartridges; she flung the shotgun aside and screamed "Run!"

Ellie saw the tunnel was a chaos of flaming, thrashing limbs: the wounded creatures had kept coming and piled into one another, and now formed a burning barricade, holding the others back.

"Move, Ellie, for fuck's sake," Charlotte screamed, shoving at her. Ellie stumbled, almost dropping Jess' body, but steadied herself and did as she was told. Madeleine had been waiting patiently, steadying herself against the tunnel wall; now she turned and broke into a sprint again. Ellie and Charlotte followed.

After that there seemed little point in looking back; Ellie just kept her eyes on Madeleine and tried not to think about how they'd fallen down a blocked shaft from a collapsed tunnel; how retracing their steps would ultimately only bring them to a dead end.

But then they veered left, right, then left again, a zig-zag course, and the tunnel began sloping upwards – steeply, too. The gradient grew punishing, slowing them down; from all around them, the screaming continued.

Ellie felt, rather than saw, a change of surroundings up ahead. A moment later the tunnel opened out, and they staggered across the bone-littered floor, towards the familiar yellow-white hummock. Charlotte's torch flashed over the heaped bones to the hole above it; the dangling rope glowed in the light.

Madeleine had stopped running, sagging with exhaustion; Ellie pulled the flare pistol from her belt, shoving it through her own waistband as she knelt to fasten the rope around Jess' waist.

"Ellie, for fuck's sake!" screamed Charlotte.

"I'm getting her out," said Ellie, thickly.

"For Christ's sake, Ellie, listen! They're coming!"

Ellie raised her head and listened, even as her fingers pulled the knots tight. The screams were getting louder, and louder, and echoing with particular volume from the tunnel they'd just emerged from. The bastards must have got past what was left of their mates at last. Even if they were still moving at that jerky half-speed they could only be minutes away.

"There," Ellie said. The rope was secure around Jess now. "I promised her," she told Charlotte. "Come on. Let's –"

But there was a click and rattle of bone, and a shadow on her. Ellie turned and fumbled for the flare-gun, but her fingers were thick and slow, and she lurched backwards as the butt of a shotgun swung at her face. She lost her balance and tumbled back down the heap of bones; Jess' stiff body swung to and fro overhead.

Grinning a bloody grin, half her face a black-and-red ruin, a single mad eye glaring down, Liz Harper steadied the shotgun and pumped a round into the chamber.

"Got you now, you bitch," she said.

There'd been a moment where Liz had almost known despair, lying broken at the bottom of the shaft with *Their* claws plucking her skin and clothes. To have served so devotedly, sacrificed so much, and to end like this, flayed of skin and cut to joints for salting – she'd have screamed in rage at it, but hadn't the strength.

And then, suddenly, the pain was gone, and the claws no longer touched her skin. She felt *Them* move back from her in the darkness, leaving her alone.

Almost alone, but not entirely. There was something with her: a Presence. A Voice.

It was a murmur without distinguishable words, but Liz had felt its vibration, deep in the bowels of her. She didn't need to understand the words: their meaning filled her. And then she could move. Her bones were unbroken. Her torch was shattered, but a minute or two's groping in the dark found the shotgun.

The Voice was still with her: *Their* Voice, or *Their* masters', it didn't matter which. What mattered was that it told her where to go, and Liz went, stumbling blindly from tunnel to tunnel. Things moved in the darkness, in robes of rustling human skin, but let her pass.

Then she'd felt the narrow walls open up and bones crunch underfoot. A thin phosphorescence had bled from the walls and she'd seen she was in the chamber beneath the Hollows: seen the hanging rope, the cairn of splintered bones.

She'd paused to crouch and grovel before the huge painted figure on the walls, then crawled behind the bone-cairn. The phosphorescence had faded and left Liz waiting, waiting, for when and if Ellie Cheetham and the rest returned...

***

And now they had, and a sorry crew they were. Madeleine Lowe, the White-Christ's useless priest: slumped and spent and good as dead. Charlotte Famu-whatsit: a spoilt little brat, a worthless little cow; Liz paid her no mind.

No, neither of them mattered. Liz could hear *Them* screaming in hunger and fury as *They* came barrelling down the tunnel. *They'd* finish the brat and the priest. No, what mattered was Ellie bastard Cheetham, groaning at the bottom of the hummock – and, dangling from the rope, Judas Jess.

So the little bitch *was* dead. Good. Liz felt no regret on that score, except for not drowning the useless whore at birth. Would've saved them a wealth of grief. Her boys would still be alive, if not for Judas Jess.

Ellie must have thought to carry the girl away, but Jess belonged to Thursdale and the Hollows: she belonged to *Them*. And *They* might have been cheated of everything else, but *They* wouldn't be cheated of this.

Or the blood of the one who'd cheated *Them*: Ellie fucking bastard Cheetham, who now lay dazed and weaponless, without a chance of escape.

Liz took aim, and her finger tightened on the trigger.

Ellie lay, dazed and mesmerised, waiting for the axe to fall.

Liz Harper barely looked human. Her ragged bloody clothes were like an old skin she was about to shed; her face, half-seared to the bone, looked halfway through the same process. There was neither mercy nor sanity in that lone baneful eye: only fury, hatred, vengeance. And then she pulled the trigger –

A blur flew screaming up the hummock of bones and cannoned into her. Liz shrieked and fell backwards; the shotgun roared, and the two figures tumbled out of sight behind the bone-heap.

Charlotte, Ellie realised. That was who'd flown at Liz. She got to her feet and scrambled round the hummock, fumbling for the flare pistol.

But she didn't need it. When she reached the other side only one of the fallen shapes was moving: the other lay silent and still. Charlotte Famuyiwa screamed and cursed and her clenched fists rose and fell, rose and fell, slamming down into Liz's face, chest, and throat. Liz's face was covered in blood; her other eye was gone.

Ellie pulled Charlotte away. A bloody clasp-knife with a handle made from an old shotgun cartridge clattered to the floor; the kind Tony Harper had used to make. It might even have been the same one Jess had fought Paul with.

Liz Harper coughed blood. Her torn hacked lips moved. Blood frothed from her nose and through her shattered teeth. "Tony," she said – at least, Ellie thought that's what she said – then shuddered and was still.

The cavern was silent then, except for the desperate groans of the tortured earth below, the cries of whatever inhabited it, and the raging screams of the creatures coming after them.

Ellie pulled Charlotte to her feet; they stumbled back towards Madeleine Lowe.

Madeleine blinked, resurfacing from the shadows she'd been sinking into. Wasn't her task done yet? She'd guided them out again; what could possibly remain?

"Madeleine!" she heard Ellie shout. "Mad! Your backpack. Quick!"

Madeleine unbuckled it and set it down. Ellie dragged it to a point between the two clear tunnel entrances. Madeleine heard a faint hiss, then the sharp smell of gas. "Get out of here, both of you," she said.

Ellie shook her head. "You go. Just see you winch Jess out too."

"What?" Charlotte – her hands and face, Madeleine saw, splattered with blood – stared at her. "Ellie, don't be stupid."

Unnoticed by either of them, Madeleine picked a heavy thigh-bone – a horse's, maybe, or a cow's – off the floor.

"It's still dark out. They'll come after you. This'll make sure." Ellie drew the flare pistol. "We've one shot left. Just get Mad out and –"

No time to waste in argument, and there was only one answer anyway. Madeleine swung the thighbone at Ellie's head, and Ellie pitched forward and lay still.

Madeleine picked up the flare pistol. "Get her out," Madeleine said. "Jess, too."

"Madeleine –"

"Go on, for fuck's sake. And tell her to look after Reuben."

"Look after –"

Madeleine smiled. "She'll know."

The pack was screeching, the sound almost deafening now. Charlotte opened her mouth to argue, then closed it. She grasped Madeleine's shoulder for a second, then ran over to Ellie and tied them together with a spare coil of rope.

Madeleine ventured towards the tunnel entrances. The smell of gas was stronger, making her feel light-headed and sick. She cocked the flare-pistol. Not long; not now.

Bone clicked and rattled. Madeleine glanced back to see Charlotte and Ellie disappear through the hole in the ceiling. On the bone-heap, Jess Harper's body lolled and shifted; that had been where the sound had come from. Then Jess stirred and began to rise, pulled up with a series of jerks on the rope.

Madeleine stepped back from the entrances.

She'd wait till they were on top of her. That was the best way. Get as many as she could in one go. The gas would be seeping down through the tunnels. Hopefully the explosion would cause a collapse, seal them in till morning at least. After that – with the Dance stopped, with the Sleepers sunk back down into the Yawning – it wouldn't matter.

The creatures were here: pale shapes crouched at the tunnel mouths, waiting, motionless. Scenting, maybe. They knew something was wrong, but not what.

She thought of Shona and Snapper, and of Reuben, who'd at least survived and would have a home, and smiled to herself. *Nunc dimittis*, she thought: *Lord, now lettest thou Thy servant depart in peace.*

"*Fiat* fucking *lux*, you bastards," said Madeleine, and they rushed forward. She raised the flare-pistol and fired.

There was a flash of red light; then a wash of orange and blue swept through the air. And then there was only white light and a kiss of brilliant pain, followed by a sound of thunder that swept Madeleine Lowe somewhere far beyond its reach.

PART IV
The old stars

22nd December
Sunrise: 0818 hrs
Sunset: 1551 hrs
7 hours, 32 minutes and 19 seconds of daylight

66.

It had been the longest, strangest night Milly could recall.

When the creatures' terrible, desolate screams – like cries of agony, although they'd been physically untouched – had finally died away, the ones clinging to the window frames slumped and sagged, dangling from their stickish limbs. The rest had remained crouching, motionless, among the tombstones.

She'd waited for them to attack, but they hadn't; later, a massive dull explosion sounded in the distance, making the church shudder as if something had stirred and settled under it. Then all had been still again, and as the night wore on she'd felt first hope, then certainty, that – surrounded though they were – no attack would come.

No sound and no movement from the creatures, all through the night. It still hadn't been easy; the cold had been bitter, their few dying lights a pitiful shield against the dark. At times her conviction they were safe had wavered, and from the sobs and gasps around her she knew that some didn't have it at all. But still the things didn't move.

When the inside of the church began to lighten she didn't believe it; thought it must be her eyes acclimatising to the dark. But soon she could see the churchyard more clearly, the landscape start disclosing itself in the grey-silver dawnlight, and still the monsters neither moved nor made a sound, even when the steam began rising from them.

The stench of their dying filled the church as the dawn brightened and the sun rose. The steam now boiled from them in clouds; their skin wrinkled, sagged and fell away. The worst part was the patient silence with which they let the sun kill them. In the end Milly looked away. The smell was bad enough; Reuben slunk away from it, whining, and hid behind her.

Head pillowed in Noel's chest, Milly thought she might have slept, if only for minutes, here and there. At some point, anyway, the smell had faded, and when she looked up, the church's shattered windows were empty with the sun shining through them, lighting the last curls of steam. Outside the door were scattered bones, cracking and crumbling as she looked at them, and a rime of bubbling scum upon the grass. Soon enough, steam, stench and bones were gone, leaving only a pale crusty layer on the ground where the last of the residue had dried out.

Noel helped Milly to her feet. Slowly she went to the doorway and stepped outside. The winter air was fresh and cold and clean. Her feet crunched briefly in the creatures' remains, and then she was on the grass. Footsteps shuffled behind her as the others crept blinking out into the light, and stood silent in the day they'd never thought to see.

It had been a long night too in Barrow Woods.

Having dragged Ellie out of the Hollows, Charlotte went back for Jess' body; couldn't do otherwise, after how Ellie had fought to get the poor kid out of there. She'd barely made it through the gap in the embankment when the explosion had gone off, staggering as flame gouted from the sinkhole behind her and the ground shuddered and collapsed.

She'd dragged Ellie into the trees. Not far: the woods were a maze, Jess couldn't guide them now, and there was no telling how many of the monsters were still out in the night. She'd dragged Jess too. Charlotte could have left her – they'd been clear of the tunnels, and the things had no interest in the dead – but it hadn't seemed right.

She'd been afraid they would freeze, but had managed to rig up a bivouac amid a small clump of trees and grub together a fire. Not much, but it had got them through the night.

Charlotte had worried about Ellie too, at first, after the blow Madeleine had given her; a thump powerful enough to knock you out could often cause far worse damage. Although Ellie hadn't seemed concussed, Charlotte still hadn't been sure if she should let her sleep, but the third time she'd shaken her awake Ellie had kindly offered to kick her arse.

Well, Ellie Cheetham had earned a rest if anyone had. The two of them huddled together for warmth; Ellie hugged Jess's body tight to her, like a doll. Determined not to let go, maybe, till Jess was safe away from Thursdale, once and for all.

Finally, it was morning. The fire was dead; sunlight fell through the branches; the few birds that hadn't fled south for winter sang. Charlotte felt stiff and sore and her clothes reeked of smoke, but she could live with that. She had far worse to live with, after all. Her parents' deaths, for a start. Dave's, too – even if she'd always really known he hadn't been worth much – and everything else she'd endured the past few days, from monsters human and otherwise. But you could do that, if you were alive.

Which was more than Jess Harper was. The poor kid lay in the crook of Ellie's arm, moulded against her. Which was weird, come to think of it: shouldn't she still be stiff? On an impulse, Charlotte brushed the hair back from Jess' face. Pale, blood crusted on the lips –

The lips.

Charlotte blinked; leant forward. No way. Couldn't be.

But when she leant close and watched, a tiny curl of steam escaped Jess Harper's mouth.

"Fuck," she said. "No way."

Ellie stirred. "Whuh?"

"We've got to get back," said Charlotte. "Find Milly."

"What's wrong?"

"It's Jess. I think she's breathing."

Ellie stared. "She can't be."

"I know, but – look."

Given the condition of her chest neither of them wanted to check Jess' heartbeat, but Charlotte found a throat pulse when she felt for one: faint, sluggish but present nonetheless. Ellie picked Jess up, and they set off.

There was no smoke from Barrowman Farm's chimney, but even had there been it would be a colder day than this in Hell before she went in there again, even if, according to Jess, Dom Harper wasn't so bad. The worst of them, like the creatures, were gone now. Liz, Keira, Paul, Frank – all gone. But for Jess to stand a chance, they needed Milly, assuming she or anyone else in Barsall was still alive.

They trudged over Thursdale and up on to the footpath to the Height. Just as they reached the top, the bells of St Alkmund's began to ring.

When they saw the state of Groveley Meadow they all froze, thinking it had been a cruel trick and no one remained after all. But the bells kept ringing, so on they went: up the High Street and down Church Street – Charlotte kept her eyes determinedly ahead as they passed the Chapple house – to the church and the small crowd outside.

"Milly?" called Ellie, pushing through the lychgate.

"Ell!" Milly ran up and hugged her, then cleared her throat and stepped back. "Nice to see you, cock."

"You too. Up to seeing a patient?"

Ernie Stasiolek had organised a few small fires in the churchyard – Charlotte doubted Madeleine would have minded – and the survivors huddled round them in small groups. No one was really talking yet; no one wanted to hear what had happened under the hill. Maybe they were afraid to, in case it wasn't over and there was another night of hell to come.

Maybe there was, for all Charlotte knew. There were still more of the things down there; with their Dance stopped, they might want revenge. But she didn't think so, somehow. Milly had told them about the creatures at the church. How they'd just given up, let the sun kill them. That sounded like an ending to her.

She and Ellie joined Ernie Stasiolek around a tiny fire of his own, shared out the few remaining cigarettes and smoked them, one by one. Charlotte glanced around the churchyard, at the other survivors. The faces she knew, the ones she didn't. The ones who weren't there, like Julie Robinson. Or Kate Beck. Charlotte had liked the girl, without ever really getting to know her. Madeleine was gone, too. Too much loss to even begin processing just now, even setting aside the very personal ones Charlotte herself had so lately sustained.

Tara Caddick came over, cradling baby Joel in one arm and supporting her mother with the other. "Hey," Laura said.

Ernie managed a smile. "Hey yourself."

Laura nodded towards the church. "How's the little one doing?"

Charlotte realised she meant Jess. "Milly's doing what she can, but..." She didn't finish the sentence. Remembering the damage done, it seemed impossible Jess hadn't been killed outright, let alone that she stood any chance of survival. Milly was a GP, after all, not a surgeon, and one with pitifully few resources at her command.

"What happened down there?"

Ellie tried to speak, but couldn't. Charlotte told the Caddicks the basics, including what had happened to Jess. "Jesus." Laura looked off nowhere in particular, and sniffed. "Tough little thing, isn't she?"

"Yeah."

"And Madeleine," Laura added. "She was a good un. I'll miss her."

"We all will," said Ellie.

Milly came out of the church, cleaning her hands on a rag.

Ellie took a deep breath, ready for the worst. "How's she doing?"

"She's fine."

"*What?*" said Charlotte. Milly shrugged.

Ellie shook her head. "Liz got her smack in the chest with a twelve-bore. Buckshot."

"What can I tell you, cock? Must've been a duff round. Fuck-all powder charge. Pellets broke the skin and she's bled a lot. *Maybe* a couple of cracked ribs. But that's about it."

"But she was coughing blood."

"Bit the inside of her mouth. Banged her head too – there's a big fucking lump on it – probably passed out from that, but no sign of concussion. No serious damage at all."

"But she wasn't *breathing*," said Ellie. "I'm sure of it. And – Mill, I saw her chest…"

"Trick of the light, maybe. As for the rest – maybe she was just breathing shallow. And the cold might've slowed her metabolism down…" Milly trailed off, knowing it sounded like clutching straws. "Look, would you rather she was dead?"

"No," said Laura Caddick.

"*Fuck* no," said Tara. Laura gave her a stern look, then the pair of them began to laugh.

"Well?" said Milly.

"Definitely not," Ellie said.

"Well, then. Important thing is she's okay." She grinned. "Maybe it's a miracle, eh? Right time of year."

"Oh, bugger off," Ellie groaned.

67.

Jess woke, and thought she'd been buried. It was dark around her, and there was stone: she was dead and under the earth.

She cried out; a hand squeezed her shoulder. "It's all right, love," Milly said.

"Is it? Am I? What?" She remembered the Hollows, the tunnel – then Mum, the shotgun's flash, the impact like a giant fist crashing into her chest. Ribs cracking like stale bread. The bitter copper taste and smell of blood in her mouth, even as she aimed the flare pistol at Mum's snarling face and fired. Choking, unable to breathe.

Her chest was still sore, especially if she breathed deep, but breathe she could. She blinked up at Milly, dazed. "I was dead. I thought I was dead."

"Came bloody close," said a voice. "What I heard, anyway."

Jess looked to her right, and saw Laura Caddick sitting on the floor. Tara sat beside her mother, cradling Baby Joel. Jess smelled beeswax polish. The ceiling overhead was high and vaulted. Broken arched windows. "Where?"

"Church," said Tara. "Pretty much the last place standing."

"Wanna sit up?" said Milly.

Jess nodded; Milly and Tara helped prop her upright. "Wanna hold him?" Tara held the baby out.

"Hey, you," whispered Jess. Joel blinked up at her, then gurgled and laughed; she wanted to cry. Then she saw she had more company.

"Hey," said Ellie Cheetham. The little grey dog sat beside her. He had warm, melting eyes; not like Dom's dogs at all.

"Hi."

"Glad you're okay."

"*You're* glad." Jess managed a weak laugh, but it died quickly. Wasn't something to joke about, who'd lived and who'd died. Stupid Jess. Stupid.

"We need to talk," Ellie said.

Something clenched in Jess' belly; what now?

"We think it's finished," said Ellie. "Won't know for sure till tonight. But – we stopped the Dance, and Madeleine..." A moment's silence. "Madeleine brought the cavern down, the one in the Hollows. Blocked their way out."

They all knew that wouldn't stop *Them* finding another, but Jess didn't say anything. "Madeleine?" she said. "The vicar? Is she...?"

Ellie nodded, and stroked the grey dog.

"I'm sorry." Jess shrank in on herself. Another one dead, and all her fault – that was what they'd think now, wasn't it, now it was over and they didn't need Jess any more? She was a Harper again, an outsider, to be kicked out and –

"It was what she wanted. She was –" Ellie broke off and shook her head. "Anyway. With any luck, it's over. But they're still down there. So we're gonna need people to keep watch."

"Oh." Jess' eyes prickled; the clenched hollow weight inside her sank, threatening to drag her back to the floor. That was it, then: *back in your box, Harper scum; back in your hole.* After all this, after everything, they were packing her back to Barrowman Farm – assuming Dom even let her in the door – to do the crap they didn't want to. Watch for *Them* coming back and be the first one standing in *Their* way if *They* did, the first one to die. She felt sorrow and betrayal, then anger; her fists clenched. She understood Mum now, her bitter rage and spite against the world outside. *Fuck them all, it's just us, even if us means Keira and Paul. At least we stick together. At least we've got each other's backs.* Was that what they wanted of her now, to become Mum?

"No," said Ellie, "not you."

Had it been that obvious? But then Jess had never been good at hiding things.

"Ernie's volunteered to live at Barrowman Farm," Ellie said. "Help run it. Keep watch. Charlotte, too."

"Charlotte Famuyiwa, breaking her nails on a farm?" Milly laughed. "Can't tell me you don't believe in miracles now, Ell."

"I heard that," called a familiar voice. Milly grinned and blew a kiss in its general direction.

"Maybe some others, too," said Ellie. "You won't have to live there again, Jess. But – there's Dom."

Jess waited.

"We can't just send strangers in to live there," said Ellie. "So –"

"You want me to go back there?"

"Just to talk to him. Tell him how things are now. It's still his home. No one's taking that from him. That's all we want you to do. Help… smooth things over. Make the change."

"And what then?" The scrap-heap for you, Jess Harper. No one wants you around, so just fuck off –

"God knows where anyone'll be living after all this, state the village's in, but –", Laura Caddick looked at Tara, then at Jess. "We were talking it over, and – well – if you want, when we've a home again, you're welcome to stay with us."

"What, like a servant or something?"

"Nothing like that," said Tara. "You'd be family. Joel too, obvs."

Obvs. The simplicity and totality of the offer was too much to take in; Jess tried to speak and was afraid to, because this surely couldn't be right. They couldn't be offering her *that*. A home. A place. They *couldn't* be offering something that meant so much to Jess when they hardly knew her.

"You deserve a sight better than you've had," said Laura. "So we thought – 'bout time someone did something about that. So if it's what you want, it's yours."

They meant it; they really did. Jess tried to speak again, but could only cry. But these were different tears than any she'd cried before.

Later on, when Milly could find no more to do, she sat back against a gravestone beside an untended fire and shut her eyes, glad to be left alone just for a moment.

"Here you go, love."

She looked up, scowling, but it was only Noel, holding out a packet of Craven A, still sealed in the plastic wrapping.

"Fuck me sideways, Jones, where'd you get these?"

"I have my ways." Noel put an arm around her shoulders.

"All right, International Man of Mystery. S'pose you want one?"

"Wouldn't say no."

Noel lit their cigarettes, and Milly put her head back against his shoulder, looking up at the sky. "Guess what?" he said. "Someone found a working radio."

Milly sat up. "And?"

"There's people out there all right. We can hear them, even if we can't make out what they're saying. Hopefully, we'll have company sooner or later. God knows what we'll tell them."

"Might not have to tell them anything," Milly pointed out. "All we know, it wasn't just Barsall where this was happening."

"A new world of gods and monsters," Noel said, which sound like a quote from something, though Milly'd no idea what. "Be a very scary world to live in, wouldn't it?"

A fallen world always was, Milly thought but didn't say.

"If it *did* just happen here, though," said Noel. "I mean, this has happened before, hasn't it? Or something like it. And they kept it quiet."

"Think they were right, doing that?"

"I honestly don't know, love."

"Me neither."

Milly huddled closer to him.

That afternoon, when the sun hung low and red, Jess, Ernie and Charlotte walked along the hill road, then down from the Height to Barrowman Farm. Tara was looking after Joel again; Jess would take over when she got back.

Her chest still ached, but that was all. Bruises and two cracked ribs, Dr Emmanuel said. Jess knew, like Ellie and Charlotte, that it had been more and worse. None of them would ever say so aloud. But they'd always know.

Ernie limped, leaning on a stick. They climbed the wall and crossed the snow-covered fields, still marked by Jess and Charlotte's footprints. This time, though, instead of making for Barrow Woods, they went the other way, towards the farmhouse. And this time, they hadn't a gun between them. Which might or might not prove a good idea when they encountered Dom.

Smoke drifted from the chimney, across the dim pale sky. As they reached the back yard, the door opened.

Ernie Stasiolek drew breath in through his teeth. "Easy," Charlotte whispered.

Jess held up a hand and went forward alone.

Dom stepped outside, the dogs slinking at his heels, a shotgun in his hands.

Jess stood, looking at him.

Dom looked from her to the others and back again. He stared at her for what must have been nearly a minute, and Jess stared back. And then, at last, Dom broke the shotgun, raised a hand, smiled shyly and waved.

68.

Ellie Cheetham caught a few hours of fitful sleep, then spent the last of the daylight hacking at the frozen ground of the Vicarage's garden with pick and shovel, till she'd dug a hole a couple of feet deep. In it she placed the cold, stiff bodies of two dogs, an old black Labrador and a little Jack Russell terrier, before shovelling the earth back on and piling a few chunks of rubble atop the grave. Reuben had sat there throughout, watching.

Now, as the sun set, Ellie left the village, walking down the icy road to the Height, a packet of cigarettes in her pocket – tomorrow she'd quit – and Reuben trotting at her heels.

She carried her torch, her AirWave and a phone that still had some charge. One question remained unanswered – two, if she included that of what this night would bring. She'd wait for both answers out here, away from the others. She'd fought enough and done enough; if the Tatterskins returned tonight there'd be no chance for any of them.

There was a third thing, too; not a question, but a knowledge she wouldn't share. Not for a long time; perhaps never. Depended on who, if anyone, needed to know.

At the Height, she swept ice and snow from a picnic table and sat down. She had a handful of treats in one jacket pocket; she fed a couple to Reuben, stroking his hair, and he rested his head on her thigh. *He likes you*, Madeleine had said.

She wouldn't think of Madeleine, not just now. There'd be time enough for grieving in the days to come.

The sun became a line of red and disappeared; the sky turned black. A million or more pin-prick stars spread out across it like glittering dust. Down in Thursdale, Barrowman Farm's windows glowed.

Reuben whined and nuzzled her, so she fed him again. Well, she'd been considering getting a dog for a while now. Might do her good, to let someone in at last, through the closed doors of her home and heart.

Ellie put the AirWave and the phone on the table, pondering which to try first. In the event it was neither, because she heard a faint noise: a steady, regular beating. She didn't dare admit she recognised it until she saw the helicopter's navigation lights in the distance, travelling slowly towards the Height.

Ellie fed Reuben another scrap and ruffled his hair again.

"No point telling them," she said. "Is there?"

Reuben looked at her, tongue lolling, eyes bright. His only concern just now was how long it would take before he received another treat. Hard not to envy that.

And what would she tell them, anyway? Any of them? How the Eye had stared into her, she into it and how they'd understood one another? How she'd realised that it had closed not because they'd stopped the Dance, but because the time simply wasn't right yet? The Tatterskins could have danced all week and still it would have slept on – for a month, a year, a century, a millennium, Ellie didn't know. That was the worst of it. All the death, Madeleine's sacrifice – none of it had mattered. Next winter, the one after, the one after that, it would start again. Another frozen body in the snow. And in a year, a century, a thousand years, beside one particular body, etched in charcoal, would be the Phoenician letter *hē*.

How did you go on with that in your head? That every scrap of creation was on borrowed time; that one day, down in the Yawning, they'd wake and rise and wipe it all away?

How did you go on with your child dead, your husband gone, your life emptied of light and love? You carried it; that was how. Because you had to. As she'd carry this, and be glad of what she had. And throw the doors open, all of them – save for that one locked door she'd hide her knowledge behind – and let in all the world, good and bad, for as long as it was there.

Reuben whined and licked her hand.

"It can't be so bad a world," sighed Ellie. "Not if there's dogs."

She fed him another scrap, then stood, switched on her torch and waved it to and fro. The helicopter and its lights veered towards her, rotors beating, and beyond it, overhead – for now, at least – the old stars remained in the sky.

Acknowledgements

My wonderful wife, Cate Gardner, for listening to the first (MUCH longer) draft of this whole thing.

Emma Bunn, who beta-read the manuscript and gave a great deal of incredibly helpful advice.

Debbie Pearson, Peak District and Derbyshire native, who made sure the place and setting rang true.

Dave Polshaw, Liz Williams, Harry O'Rourke, Paul Flewitt, Kevin Redfern, Ryan Whittaker, Andrew Freudenberg, Anthony Watson and Roy Gray for information about house fires.

Priya Sharma, (aka 'Priya Poppins, Practically Perfect in Every Way') for (hopefully) ensuring I haven't made too big a fool of myself with medical details. (If I have done, it's my fault, not hers.)

My amazing agent, Anne Perry, who helped shape the novel into its ultimate form and found it a home.

Simon Spanton, Caroline Lambe and Gemma Creffield at Angry Robot, and publicity whizz Sam McQueen.

Countless friends and family, for many kinds of support both during the writing of this novel and over the years.

Anyone whose kindness, advice or help I may have forgotten.

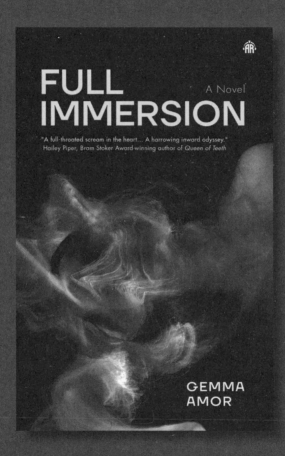

WORDS ON A PAGE

To: The Department of Virtual and Experimental Therapy
University of Bristol
One Cathedral Square
College Green
Bristol

JUNE 26TH, 2019

Dear Sirs,

It has taken me six months to write this letter.

You should know I have tried everything else. I have tried medication, counselling, cognitive reprogramming exercises. I do yoga, and I paint. I take long walks. I sleep for eight hours a day, read self-help books, listen to soothing podcasts and ambient, lyric-less music. I have a therapy app on my phone, in fact I have three. I masturbate frequently and stay hydrated.

None of it works.

Because I still wake up every single day without exception and think about throwing myself off the Bristol suspension bridge.

It's not an idle thought, nor a romantic one. I don't wake up and wonder what it feels like to fly, or how the cold metal suspender cables will feel in my hands as I climb up above the bridge deck, or whether the impact of hitting the river will kill me before I drown, pushing my bones out through my skin, snapping my neck. It isn't a dramatic response to stress, or a morbid fascination, or an indeterminate sense of melancholy, or even a cry for help (unlike this letter).

It's a compulsion. It's like I am being called. It's relentless.

And I just don't know *why*.

That's why I need your help.

I know about your department and your Virtual Experimental Therapy programme. My husband keeps up with that sort of thing – he has a vested interest now, I imagine. I first read about you in a magazine of his, then did some digging. I understand that you are widely considered "unorthodox".

Well, maybe unorthodox is exactly what I need, because Christ knows nothing else is working.

I understand you accept a limited number of patients on a deferred payment plan basis. I need you to consider this letter as my application to be one of those patients. You see, the thing about my condition is that I can't hold down a steady job. This means I have no money. I can't ask my husband for any more help; I have taken enough from him already.

But without money, I can't afford your services.

So again, these words:

Help me.

Words are funny, aren't they? They're like little pieces of yourself, given away. Like the words in this letter. Are they persuasive enough? I hope so. I was a writer, in my better days. I don't really know what I am anymore. A shadow, perhaps. An echo. An impression of a person, rather than the whole.

I'm drunk, writing this. Ten minutes before putting pen to paper I chased the booze with some of those pills various doctors keep giving me, the ones that don't help much at all. I keep telling them, *these don't help,* but all I end up with is a fresh prescription, a different type of pill. If you listen carefully enough, you might hear me rattle, I am so full.

But you don't want to hear all that.

There is a point to this.

The point is "The Question".

And "The Question" is always the same. People always want to know the same thing.

"Why do you want to kill yourself?" they ask.

And I never know how to answer.

Because leaving everything behind would only make sense if there was a *reason* for me to want to do so, surely.

"Did something happen to you?"

This is The Other Question that people always ask. They're also looking for "A Reason", an exposition. Maybe a trauma, an event, as described, something that perverts my brain away from its vital task of the everyday, and makes it weaker, and tired, and colours everything grey.

And this question is actually a "Good Question".

Because, sure, lots of things have happened to me. Things I can consciously recall. Bad things. Good things. Awful things, surmountable things, shameful things.

But what if something happened to me that I *can't* recall? My memory feels like a beach bathed in fog.

Or worse, what if I did something? Something wrong? Something bad? Something I've forgotten. What if there is a dark secret lurking in my head?

And if there were, could you help me uncover it? Your programme seems ideally placed to do so.

If there *is* no grand, insidious secret, if it turns out that life is just a steady trickle of events, a slow and creeping succession of little traumas, a collection of hurt, if you will, then your treatment may also help me come to terms with that.

Either way, my mind is being eaten away steadily. In the better hours, I can just about remember my name, and that I am married, and that I used to be a Mother, have a life. Other times, the words escape me. Because words are tricky, aren't they? In the time it has taken you to read this far, I have told you that I no longer want to live. Perhaps I'm already dead. Who knows? You can't see me, you can only see my words, like footprints left behind in the sand.

Do you believe me? Why would you? If I was serious, then I wouldn't be sending this letter, would I?

God, I'm tired of myself.

I'm writing with no expectations, only desperation. Words, marching quickly across the white page like dutiful ants going about their business, and that business is this: alive, or dead.

Heads, or tails. Black, or white.

Seems simple, doesn't it?

It isn't.

Please help me.

Yours, with hope,

M

2

VOYEURS

In a dark, modestly furnished room that smells of hot coffee and hot metal and hot plastic, two technicians sit side by side, crammed up against the far wall. They are pinned in place by a vast array of electronics and equipment: wires, screens of varying sizes, VR headsets, headset base stations, a projector, routers, laptops, a scanner or two, mounted panels with flashing, multi-coloured LEDs, keyboards, speakers, wireless controllers, a strange, square, multi-parameter monitor with a built-in printer, and other things that are difficult to make out in the low light. It's a mess, but one the pair seem comfortable with. On three walls of the room, polished whiteboards hang, graffitied with scribbles and doodles. On the last wall, closest to where the Techs and their equipment huddle, a large expanse of glass stretches from corner to corner: a window, or, more precisely, a reciprocal mirror, reflective on one side, transparent on the other.

The team of two speak in a hushed, absent-minded way to each other as they fiddle with their gear, fully absorbed in their work, wiring themselves up, slotting headphones over their ears, plugging themselves in with the practiced seriousness of astronauts preparing for launch. They have an important task to perform. A new project. They are the watchers. The moderators, the Behind the Scenes team.

They are the Control Room.

They have been doing this for some time now, spying out

in the open like this. It is as legitimate as voyeurism will ever get. They have letters after their names and paperwork that gives them agency to do so, day in, day out, and get paid for the pleasure. Infiltration in the name of science. A rum job, but someone has to do it. At least, that's what they say to each other, jokingly, but the reality is much more serious. They are not spies, not really. They are an intervention. A rescue team. White knights, of a sort.

Before them, that tinted glass window yawns. They can see perfectly well into the neighbouring room through it, but no-one can see them from the other side.

Not that the occupant of the adjoining room is in any condition to try.

She hangs in a hypnagogic state, hovering somewhere between wakefulness and sleep, thin steel wires, pulleys and cables keeping her form amply suspended in the air about four feet above the ground. Her limbs are supported at the joints by soft fabric cuffs attached to the wires. Her body (thinly clothed in paper pyjamas), neck and the back of her head is braced by a strong silicon cradle, articulated and moulded to fit the contours of her spine closely. The cradle is held up by more steel cables that are mounted to a moveable track on the ceiling. She looks like a dangling marionette in storage, waiting for a performance to start, which is precisely what she is. Tubes of varying sizes crawl into her mouth and nostrils and other hidden parts of her body, and there is an IV drip plugged into a vein on one thin, bruised arm. A forest of wires protrudes from her shaved scalp, attached to dozens of biomedical sensor pads held in place around her skull by an elaborate headband. A wide curved visor covers her eyes, which are blue in colour and held open by tiny eyelid retainers and special adhesive strips to keep the eyelashes clear. Small white buds nestle into the hollows of her ears: wireless headphones. Her hands, which hang loosely by her sides, are sheathed in fingerless gesture control gloves, and her feet are clad in thin, membranous boots wired to a massive unit standing off to one side. There are several of these large black units positioned around the edges of the room, monumental things that hum as they process, emitting a low, keen non-sound that can only be heard if a person were to focus on it, a white rush of noise that is as absorbent as it is abrasive. The patient will not be able to hear it beyond the ambient sounds trickling into her brain through the headphones.

The Observation Room in which the patient hangs feels cavernous: a large, clinical space that has been kept purposefully clear so she can move about, enact things freely at the end of her wires. Being able to do so will reduce the cognitive dissonance between a sleeping, immobile version of herself and the notion that she is free to move, explore, react. More headsets dangle from the ceiling behind her like strange redundant vines, not needed for this scenario, and an organised mass of colour-coded cables snake around fluorescent strip lights that are currently switched off. The floor is black vinyl, easy to clean and sanitise. Patients in this room often secrete fluids: vomit, piss, sweat, it's all been thought about and catered for.

A nurse in a crisp white uniform makes herself busy attending to the patient, reapplying anaesthetic eye drops so she doesn't feel the subconscious need to blink, adjusting wires and cuffs, checking pulse rates and blood pressure, smearing barrier cream onto any parts of her body that can chafe, gently rubbing at hands and feet to keep the circulation flowing. It is tricky to manoeuvre around the wires and tubes, but she knows what she is doing. This is not her first rodeo. She notes things down on a tablet with a stylus as she works, her handwriting neat and precise. The notes pop up onto a small monitor in the Control Room next door. The team within ignore them. The patient is stable. If there was something wrong with her vitals, they would know about it. The system has been designed to panic at the first sign of physical instability. Lawsuits are an ever-present threat to experimental medicine, so they are taking no risks. Not that the woman could sue if she *did* die. Angry relatives on the other hand, are a different kettle of expensive fish.

The patient breathes softly in and out, unaware of her surroundings and the gentle bustle of the Nurse. Unaware of anything much, except a deep, dull ache in her heart, an ache that straddles both the sleeping and wakeful parts of her. Luckily, the people behind the glass claim to be adept at administering to aches. The patient is here for that reason, and because she wrote them a long, painful letter that rambled and ended with three devastatingly simple words:

Please help me.

And so, the techs will endeavour to do so.

It is not a completely selfless act: these are salaried heroes who are encouraged to maintain a professional distance from the patient herself. Boundaries are important in this industry – their efficient, business-like demeanour is therefore not due to a lack of sympathy. As technicians, they are encouraged to see the disease, rather than the host, as many doctors are encouraged to triage and treat symptoms before delving into causality.

Still. It is hard for them to not feel some pity for the woman who hangs, lightly drooling, before them. Her thin, bruised state acts as an incentive. The most desired outcome is, of course, a long, happy continued life for the patient. After that, words like "Fellowship" and "Royal Society" and "research award" and "pay rise" flit through the technicians' respective minds.

Around them, monitors display a variety of scenes from what looks like a live video feed, cycling through high-definition snapshots of the world outside the darkened room in quick succession: a river, over which a vast, curved bridge hangs suspended, a meadow, an island, a huge, colonnaded space like that of a museum, or an art gallery. A small laptop resting on one of the tech's knees shows strings of code moving up and down, living digits that crawl across the screen like insects, like ants. Not words, but cipher. Soul cipher, although the techs don't know that, not yet.

Eventually, with all routine checks completed, the pair lean back in their chairs, stretch out sore arms and roll their heads around uncomfortably on stiff necks. Then, in unspoken agreement, they turn to one another.

"Ready?" says the first into a small microphone mounted on her desktop. She is dressed in a pinstriped shirt that pulls a bit around her shoulders, and brown corduroys. In her late fifties, she is ageing well, skin still smooth, at odds with her thick silver hair. She speaks to her colleagues as a Boss speaks to a subordinate: gently commanding, professional, but pulling rank with every syllable.

The Nurse in the next room completes her last check, adds a final note to her tablet, smiles, rearranges a wire or two, then makes a thumbs-up gesture.

"Thank you," the Boss says.

The Nurse leaves the room quietly and the sleeping-yet-awake patient is alone, at last. She sways gently as the wires settle; a human pendulum headed for equilibrium.

"Ready?" The silver-haired woman repeats the question for the man sitting next to her, who wears a security tag on a lanyard about his neck on which the name "Evans" can be read.

Evans takes a deep breath, reaching out a single finger and letting it hover it over a large red button anchored to a Perspex safe-box on his desk.

"As I ever will be," the younger man replies, and, with that, his finger descends and he pushes the button.

A loud, long beep fills the air between them. The woman suspended mid-air twitches, just once, and then settles.

The session has begun.